PRAISE FOR
JOHN FARRIS

"*Sacrifice* is a truly remarkable novel and John Farris is a truly remarkable writer. Or let's put it another way. *Sacrifice* is THE MOST EXCITING SUSPENSE NOVEL I'VE EVER READ."
— Robert Bloch, author of *Psycho*

"Nobody RUNS THOSE ICY FINGERS UP AND DOWN MY SPINE like John Farris who has done it again brilliantly."
— Naomi M. Stokes on *Sacrifice*

"A GENIUS for creating COMPELLING SUSPENSE."
— Peter Benchley

"His paragraphs are SMASHINGLY CRAFTED and his images GLITTER LIKE SOLITAIRES."
— *The Philadelphia Inquirer*

"Farris has remarkable ability to JAB HIS LITERARY ICE PICK INTO THE BONE MARROW. With uncanny reality he depicts raw evil, particularily the sort that masquerades as innocence. It is genuine terror, and Farris provides it with an attribute lacking in the work of most contemporary storytellers: style."
— Brian Garfield

"He proves that black print on white paper can literally CHILL THE BLOOD."
— *Springfield News & Ledger*

"MARVELOUS SKILL."
— *Associated Press*

Tor books by John Farris

All Heads Turn When the Hunt Goes By
The Axman Cometh
The Captors
Catacombs
Fiends
The Fury
King Windom
Minotaur
Nightfall
Sacrifice
Scare Tactics
Sharp Practice
Shatter
Son of the Endless Night
The Uninvited
When Michael Calls
Wildwood

SACRIFICE

JOHN FARRIS

A TOM DOHERTY ASSOCIATES BOOK
NEW YORK

This is a work of fiction. All the characters and events portrayed in this book are either fictitious or are used fictitiously.

SACRIFICE

Copyright © 1995 by John Farris

All rights reserved, including the right to reproduce this book, or portions thereof, in any form.

Rollout photograph copyright © 1980 by Justin Kerr

A Tor book
Published by Tom Doherty Associates, Inc.
175 Fifth Avenue
New York, N.Y. 10010

Tor® is a registered trademark of Tom Doherty Associates, Inc.

ISBN: 0-812-50956-0

First edition: September 1994
First mass market edition: June 1995

Printed in the United States of America

0 9 8 7 6 5 4 3 2 1

GREG WALKER'S NARRATIVE

ONE

February, 199–

I was finishing my laps around the lake about seven o'clock when Doyle Kindor's youngest boy, Ricky Gene, shot me in the head with Doyle's old Colt Woodsman.

Ricky Gene was only ten, and he shouldn't have had the gun at all without his older brother or Doyle along with him, for safety's sake. As I found out later, Ricky Gene sneaked the Woodsman out of the house to do some target shooting with a couple of his fifth-grade friends.

The how and why of it weren't important to me, of course; the fact is that a .22 caliber, unjacketed lead bullet went astray and struck me six centimeters from the temple, just above the left eye, penetrating the skull at a slight upward angle, splitting apart on impact with the bone (I have well-calcified bones). Pieces of the bullet then plowed through the left hemisphere of the cerebral cortex and Broca's area. One fragment traveled as far as the cerebellum.

The solid blow to the forehead snapped my head back. I was in stride and on a slight incline; the impact of the little bullet turned me sideways and I lost my footing, fell backward at the water's edge. I didn't lose consciousness. But I was partially paralyzed and unable to get up again. I had uncontrollable spasms down my left side; I couldn't feel my left hand at all.

Spud Morris, doggedly trying to drop a lot of excess poundage, was trudging along the lakeside path about forty yards behind me. He undoubtedly had heard the little firecracker pops of the Woodsman too, and as soon as he crossed the shelf of limestone that juts out over the weedy cove where the bream are most likely to be biting early in the morning, he saw me and realized what had happened.

"Greg? Greg, Jesus!"

I was faceup, lying back on one elbow. I could hear and see Spud okay. At first I didn't know, or want to believe, that I was seriously wounded. I thought I'd run into something in the twilight, like the blunt end of a dead branch protruding from a tree. But Spud, who had done two tours in Vietnam, left no doubt as he knelt beside me.

"You've been shot, you've been shot!" he said. "Damn careless kids!" Staring at the hole in my head, fear in his eyes, he put a burly arm around me. Sweat dripped from the tip of his nose. Spud tried to catch his breath, and didn't seem to know what to do next. He dabbed at the blood on my left cheek with one of the terry-cloth wristbands he always wore when jogging, and raised his head.

"Hey, you kids! Run, get help quick! Nine-one-one. *Nine-one-one*. Mr. Walker's shot, he's hurt bad!"

Spud has a bass voice, and it carried like the baying of a bloodhound across the placid lake to the homes on Thornhill Road. The neighborhood that Caroline and Sharissa and I had moved to not quite two years ago, after a decade of hard work, planning, and a lot of scrimping to make it all possible. We were in our dream house, and now this had to happen.

The spasms had lessened; I felt inert and cold to the bone, as if I were crystalizing in a snowbank. Maybe it was the way Spud was holding me, but I found it harder to breathe with every passing moment. His face was close to mine, his lips crimped in a concerned smile as he tried to reassure me.

"Hey, Greg, hey, it's gonna be all right! You're gonna

make it, son! Kids have gone for help! You just hang in there!"

I hung in there, perhaps surprising us both. Spud kept talking, embracing me firmly, telling me tall tales about his golf handicap and his ability to pick stocks that tripled in value—as his wife put it, the only thing that could shut Spud up was an oral contraceptive. Meanwhile, he kept me in a sitting position, something he'd learned dealing with grievously wounded men in his command and which, under the circumstances, was the correct thing to do.

I was fortunate that the paramedics from the nearby fire station got to me in less than eight minutes. The emergency medical units were something new in Sky Valley. Caroline, my wife, was largely responsible. She had spent three years lobbying the City Council, getting the necessary community support: four thousand signatures on a petition. We have a fine hospital, too, for a city our size.

One of the medics was cowpoke-thin, with a jutting chin like the joker on a playing card; the other was a gum-chewing half-pint young woman who didn't look much older than my daughter. I can't imagine that even Mother Teresa had more caring hands. They didn't waste a second. On advice from the trauma center at the hospital, the medics put me on oxygen, sodium pentothol to decrease the brain's metabolism, and lidocaine to reduce intracranial pressure.

But my brain was rapidly filling with blood. I still didn't feel much pain, and I couldn't feel anything at all on my right side. I was blinking and woozy, the lashes of my left eye sticky from blood and leaked brain tissue, but as they carried me on the wheeled stretcher, still sitting up, around to the other side of the lake, I saw a couple of cops talking to Ricky Gene and his friends. Those kids had the sickest, scaredest faces I've ever seen.

Unlikely as it seems, I wasn't worried about myself—shock, I suppose—but I felt sorry for Ricky Gene. He was a good boy. It was always "Yes, sir" and "No, ma'am" with Ricky Gene.

I guess the sodium pentothol took effect quickly, because I was drifting off by then. Spud Morris kept shouting at me as they hurried me to the ambulance. Something about finding Caroline and Sharissa right away. The roof of my mouth was swelling and I couldn't talk, so I wasn't any help there. It was a primary month in Georgia and Caroline was off in another congressional district, ninety miles south, working on Claude Gilley's campaign for the United States Senate. She hadn't expected to be home before ten o'clock. Sharissa, I thought, might still be at the country club playing tennis after her shift as a lifeguard. I assumed she'd arrive at the hospital first. But I didn't want my baby to see me with a hole in my head.

The traumatized brain always swells from bleeding. Most severe head injury cases arrive at the hospital with no neurological functions, and if they don't get fast, expert treatment, the swelling brain herniates, forcing the brain stem through the bottom of the skull and compressing it to the point where it can no longer function. Then the lungs and the heart stop. Pure oxygen to slow down the heart, regulate the violent pumping of blood to a brain that already holds too much, is the first requirement. Then emergency surgery to relieve internal pressure, suction off the necrotic tissue, all the bone and bullet fragments that can cause trouble later if the patient survives the initial trauma. But only one in ten ever do. After that, the neuro team replaces the bone they removed to get at the brain, and hopes for the best.

Eighteen hours after the accidental shooting, I came to in the Intensive Care Unit.

I had shrieking-teakettle sounds in both ears. At first I couldn't make any sense out of being hooked up to a respirator, some monitors, and three drip feeds. A humidified re-breather covered my nose and mouth. I had drains in my head and my left eye, which had swollen shut. My right eye was little more than a slit. I couldn't lift either hand or move my head. The last thing I remembered was dropping the Honda off at Ed Reedy's dealership for an overdue brake job. But that had been more than a week ago.

The first face I saw was Dr. Jesse Fernando's. Jesse and I used to play racquetball doubles at the Y until his back went out on him. I hadn't seen him in quite a while. He had put on weight, added a chin, some silvery gray at his temples. He was wearing a clean set of O.R. greens.

"Do you know me, Greg?" he asked. "Just squeeze my right hand once for yes, twice for no."

I moved my lips, but my tongue wasn't mobile. It filled my mouth like a rubber stopper in a sink. And it was news to me that he was holding my hand.

"Just squeeze," Jesse said again, not looking hopeful about my ability to do so.

I had to concentrate, thinking *right hand, right hand*; thinking created pain, a lot of it, but then I was able to tighten my fingers.

Jesse looked relieved at this rudimentary communication. There were a couple of nurses at bedside, faces blurred at the limits of my severely restricted vision, checking this, checking that, jotting things down.

"Caroline and Sharissa are outside," Jesse told me. "I'll let them see you for a few minutes. But I wanted to talk to you first. If that's all right, squeeze my hand again."

I applied enough pressure to make him smile, incredulously. I didn't know what kind of medication they were giving me, but I needed to tell him that I was feeling a lot of pain. I tried to get at the re-breather with my hand and pull it off my face. Jesse restrained me, said something to one of the nurses I didn't catch: the teakettles were making too much noise.

"You're in the hospital, Greg. I expect you know that much. I had you in the operating room for five and a half hours. You were shot accidentally in the head ..." He went on, describing how that little bullet had fragmented and done a lot of damage, shearing an artery, which in turn resulted in a massive blood clot. "But the brain looked good," he said. "Once I cleaned it up. Only one small fracture of the brain floor. So far I don't have any reason to feel discouraged. It's a sizable miracle that you're conscious already. We have every reason to believe you'll pull through."

Jesse didn't go into paralysis or permanent speech impairment or any of the other expectable consequences at that point; he grasped my right hand reassuringly and smiled and said, "Here's your family."

I got some idea of how long they'd been waiting from the puffiness and discoloration around Caroline's eyes. By then she probably hadn't slept for forty hours. She couldn't hide her horror or stop crying. Sharissa was trying to be brave, but it was obvious my appearance sickened her. Later she described to me how I'd looked: big turban of bandages, the rest of my face swollen and discolored like a prize eggplant. Her lips were bloodless, the skin ragged from being chewed.

Bobby Driscoll, the boy she'd been dating exclusively for a year or so, was with her: tall, wide receiver on the football team, smart too—the sort of boy I would've liked for a son, if Caroline and I had been blessed with another child.

Caroline and Sharissa took turns kissing me and squeezing my right hand. The vision in my right eye, already blurry, was made worse by tears. I tried to smile beneath the re-breather mask, but my lips wouldn't cooperate. Neither of them had much to say, except that they loved me and I shouldn't worry.

I couldn't worry about anything. I was in twilight by

then. Dreaming the dreams of near-death, whatever they may be. I had no recollection, afterward, of the intensely bright, otherworldly light reported by others who have been in my precarious state. There were no figures of old friends calling to me, or angels that glowed like gaslight in a somber haze at the end of a long tunnel.

There was only a man, a man with a stocky peasant's body, in my near-death dreams. The landscape was clear and sharp-edged. The sun shone painfully bright (so brightly I could not open my eyes all the way) where he stood near the base of a flat-topped pyramid. He was wearing a black suit with a white shirt unbuttoned to the breastbone. I could make out the gleam of a gold chain around his neck, and the cool green of jade in the form of something winged, ancient, chimerical. He had an old-fashioned stem-winder pocket watch in his hands. It gave off sizzling glints in the sun.

I was fascinated by the timepiece; all of my attention was focused on it. But when I tried to approach the man he raised his head and stopped me with his gaze. His face was flat and seamed, oiled and coppery-dark; his hair shock-white and full as flowery grief. His eyes were star-less night, as forbidding as the depths of space. He shook his head slowly, then lowered his eyes and, methodical Timekeeper, continued to wind the watch.

I only had meant to ask him how late it was. Late for what, I didn't know.

The next face I saw was that of one of the nurses, a slim mocha-colored girl.

I watched her through the slit of my right eye for a

while. Her back was to the bed. I reached up and pulled off the re-breather. She heard the hissing of oxygen through the mask, and turned.

"Guh morning," I said. The steam-whistle noises in my ears had faded. "Or is it . . . morning?"

She just stared at me, then shook her head. I found out later it was midafternoon, two days after the shooting. The nurse smiled, but she looked shocked. She stopped what she was doing with the tree of drip-feed bottles and quickly went away.

When she came back there was a doctor with her. He looked very young to me, but he'd already lost half of his hair.

"Mr. Walker, I'm Dr. Kiddfield. Senior neurological resident here at the hospital. I understand you spoke to Ruby."

"Sure . . . I did," I said. My voice sounded thick, but at least I was understandable. "Why not?"

"Well—" he rubbed his high forehead as he consulted my recent trauma history on his clipboard, grimacing a couple of times while he read. "According to this, you suffered significant damage to Broca's area."

"What . . . does that mean?"

"Broca's area controls the necessary muscle movements that enable you to pronounce words. There's more to speech than that, but in a nutshell—"

I went on producing words, although some were garbled. "Maybe I'm not hurt . . . bad as everybody thought. I feel pretty good, actually." I reached up with my right hand to rub the stubble on my cheek. It was like someone else's hand—trembling, no strength in it. "Could use a shave," I said.

Kiddfield watched me, then pored over the information on his chart again. He looked as thoroughly confused as any human being I'd ever seen.

"I'll be back soon," he said. "I just want to have a good look at your EEGs and, uh, the preliminary CAT scan again."

That evening, after another CAT scan, I was moved from Intensive Care to a private room.

Except for a persistent headache and a fluctuating fever, I was steadily improving. I continued to feel very tired and sometimes nauseated. It was an effort to move any part of my body (and impossible to lift my head, which seemed to be huge but insubstantial, like a hot-air balloon). My head was wrapped in bandages from just above the eyebrows; my lips were fat and my swollen left eye, which was still draining, stood out from my face like a piece of hard, unripened fruit. But the swelling had stabilized. As I'd already proved, I could move and guide my right hand; feeling had returned to my right leg as well, although I had no control of it.

Now I was conscious much of the time, despite the painkillers and what my daughter described as "majorly amounts" of antibiotics. Less than seventy-two hours after I'd been brought to the hospital, I was sitting up for as long as an hour at a time.

For the next couple of days it seemed as if there was a different doctor in the room every ten minutes. I was the guy who should have been, at the least, brain-dead. I didn't know if my apparent escape from horribly debilitating damage was an inspiration to them; but most seemed skeptical even when they were talking to me, as if I were some sort of hoax perpetrated by Jesse Fernando.

Jesse said, "I've been a neurosurgeon for fifteen years. I still don't know a hell of a lot about what goes on in here." He tapped his forehead with a finger. "I'd have an easier time explaining how Jesus walked on water. What I do know is, the brain has a lot of excess capacity, and for that we can both be damned grateful, Greg."

I wasn't grateful for the gaps in my memory: our second-honeymoon trip to Captiva, phone numbers, the recent death of a former business associate, all of it was gone. I could not recall Caroline's parents' names, the floor plan of our new house, or even what Thornhill Road looked like. For the most part, the blanks occurred in memories of the last two years. Going back much further, everything I needed or cared to recall was still intact.

Thanks to the skill of Dr. Jesse Fernando, who had been forced to invade my brain in order to save my life.

But frequently such invasions can result in a permanently lobotomized patient. As one of the residents under Jesse cheerfully explained to me, "See, if you get just a little bit of suction in the wrong place, it's like 'Oh-oh, there goes high school.'" Or college. Or the ability to remember the faces of loved ones. Or the inhibitions that enable us to function acceptably in society and which, perhaps, separate us from the beasts.

Caroline raised hell with Jesse about the unauthorized consultants; Jesse raised hell elsewhere, and, because the NO VISITORS sign was still up for all but immediate family, I had some peace. Even though I was attended by nurses around the clock, Caroline and Sharissa took turns keeping an eye on me until finally I made each of them go home to get a decent night's sleep. I could see in their eyes that they were afraid to leave, afraid that I would take a sudden turn for the worse and be gone, or in a coma, before they could get back to the hospital.

I was more concerned about them than I was for myself. Obviously I was going to be laid up for a while, months perhaps. But I'd had some luck, and I had learned a long time ago how to adjust quickly to whatever circumstances fate handed me.

M r. Walker? I know it's kind of late, but Dr. Fernando said it might be okay if I had a few words with you?"

I thought he must be another doctor. But he was wearing a loud Madras sports jacket that looked a size too large for him, and was years out of style. He didn't have a hospital ID tag attached to a lapel.

Instead he showed me a folder with a gold badge inside.

"I'm Sergeant Butterbaugh. C.G. Butterbaugh. Sky Valley police. Say, you sure do have a lot of flowers." He hastily pulled a handkerchief from his hip pocket and caught a sneeze in time, then glanced at me in apology as tears came to his eyes. He looked around the room again. "Sorry. Any roses? Yep, thought so. Roses get me every—"

He sneezed again, lustily, jogging his eyeglasses askew on his face. The black rims contained lenses like blastproof ports. I wondered how he could see well enough to qualify for the police department, even in Sky Valley, where the crime rate was less demanding on the abilities of our officers.

"Maybe I could just set those outside while I—" He looked at me for approval.

I nodded and put down the three-pound hand weights my physical therapist had given me to work with. After four days the left hand and arm were coming around. I was also looking forward to my first walk down the hall in the morning.

Sergeant Butterbaugh carried the vase of yellow roses at arm's length to the door, stifled another sneeze, and closed the door behind him. He had the upper body of a large man and unusually short legs, a youthful face not favored by a strong chin line. His sandy hair was so fine there was probably no use in combing it; the hair just seemed to drift where it wanted to go.

"The roses . . . are probably from the Kindors," I said. My voice was still hoarse and sometimes I had to think about what my next word was going to be. "Meghan raises them."

"Oh, the Kindors. Yeah, I spoke to them? He's getting rid of that Woodsman, by the way."

"Good idea, a little . . . late. I hope . . . Doyle's not being too hard on Ricky Gene."

"From what I gather, Ricky Gene's hard enough on himself. He's hardly been out of his room since it happened."

"I should give him a call," I said.

"I'll bet that'd help. Well, like I said, Mr. Walker, don't

want to tire you. I'm just wrapping up my investigation of the incident, and I wanted to ask you a couple of questions?" He had a lightweight though not a girlish voice, and the cadences, if not the typical highlands twang, of a North Georgia native; many of his sentences ended on an interrogative note. "Why don't I pull this chair over—"

"Sure."

Butterbaugh had a palm-size tape recorder with him. He sat beside the bed and put the recorder on the stainless-steel tray near my pillow.

"I don't think I . . . I'll be of much help to you. I know I was . . . jogging. I jog most evenings around the lake. But getting shot—that's all a blank to me."

Butterbaugh took off his glasses and cleaned them with a tissue from the box on my tray. "Sure, I understand. I was out there today and took some photographs. After talking to the kids, I've got a good idea of how the shooting happened."

"Let me in on it."

He straddled a chair, arms on the chair back. "Well, Ricky Gene and his buddies weren't very good shots to begin with. They'd pinned up a target on his shagbark hickory that grows on the crest of the rise; it sort of leans out over the path around the lake? I found seven hulls on the ground, but only one shot hit the target. The kids were standing forty-two feet away. Now, where the path you took crosses that limestone ledge, I expect you know the ledge I'm talking about—"

"Yes."

"A man your height, jogging, would be exposed from the waist up for just about three seconds as he crossed that ledge. I had one of your neighbors, Mr. Bromley, who is also six-one, run the path for me so I could be sure of that. He ran it three times at different speeds. I took my photos with a 500-millimeter lens at three different ASA levels. Photography's a hobby of mine? I've won some prizes, mostly local shows. Mr. Bromley's head was to the right and on a line from where the kids pinned their target and exactly thirty-four feet behind the tree. Given that it was twilight and the way the sun was reflecting off the lake surface, and that there was some understory in the way, I was able to conclude the kids might well not have been aware of you while Ricky Gene was potting away in the direction of his target. So that part of their story checks out, wouldn't you say?"

"You're very thorough," I said. "You made all those measurements, and—"

"Oh, yes, sir. There's a lot of ramifications to a shooting, even when, as in your case, the victim survives. And if I'm going to be in court testifying—"

"Why would you be . . . in court?" I asked him.

Sergeant Butterbaugh hesitated, and shrugged. I couldn't read his eyes; the light from my bedlamp was flaring on the lenses of his glasses.

"I'm not here as your attorney, Mr. Walker. I'm only saying that sometimes there are court proceedings, and that's one reason why my investigations are as complete as I can make them."

"It was an accident, pure and simple, and I don't—I've never given a thought to—"

He held up a hand. "You understand that it's my job only to determine if the shooting was, in fact, an accident."

"What would make you think—"

"But I don't have any preconceptions, Mr. Walker. I just met you, and I've talked to Ricky Gene twice. I guess I haven't been at my job long enough to claim any special insights into people. I *have* investigated a lot of shootings. I took a degree in Police Science at Cal State L.A. and I was on the force in Los Angeles for two years, until family matters brought me home to Sky Valley. I was in a "crash unit" most of the time. Seventy-seventh Division? That's South Central L.A. Juvenile gangs everywhere—Crips and Bloods. They all own guns. Kids not as old as Ricky Gene have them. MACs, Glocks, Uzis. One time I took a Desert Eagle auto away from a boy who could barely hold it level in both hands. This model was a .44 magnum. If he ever managed to fire it, the recoil would've broken both wrists and probably dislocated a shoulder. Matter of survival for most of them. Blood on the streets almost every night, shooting at shadows, strangers, rival homies, anybody wearing the wrong colors in the wrong place. No thought about the human consequences. What does a kid that age know about death? Or care?"

He had to stop to sneeze, smothering it in the crook of his elbow. His chubby face had a high color, a sheen of perspiration. His voice was strained, from his allergy, perhaps; or it might have been from the passion of his indignation.

"You follow, Mr. Walker?"

"I—I don't know. You mean you had the notion that Ricky Gene might've—"

Butterbaugh shrugged. "Sometimes a kid will bear grudges for reasons that aren't very clear, even to the kid himself."

"Ricky Gene isn't . . . that sort of boy, and I . . . only know him to say hello to. I've been to his house a few times. We used to be a foursome with . . . the Kindors for bridge, one Friday night a month. They're a . . . good family, Sergeant. Ricky Gene couldn't mean me any harm, and I . . . certainly don't have any ill-will toward the Kindors! It's ridiculous even to suggest . . . that Ricky Gene might have shot me on purpose."

Butterbaugh nodded, as if he were anxious to agree. He blew his nose again, then took off his glasses. I saw his eyes differently—or saw them for the first time. They were olive green in color and there was something implacable in them—the eyes of a cutthroat competitor. I also noticed the size of his hands, and the muscular thickness of one wrist—his right wrist.

"One thing you learn quickly in police work: nobody really ever knows anybody. You understand that I have to ask these questions. I wasn't making allegations."

But he had been strongly implying, and I was resentful, or perhaps defensive, because in Butterbaugh's speculation there seemed to be a buried hint of guilt on my part, as if somehow I might have been responsible for Ricky

Gene shooting me. On the other hand, maybe all of us, even the law-abiding, feel defensive when someone connected with the police is asking personal questions.

I was spared further questions when Kelly Dorminy, my night nurse, came in.

Kelly was a strawberry blonde, a pretty girl with a wry mouth. She was a little on the plump side but had the nervous energy, the dash of a whippet. With my face still swollen and bruised, I didn't think she could have detected any displeasure in my expression. But after one glance at me she turned to Butterbaugh and said, cheerful but firm, "That'll have to be all for tonight. Old Ironhead needs his rest." That was my nickname on the floor. I had become a little vain about it.

"Sure." Butterbaugh scraped his chair back. "Thanks, Mr. Walker. I guess this wraps it up for me." He retrieved his miniature recorder and shut it off. I felt a measure of relief as he prepared to leave.

"Do you play a lot of tennis?" I asked him, just to be saying something cordial.

"Sir . . . ? As a matter of fact, I do. How——?" He pocketed the minicorder, gave his strong right wrist a half turn and laughed. "You ought to be a detective yourself."

"My daughter started playing when she was six. She was the third-ranked G.S.T.A. junior girl a couple of years ago. Her left arm was weak, so she did special exercises to build up the muscles."

"That's Sharissa? Beautiful name. We had a nice chat yesterday when I dropped by to see how you were coming along. Sharissa told me she was doing an Advanced Placement paper on Forensic Science. Seems like a very bright girl."

"Top five percent of her graduating class. We're real proud of Sharissa."

"Now that really must be all," Kelly said to Butterbaugh, "and you have no idea how ugly I can be when I'm not minded."

"You? Nah." Butterbaugh smiled and was nearly out the

door when he hesitated and snapped his fingers. "Almost forgot. Mr. Walker, tell Sharissa I'll drop off those books she wanted in a day or two."

"Out," Kelly Dorminy said, and she closed the door in Butterbaugh's face before I had a chance to ask him what books he was talking about.

After that, Kelly checked all the medications I was receiving through tubes in my wrist and right foot, and took my temperature. The fever was coming down, slowly. Their biggest worry, Dr. Fernando had told my wife, was an inflammation of the brain, for any number of reasons, or the sudden onset of meningitis, which would be fatal quickly in my present condition.

"Don't let on to anybody that I told you," Kelly said, "but you're scheduled for some major-league visitors tomorrow: neurosurgeons from the AMA convention they're holding down there in Atlanta."

"I can hardly wait."

"Big day for you. The catheter's coming out, and so's that pipeline into your foot."

"Good. It's been itching like crazy."

"Want me to scratch?"

"Yes."

She scratched the sole of my foot for me, a teasing smile on her face. Or that's what I thought I saw. "How's that feel?"

"Feels fine," I said. "Kelly, honey, you know what? I've had me a hell of a hard-on since you walked in the room. Why don't we just take the catheter out tonight, and then you can suck Old Ironhead off big-time."

Kelly stiffened in shock; then the light went out of her pretty green eyes and they seemed suddenly vitrified. She turned away from the bed as if she had just slammed a door.

"I'll be back in a little while," she said.

"Kelly!"

"Yes?"

"God—I don't know what made me—I don't know

where that came from! I never use that kind of—that was somebody else talking, Kelly!"

She hesitated, then her shoulders drooped and she turned with a slightly bitter smile.

"Never mind. I didn't hear it. Would you like the TV on?"

"Yes. Okay." I was still mortified. "Please, Kelly. I'm really very—"

"No need to apologize, Mr. Walker. You just kind of zinged me there—I was surprised, bu I shouldn't have been. Dr. Fernando and Dr. Kiddfield explained to all of us who are on this service that—well—there could be some sudden changes in your behavior."

"Explain it to me."

"It has to do with the frontal lobes being—disturbed. Patients with wounds like yours sometimes speak and act in a manner contrary to their normal personalities. In the worst cases—and you're certainly not the worst head trauma case we've had, don't get that idea—patients will say or do anything that pops into their minds."

"Or may have been there all along?"

"Mr. Walker, it was just a—didn't mean anything, really. I get worse stuff all the time from some of the residents around here, believe me." Kelly put the TV remote control near my right hand, fussed with my pillow to prove that I had been forgiven. "News, or the HBO movie?"

The HBO movie was a rerun of *Robocop*.

"Just turn it off," I said, "I guess I don't feel like watching anything right now."

That night the old Timekeeper was back in my dreams, as was the pyramid.

There were strange-looking birds the color of the sky flying over the white, step-terraced pyramid. Something was crouched on the roof of the structure that capped the pyramid—something huge, animal-like, and forbidding. But I was far away, I couldn't make it out. The Time-keeper in his severe black suit beckoned me closer. I walked slowly across a deserted, stone-paved plaza toward the Timekeeper. It was night before I reached him, a night of drumming and the brilliance of stars. There was torchlight in the black pupils of his eyes.

"Father?" I said. He smiled at me. "Now?" I asked him.

He opened a hand that was caked with old blood. The gold pocket watch in his palm had no hands. Instead of ticking it made a windy, moaning sound, like a bull-roarer gathering velocity. He looked from my face to the top of the pyramid. I was to climb up there. I had known that all along, but I couldn't make myself ascend the seven steep levels to acknowledge the fate that was waiting for me.

I turned back to the Timekeeper. Where his head had been a harpy eagle sat clutching his shoulders, glaring at me with yellow eyes.

The next day in the hospital was, emotionally, my worst, although my spirits should have been much improved by getting out of bed and limping around for short periods of time. I had made up my mind that I was ready to go home; Jesse Fernando had other ideas.

Three eminent neurosurgeons took time out from the convention they were attending and helicoptered up from Atlanta to review my case and talk with me. Jesse didn't come right out and say so, but it was obvious he hoped

I'd make the effort to cooperate with them. I tried, but I was getting fed up with all the attention. I wanted to put the shooting behind me, go home to my family and get on with my life as soon as possible.

The eldest of the neurosurgeons, a man with buzz-cut white hair and the ruddy complexion of a construction foreman, said, "I was a battalion surgeon in Vietnam for three years. I'm confident I've seen almost everything, including one soldier who came back from the dead as they were about to prepare him for burial. But the adaptive and recovery powers of your brain is unique in my experience."

"What about the bullet fragments?" I looked at the eminent neurosurgeon from Lyon, a man named Duvivier. *"Vont ils mé causer des problems plutard?"*

He nodded and smiled approval of my French, which I was glad to learn hadn't gone down the drain with fragments of brain tissue.

"This is most difficult to say. Dr. Fernando did excellent work in recovering the majority of the fragments. But it was not worth the risk of trying to remove all of them."

"Greg's forty-five," Jesse said. "But he has the constitution of a man twenty years younger. That may be a factor in his recovery time."

"I've always tried to take care of myself. Most of my life I've worked two jobs. I always like to say, I'm too busy to get sick." I chuckled and they smiled, but I still didn't care for the way they were looking at me. As if I were an insult to their education and experience. "This is the first time I've been in a hospital since my daughter was born. I hope it'll be the last."

The Reverend Bob Justival had a little different slant on my narrow escape.

"It's a miracle, Greg!" Bob said, or rather, exulted; he has that bully, holy look of the fatted friars of old. His fervent style can wear you down after a while. Most parishoners of First Iconium refer to his wife Beth Ann as "shy," but to me she looks sort of stunned most of the time. "Jesus heard your prayers, good buddy."

"With God all things are possible," I agreed.

"A special favor," Bob beseeched me. "Would you testify at our next revival meeting?"

There was no doubt about it—I was the local celebrity of the week. Or month. I was hoping that it would stay local.

Once I was allowed out of bed and could sit up in a chair in my room, I was, as they say in the South, at home to callers. Most of them, like the Reverend Bob, obligatory.

Caroline brought the Kindors, including the repentant perpetrator Ricky Gene, to see me. Doyle had been involved in several different businesses since I'd known him—a fifty-cent car wash, a collection agency—but nothing that had been very successful. He could barely manage the payments on their house, and they walked a financial tightrope most of the time. Meghan liked to say she was in telemarketing, which meant that she was on the phone in her kitchen three hours a day, trying to sell cemetery plots for an enterprise called Beauty Rest Eternal Gardens: several undeveloped acres where no one, as yet, was sleeping off Eternity. The point is, the Kindors had no cleaners I could've taken them to had I been so inclined.

I thought that I should put on a show of forgiveness even Bob Justval would have admired, so two minutes after they came into the room we were all in tears.

I was scarcely aware that Caroline was taking pictures of me with her Sureshot. My arm around Ricky Gene, both of us smiling. No hard feelings. The next day we were on the front page of the Sky Valley *Tribune*. Caroline had taken the photos as a favor to the managing editor, her former boss.

I didn't know until much later that the Associated Press had picked up the story, and the photo, and that it was reprinted in papers around the country as well as in Canada.

So far away. But we all live in a world of instant communications. Very little that happens anywhere escapes attention, depending on how attentive one cares to be. We truly are, as a man named McLuhan said, a global village.

Having bypassed the usual expectations when a foreign object of any size passes most of the way through the human brain, I was home ten days after the shooting. I showed no signs of significant neurological impairment and I'd been fever-free for seventy-two hours. The headaches hadn't stopped, but they were no real problem. Jesse recommended at least a week of recuperation at home, and I was in no hurry to go back to work until my hair grew in. Not knowing in advance of surgery how many entries into the skull he'd have to make, Jesse's team had shaved my entire head. But my hair has always grown quickly. To keep it the length I like it, I need to have it trimmed twice a month.

Fortunately I had a boy named Bisco working for me at Walker's Authorized RCA Servicenter, a junior-college dropout who has a genius for locating the trouble in TVs and stereos that have been blitzed by sudden power surges—most people have no idea of the damage that can be caused if they leave their sets plugged in during an electrical storm, even if the set is turned off.

If Caroline hadn't been working eighteen hours a day to get Claude Gilley reelected, we might have taken some time off and driven down to Calloway Gardens or even to Hilton Head for a vacation we both needed badly. Sharissa was working as a lifeguard days at the country club and doing four nights a week at Burger King, but even so I saw more of her than I did of my wife. Sharissa made it a point to spend time with me, having sensed what I was doing my best to hide: a post-traumatic depression, a deep uneasiness at having come so abruptly to the stark realization that it was all going to end for Greg Walker, perhaps sooner than I had anticipated. Although it certainly was not my nature, then or now, to brood about death.

Caroline alternately slaved over her typewriter in her small study off our bedroom trying to come up with speeches that would put Claude back in the good graces of his disenchanted constituents, and running off to whatever club breakfast or civic forum he was scheduled for. Sharissa and I spent several weekend hours scraping and repainting the deck behind our house. Looking back, I realize that they were some of the happiest hours of my life.

I'd been married to Caroline for eighteen years; Sharissa had turned seventeen in June. In the fall she would be a senior in high school, where she was Miss Everything. She deserved all of her honors. She was a lovely girl who had inherited my slim build, Caroline's Georgia-peach complexion and also her alluring, autumnal, gilt-edged eyes, so light a shade of brown that they seemed, eerily, to have no pupils when you looked at her from certain angles. Her closest friends, boys and girls, were from our church. They were all active, personable youngsters with high ideals and rigorous moral standards—no trace of the soiled insolence that characterizes so many young people these days. In an age where numerous mental cases are on the loose and smut is a national blight, we'd never had a moment's worry as to where Sharissa was, who she was with, or what she was doing.

No matter what time of day I needed to be up—and for years I'd awakened at four-thirty A.M. to deliver the Atlanta *Constitution* locally for extra income—Sharissa was always in the kitchen ahead of me, the coffee would be perking, and she'd greet me with a cheerful, "Good morning, Daddy." She always had her own reasons for being up and around that early, but I suspected her primary motivation was just to spend those few extra minutes with me. We were no longer under severe financial pressure, like the Kindors—Caroline's spells of nervous debilitation were few and far between these days—and breakfast was now at a more reasonable hour, but Sharissa had never abandoned the small ritual that was so precious to me.

Caroline's nerves and melancholia—well, it had been a strain on the family union no matter how hard Sharissa and I tried to pretend otherwise. Who could blame Caroline? She was simply one of those high-strung persons with more nervous energy than is good for them. More than one member of Caroline's large family, going back a hundred years, had been subject to what they referred to as "sinking spells." In the old days the Crowder family manics dosed themselves with patent medicines liberally infused with cocaine, and were, perhaps, the better for it. Caroline's treatments had been more complex, and of limited value. In addition to our unyielding trust in God, what seemed to benefit Caroline most was the passage of time, and, of all things, an early menopause, which occurred when she was forty-six. Sharissa had been spared this glum and potentially dangerous inheritance, although like any teenager she could be moody. Since we'd moved to Thornhill Road Caroline had suffered only one crisis, after a tongue-lashing from the senator, whose home-district office she'd managed while he was away in Washington. Caroline put up with Claude, not only because the pay was good, but because she believed he still had value to our state—a point I was always careful not to argue with her, although I and numerous of his colleagues in Washington considered Claude to be a four-flushing son of a bitch.

Just before moonrise we finished the tedious job of hand painting the latticework around the deck, cleaned and put away the brushes. I was standing on our flagstone patio looking at the sunset-reddened lake and a flock of birds feeding in the abundant foxtail and broom sedge along the shore. Burgers were sizzling on the charcoal grill. Sharissa came down the steps from the kitchen with the hamburger buns, potato chips, and catsup. She put the stuff down on the picnic table and came over, slipped an arm around my waist, laid her head on my shoulder. As always I was ravished by the power of her art, which is called youth. I clasped her hand and sighed contentedly.

"What were you thinking just now?" she asked me. She used to ask that all the time, when she was much younger, but was out of the habit now. It was one of those special privileges and freedoms of childhood that seems to be lost once children pass through that invisible barrier into the constraints of puberty.

"I was thinking that life is good."

"Amen," Sharissa said, and tightened her grip on me, laughing, a joyous laugh that expressed more eloquently than any words or prayers the miracle that had kept us together.

Sharissa had invited Bobby Driscoll to eat with us, and after supper we played a few hands of hearts. Caroline called a little after nine, from the Hilton in Atlanta where Claude Gilley was campaigning at a state Junior Chamber of Commerce convention. She sounded tired, and they had another couple of hours to go. I suggested she take a room at the hotel instead of driving back to Sky Valley after midnight.

"I hate hotels," Caroline said. "There's nothing like being in your own bed, after a long hard week. Promise you'll let me sleep until noon tomorrow?"

"Promise. Things not going so well for Claude?"

"He's down another three points in the latest *Journal-Constitution* poll. You know how he can be when—"

"When the going gets tough, Claude looks for a cat to kick. If you want my opinion, he's going to lose this one." *And good riddance,* I thought. Claude Gilley had a grotesque amount of unearned wealth, which seemed to have deformed his ego at an early age. But eventually he was bound to be undone by the sheer incompetence of his ambition. I suppose the principal reason why I didn't like him was that he had once propositioned Caroline while they were on an airplane. A small airplane. He was the type to simultaneously insult a woman's honor and her dignity.

"I'll be unemployed," Caroline reminded me.

It wasn't an admonition, but I'd had enough lean years to be slightly on the defensive. "We're doing all right. If a new administration in Washington doesn't put us through the tax grinder, you'll have time to finish your novel."

"Do you know how many unpublished novelists there are in this country?"

"Yours will be published."

"I wish I had that much confidence in me."

I heard Caroline exhale in a familiar way. "Are you smoking again?" I asked her.

"First one today. Scout's honor. I reached that point where I had to have a cigarette, or—oh-oh, I'm being paged. Gotta run. Is Sharissa taking good care of you? Love you, Greg, don't wait up for me."

When I returned to the sun porch Sharissa and Bobby were lounging on the sofa with their heads contentedly together, watching a tennis match on ESPN.

"That was your mom," I told Sharissa. "She'll be home late. Or is that news?"

I must have sounded a little grumpy. Sharissa straightened and glanced at Bobby. "We were going to go out for a little while. But we don't have to, I mean if you want me to stay."

"No, that's okay, I'll be fine. Bobby, looks like you've put on at least an inch around the neck since they opened that new weight room at the high school."

"Yes, sir. I've bulked up to two twenty-eight now. And I've got a lot more, you know, stamina since I started the summer lifting program. I was, you know, that was my big problem last year, I had a tendency to fade in the fourth quarter against some of the real big guys, like all those steroid freaks at Mountain View."

I walked them to the front door.

"Where're y'all going? Late for a movie. Sharissa, you need more rest than you've been getting with all the upset around here."

"I *know*, daddy." She put an arm around my waist and kissed my cheek. "We were just going over to the DQ, see what's happening. I'll be home by eleven. Eleven-thirty?"

I nodded approval of the time. Bobby, I saw, was driving his brother's Chevy Maxicab—the silvery gray shade of fresh solder, with darkly tinted windows—while Kevin was at Benning training with a Ranger unit.

"Kevin sent us a new bumper sticker," Bobby said. "That one there on the left side of the back window? It says, 'Nuke them till they glow, then shoot them in the dark.' "

"Bobby," Sharissa said, "honestly, one more bumper sticker and I am not going to be *seen* with you in that old truck."

Bobby laughed. "Kevin's the family mercenary. All I want to be is a country lawyer, like Granddaddy Bub. Raise me a mess of kids while Kevin keeps the sand niggers in line."

It was the look that Sharissa gave him—as highly charged as sunspots—when he mentioned children, and the way her hand slipped into his as they walked toward the truck, that give me the chilly notion they had more in mind than a trip to Dairy Queen. They looked good together, dressed almost alike in faded jeans and polo shirts, wearing, on their left earlobes, the small gold crosses they had exchanged months ago. Bobby wore his hair long and a little straggly in back, but nothing outlandish. As I watched them from the veranda, in the glow from the gaslights on either side of the entrance to our driveway, they seemed older, exclusive to each other; and for the first time I sensed something secret in their relationship, the possibility that they were becoming lovers.

Bobby honked once as they were pulling away, and Sharissa waved. I heard Bobby singing, "Drop-kick me, Jesus, through the goalposts of life." I remained on the veranda, watching the taillights of the big truck as it drove up the street, past Meghan Kindor's black-and-silver Dodge van coming from the other direction. The moon over the lake was nearly full, bright as a searchlight.

Seeing me on the veranda, Meghan stopped in front of house.

"Hey, Greg!"

"Hey, Meghan. Doyle and the kids get off on that fishing trip?"

"Finally! Guess I'm an old bachelor girl for the next three days. You feeling good?"

"Feeling like a prince, Meggy. Look like one too, in this turban I'm wearing."

She laughed. It was abrupt and mirthless—Meghan's way of commenting when she can't think of anything to say. Meghan appears breezy and cheerful, but beneath that there's something cowed about her, even sad. This often is the fate of women with husbands like Doyle, who is a caring man and a good father but occasionally goes too heavy on the Jack and Seven, until there is something amok in him, buzzing like a maddened wasp from one side of his skull to the other.

"Well, you take care."

"You too, Meggy."

Meghan pulled into her driveway two houses away—they lived in the Williamsburg model, theirs a gray clapboard trimmed in yellow. Our house was the Mount Vernon, largest in the subdivision, featuring a narrow veranda paved in zigzag brick, with white columns. I stayed on the veranda for a few minutes, looking out over the neighborhood, savoring it: the neat hedges and Bermuda lawns and ornamental fences, the cascades of weeping willows and popcorn clusters of white crape myrtle in the moonlight. The warm air I breathed was steeped in the fragrance of our night-blooming jasmine. The Feltmans' new baby was crying, a thin distant fussing that made me nostalgic and melancholy at the same time. *Sharissa.* I had held her in my arms when she was five minutes old. I remembered her wide happy smiles as a child, mock-ferocious from missing teeth. I remembered the falls, the bumps, the scrapes and cuts. Now she was tall and flawlessly tanned and athletic, martial on a volleyball or tennis court—crouched, perspiring, lower lip pressed in a taut, bloodless line against her teeth, swaying slightly as she prepared to return a serve, the amber light of a lioness in her eyes. Deadly with a tennis racket—or heavenly in an aqua gown. So many good memories, which, thank the Lord, those little fragments of lead had spared.

On the other side of the street Erica Lashley came out of their house screaming at her hapless mother, jumped into her red Miata and roared out of the driveway. Erica was sixteen, a trampy sixteen; the Lashleys had lost their grip on her when she was still a child, and were having no luck trying to buy her back with sports cars and trips to Florida during spring break. Sharissa would just roll her eyes whenever Erica's name was mentioned. The Hulstines were having another Saturday-night party in their backyard. They were the only childless couple in the neighborhood, which meant they had both the time and the money to invest in their social life. Roddy was lithe and youthful but dour, like a Greek chorus boy; Irene Hulstine was a good fifteen years older than her husband and always dressed as if she were a finalist in a conspicuous-consumption contest. The Dutch Colonial house between the Kindors and ours, owned by Hoke and Tempie Howington, was dark. Hoke was retired from Coca-Cola and when they weren't on the road in their Airstream they usually hit the sack by nine o'clock.

Another car was coming up the street, one I didn't recognize. A coffee-brown sedan, Buick or Oldsmobile or

Pontiac: without their respective corporate emblems nobody's been able to tell them apart for the last thirty years. The car hesitated at our driveway, then pulled in.

Detective Sergeant C.G. Butterbaugh of the Sky Valley police department got out. He was wearing walking shorts that emphasized the almost comical brevity of his hairy legs, and a baggy tennis sweater.

"Hello, there! Mr. Walker?"

"Yes."

He had a couple of books under one arm. I remembered Sharissa talking about the paper she was working on for school, and how helpful Butterbaugh had been in providing her with source material.

"Good to see you up and around. Sharissa tells me you're doing real well?"

"Some headaches, a little dizziness, memory lapses; but physically I'm nearly as good as I ever was. I'll know for sure when I start jogging again if I'm going to be a hundred percent. Would you like to come in, Sergeant? Sharissa's not home."

"Oh." He was obviously disappointed, and I tried not to smile. Another one my daughter inadvertently had caught in her gossamer net. Then I thought of Sharissa with Bob. There was a bad taste in my mouth—bitterness, gall. Since the shooting I had been prey to sourceless, unpleasant odors and tastes, possibly the result of minute malfunctions somewhere in the abused areas of the brain. On a couple of occasions the olfactory halluncinations had been powerful enough to trigger my gag reflex. I put a hand over my mouth and tried to clear my throat. I wasn't much of a drinker, but usually a shot of something dark, syrupy, and potent, like apricot liqueur, was necessary to clear the palate.

"How about a beer?" I said to Butterbaugh. "I was about to have a nightcap myself."

"Sure, I wouldn't mind a beer. I've got a little time before I need to get back to my folks." He hesitated, perhaps wondering if an explanation was called for, then offered, "They're old, and, not exactly bedfast, but housebound, and I can't afford to have somebody stay with them all the time. So, when I'm off duty I like to spend as much time with them as I can."

"Is that the family business that brought you back to Sky Valley?" I asked him as we went into the house.

"Yes, sir. In a way I don't regret coming home, but I was already accepted by the Bureau when my dad had his stroke."

I coughed into my fist, still trying to clear my throat, and took a can of Heineken from the refrigerator. "Bureau? You mean the FBI?"

"Yes, sir. Lifelong ambition." He put the books he'd been carrying on the butcher-block table in our breakfast room; one of them had to do with the FBI's crime laboratories. He saw me glance at the cover. "Sharissa was particularly interested in DNA typing as admissable evidence in court cases."

I nodded as if I were interested as well, or even knew what he was talking about, opened the pantry and took out my bottle of apricot liqueur. We maintain a small store of liquor for Caroline's drinking friends, co-workers, or buddies from her days as a reporter, but we're a Baptist family and like most Baptist families, if you have it in the house at all you don't flaunt it.

We went outside. The Hulstines' party was going full-blast around their oval swimming pool. We sat in the small gazebo at one end of the deck. The smell of fresh latex paint was still strong here. I thought about the shade of beige I'd chosen, wondering if I was still going to like it in the morning.

"Been trying," Butterbaugh said thoughtfully, "but I can't place your accent. Not from around here?"

"Balamer," I said.

"Oh, Baltimore. Lot of family living there?"

"I'm afraid not. At least as far as I know. I was a foundling."

"Tough break," Butterbaugh said, with a little wince of sympathy. "You've certainly made out okay. Couldn't have been easy for you, alone in the world."

"I realize it's trite to say. But the love of a good woman has meant everything to me."

He nodded. "Sure, I know what you mean. Wouldn't mind being married myself. Don't put enough effort into it, I suppose. I mean, looking for the right girl." Frowning, he sipped his beer. "Sharissa's out on a date?" he said.

"More or less. She's with Bobby Driscoll. Maybe you met him."

"The tall boy? Wants to be a lawyer? Yeah." Thinking about Bobby seemed to weigh on his spirits; he sighed softly and changed the subject. "This is really a nice place you have here, Mr. Walker."

"Thank you. Why don't we make it Greg, and—what's the C.G. stand for?"

"Collins Gosden." He shrugged, with a little deprecatory change of expression, as if from long habit. "My mother had me late, and because they both knew I was going to be their only child, they paid off both sides of the family. Actually, I have three names; but the other one is so awful I don't want to be reminded of it by using the initial." He shrugged again. "Three initials are too much anyway. Unless you're British." His eyes moved often—not shiftily, but with a certain thoroughness of scrutiny, as if something he'd been anticipating all of his life was about to materialize from shadows. "In high school," he said, "they called me 'Butts.'" He sat up a little straighter and swiveled a half turn in the cushioned patio chair. "That reminds me, I reserved one of the school courts for Wednesday at six. Sharissa said something about taking me on if we could work out a time."

"I'll mention it to Sharissa; but maybe you ought to give her a call yourself."

Butterbaugh glanced at the time with a look of resignation. He wore an old-fashioned gold strap watch with Roman numerals and an enameled black bezel which I recognized as a Hamilton. The Piping Rock model, introduced about 1925. It may have been because I had nothing in the way of family heirlooms or keepsakes myself, but I liked old things; and I hadn't seen a watch like his for many years.

The dark taste in my mouth was nearly gone. I brooded on the sapphire lozenge of pool in the Hulstines' backyard. We listened to "California Dreamin' " from numerous speakers. The Mamas and the Papas. I had enjoyed their music once, but I couldn't remember anything else they'd done. This lapse of memory made me uneasy, even anxious. As if little pieces of my brain were still crumbling away, and eventually there would be nothing but a void inside my head.

"Do you think you might get another shot at the FBI?" I asked Butterbaugh.

"It's not likely. The best time to apply is after you've been in uniform a year, eighteen months. After three years you're what they call 'tainted.' Too much time as a cop or something. Anyway, I'll be thirty-two in September, and that's—"

He finished his beer instead of the thought. I discovered that I liked Butterbaugh, or at least empathized with him very strongly. How many of the young fail through the tyranny of circumstances to develop their dreams, explore all the potential that life has to offer? "Now my days are swifter than a runner; they flee away, they see no good. They pass by like swift ships, like an eagle swooping on its prey." There is much in the Bible to give us comfort. And so much wisdom that is harsh, unyielding. I found myself thinking not of my own life but of the days of my daughter. She passed then, distantly, through my field of inner vision, and I was numbed by her beauty. So short a time for the work to be done, for the pleasures we seek. What is life but what we hope it will be—in other words, an illusion.

I made some sort of inarticulate, despairing sound. Butterbaugh was staring at me. I realized then that I was crying.

It was a little before ten on that Saturday night when Butterbaugh took his leave. I felt tired without also feeling the need to sleep. I could have gone jogging, but Jesse Fernando had forcefully warned me not to overexert myself.

As a compromise I jogged in place for five minutes, then worked out with my hand weights for fifteen minutes more. My left hand was still understrength and my fingers felt wooden after any sort of physical effort. I could not straighten the last two fingers, which curled stubbornly in toward the palm without actually touching. I didn't want to believe this might be a permanent consequence of the shooting. An admonition from Ecclesiastes came to mind: "That which is made crooked cannot be made straight." I was in a poor frame of mind. I wished Caroline were home. Or Sharissa.

The Bible also says (Ecclesiastes again) that a man shall see good for all his hard work. The good of my life was the love of my family, and I was always deeply aware of that. The intelligence, strength, and chastity of my daughter was a matter of great pride. Too much pride, perhaps.

My head hurt. I was filled with a terrible, unappeasable nervous energy. I paced through all the rooms of the house as if looking for something unwittingly lost, that I couldn't name. Several times I paused just inside Sharissa's room. Like most girls her age who are always in a hurry to be somewhere else, she was not particularly neat. Tonight there were odds and ends of clothing strewn on her rumpled bed. The mirror of her vanity had a cold cream smear on it. There was a heap of schoolbooks beside her desk in what builders like to refer to as the "bonus room." I picked up a physics notebook, saw Bobby's name doodled in many ornate styles on an inside page, put the notebook down. *Where her thoughts were. Where her heart was.* It was only an infatuation. Bobby was an upstanding boy whom I liked and admired. I had to trust my daughter, trust her. I had never doubted Sharissa's moral integrity; why was I doubting her now? It might have been only a sea-change in Bobby's blue eyes when he looked at me while holding my daughter's hand, casual as a cat holding a mouse by the tail.

I had Percodans, but I didn't like to take them. With the lessening of pain came a gray fog, and things that crept in the fog, crept and crouched and waited to be recognized. I bore the pain and went into Sharissa's bathroom, which was still a little muggy and shampoo-fragrant from her last shower. One of her lipsticks was open on the counter, a rusty-red shade. I touched a finger to the thick bullet of lipstick. The slim gold cylinder, that firm but oddly fleshy, rounded head, like a prim little penis women put to their lips every day. I smeared my finger slightly and held it to my nose. Sharissa, her scent. She used makeup sparingly, for mild and, I thought, unnecessary enhancements on date nights. I stared at myself in the moist mirror, disliking the ugly flesh-colored turban more than ever. It seemed constricting, putting pressure on my tender skull, the unwell and seething brain. I felt tortured, as if my head were being squeezed in iron tongs. To my right I was blown all out of proportion in a magnifying mirror, like a blurred giant trying to see through the small window of a doll's house.

Sharissa had been reading in her bathroom, one of the fashion magazines she'd studied avidly since she was twelve, and nourishing a nascent ambition that eventually had faded, to my relief: I had never been able to picture my daughter as one of those unearthly child-women looking up from covers of *Vogue* with the bland power of killer sharks.

I picked up a months-old copy of the magazine from the mat beside the tub and saw that she had folded a page back. The slick paper was wrinkled from water drops. The page was an ad, in tasteful pastels, for a woman's contraceptive cream.

My hands were shaking. They shook too easily, since my release from the hospital. I closed the magazine and put it in the wicker basket with other magazines and paperbacks she liked to read while soaking in her tub, a habit she'd picked up from Caroline. I don't know what was in my heart just then. I don't want to remember. After a few moments I'm certain I rationalized that it was merely passing curiosity on Sharissa's part, something she planned to discuss with her mother when the opportunity arose. My daughter was, after all, seventeen, more woman than child. She was sound of mind and body, healthy of spirit. I tried to tell myself that it was my own spirit and emotions that were betraying me, causing me to think evil of her. An aftereffect of the shooting, a brooding pestilence in mind and blood.

I sat in the kitchen drinking black coffee while the two-hundred-year-old cabinet clock, a Crowder family heirloom, ticked relentlessly in our entrance hall. I counseled myself as the Bible counsels: "Do not let yourself be conquered by the evil, but keep conquering the evil with the good."

If Caroline had been home we would have talked, and then I think it would have been all right for me.

But I was alone and, I was certain, in peril.

At ten-thirty I took out the staples and unwrapped the turban of thick gauze from my sweaty, itching, nearly bald head, put on a corduroy cap I found on the shelf of the hall closet, and, with my red pinched-together scars only partially concealed, went looking for my daughter.

Sky Valley, in northwest Georgia, has a population of a little more than thirty thousand; but in the last thirty years that population has scarcely increased at all. In fact, as the twentieth century enters its last decade, Sky Valley is one of numerous small cites everywhere in the country having trouble maintaining their economic bases. This part of the state is not prime farmland, and, although the setting is attractively hilly and forested, it lacks the scenic qualities that promote tourism. Sky Valley, some twenty miles west of Georgia's north-south interstate highway, is too remote from metropolitan Atlanta to become a bedroom community. Two carpet mills have closed recently. If not for a Japanese firm that opened a small factory to manufacture parts for their line of motorcycles, our unemployment rate might have been close to nine percent this past year. The county government is complacent, and only the Chamber of Commerce lobbies vigorously, on a limited budget, to obtain the light industry Sky Valley must have. The alternative is to slowly lose the young people, the leadership of the future.

In spite of the fact that I had had my share of difficulties in establishing a going business, I'd never considered moving anywhere else after my marriage to Caroline. I loved Sky Valley—the sense of community, the deliberate pace of life there. I felt no shame in admitting I was not an ambitious man. I was largely, because of my circumstances, self-educated. My one talent, or knack, shall we call it, was a facility for languages, which, perhaps, was coefficient with a love of books and reading—although no one would consider me a bookish person. Caroline had always said I could be an excellent writer if only I applied myself. But, again, the matter of ambition: I left the writing to her. I had picked up a satisfactory knowledge of electronics, of microcircuitry and software, without taking courses. I belonged to several businessmen's organizations and had chaired a couple of committees at First Iconium Baptist Church. I swam, jogged, played tennis with my daughter (although I was no competition for her by the time she reached puberty), went fishing three or four times a year.

As to personality, I am the sort of man who has many acquaintances but few hard-and-fast friends. Truthfully, I had no close male friends because I lacked the interest to put myself through the traditional male-bonding rituals that were necessary to acquire them. I preferred spending what free time was available to me with my wife and daughter. When it came to women, I had to be careful. I have always been sexually attractive to women. I don't know why. I like talking to women, and listening to them. But I've never pursued them. I certainly don't have the kind of looks that stop women in their tracks. I'm taller than average, dark, unblemished and, blessedly, not burdened with a heavy beard. I'm not all that outgoing, but I tend to be comfortable with myself; and I notice that quality in very few of the people I meet. The actors we remember and like seem to have this quality as well; in show business I believe it's called "presence."

That's about it: the sum and total of Greg Walker. The fact remains that, although I was obviously a married man, I would occasionally find a note beneath a windshield wiper blade of my car in the Kroger parking lot, from someone I couldn't recall having met at all, or a shop clerk I knew only casually. Other women, at least two of whom were from my church, had come into the store, and—"I'd like to get to know you better, Greg." Eventually I heard something like that. Said nervously, or with a laugh, or with just a look, a long, steady look that disdained pretense, or caution. I had no desire to take advantage of whatever opportunities they were offering. Perhaps for the idle or the bored a superficial relationship is better than nothing, but not for me.

I was, inevitably, at some distance from Caroline's family, in spite of my best efforts. They had always considered me to be some sort of homeless drifter, which, in point of fact, I was, when Caroline and I met: twenty-seven years old, lately discharged from the Army, with some money carefully saved but no prospects. The obvious success of our eighteen-year marriage had not made a significant difference in their deep-seated attitude. The unavoidable lack of family was, as far as they were concerned, an ineradicable flaw in me. Even so, I had no complaints about my life in Sky Valley. Until the errant bullet from Doyle Kindor's Woodsman pistol brought this life to an end, although not in a foreseeable way.

On the Saturday night that I went looking, in a kind of panic, for Sharissa, I drove mostly with my right hand through the streets of Sky Valley, my left hand with the two curled-in fingers resting in my lap.

The Dairy Queen that was two blocks from the high school, out on Old Chestnut Pike, stayed open until eleven on Saturday nights. It was a popular spot for teenagers to congregate, so popular that there was a private patrolman on duty weekends to prevent cruising and the fights that sometimes break out when kids have nothing else to do.

I couldn't see the Chevy truck from the street and had to circle the driveway myself to make sure they weren't there. Other than the Dairy Queen and a McDonald's nearby, there was no place else to go this time of night except home. Or to someone else's home. But we had a standing rule: if Sharissa changed her itinerary on date nights, she had to call and let us know.

I assumed I had missed them, and turned right out of the Dairy Queen lot. Bobby lived north of downtown, in an older, slightly seedy but still presentable neighborhood of mixed bungalows and two-story frame houses shaded by lovely old oaks and hickory trees. His father managed an auto parts store; I knew him from Rotary luncheons. Bobby's mother was a hospice volunteer. They were solid unassuming people, like Bobby himself. I tried to remember the name of the street where the Driscolls lived. West Fourth, or Fifth. If they had gone to Bobby's from the Dairy Queen, then she would have called me. We had few rules for Sharissa, and she has never broken any of them. So she couldn't be there. She hadn't gone home with Bobby.

There was a Texaco mart on the corner of Old Chestnut and Rockmar. A big silvery tanker truck was replenishing underground storage tanks. I slowed on the street, almost stopping, then turned in. I parked away from the pumps on one side of the building and went inside.

A glum young man with moles like watermelon seeds on his face was nursing a diet cola and complaining about his life to the cashier. She had sulfur-yellow hair as wiry as an Airedale's. She gazed steadily away from him with bored blue eyes, watching instead the postcard-size screen of a television on the counter, winding a strand of pink bubblegum around and around her little finger. She was watching a home-shopping program.

"I wouldn't mind having one of them pear-cut dia-mondette dinner rings," she said, mostly to herself. She examined the bare fingers of her left hand. "It's fourteen-carat gold, too. I'm talking about genuine. My ex never gave me nothing that good when we got married. No, I wouldn't mind. But shoot, you got to have a credit card to order something off them home-shopping people."

"I allow they'll take a check. Won't they?"

"Well, now, you got to have a bank account to write a check. Of course that little detail never bothered my ex. Which is why he's where he's at for the next year and a half."

I looked up the Driscolls' address in the phone book. Five forty-two West Fifth. I was about to call, but then I glanced at the clock behind the cash register. It was six minutes to eleven. The young man asked the girl if she could let him have a pack of Camels and he would pay her tomorrow. She chewed gum and shook her head and didn't look at him.

"Here they go again with the solid-brass cordial sets. Reckon where do they get the people to buy tacky stuff like that?"

The taste was back in my mouth, black and bitter as coal tar. It went with the headache that was hammering me with every step I took. I pulled a can of Orange Crush from the wall-size refrigerator unit beside the counter. I almost never drink sodas, but the taste in my mouth was vile and I needed something like the soda—brutally sweet and artificially citric—to wash the blackness out.

"Looks like you was in a good'n," the young man said as I sorted through change to pay for the soda. "You total that son of a gun?"

I dropped the coins on the counter and pulled the tab on the can. I turned and looked at him. I didn't say anything. I couldn't have, because my tongue was thick with the terrible taste my erratic brain was producing for me. I drank some of the soda, not getting my mouth on the small opening in just the right way, so that I dribbled down my chin. I was staring at him, but barely paying attention. He didn't mean anything to me. The remark was just harmless conversation, an attempt to be sociable. Or sympathetic. I don't know. But as I looked at him he backed away. In the manner of a man about to be suddenly dead backing away from the muzzle of a loaded gun.

The blond cashier was looking at me too, with her chin up in a startled way. "Orvie," she said, "sometimes you need to take a tuck in it, son." And to me: "Don't pay him no mind. He's just my sister-in-law's cousin from Brash Fork."

I lowered the can of soda and wiped my chin with the back of my other wrist. That hand, the arm itself, was shaking. I didn't know what was wrong with me. I was, literally, seeing red. I reached out and set the can on the counter. I said to the blond girl, "What are you staring at?" It was a voice I wasn't at all familiar with.

She wanted to drop her eyes. She couldn't, because I wouldn't let her. Her mouth fumbled and finally she said, "Well, nothing, really. Now look, what we don't need here is trouble."

"Do I look like a troublemaker?" I reached up again with the trembling hand, to wipe away the sticky track of soda. It came away smeared with bright warm blood. I had no idea where the blood came from. I wasn't frightened or particularly disturbed. I was infuriated by the blond girl, her washed-out blue eyes and thin beaky mouth. I felt contemptuous of her, for being frightened of me.

"I was shot in the head," I explained, trying to be reasonable. "See the bullet scar?"

"Lord," she said. "I see it! That little puckery place there? Lord, yes." Her eyes narrowed in speculation. "Now I know, I seen all about you on the Channel 12 news! What was it, about a week ago? Didn't you see him there on the TV, Orvie?"

Orvie said, "Who, me? Not hardly. I don't pay attention to it."

"I didn't ask for this," I said. Still reasonable, if not benign. "Getting shot wasn't any doing of mine. But I'm all right. I'll be fine, once my hand straightens out and—" It seemed very necessary for me to reassure them, two strangers who saw me trembling and bleeding, as if I'd cut my lip on the soda can. I wanted just to go away, and find my daughter. I explained that to them, too. "I'm looking for my daughter," I said. "She—well, it's late. And I'm not—I just want her to come home, I need her."

The blond girl nodded, a little too vigorously. "Want us to call her for you, then?"

"If I knew where she was, I'd call her myself!"

"What's her name?" the girl asked, getting up the nerve to smile a little. But I was still scaring her. I couldn't understand why. I couldn't imagine anything frightening about me. Not even my scars. Not pretty, no, but not frightening either. A lot of people had scars. Mine would go away.

"Sha—" It was all I could say. There was a lull. A sensation of nameless disaster held me in paralyzed suspension. I had awareness—of the blond cashier and her sister-in-law's cousin from Brash Fork, of my immediate, harshly flourescent surroundings—but in the immeasurable outback of my mind where there had been volcanic thunderclouds, lightning and acid red downpours, now nothing stirred or shone with even the faintest radiance. I felt tightly bound and shrunken inside my own body, like a mummy in a case. The dark, *the dark*! I was shuddering—with fear, not violence. "She's—" I stopped, and my heart wanted to stop as well, to end this agony. "My life," I said.

There was heat lightning, like a remnant of flame sinking in a lantern, to the north above the Saurian tailbone of the Appalachian Mountains that lay across our corner of Georgia. I drove away from the Texaco Mart and turned north on the next street. Two blocks away I crossed the railroad tracks that bisected the city and the now nearly still heart of downtown. Only the Manhattan Restaurant, on the second floor of a Civil War-era building on the northeast corner of the square, showed activity, although the Manhattan, like almost every other establishment in Sky Valley, closed by eleven o'clock.

Moonlight glimmered on the overflow of water from the bronze basin of the fountain that occupied the center of the square, a place of some historical distinction: a detail of horse soldiers from General Sherman's army had skirmished here with a collection of local irregulars during the war. A couple of the oaks that were around at the time are said to contain shot vainly fired in the short-lived defense of the town, known then as McCauseland Station. The brick of the pathways in the square had come from demolished buildings of the era. Of course there were cannons with semi-erect barrels, and the seven-foot statue of a young man on picket duty with rifle and bayonet in an upraised fist, his other arm in a sling. His expression, combining anger and a fierce joy to fight, had scarcely been softened by more than a hundred years of weather (the statue, local historians believed, had been modeled after sketches provided by Frederic Remington).

I'm not a Civil War buff, but I often stood in the doorway of my shop just off the southwest, lower corner of the square, where my business had been located for nine years. From this vantage point I could see the wounded Confederate against an oblong of sky between two buildings. I had watched him in sun and snow and blazing autumn weather with leaves slashing by, in every change of light the seasons had to offer. He was a symbol to me, I suppose, of what was durable in man, and worth honoring. I had no grand philosophy, no deep insight into the tragedies, the beguiling enigmas of life. I only wanted to work hard, educate myself, and be loved in my allotted time. I thought that I knew my limitations. If, by the grace of God, I could be bronze, I had no desire to become steel.

Fifth Street was five blocks north of the square, and I made a left turn off Larrimore. The Driscoll house, white frame with red shutters and a shingled roof in a darker shade of red, was architecturally distinguished by two turret-style porches on the corners facing the street. There were entrance doors, each with an oval of curtained glass, on both porches, but no true front door. The driveway, two parallel strips of badly crumbled concrete, was to the left of the house and went on back to a free-standing garage that had once been a carriage house. The light of the porch next to the driveway was on, a muzzy yellow sun with flickering orbits of insects. But the house appeared to be totally dark.

The Maxicab that belonged to Bobby's brother was parked in the drive toward the rear of the house, in front of a black sedan. I parked by the curb a couple of feet from the driveway entrance, looking at the back of the pickup truck with its half-dozen belligerent, bragging, typically proletarian bumper stickers. *Nuke Them Till They Glow. Abandon Hope All Ye Who Ride My Bumper. Damn I'm Good!* My right eye was tearing, and the panic that had compelled me to come this far was still feeding an indestructible headache. The window was halfway down on my side and I heard the fitful music of tubular wind chimes somewhere, the low momentum of thunder as wind poured through the crowns of trees along the street. It had been a warm and humid evening; now the air smelled refreshingly of rain.

Bobby Driscoll was already home and, I supposed, in bed. If I had had the presence of mind to call my own home from the Texaco Mart, I would have found Sharissa there. This is what I thought; but something still nagged at my heart, my confidence.

I got out of the Honda, wondering if they had a dog. If I aroused one by walking up the driveway, if anyone appeared at the door, I didn't know what explanation I could offer without sounding foolish. The way I looked— little knotlets of surgical thread clustered like spiders on my discolored forehead—would not have helped. I came to the Maxicab and paused there, looking at the carriage house thirty feet away. There was a netless basketball goal over the double doors that sagged on their spear-point hinges; the paint above the goal had been nearly worn away by the repeated impact of the ball. A flight of steps went up to a narrow covered porch along one side of the carriage house. There was a cat on the porch. I saw only its creature eyes, a dazzling greenish gold, as if they had been ignited by a faint light leaking around a window shade.

I moved closer to the carriage house and looked up from the bottom of the steps. Little shards of light like razor cuts gleamed in the denseness of an old green window shade. The sky lit up. The wind died. I heard a different, fainter, fondled sighing.

"Bobby."

"Don't you want to?"

"Yes. No. I better not."

"I'm dying to."

"Uh, Bobby. No. Don't put your hand . . . there."

"I love you."

"I love you, too. Please stop, it makes me crazy."

"Uhh, God."

"It's so late. I'd better get home."

"Not yet. A little longer."

And silence. From them. As the wind returned, a ferocious exhalation scaring up the leaves of trees. The hair on my forearms was standing too. I bit where I had bitten before, where my lip was cut, and a drop of blood spurted onto my tongue.

I looked around. There was a trash can nearby, against the backyard fence. I went to it and tore open the sack of garbage on top and found cans, a nearly empty catsup bottle. I flung the empty cans up there, on the porch, where they clattered and rolled. A dog in a neighbor's yard began barking. For good measure I hit the blank front wall of the building above the basketball goal with the heavy catsup bottle. It left a red smear.

Then I ran down the driveway to my car. I felt half scalded, half frozen. The loose and crumbling drive might have thrown me, causing worse damage to my healing head than Ricky Gene's bullet. But I made it to the Honda.

The sky flashed as I got in, let off the brake and rolled backward. Half a block from the house, I started the engine, drove in reverse to the intersection, no lights. Even so Sharissa might have recognized our family car. But neither she nor Bobby appeared in the driveway. I had not been seen getting away from there.

Would it be enough, I wondered—the racket, the interruption. Would it have awakened her from the fevered bliss of seduction, would she come to her senses now?

My alternative had been to walk up the sagging steps and find the door to the carriage house hideaway, walk in and put an end to their groping without saying a word.

But I couldn't have faced either of them: boy and girl partly or fully unclothed, entwined on some musty piece of discarded furniture, their skins shining from perspiration in the dim light. Sharissa's lips, her nipples, swollen from kissing, being kissed . . . if I had discovered her like that, it would have shattered us both. Love, respect, trust, all in ruins. At least she deserved a chance to think twice about her foolishness. The upstairs of the carriage house the equivalent in privacy of a cheap and anonymous motel room—what had possessed her to go up those steps with Bobby? How well did I know my daughter, after all? And why had I ever trusted *him?*

If they had not had intercourse tonight (and despite my anxiety, I could be reasonably hopeful that before I arrived Bobby and Sharissa had only indulged themselves in what used to be called "heavy petting"), then almost certainly in the near future Sharissa would find herself in a similarly compromised position, on another delicious joyride, all twists and turns and no stopping place. Bobby would see to that. He already had broken down most of her defenses. He wanted Sharissa, and he was going to have her.

I was angry with Bobby, yet I couldn't condemn him. I had seethed with the same brutal longings in my time.

I couldn't bring myself to consider the likelihood that Sharissa wanted, with equal passion, to make love to Bobby. I could not visualize her on those terms. This was not the daughter I had raised and cherished. She had scruples and an impressive personal dignity, the beauty, breadth, and grace of a virgin goddess. She was a role model for younger girls. She taught a class at Sunday school. She had informed my days with a parental contentment that now, burdened with her lubricious secrets, I seemed destined to lose. Unless there was some action I could take that would not turn her against me.

Rain began, midway of my brooding drive home to Thornhill Road.

If I stayed calm, I thought, then I could reason with her. I might have the opportunity to appeal to Sharissa's better nature, before it was too late.

I tried to frame adequate beginnings to such a conversation. Father to daughter. But we had never talked about sex. I hadn't seen her fully naked since she was seven years old, scampering from the hall bath to her room in the small ranch house we'd rented in Sherwood Forest: soap bubbles clinging to winglike shoulder blades, the edges of her hair drenched and slicked down on the lucent skin of her breast. Adorable and asexual at that age; womanly now, steeped in the ardor of her boyfriend, already half-corrupted by his powerful musk.

She would listen to me, for a while: grim and embarrassed and downcast.

Then Sharissa would say, *How could you spy on me?* And I would have no appropriate answer. However unfair her accusation might be, my credibility would be destroyed by those few words.

Together Caroline and I could enforce our demand that Sharissa drop Bobby, not see him socially. But it was the sort of edict that bred rebellion in teenagers; it would only serve to make Bobby more attractive to Sharissa, even necessary. They would find ways to be together, and the urgency of their furtive meetings might only lead more quickly to what, at any cost, I had to prevent.

I arrived home at eleven-fifteen. I hoped Sharissa would be only a few minutes behind me. But I didn't want to see her when she came in.

My head was killing me. The pain was so bad I vomited, which left me tingling and cold. I needed to take two Percodans, if there was to be any chance of my getting to sleep. I realized, too late, that I shouldn't take them on an empty stomach. I knew I had pushed myself beyond the limits established by my head wound. Which only made me feel incompetent, and this sense of helplessness served to increase my anger at the predicament I was in. Everything seemed to be going against me lately.

Lightning flashed outside the kitchen window; my field of vision, dark at the edges, was filled with sparklers.

When I could see clearly again I was aware of the lighted kitchen window in the Kindors' house, and Meghan Kindor's face at the window, as if she was peering out at the sky. I knew that thunderstorms made her as nervous as a child. And she was alone tonight.

The rain swept across the lake behind our homes and I was drenched and shivering by the time I let myself in through an unlocked patio gate and knocked at their kitchen door.

The outside lights came on. Meghan looked out apprehensively through frilly polka-dot curtains, then unbolted the door.

"Greg? Good Lord. What—"

"Could I come in? I know it's late—"

"It's not *that* late!"

Meghan stood aside for me. She was wearing a short, flowery, snugly fitting kimono. Without her shoes Meghan was exactly five feet tall.

I entered the kitchen, dripping on the floor, and leaned against a countertop. Tricky Dick, the Kindors' ancient mongrel, lifted his gray muzzle from a corner of the rag rug he slept on in the keeping room, looked at me with half-blinded eyes, gave an obligatory bark, and fell back into a doze.

"Isn't this something?" Meghan jumped at thunder and laughed her high-pitched, staccato laugh. "Whoops! There goes another one. I'll get you a towel. Sit down, Greg. You look—tired."

"Sorry to make a mess," I mumbled to her back as she went down the hall to the powder room. There was an opened magazine and a half-eaten apple on the tiled range counter in the center of the kitchen. Above my head lightning bloomed; rain streamed down the skylight and I noticed a slow drip, from a badly flashed corner of the skylight. The kitchen smelled of freshly baked cinnamon bread. It had been a long time since Caroline had had the leisure to do any baking, and I missed those appetizing odors in our own kitchen.

Meghan came back with a monogrammed hand towel, looking closely at my face. I blotted it slowly. The lights dimmed momentarily, and Meghan's eyes flashed wider in alarm. She grinned. She has a pretty mouth with a high arch to it, arched eyebrows and a droll, semi-drowsy expression most of the time—I think it must be the way her eyelids are tucked and folded at the corners. Her eyelids were tinted a vivid blue tonight, but her lips were nearly colorless.

"You should have brought an umbrella."

"I didn't realize . . . it was raining so hard."

"It is *really* coming down!" she said, with an ecstatic shiver. I was trembling too, my jaws locked together. "Let me get you a sweater of Doyle's. Pull that wet shirt off, Greg? I'll throw it in the dryer for you."

"Hope it isn't too late for you, Meggy."

"No, no, I barely sleep a wink all night with Doyle and the guys out of the house. It's just too darn *quiet.*" Her voice faded as she rummaged in the coat closet in the foyer. "Where's Caroline tonight?"

"Atlanta Hilton. Political dinner. She won't be home much before two."

"Poor thing. The *hours* she puts in."

I looked through the bow window of the breakfast corner as another filament of lightning, like a deep crack in a block of black ice, split the sky. I saw the Chevy Maxicab pull into our driveway up the hill.

"She loves her work," I said of Caroline, as Meghan returned with a V-neck cotton pullover.

"Well, I really envy her, you know." Meghan held out her hand for my shirt and I unbuttoned it, pulled it out of my khaki pants. She looked at the soaked cuffs and my wet docksiders but didn't comment on them. "She has a *career.* I wish now I'd finished college."

"Why didn't you?" I said. I started to pull the sweater over my head, then remembered and took off the corduroy cap. Meghan stared for a couple of seconds, then looked deliberately away.

"Frankenstein," I said.

Meghan laughed, ha-HA, chopping it off abruptly. "You look—I mean, for somebody who . . . what I'm trying to say is, I wish Doyle kept himself in as good a shape as you do." KA-BOOM. Meghan seemed to shrink a size smaller. I saw the tilt and pucker of her nipples against the synthetic kimono fabric. The lights almost went out, dimming to a coppery glow before returning. "Maybe I ought to light us a candle," Meghan said.

"Good idea."

I managed to get the sweater on over my bandaged head. I was feeling calmer, although my hands still trembled annoyingly. Calmer, slightly hazy, vaguely adrift. The Percs were working. My stomach had settled down. I needed to go to the bathroom, and went without saying anything to Meghan.

When I came out she was standing in the hallway between the den and the kitchen area, with its keeping room and breakfast nook, one side of the hall all windows facing the stake-fenced patio. She had a candle with her, in a glass holder shaped like a swan.

"We could sit in the den," she suggested. "Would you like something to eat?"

"Is that cinnamon bread I've been smelling?"

"You bet! Baked it an hour ago. I just got the urge. I must have known you were coming." Ha-ha-HA—

"Meggy?"

"What?"

"You're a lot more attractive when you don't laugh like that."

She bit her lip and looked chastened, her face paling in the sizzle of another lightning stroke.

"I know. It's just something—stupid nervous habit, I don't even know when I'm—"

"I shouldn't have said anything. I'm sorry."

"It's okay! I don't mind. I know you're not criticizing,

you're not like that. You're—not like any man I've ever known, if you want the truth."

That made me smile, what I hoped was a pleasant, encouraging smile. "I'm not? Why am I different?"

"Oh, that would take a book!" She scribbled in air with an imaginary pencil, then gestured hopelessly. "If I could write, which I can't."

"Would you try to tell me? I guess I need to hear some good things about myself tonight. I'm feeling on the low side, Meghan."

"Funny. I've been feeling the same way."

"Have you, Meghan? Why?"

"Well. It didn't start with you . . . getting shot." She took a deep breath, held it, then said in a rush, "Goes way back . . . we're neighbors, but I'm sure you have no idea what it's . . . been like around here, for me. I don't blame Ricky Gene so much, it's Doyle and his . . . his damn guns and his . . . *attitude.* Anyway, the accident was almost the last straw, but, thank God, you pulled through! I still can't believe we . . . you . . . were so lucky."

"Give God most of the credit."

"I do, I do!" She touched me, near the shoulder, solemnly, not a nervous touch but as if she needed to be firmly convinced I was flesh and blood and not the climax of a nightmare. "Thank you, God," Meghan said in a small tearful voice. "Greg's still here." I almost put my own hand on top of hers, but I didn't, and slowly she withdrew it and dry-washed both hands. "Come . . . sit down, watch TV if the cable didn't take a hit with all of this lightning."

"I don't watch television very often."

"I do. Unfortunately. It's just another one of my stupid, boring habits. I'll get the bread, and—how about some hot cider?"

"Perfect."

Meghan was in the kitchen loading a tray when the lights went out, without warning. The lightning flashes had become less frequent, the thunder no longer rattled the glass in the windowpanes.

"Yike!" Meghan said. "Greg? Can you bring the candle?"

In the kitchen I gave Meghan the candle and followed her, carrying the tray with cider and half a loaf of fresh cinnamon bread and crock butter back to the den. I placed the tray on their big square coffee table, which is like a low alterpiece with a veneer of fossil stone, very handsome. We sat side by side on one of the loveseats, not touching but not far apart either: well within each other's private space. The kimono just covered Meghan's hips when she leaned forward, knees together, to slice bread and butter it generously, pour cider for us.

One of the french doors was open a few inches to the cedar deck outside. Rain splashed down, dwindling slowly. The cool air flowing inside felt good, like the alcohol baths I'd had while in the hospital. The candle put out a tall, guttering flame that constantly altered the shapes of things, the depths and surfaces of our faces. Changing how we appeared to each other from moment to moment. We were Greg and Meghan, and we were not. Familiar strangers. My headache wasn't so bad anymore. The Percodans, as usual, had made me pleasantly tipsy. I had to do a mild balancing act to keep from swaying on the satiny loveseat. This amused me. The skin on my forearms prickled. My head felt more like a shimmering glass sphere than a bowling ball. Drained of all the impure, rankling blood that had been causing me such torment. But blood must pool somewhere: I had an erection that felt like an I-beam. This amused me too.

Meghan sipped from her cider mug, winced slightly, put it down and got up from the sofa.

"Needs a little something," she said vaguely, and she went quickly to the built-in cabinets on the fireplace wall. She bent over to open double doors. The hem of the kimono was right at the bottom of her taut cheek line when she did that. Of course she knew I was looking at her thrust-out ass. I was amused by Meghan too, as I would have been amused by a playful cat or a particularly cunning teddy bear in a toy store window.

She found whatever it was she wanted in the liquor cabinet, came back and, still standing, poured an amount of black Jack into her cider that would take the rest of the night to burn out of her system. She looked at me, smiling as if she were doing something daring.

"I thought that was Doyle's weakness," I said.

Meghan sat down again, differently this time: facing me, legs tucked under her.

"I don't like it straight up, but it goes good with cider, I found out."

"So now you drink a lot of cider."

Meghan laughed, but it wasn't her usual laugh. There was something rueful about her humor.

"I had this dream the other night. I dreamed I was the one who took the pistol from the house. I was trying to kill a snake with it. Instead I shot Doyle in the foot. He was hopping around on the other foot, just hopping mad. I laughed and laughed. Oh, we were on the front lawn of the church and the minister was watching, so Doyle couldn't swear the way he usually does. He had to make up a lot of strange-sounding swear words."

I thought about the Doyle I knew, hearty and obtuse, a man astride his native ignorance like a big, American horse.

"What's Doyle doing to you?" I asked her.

"Lately? Oh, hiding money when I can't even pay the phone bill, and spending it on women. Ignoring *me*."

"In bed, you mean."

Meghan turned her head aside, to the candle flame, which seemed attracted to her and trembled at a nearly horizontal angle. Her arched lips pressed tighter and higher, and her petite chin wrinkled like a baby's.

"I think we're getting en*tire*ly too personal," she murmured. She raised the mug to her lips.

"Bullshit, Meghan."

Her eyes closed halfway. She opened and closed her lips on the rim of the white mug. Her face relaxed as her attention withdrew—from me, from the husband who infuriated and insulted her, from the house they couldn't afford to maintain, from the responsibilities of children and the chaotic, threatening environment of modern life that only occasionally rewarded the odd struggler with a bolt from the blue.

"I'm thirty-six years old," Meghan said thoughtfully. "And I deserve something. I'm not sure what it is, but . . . something."

"Cheap affairs are never worthwhile."

"It doesn't have to be cheap . . . Greg."

"Finish your cider," I told her.

Her lips turned up in an ironic smile. "Those who deliberate on sin/ will be late getting in/ on all the fun." She drank the cider slowly and steadily, then threw the cup over her shoulder, not caring where it landed. "That was one of my daddy's sayings," she added. "He was a sly dog." She gave me the merest hint of a sly look herself, then opened her kimono and crouched on the sofa, almost facedown in my lap. One hand finding, clutching me. I looked past her breasts at tan lines, the gleam of underbelly, pitch-dark pudenda.

"You want to know . . . what it is about you, Greg? You have eyes that say to a woman, 'I'll fuck you better than any man has ever fucked you before.' "

"That's the Jack Daniels talking, Meggy."

I put a hand on her small head. I have large hands. I tightened my grip on her head as she was rhythmically tightening and releasing my cock. She went after it as if she were strangling a chicken in a sack.

"All the women know it. They talk about you. They all wonder if you—but you've never cheated on Caroline, have you? At least not around here."

"I take my wedding vows seriously, Meghan."

Gradually her hands stopped squeezing my cock. Her attention had had an unusual effect, in that I was detumescent without having achieved an orgasm. I lifted her by the short hair of her head, not hurting her very much.

Meghan's face was inches from mine. She was perspiring. Her face was the face of a drowned thing, but she breathed quite heavily. Her kimono hung from her shoulders like untidy drapes. Her breathy heated aroma, laced with sweet apples and strong Tennessee sipping whiskey, with the sharp fatty tang of sweat and subtle but distinctive labial musk, had the spicy flavor of women in the tropics.

"Caroline's given me everything I wanted," I said to Meghan. "The least I can do is not betray her."

Meghan, as if collapsing, slipped part way off the sofa. One of her pale breasts came momentarily into the palm of my hand. It felt as small and light as a baby bird. A bare heel repeatedly kicked a leg of the coffee table, as if she were starting a tantrum from the ground up. Then she burst into tears.

"You must think I'm awful, just *awful!*"

"I don't."

"Let go. Please."

I let her go. She kneeled on the rug beside my knee, shoulders hunched, sobbing, a hand across her throat. She wouldn't look at me.

Outside the rain had stopped. I stared at the now-steady candle flame above the altarlike table with its veneer from the shells of incredibly ancient sea life, and felt at ease. I had come to a decision, about Sharissa and Bobby. I knew what to do, so that my relationship with my daughter would in no way be jeopardized.

"I never had a chance to meet a man like you," Meghan said bitterly. "I had to go and get *pregnant*, the second week I went out with Doyle. Two years of college left. You know what I *should* have done?"

I looked at her for a time, and at the shadow gang of doubts and false persuasions surrounding her, and thought, as I have many times, that the only true success in life is contentment. It was uncharitable of me, but by then I was bored with Meghan.

"Don't say it, Meggy. They're great kids, both of them.

You'll work things out with Doyle. I think I'd better go home now."

The lights came back on just as I finished speaking. Meghan flinched, then pulled her kimono together in her fist and stared at me, appalled. I had seen the same expression on the face of our cocker spaniel, named Corky, just after she ran into the street and was fatally injured by a car. Not so much pain as guilt: *Well, I really messed up this time, didn't I?*

But Meghan called to me as I was leaving by the kitchen door.

"Greg, take the rest of the cinnamon bread home with you! It'll just go to waste, there's more than I can eat."

───────────────

We never lock doors inside our house. I looked in on Sharissa, as I always did, before I went to my own bed. I thought I was being quiet. Or maybe she had a lot on her mind and hadn't fallen asleep.

She raised up on an elbow and looked over her bare shoulder at me. Except in winter she wore only a tank top and underpants for sleeping.

"Oh, hi. Mom home yet?"

"No, she's not here. Are you okay?"

"Sure. How about you?"

"My head was bothering me earlier, I took a couple of Percodans."

Sharissa yawned. "Couldn't find you when I came home."

"I was at the Kindors'. Meggy made cinnamon bread. I brought some. Are you hungry?"

"Huh-uh."

"How was your evening?"

"Okay. Nothing much doing."

"Well, good night, honey."

"Good night, Daddy." She stretched and started to lie down, turned her head again. "Daddy?"

"What?"

"Do you like Bobby?"

"Why do you ask that?"

"Sometimes I get the feeling you don't."

"I suppose the more serious you two get, the more reservations I have."

"Oh."

"It's just the way fathers are."

"Dad? Come here. I could use a hug from you."

I sat on the edge of her bed, and she put her long arms around me.

"I'm going to Vanderbilt," she said. "And Bobby's probably going to UGA, so—who knows what'll happen?"

"But in the meantime," I said, "it's really serious."

Sharissa looked me in the eye, and smiled.

"I promise that we're not going to run off and get married or do something stupid."

I touched my lips to the purplish-brown scar on her right shoulder, where a brown recluse spider had bitten her when she was nine. She'd been a very sick girl for a couple of weeks.

"I know. I have a lot of confidence in you, baby."

Sharissa kissed my cheek and touched the side of my head lightly, where the hair was growing back.

"I love you. Wake me up for church?"

"I sure will. Probably I'll let Mom sleep, so there'll just be the two of us."

I left her then, as I had left her so many nights, curled up on her right side, head on her pillow, right hand cupping her forehead as if she were meditating, her outstretched left hand near the dilapidated penguin named Chilly-Willy, who had been her nighttime companion from the age of three. And all was as it had been, as I wished it to be, in our house; I felt upheld in my love for Sharissa, and my judgment of her, and content in my purposes.

———

Two days after I returned to work, the madwoman came to town.

It was unfortunate that this was also the day Caroline was able to steal enough time from Claude Gilley's campaign so the two of us could have an early dinner at the Ovenbird.

I had first seen the woman earlier in the day, outside my store. I noticed the car she was driving before I paid any attention to her. It was a vintage Pontiac that had seen plenty of miles and a lot of bad road. Mud caked in the fender wells, cracks in most of the windows, a redneck's squalid car. I was on the floor trying to convince Carmack Knox to splurge and buy the big-screen projection model he'd been hankering after for months. He said he just might try Circuit City and see what they were getting for their TVs. The woman drove her Pontiac past my store at least four times, slowly enough to annoy the drivers behind her. She appeared to be almost too elderly to be driving at all. She obviously was looking for something, or someone, but she probably couldn't see inside the store: on sunny days I don't keep all of the overhead lights on, to pinch a dollar or two.

I told Carmack to shop Circuit City, then I'd meet any price of theirs. I made a service call out on Balm of Gilead Road, and returned to town at one-thirty. The dirty red-and-white Pontiac Eight, one of those with the Big Chief ornament on the hood (which does go back a few de-

cades), was now parked in one of the diagonals that sur-
round the square.

I didn't see the woman who owned the Pontiac on my
way to the bank. She might have been eating her lunch
with other retirees on one of the benches around the
town gazebo. Or shopping at Goldblum's. Goldblum was
slashing prices again at his old-fashioned clothing empo-
rium, hoping to lure a few customers away from the mall.
He's been on the square for fifty years and is always crying the blues. Fact is he owns half of the choicest commercial property in downtown Sky Valley.

Mindy Lockard, one of the loan officers at Sky Valley
National, came over to chat while I was in line to make a
deposit.

"Did she find you?"

I was wearing a Braves baseball cap and I still had a big
caramel-colored elastic patch covering most of my forehead. The cap was new and making my stubbly scalp itch,
so I took it off briefly.

"Who, Mindy?"

"The woman who was looking for you. She came in to
cash a traveler's check. Royal Bank of Canada. She had
your picture that she cut out of a newspaper. Your famous
picture? Hey, your hair's really coming back fast. Without
that part on the left, you look young enough to be one of
those Aryan Brotherhood kids who hang around the mall
wearing suspenders and paratrooper boots."

"Wish I felt that young, Mindy."

"Don't we all," Mindy said, looking wistful. She played
tennis nearly every day to keep her figure. Her weight
was down, but she had serious sun-wrinkles to go with
her tan.

"By the way," I said, "thanks for the flowers."

"Our pleasure. You really scared us, Greg. You're one
for the books, I guess."

"I've heard of men who have survived worse. Did she
tell you what her name was?"

"Oh, the woman who—no, Sandy cashed the traveler's

check for her. Sandy could tell you. But it looks as if she's on her break right now."

"Well, whoever it is, I expect she knows where to find me. What does she look like?"

"Old." Mindy shrugged, and elaborated. "White hair. I'd say seventy, or better."

On my way back to the store I cut across the square.

The Pontiac was still in the same slot. The red flag was up in the meter window. The owner would be getting a ticket as soon as Alma, our parking control officer, cruised by on her scooter.

I looked at the license plate in passing. It was as dirty as the rest of the lower half of the Pontiac, but I could tell that the car was registered in British Columbia.

I had the uneasy feeling I was being closely watched as I continued on to my store. But a lot of people had been staring at me since the shooting accident. I was still considered to be a freak of nature by some people in town, but what could I do? Go about my business and assume it would all be forgotten soon.

They had a good crowd in the dining room of the Ovenbird by the time I got there, at a quarter to seven. Caroline was late, but we both had expected her to be. Our favorite table overlooks the walled garden, in an alcove away from the traffic patterns. I sat where the quarter-inch of stubble on my head wouldn't be conspicuous and had a Campari and soda.

Caroline showed up ten minutes later, escorted by Fog Hatley, one of the Ovenbird's owners.

"How're you, Fog?" I asked him.

He was a slow-talking man, who squinted judiciously in consideration of every question put to him. "Still payin' top dollar for my sins. How 'bout them Dawgs?" Fog is such a big fan of UGA football that he travels to intrasquad scrimmages. The college football season wouldn't begin for another three weeks.

"Heck of a recruiting year," I said, as if I hadn't said it a dozen times already. "Two high-school All-Americans. How's Casey handling that switch to running back?" Casey was one of Fog's numerous nephews.

"Blows through the line like salts through a widow woman." He seated Caroline ostentatiously and batted his eyelashes at her. "What can I do you for, darlin'?"

"Coke and four aspirin," Caroline said with a husky sigh.

"Gonna pull old Claude through this time around?"

"It'll be a squeaker," Caroline said, and added cautiously, "you didn't hear it from me."

"Gotcha," Fog said, with a wise squint of one eye, and he went away. We heard him say, "How 'bout them *Dawgs?*" from across the room. Caroline and I smiled at each other, and the tension of a day on the run began to leave her body. She'd lost at least ten pounds in the past couple of weeks, which was to her advantage; but her cheeks looked sunken as a result, and the lines around her mouth had deepened.

"You're coming straight home with me tonight," I said. "I'm unplugging the telephone and locking up your typewriter."

She smiled again, gratefully. "I just keep telling myself, Tuesday week, Caroline, it'll be over in ten more days. Then we're home. November'll be a breeze."

"Love you," I said.

Caroline reached for my hand on the table.

"I know I've been impossible these last couple of months. But if it wasn't for politics, well—"

"We don't have to talk about it. Your income's important. Sorry I gave you such a bad scare."

"Scare?" She squeezed my hand; I felt her nails digging in. "That's the understatement of the century. But we're not going to talk about that, either. We're good people. We deserve to be blessed."

"Not another word," I agreed.

"Pardon me," the madwoman said. "This man is my husband, and I need to talk to him."

Caroline and I looked up simultaneously.

She was standing a little behind me, a large woman with permed white hair. Her eyebrows were newly plucked and penciled; in fact she looked as if she'd just paid for the works at Lauralee's downtown. But she had on too much rouge and a purple eyeshadow that was not becoming. Her upper lip was pleated like a boudoir lampshade. The sunlight splashed our way by the fountain in the Ovenbird's garden revealed liver spots through her vivid peach makeup base. She wore a purple silk suit, a frilly blouse, and a big gold locket on a thin gold chain.

The woman was staring at Caroline. We were still holding hands across the table. Then the woman smiled, revealing goldlined teeth that didn't appear to have been worth saving in the first place.

"Let go of him," she said, still smiling, but ominously. "He don't belong to you. I staked a prior claim, honey, and believe me it'll hold up in any court of law."

Caroline blinked; she's a quick-witted woman and almost never at a loss for words. Her hand, covering mine, twitched a little, the baguettes in her wedding band reflecting a dancing light over the enameled rose in the bud vase.

"Excuse *me*," I said. "This is our table and my wife and I are having a private conversation. Whoever you are—"

The woman looked at me. She had a strong beaked nose and cheekbones bold as a squaw's. I could see that, much younger, she would have been a roughhewn beauty. But longing was weighty in her, and toxic as a tumor. I was rapidly becoming more concerned than indignant.

"Stuff it, Frederick," she said. "It's been a long time, but the giveaway is, see, you haven't changed a bit. Always been the problem with you, hasn't it?"

She laughed. Her voice hadn't carried, but the laughter—coarse, uninhibited—attracted attention. It was almost impossible to detect that she was putting on an act. But blue veins showed on each white knuckle of the hands that gripped her purse. And something—a long-held sorrow, remorse—ghosted the dense black pupils of her eyes.

"Greg—"

The woman turned her head sharply when Caroline spoke.

"Not Greg. Not *Walker*. That's all hooey, sweetheart. His name is Frederick Sullivan. I'm Mrs. Roxanne Sullivan. We were married September 3, 1954, in New Lost River, British Columbia. Married eighteen years. Until—until—" It was then her voice cracked, pathetically. She sniffed. "Do you want to tell me what happened, Frederick? I sure as God deserve . . . an explanation, don't you think?"

I looked at Caroline, furrowing my brow significantly. She got the message and stood up at once.

"Excuse me," she said, and left the table. The woman turned to watch her as I unobtrusively moved my chair so that I was not sitting trapped sideways between her and the garden windows.

"Didn't do so bad for yourself, huh, Frederick? Of course she's beginning to show her age some. I guess I did too. Was that it? Was that all there was to it—" And now she looked at me with one of those disconcertingly quick turns of her head, "—you *bastard*?"

"I don't know you. I don't know what you're talking about. I'd advise you—Mrs. Sullivan—"

"Got a proper Southern accent, 'n everything," she sneered. "But I'm not fooled. As for your advice, hooey. You can stuff that too. You're coming back with me. To New Lost River. Nothing's left. The house, the lounge—gone. But we can start over. I've got some good years left,

Frederick. I knew as soon as I saw your picture in the Vancouver paper I was willing to forgive you. All you need to do is tell me—"

Caroline was coming back, with Fog Hatley behind her. Fog is six-five and stopped weighing himself when he hit three hundred pounds. I relaxed at the sight of him. I didn't know if there was any real danger in her, but Fog would have the woman out of his restaurant in a matter of seconds.

Possibly she sensed, from my eye movements, what was going on. She moved quickly for her size and age, slipping into Caroline's vacated chair. At the same time she drew a small nickel-plated automatic from her purse. Her eyes flickered to Caroline and Fog.

When they were ten feet from the table I waved them off.

"Tell that tub of guts to stay put," the woman said. "Or I'll put one through your eye, and we'll see how quick you get up and walk away from that! Remember how good a shot I was, Frederick? Maybe you don't think I've still got what it takes."

"This is really—not very smart of you."

"I'm smart, all right. I'm *very* smart. It was me made such a big success of the lounge, remember? All you ever did was tend bar and fool around with the strippers. Couple of those young slimhipped cowpokes, too, as I recall. Never mind. It's all bygones with me. Got myself all fixed up for you this afternoon." She preened, her smile striking gold again. "I still love you, Frederick, or I wouldn't be here."

Her gaze swarmed on me, like a cluster of bees around a honeyed fingertip. Quite obviously, in my own eyes she saw nothing but disgust.

She stopped smiling. There was a quirk of malevolence to her pleated lips. She made an odd clucking sound.

"What happened to Bonnie? You know where she is? She never came to visit me even one time, after they locked me away."

"I don't know anybody named Bonnie," I said, looking at the muzzle of the pistol and ready to explode from frustration.

"Don't know your own daughter?" She clucked again, out of the side of her mouth. "Fat chance. Well, you're crafty, Fred, I'll hand you that. But I've got the goods, lover. Tell those two to get over here toot sweet, and let's get this show on the road."

"What show?"

"Don't try my patience! No more bum steers. What's her name?"

"My wife?"

"I'm your wife! She's—she—doesn't count."

The woman faltered then; there were flecks of saliva at the corner of her overly colorful mouth, the side that tended to fly out of control when she made the clucking noise. She had the slick, devoted expression of one who is listening, suspensefully, for her heart to start pumping after a hiatus. But her grip on the automatic was still solid.

The tables on either side of us were empty; so far, the madwoman hadn't attracted much attention. The fist with the little automatic in it was on the table in front of her, the muzzle angled up at my face. I thought, with a dread that was beginning to freeze at the edges, *not again*.

A waiter approached, and Fog Hatley sent him off with a curt motion of his head. We looked at each other. I tried to smile, but it was a poor effort. Fog backed off a step but Mrs. Roxanne Sullivan caught the movement out of the corner of her eye and said, "Stay standing where you are right now, fat stuff. You—Mrs. Bogus—come on over here."

Caroline advanced slowly to the table. I could tell, by the tightness of her eyes, how frightened she was. I knew I'd better do something, and quickly. I could shove the table toward the Sullivan woman, knocking her off balance, maybe out of the chair. But if there was a possibility that the stubby automatic would go off . . .

"If you've convinced yourself that I somehow mean

something to you," I said to the madwoman, "why threaten to kill me?"

She looked vague for a few seconds. She licked her lips.

"That's a bum steer," she said finally. I didn't know what she meant. But I wasn't particularly skilled at talking to, trying to reason with, the mentally disoriented. To Caroline she repeated, "Open my purse. Take out the envelope. Like I said, it's all there. Marriage license. Pictures of me and Frederick together. Have a real gander. Then tell me if you still think your claim's any good."

"Please—I wish you wouldn't do this—please, he's been hurt already, put your gun away."

"Fat chance, Mrs. Bogus. I said, open the envelope! And get set to piss in your pants." A tremor of excitement agitated her garishly painted features. I was, for the most part, keeping an eye on the pistol. I wasn't all that afraid now. I just felt very, very tired, and a little depressed.

Caroline did as she was told. There was a large packet of photos secured with a thick rubber band. A newspaper clipping fell to the table and I carefully reached for it. The familiar photo of Ricky Gene and myself in the hospital room, reprinted in a Vancouver newspaper. I was wearing my postoperative turban. My face was still a little swollen. The quality of the photograph wasn't exceptional. How Mrs. Roxanne Sullivan could have decided I was her long-missing husband was beyond my ability to comprehend. I have strong features—a Roman nose, high cheekbones, heavy eyebrows, rather penetrating brown eyes. So do a great many men.

Caroline passed me a black-and-white photograph. This one showed a far younger, busty Roxanne standing in front of an ordinary-looking corner bar with glass block on either side of the padded doors, her arm around the sought-after Frederick.

He resembled me, superficially. I didn't care for the way he grinned at the camera. The cocky, lady-killer type. I could read a history of a knock-about life in his face.

There was a row of B-girls behind them, bartenders, kitchen help. The cocktail lounge was called the Pigalle. A hand-lettered GRAND OPENING banner hung from a tacky marquee. Snow-covered mountains were visible in the background.

I laid the photo and the newspaper clipping down. Caroline was shaking her head slowly, unnerved by the deadly threat in this ludicrous situation.

"When did the Pigalle open for business?" I said to the madwoman, keeping my voice low and matter-of-fact.

"September 1954. As you very well know."

"How old was—Frederick then?" I asked her, seeking a chink in the hard fortress of her self-deception, a means to yank the entire edifice down.

"You were thirty-four, lover."

"Then I—I mean Frederick—would now be nearly seventy-three years old. Don't you ever stop to think about—"

"Sure I thought about it! Being as you never aged a day in the eighteen years we were married, I didn't see any special reason why you would have aged since then."

My mouth was dry; I reached for a glass of water. The muzzle of the pistol snapped up alertly. The madwoman clucked, and clucked again; some spit flew from the corner of her twitching mouth. Her eyes looked different to me. They seemed to be peering backward, past old ecstasies into the darkness of her pathetic soul.

I glanced at Caroline, who, I was afraid, might do something reckless out of sheer frustration. But she hadn't moved. A tear ran down one cheek. Fog Hatley loomed behind her, close enough to grab and hurl her aside if Mrs. Roxanne Sullivan aimed the pistol her way.

The madwoman's eyes flicked back to the here and now.

"Time for the pièce de résistance," she said. She pronounced it correctly. "Nobody believes their own eyes, hey? Okay, Frederick. Remember how you earned your living at the sawmill before you cozied up to me and got your hands on my nest egg? You had an accident that almost cut your arm off. Left a wicked scar midway of your left forearm, didn't it?"

I heard Caroline react, a sharp intake of breath.

And I heard, from the madwoman, "Peel back your sleeve. Here comes proof positive you're who I say."

I unbuttoned the left cuff slowly, and rolled it back.

She clucked again, triumphantly.

"That's how you always did it, just before you tended bar! Peeled back those cuffs in such a dandified manner. Still keep your hands nice, don't you, Frederick, the nails all buffed and—"

I suddenly pulled the sleeve back as far as my elbow. Of course there was no scar.

She stared at my unblemished forearm, then reached quickly with her free hand and clutched at me, her recently manicured nails digging in. I could have disarmed her then with little potential danger, but as she touched me I looked deeply into her eyes and saw her mind fall apart, almost like a slow-motion study of a calving glacier. A momentary churning, then nothing was left behind her eyes but a great white void. Her fingers on my forearm lost their strength.

I easily took the little automatic from her other hand. She was leaning forward against the table. Her mouth had sagged open, and she'd begun to drool. She didn't make a sound.

The Ovenbird's patrons scarcely had been disturbed by the drama taking place in our alcove. Fog Hatley had a screen set up around the table. The police came in the back door, and carried Mrs. Roxanne Sullivan away, still seated in the chair. She was completely rigid, in some kind of terrifying—but oddly funny—psychologically paralyzed state. Even so, I was glad to see they took the precaution of handcuffing her.

After Detective Sergeant Butterbaugh finished looking through the photographs and documents that Roxanne Sullivan had brought with her from British Columbia, he picked up the car keys from her purse and said, "Let's go see what else we can find. Unless you want to finish your dinner."

"We never got started," I said. "And right now I still have a hard time swallowing."

He nodded sympathetically. "So would I."

We left Fog Hatley's office and went out to the parking lot. Fog was with Caroline in the Ovenbird's bar, diverting her with bourbon and gossip. I was sure she didn't feel much like eating, either.

A police car was parked in front of the high-profile old Pontiac I had seen earlier in the day.

"Looks like about a '50, '51 model," Butterbaugh said. "I recall my Uncle Chase, from Hahira, Georgia? He had one of those V-8s, only in blue, with whitewall tires. He had whitewalls before anybody else in Hahira had them. What time did you say you first noticed Mrs. Sullivan driving around the square?"

"I think it was about eleven-fifteen, eleven-thirty."

"How many passes did she make by your store?"

"Four that I counted. I wonder how she knew where we were having dinner tonight?"

"She was in the bank, asking about you? She might have asked all over town. Didn't notice her anywhere around your neighborhood, did you?"

"No. But it wouldn't have been any trouble to find out where we live. I'm in the book."

"Let me have your flashlight, Lanier," Sergeant Butter-baugh said to the uniformed policeman who was keeping watch over the old Pontiac.

"What do you think will happen to the woman?" I asked him as he unlocked the dirt-encrusted front door of the car.

"Tonight? She'll be locked up in the mental ward at the hospital, probably in one of the padded detox or suicide cells, with somebody keeping an eye on her all the time. If she remains in the condition she apparently was in when she left here, then I'd expect the court will send her straight to North Georgia Mental Health Center for a thirty-day-mandatory. After that, it's anybody's guess. If she proves to be competent, then we'll take her back and the District Attorney's office probably will bring charges. Pointing a pistol at someone is aggravated assault. But there may be priors back home, an outstanding warrant or two."

Butterbaugh flashed his light on the front seat of the car, which smelled rancid from the smoke of many cigarettes. There was a half-smoked carton of unfiltered Camels on the seat, along with wrappers and foam coffee cups from fast-food restaurants, and an empty one-pound box of Go-diva chocolates. A large rabbit's foot dangled on a chain from the rearview mirror. The knob of the gear-shift lever was a plastic skull with ruby eyes rimmed in black—a bizarre touch, I thought. Since the danger had passed, I'd fought the disconsolate urge to laugh and laugh and laugh at the oddity, the surreal nature of the Sullivan woman's intrusion into our lives. I recognized the urge for what it was: aftershock, combined with a distant early warning of hysteria.

The gray felt seat upholstery was worn to the springs in places, and there were several cigarette burns where her right hand might have rested on the seat as she drove south from Canada, drowsy at night on the lonely roads of the high plains.

In the glove compartment Butterbaugh found a box of cartridges for the .25 caliber automatic.

When I saw those I said, "What I really want to know is, what are the chances she'll just be let loose and turn up on my doorstep?"

Butterbaugh examined a plaid lap robe on the backseat, where the madwoman may have slept for an hour or two at a time, in parking lots or at interstate rest stops. A squashed chocolate-covered cherry was stuck to the blanket. He shook out a couple of dead flies.

"Don't think that'll happen. Obviously she's delusional, or worse. According to your statement, she made reference to having been 'locked away.' Institutionalized. We'll find out where and what the circumstances were."

He backed out of the front seat and closed the door, went around to the back of the Pontiac, and unlocked the trunk.

"No, whether she stays as the guest of the state of Georgia or we ship her back to the authorities in British Columbia, she won't be in a position to cause you any more trouble." Butterbaugh smiled. "Who knows? She might pick up another newspaper a month from now and see the photo of somebody she thinks is her long-lost daughter. Forget all about you."

I didn't smile. He pulled out an old-fashioned carpetbag with brass fittings, put it down and searched the trunk with his flashlight. He found nothing of interest, and closed the trunk lid.

"What will happen to her car?"

"Impound. We'll take everything out and store it, along with the luggage and the contents of her handbag. Well, I guess that's about all there is to do here. By the way, how's Sharissa? We can't seem to get together on a time for that match."

"She's competing in the Southeast Junior Regionals, beginning next weekend. Seeded second, as a matter of fact."

Butterbaugh pitched the flashlight to the cop on duty and we walked back to the restaurant.

"Like to see her play," he said. "Where's the tournament going to be?

"Chattahoochee Tennis Club in Atlanta."

"Maybe I can—"

His foot struck something on the asphalt pavement and sent it skittering, a flash of gold in the lights above the entrance to the Ovenbird's kitchen. He retrieved the object from the edge of a big dumpster and held it up. I recognized the half-dollar-size engraved locket Mrs. Roxanne Sullivan had been wearing.

"It's hers," I said. "The chain must have snagged on something when they were carrying her outside to the ambulance."

"Let's have a look." But he couldn't find the hidden catch to open the locket.

"Probably nothing much inside," I suggested. "Another picture of Frederick."

"Yeah. I'll put it with her other effects." He separated a plastic sandwich bag from several that he carried in a coat pocket and dropped the locket inside.

"Do you need me for anything else?" I asked Butterbaugh.

"We'll want you to sign a complaint. I'll bring it around to the store tomorrow; you're only a couple of blocks away from the Hall. Hope you can salvage something of your evening out."

But I already knew there was no chance of that. Caroline was anxious to leave and Fog Hatley couldn't coax her to stay, even though he assured us everything would be on the house.

On the way home I broke a bad silence by saying, "Another close call."

Caroline had her hands over her face. "Stop," she said. She hissed when she breathed. That made me uneasy. It was a familiar symptom, recurring when she was near an emotional crisis. "This was . . . too much, don't you see? I don't even want to think about . . . that woman."

As soon as we were in bed, I began, with an urgency that surprised us, to make love to Caroline. We'd always had good sexual relations, except for those down times in her life when it was useless to approach her. We started all right, she was very responsive; then she just turned off. Her eloquent fingers were poised lifelessly at the base of my spine as if she had forgotten not how, but why. She didn't ask me to stop, knowing I was closer to my climax than she had been, but, burdened with the sudden blankness of her flesh, I couldn't keep on, so it was one of those rare fizzles for us.

We lay side by side on the bed with the moonlight on our bodies, holding hands.

"You haven't changed, either," she said.

"What, honey?"

"We've been married eighteen years, too."

"I thought we weren't going to—"

"Look at me. Everything sags, or puckers. I have to have a rinse twice a month or I'd be as gray as my own mother—"

"Don't," I said.

"But *you're* still the same. Your body is—"

"Usually I run thirty miles a week, minimum."

She was quiet for a long time, but because of the rhythm of her breathing I knew she hadn't fallen asleep.

"Ever been to British Columbia?" Caroline asked me.

"I was up there just last week, scouting for a nice little topless lounge to buy."

She rolled to her right, then rolled back and hit me with a pillow, her usual response to my occasional absurdities. I tickled her. Finally she begged me to quit.

''Sharissa'll hear us."

"I don't think it'll do her any harm to know we have fun in bed. After all these years."

Caroline, pleasantly warmed and dampened from our exertions, snuggled against my chest and reached lower. I was fully erect.

"I could—if you want—you know—what you like?"

"And I'll do what you like." Although, after eighteen years of marriage, she was still too bashful—prudish, I suppose—to admit that she liked it. The mutual act we performed, to our complete satisfaction, is still a felony in the state of Georgia, and men—but no women that I know of—have done long stretches in prison for their pleasures. The Baptist church was against it, too, I'm sure. I tithe, and attend our church faithfully. But no sensible man would allow his religion to regulate his sex life.

"How did you ever learn to make love like that?" Caroline murmured, when we were finished. She had said it many times before, not really expecting an answer. Just contented, I liked to believe.

And my stock reply was, "Curiosity and unlimited opportunities with the woman I love."

S oon the old Timekeeper was back, in my dreams.
On a cloudless morning with the sky tinted gold and rose by the newly risen sun, we were making our way up the seven levels of the stone pyramid on the east of the great plaza I had crossed in a previous dream. The plaza had been deserted before, but now I was aware of the presence of thousands of people, congregation for a sacred day. I felt the music they were making through my skin, for I was naked except for a pure white loincloth. Naked, my skin ritually oiled, and barefoot. My hair was long in the dream, but tied above my head with a panache of feathers that hung down between my shoulder blades.

The stairway rising before us was wide and steep, and slippery, from blood that had dripped on the steps, the blood of ritual sacrificers who had preceded us. The odor of blood enflamed me: I was in a state of drug-induced ecstasy bordering on delirium, yet I continued to climb steadily behind the Timekeeper, the ticking of his antique watch resounding in my ears, hammering me on and upward. The Timekeeper carried a deerskin bundle under one arm. Where there was no blood, the loaf-shaped stones of the pyramid were gleaming white from smooth layers of gesso. The Timekeeper, despite his great age and the steepness of the pyramid steps, moved with no show of effort toward the temple at the top.

Smoke rose in many columns from censers placed within the unroofed temple. As we reached the last level, I saw Caroline. With two attendants flanking her, she came through a portal of the temple and walked toward me, eyes wide and tranced, an expectant smile fixed on her face. She wore a headdress of flowers and a jade-green shoulder cape over a flowing white robe of a gauzelike material.

The Timekeeper placed his gold watch and the deerskin bundle on a stone altar decorated with painted masonry figures. Behind the altar there was a massive stone head, part human and part monkey, with a gaping mouth that revealed many teeth. Despite my own state of ecstatic entrancement, I was afraid to look for more than an instant at the face of the deity.

As I took my place at one side of the altar, and Caroline stood opposite me, the Timekeeper, seeming so out of place in his shabby suit of dull black cloth, unwrapped the deerskin bundle, taking out sacred objects carved from rock crystal or bone, and a loaf of chocolate in rice paper. The chocolate he placed in the mouth of the stone diety.

The other object in the bundle was the razor-sharp spine of a stingray.

The Timekeeper passed a shallow ceremonial bowl filled with strips of beaten-bark paper to an attendant, and gave the rope the thickness of Caroline's little finger to the other attendant to hold. Then he approached Caroline and placed a hand on her bare left shoulder.

Caroline, staring wildly with the pupils of her eyes as large as plum stones, swaying a little to the sounds of drums and conchshell trumpets from the plaza far below, put her tongue out of her mouth as far as it would reach, and kneeled. The attendant holding the ceremonial bowl placed it at the level of her breasts. Caroline grasped the rim of the bowl lightly with both hands. Then the Time-keeper drove the point of the stingray's spine down through the middle of her tongue.

Her throat bulged slightly but she made no sound, gave no indication she had felt the cruel spines of the stingray as they penetrated one of the most exquisitely sensitive parts of her body.

The Timekeeper took the rope from the other attendant

and threaded it through the slit in her tongue. One end of the rope hung over the ceremonial bowl. Caroline was bleeding freely and her chin was covered with her blood, which dripped steadily from the end of the rope until it saturated the paper in the bowl.

At a signal from the Timekeeper an attendant removed the ceremonial bowl and brought it to me. Caroline remained kneeling, and with glazed eyes still unfocused, reached up and removed the length of rope from her tongue. She coiled it ritualistically, and placed it in the hollow of a jaguar's skull handed to her by the Timekeeper.

It was my turn. I placed the ceremonial bowl between my bare feet and squatted. The already-bloodied spine of the stingray was handed to me. I pushed my loincloth aside and took my penis in my free hand. It was semierect, the foreskin beginning to tighten at the base of the darkening glans. With the needle point of the stingray spine I pierced the foreskin around the glans three times, then took fresh strips of bark paper from a plate offered me by an attendant and threaded them through the foreskin slits until the ends of the paper hung down from my partly tumescent penis. I watched the papers slowly become saturated with my blood, until they could hold no more; then the first drops formed, grew fat and fell into the bowl where they mingled with Caroline's own shed blood . . .

I started up, hearing Sharissa crying in her crib, and got out of bed with fewer than half my senses functioning properly. Caroline wasn't there. I wondered if she had gotten up to warm Sharissa's bottle, but I realized, dimly, that Sharissa was five months old now and had been sleeping through the night, after her last feeding at eleven. I made my way down the dark hall from our bedroom, finding everything strange, unfamiliar, but still hearing the wail of my precious baby . . . threw open the door to her room and stood blinking in the glow of the nightlight in the socket at the foot of her bed. Not her crib. What the hell had happened to—

Sharissa sat up slowly and gave her tousled hair a shake.

"Daddy? What's the matter?"

"I . . . heard . . . I thought I heard you crying."

"Me?" She yawned and stretched. "Uh-uh."

"Then I was dreaming. Dreaming that you were just a few months old."

Sharissa laughed. "Oh, Daddy. What brought that on?"

"No idea. Sorry I . . . woke you up, sweetheart."

"Don't worry. Go back to bed. See you in the morning."

In the hall I heard Caroline coughing downstairs. I found her in the living room sitting cross-legged on the sofa in her short nightgown, hunched over a photo album in her lap. There was a pack of Kents on the coffee table. She was smoking, holding the cigarette with a pinched craven intimacy, and there were butts in the coffee mug she was using for an ashtray.

A hunger for tobacco had always been a prelude to one of her depressive phases. She turned the stiff gray pages of our wedding album with a robotic, mildly distressed monotony, her normally clear, light brown eyes hazed by smoke. She smiled sadly between puffs on her cigarette.

" 'Til death do us part,' " I heard her say.

"Caroline?"

She looked up, not surprised. "Oh, hi." Her gaze wandered; she cocked her head, as if my image had appeared, mysteriously, near the crown molding. Or some other image of great interest to her.

"Where did you get the cigarettes?" I asked from the doorway.

"Oh, Jim Shively gave them to me to hold. He said absolutely not to give him one even if he begged, he was turning into a human chimney."

"So now you're turning into a human chimney."

"I'm having just this one," she said blithely. "Then I'll quit."

My expression accused her of nothing, but she lowered her gaze and fidgeted while slowly returning her attention to the wedding album. There were other photo albums on the coffee table. She had taken them all from the breakfront cabinet and was making visual contact with the flash-frozen past. First car, first home, first and only cherished child. I wondered if there was any Xanax in the house. She'd always been able to get out of the darker corners of her mind with the help of suitable medication. I'd opposed the suggestions of her doctors that Caroline undergo psychoanalysis. Aside from the expense, in my view the story of psychoanalysis is basically a history of windy theory, intellectual thuggery, and cunning emotional intimidation.

"How many did we have at our wedding reception?" Caroline said. "A hundred sixty-eight guests? Look at this. Here's Maceo Hubbard and Roy Starke. I went to school with both of them." She looked up at me earnestly, trying to share her ordeal. "Maceo's dead."

"I know. Heart."

Her breath hissed hotly as she smoked. "I saw Roy the other day. He looks bad. Most of his hair's gone. He's at least fifty pounds overweight. I think he said something about having a vein-stripping operation."

"Sweetheart, please come to bed."

"In a minute," she said sharply, turning a page. "And here you are."

"No," I said, moving closer to the sofa. "This is me; and that's a picture in a wedding album. And I'm not just the same as I used to be. I'm older and better."

Caroline nodded slightly and turned another page.

"One hundred sixty-eight guests. Each of them a friend or relative of mine. Where were your relatives?"

"I didn't know then, and I don't know now. What are you trying to do, Caroline?"

One of the pages came out of the album as she turned it. She held up the page with an apologetic smile and mumbled, "Coming apart."

I reached down, taking the page and then the album it had come from out of her hands. She didn't resist me. I put the wedding album on the coffee table with the others. I sat down beside her. She surrendered the cigarette, holding it upright like a tiny torch, and I took that too, put it out in the coffee mug. We sat side by side, not looking at each other, like two strangers about to take a trip.

"The long and short of it is," Caroline said, "I don't know who you are. You're somebody from Baltimore, Maryland, who did his service at Fort Belvoir, was discharged from the Army, and settled in Sky Valley."

"Because I loved it here. The first time I saw this town, I knew I was going to stay."

"And I fell for you like a load of bricks. Didn't care where you came from, even though Mama and Daddy had their objections. I married you because you were a kind, decent, loving man, and you've taken wonderful care of me. Sharissa and I adore you, Greg. But *who are you?*"

"Just a guy who's had a little luck in his life, after a bad beginning."

"Did you ever make any attempt to find out who your father was, what happened to your mother after she abandoned you?"

"You know the answer to that."

"But why not?"

The residue of tobacco smoke in the air was giving me a stuffy nose. The cabinet clock in the center hall struck three-fifteen. I didn't want to be angry with Caroline; lately she'd been under more stress than any human being should be asked to cope with. Much of it I had unwittingly provided.

"I think it's obvious no one wanted me when I was born. Why should I care about them? I have all the family now I've ever wanted, or needed. It would be just too painful for me, Caroline. Please try to understand that."

She glanced at me uncertainly, mollified if not content. I took her hand in mine. Caroline touched the bandage that covered my forehead, then the fingers of my left hand that were beginning to straighten. In a few days, when the stitches came out and I had the full use of my left hand, I hoped there would be no further reminders of the unfortunate accident.

"A little luck," she said. "Yes. That's all there is to it sometimes . . . isn't there?"

"Good morning, Daddy," Sharissa said. She was poaching eggs and making French toast. The purple crape myrtle outside the breakfast room windows was full of towhees telling us to "drink-your-tea!" I saw a blur of wings near the hummingbird feeder on the back porch. The surface of the lake was a misty early-morning gold.

"Good morning, babe." She had on her running shoes and summer-weight track warmups. "Where're you off to?"

"Bobby's coming by for me. I need to put in five miles every morning until the tournament starts. Did I tell you? I drew Jan Cassiday in the first round?"

"You've always had trouble with that left-handed serve of hers."

"It's not Jan's such a great player, but she doesn't make many mistakes. I can't let her wear me down."

"I know how much you hate running."

"Well, it won't be so bad with Bobby along. He's been running all summer out at King Forest."

"Maybe I'll join you in a couple of days, when Jesse gives me the okay."

Sharissa served up eggs and French toast for us and we sat down in the breakfast room. She poured fresh orange juice from a chilled pitcher and we dug in.

"Mom left at five-thirty," Sharissa said.

"The senator's barnstorming north Georgia today. Seven stops in ten hours."

"That old fool," Sharissa said, which was uncharacteristic of her. "And don't give me that look, I know how *you* feel. Mom's wasting her talents. I wish she'd go back to work for the *Tribune*."

"So do I. But she loves politics."

Sharissa ate a bite of egg, spread thick maple syrup over her French toast, and looked up at me speculatively. Her eyes, in that smooth tanned face, could still startle me: I felt certain that no artist had ever lived who could duplicate so subtle and ravishing a color, or combination of colors, because her eyes were ever-changing, according to the light; and I felt with a wrench of the heart that perhaps I was seeing my daughter, in this season of unexpected and violent trouble for the Walker family, at the peak of her freshness and beauty.

"After you woke me up," Sharissa said, "I went to the bathroom. I heard you and Mom talking. She sounded . . . depressed." Sharissa paused and put her chin on her folded hands, wanting me to confirm her suspicions.

I decided to tell her about our aborted evening out, the close call with Mrs. Roxanne Sullivan and her pathetic delusion.

It shocked her. Sharissa had no further interest in her breakfast. Tight-lipped, she blinked at me, as if she were trying to communicate in code.

"Mom must have been petrified. What about you?"

"Sure, I was scared. Having another gun aimed at you so soon after being shot is not an experience I'd recommend."

Bobby Driscoll appeared at the kitchen door and looked in through the screen.

"Hey, Sharissa! Morning, Mr. Walker. Am I interrupting anything?"

Sharissa glanced at him. "No, Bobby. I'm ready. Would you mind waiting for me in the truck?"

She got up and scraped her plate in the Disposall, picked up her gym bag, then came over and hugged me.

"Don't let Mom . . . you know. Crash-dive again. I don't think I could stand it."

I held her for a few moments. I thought I could feel her heart beating. Or maybe it was two hearts together.

The bandage came off and the stitches came out of my forehead. Jesse Fernando had done a neat job of sewing the big flap of scalp back. He told me that after a few months, a year at most, the scars would barely be noticeable—a thin, white, sealed doorway into the brain.

I had continued with my physical therapy. Jesse, always cautious, did a full physical workup before he would let me run again. Some of the test results obviously troubled him, although he wouldn't tell me what they were over the phone. I wasn't feeling badly—a touch of vertigo now and then had been my most serious complaint—but I was worried when I sat down with him in his office at the medical center across the street from Sky Valley Memorial Hospital.

"What is it, Jesse?"

He pushed his reading glasses up on the crown of his head and glanced at me, then smiled at my expression.

"Nothing to be alarmed about. Your EEG was fine; some slight but probably not significant abnormalities in the regions affected by the bullet fragments." He looked through the folder in front of him for other test results. "It's your blood screens I wanted to discuss with you. Specifically, a very high cholesterol."

"Oh-oh. High cholesterol's not good for me, is it?"

"Depends on which form of cholesterol we're talking about. There's high-density lipoprotein, HDL, and low-density lipoprotein. HDL is the good form of blood cholesterol. It probably prevents the clogging of the arteries that cause most heart attacks. An HDL level above forty milligrams per deciliter of blood plasma would be ideal for most of us. Your HDL level is more than five times that high."

I shrugged. "Good news for me. I guess."

"The best news is your LDL level—low-density lipoprotein, the "bad twin" of the set. It's about ninety milligrams. One hundred sixty milligrams is considered outstanding for someone of your size and age."

"What all this means is, my brain could use a little work but I have one hell of a healthy heart."

"There's more to it than that, Greg. An HDL level as high as yours is an extreme medical rarity. I ran your test results by a colleague of mine at the National Heart, Lung, and Blood Institute in Bethesda, Maryland. They have a lab there for the study of cholesterol abnormalities at the molecular and genetic level. He confirmed that an HDL level of four hundred or better indicates the presence of a variant gene that no one's been able to isolate yet. Dr. Pensky called it the "Methuselah gene.""

I smiled. "If I have this gene, it means I'll live to be nine hundred years old? Come *on*, Jesse."

"Well, considering the state of the environment and the stress we all live under these days, maybe nine hundred years is asking too much. If you continue to take good care of yourself, and don't get in the way of any more stray bullets, the odds in favor of you cracking a hundred are very damned high. The real test is how long members of your family have lived—mother, father, grand-parents on both sides. If we know their respective ages, then we can tell which side is passing along the gene variant that's raised your HDL level so high."

"I don't know who my parents were; and I have no interest in trying to find out."

Jesse looked perplexed. "Even after what I've just told you? Look, Greg, there may be more than one mutated gene at work here. Genes that literally have saved your life. Here you sit across the desk from me with only a bad haircut to show for getting shot, when I ought to be looking at a man in a terminal coma. Or looking at your grave."

"It was pure luck, Jesse. Or the grace of God, or both."

"I don't want to use any words with bad connotations—"

"Like 'Guinea pig'?"

Jesse knotted his smooth surgeon's hands together, locking down his urge to be relentless in pursuit of scientific truth. "If you could give the people at Bethesda just a few days a year, who knows what they might find out?"

I stared at him for several seconds. "I see myself as an ordinary man, Jesse. Nothing unusual about me, in spite of what you say may be hiding out in my bloodstream."

"What I believe is there could ultimately save hundreds of thousands of lives a year, the lives of the genetically underprivileged, once the lab guys find the gene or genes that make you unique and learn how to duplicate them."

"Now I'm unique? I thought I was just a rarity, like your average two-headed calf."

He accepted my surly humor with forebearance, blinking mildly.

"Would you give this serious consideration, Greg? Maybe we can talk again in a month or two."

"In the meantime, I suppose my case will be turning up in medical journals all over the country. Or on the front page of *The New York Times*. I'd better change my phone number."

"You know I'll respect your privacy, Greg," Jesse said firmly, as if I had, finally, hurt his feelings. "I haven't given your name to anyone else, even Dr. Pensky."

I nodded. I tried to think of a way to explain, to expiate my rudeness.

"I'm a den animal," I said. "I've never craved attention. I resist anything that complicates my existence or will give my family notoriety they don't want."

"I understand that. And you've been through a severe trauma. It's natural for you to want to retreat and close all the doors while your emotions catch up with events." He closed the file. "This goes in a locked drawer. I'll only bring it out again with your permission. Your blessing."

My hair was growing faster in some places than others; not enough yet to shape, but at least I could have it neatened on all sides. I was in the middle chair at Pete's on the square when Detective Sergeant Butterbaugh caught up with me. After Pete had me looking presentable without the necessity of hiding my head under a Braves cap, I walked down the street with Butterbaugh, and we stopped in at the Peacock for midmorning coffee.

Butterbaugh took three heaping teaspoons of sugar in his. I didn't say anything.

"Mild hypoglycemia," he explained. "Doesn't affect my work." Then he said, "I dropped by Burger King last night? It was slow; had the chance to talk to Sharissa for a few minutes." He seemed proud of this, almost as if they'd been on a date. I was getting the feeling that he had become one of the family, insinuating himself like a stray dog who won't budge off your porch.

"What did you talk about?"

"Oh, mostly tennis. Sharissa said she's been getting scholarship offers since she was fourteen. Vanderbilt's package is worth $80,000 for four years?"

"Something like that."

"Maybe Sharissa ought to consider the pro tour, like Capriati? Some of those kids are worth millions, and they're not old enough to vote."

"She'd have to have the national ranking, which means you work at tennis full-time, a one-track program at a good tennis academy where the competition is really first-rate. Maybe we could have scraped together the money for Bolletieri or Rick Macci's. No way Caroline and I could have started over in Florida, so we wouldn't have seen much of Sharissa during some very important years. We let her make up her own mind, but I'm damned glad she decided her home and family and education was more important to her than a pro career."

"Sharissa's one in a million," Butterbaugh said, almost reverently. "Very analytical mind. She wants to be a federal court judge some day?"

"I know," I said. "We've talked about it. We talk about everything."

Butterbaugh had a couple of sips of coffee. He was one of those people who can't drink quietly from a cup. He decided to add more sugar. Then he noticed that his watch had stopped, and he took it off to wind it. He treated the old Hamilton with loving care.

"They don't make them like that anymore," I said.

"No, sir. This one belonged to my father's father? I probably shouldn't wear it on the job. I've got another one, an Elgin officer's model from World War I, those came with detachable shrapnel covers. But the jewels are worn and it loses too much time every day." He strapped the watch on, lifted his cup and swallowed noisily. "You look a hundred percent, Greg. That's not a word of a lie. My maternal grandfather did some boxing, trying to make ends meet during the Depression. I expect he took his share of jabs to the head? Died years later of an embolism nobody was aware of."

"That's something to look forward to," I said, a little coldly.

"I wasn't drawing any parallels," Butterbaugh said hastily. "I've been thinking about how fragile the human brain is. Or the human mind. I went down to the mental health center to see Mrs. Sullivan."

"Do we have to talk about her?"

He looked a little surprised. "Why not?"

"I've been trying to put that—distasteful business at the Ovenbird out of my mind."

"I just thought you might like to know, we've come up with a few things."

"I suppose she's still claiming that I'm her husband."

"Oh, no, she's not talking. Can't or won't, nobody can be sure. They've diagnosed her as catatonic schizophrenic. It used to be the most common form of the disease, in the horse-and-buggy era. Nowadays schizophrenics tend to be paranoid—everybody's out to get them, aliens are programming their minds, that kind of thing? The more technologically complex our society becomes, the more paranoids we have. But Roxanne Sullivan is just the opposite. She's unreceptive, unresponsive. I saw her. Gave me a chilly feeling. As if the soul had shed the body and left it like a snake leaves its skin hanging on a bush somewhere. Snap your fingers in front of her face, she doesn't blink. Long rope of saliva hanging down from one side of her mouth."

"C.G.! For Christ's sake."

"Sorry. Anyway, this is the same mental illness that put her in an asylum in Canada for years."

"How do you know that?"

"LETS."

"Let's what?"

"Law Enforcement Teletype System. We know everything Canada had on her in a few hours. Mrs. Sullivan was a borderline alcoholic most of her life. But when her husband, what was his name—?" I looked blankly at him. He scratched an eyebrow and the name popped up in his mind. "Frederick, walked out on her, she really hit the sauce hard. We couldn't locate much in the way of family up there, nobody willing to be responsible for her. Frederick and Bonnie were her immediate family—"

"Bonnie?"

"Their daughter. Adopted when she was a couple of years old. Mrs. Sullivan couldn't bear children."

"You did a very thorough investigation."

"Almost everything about an individual who's lived during the past forty years is in somebody's computer somewhere. You'd be amazed. Getting back to Frederick Sullivan: Frederick apparently wanted a child more than she did. He wanted a girl, too. Had to be a little girl. We don't have actual proof of any child abuse, but Mrs. Sullivan complained to a social worker that Frederick and Bonnie's relationship was a little too intimate, once Bonnie reached puberty." I must have grimaced. "Maybe it was jealousy. The story is, Roxanne used to beat the girl up when she'd been drinking. An all-too-familiar domestic situation. But Bonnie obviously cared more for her adopted father than she did for Roxanne. She split with Frederick after he cleaned out the bank accounts he had with his wife. That was a few days before Bonnie's sixteenth birthday. Nobody wanted him for anything; he had a few old misdemeanors on his record. He was just another good-looking low-life, according to all reports."

"But he had something that Mrs. Sullivan continued to fantasize about, for almost twenty years. Until her fantasy got the best of her."

"It's sad, when you see her where she is now. On the other hand, she might have killed you. The love-hate thing. There's a ten-dollar word for it. Erotomania? Something like that."

"What's her prognosis?" I asked him.

"They've tried a couple of the new psychoactive drugs. No results yet. What's for certain is, her liver's failing. All the years of boozing it up. So at best she's got another eight, ten months to live."

"Oh. What do you think happened to her husband and the girl?"

"They probably could be traced, if somebody had the time or the motivation. Why bother now?"

"No reason," I said. I looked at my wristwatch. "I'd better get back to the store. That new Sam's Wholesale Club out on Old Alabama has me in a discount bind. My repair business is falling off, too."

"They just make them too good these days."

I paid for our coffees and we parted company on the sidewalk. He started across the street to the municipal building at Second and Ramer, then called back to me, "I forgot to tell you, I found out what was in the locket."

"Her favorite snapshot of Frederick?"

"No, a lock of hair. Dark brown."

"The girl's?"

"Bonnie Sullivan was blond. I have all of those Sullivan family photos in my office, if you're curious as to what Bonnie looked like."

A car turning the corner almost hooked him with a fender, and he skipped out of the way, backing up.

"I'm not," I said.

"So it must be Frederick's hair. See you Friday night!"

"You will?"

"Sharissa invited me to dinner!" Butterbaugh said, and he went whistling on his way back to work.

The next morning, Wednesday, Caroline could barely lift her head from the pillow. Exhaustion from her long days and nights on the campaign trail, combined with a summer cold. We had a brief argument about her staying home for the day, which I think she was happy to let me win.

I fixed breakfast for Caroline, but when I took it up to our room on a tray she was sound asleep again.

"Mom's not feeling well?" Sharissa asked me when I returned to the kitchen. She was wearing a silvery tank top and feather-weight, bright red Nike shorts.

"She's about run herself into the ground. Claude ought to be able to get through one day without her. I'll call campaign headquarters in a little while."

I put plastic wrap over the glass of orange juice I'd squeezed for Caroline and placed it in the refrigerator. The eggs wouldn't keep, but I could make a sandwich of them for my own lunch.

"How's the roadwork coming?" I asked Sharissa.

She looked a little grim. "First week's the hardest."

"Bobby's not showing you any mercy?"

"No, but I wouldn't want him to." A minute later we heard his truck in the driveway. Sharissa grabbed her gear and gave me a quick kiss. " 'Bye, Dad."

"You're limping," I said, as she went out the door.

"It's just a stone bruise. No problem."

I got out the bread, made myself a fried egg sandwich, and added a carton of fruit juice to the brown-bag lunch. When I went upstairs to our bedroom I saw that Caroline hadn't changed her position. She was still snoring lightly through a stuffy nose. I left her a note, explaining that I would call in sick for her.

The Zeiss binoculars, my Christmas present of two years ago, were on the shelf in the hall closet. I took them with my lunch outside and, after a few moments' consideration, decided to drive Caroline's old Volvo. One hundred sixty thousand miles on it. Cartons of campaign literature on the backseat, but she wouldn't be needing any of that today. As usual, the Volvo could've used a wash job and was low on gas.

By the time I'd filled the tank and gone through the free car wash at the Amoco station four blocks from our home, it was close to seven-thirty and the day was already heating up. Sultry and hazy. I knew it would be cooler beneath the big trees of King Forest, along the trails where Sharissa jogged with Bobby Driscoll. I'd run there myself, although it probably had been a couple of years. A little too far to drive when I was busy. Weekdays, early, you could run for half a mile or more through the glades without encountering anyone. On weekends the trails were well populated with nature hikers, too many of whom didn't pick up after themselves.

Bobby and Sharissa were seventeen minutes ahead of me. Too far ahead to catch up if I wanted to run with them. But exercise wasn't my reason for going to King Forest today.

There were a couple of lots for public parking at King Forest. I located the blue Chevy Maxicab with the provocative bumper stickers (which someone has characterized as "one of the few native American art forms, along with Navaho blankets and comic books"), drove by Bobby's truck, left the lot, and took a narrow blacktop road to the top of the modest mountain that afforded an overview of much of the forest: the swimming lake, almost invisible beneath a blanket of mist, the campgrounds and winding trails through the lowland sections. There were tougher hiking trails in wilder parts of the forest, but I was hoping that Bobby and Sharissa would stay on the well-beaten paths where the mileage was conveniently marked off.

Mine was the only car in the half-moon of parking lot near the summit of the mountain. A couple of flights of steps took me down to the level of a limestone jut with the area of a tennis court. It was enclosed by a four-foot concrete wall with a pipe railing on top of that. The drop here was a nearly perpendicular three hundred feet.

I got out the binoculars and sighted in on a covered bridge at the north end of the lake, about three-quarters of a mile away. The binoculars moved the bridge to within a couple of hundred feet. The bridge was about one hundred sixty feet long and spanned a rocky stream that splashed down into the lake. River birches and wild mountain laurel grew thickly to the edge of the water below the bridge.

I saw a fit-looking gray-haired couple in jogging suits on the trail. They disappeared into the bridge and emerged eighteen seconds later in the misty early-morning light; they were setting a good pace for themselves.

No one else appeared on that part of the trail for seven minutes. I lowered the glasses and rubbed my eyes. When I focused on one end of the bridge again I saw Bobby and then Sharissa, probably twenty yards behind him but running well on the packed red clay of the wide trail.

At the mouth of the bridge he looked back at her; he seemed to be laughing, but I wasn't sure. She slowed momentarily, then sprinted the last few yards after him and disappeared from my view.

Ten minutes went by. Twelve. They didn't reappear. No one else came along. It was stressful holding the binoculars steady. The sun was higher, and there was no breeze. I heard a hawk in the sky.

I began to feel light-headed. The sweat that ran down the side of my neck was cold. I was breathing through my mouth, but still not getting enough air.

When I saw them again they were walking. Each with an arm around the other at the waist. Sharissa leaned against Bobby. They stopped and gazed down at the tumbling stream. Then Bobby put his arms around her and they kissed, again, or so I assumed. What else would they have been doing for so long under cover of the old bridge? Sharissa had her back to me. Bobby's big hands slipped down inside the waistband of her shorts. Holding her like that, a hand spread on each cheek, he pulled her very tightly against himself. And she didn't resist. Up on her toes, Sharissa clung to him like a moth on a screen.

I put the binoculars back in the case and went up the steps to the parking crescent, the sun in my face. There was nothing more I wanted to see there, or needed to think about. The moments of vertigo had passed. I was neither bitter nor angry. I could never be angry with my daughter. I couldn't find it in my heart to blame Bobby, either. They both were possessed, and too young to believe that any harm could come of it if they really loved each other. They would never know what they were about to do to me.

The sickness swept over me so quickly I was almost helpless: the rising gorge, the indescribable, gagging vileness. I was able to stop and keep my foot on the brake while I opened the door, leaned out and vomited in the road. It was almost like losing blood; I had the sensation of my life receding, draining away in a violent whirlpool. I heard a terrible moaning that turned into a yowl of misery, of unbearable grieving. Nothing animal nor human could have sounded like that: it was a cry from a threatened soul, from the torment of limbo.

My agony ended soon enough, and was replaced by a throbbing in my skull, by bleakness. And a vaguely dreadful sense of unreality, as if I were separated from all that was familiar in my life—the streets of Sky Valley, the interior of my store—by a thick pane of glass. Everyone who spoke to me sounded distant to my ears. My skin tingled from time to time. I would touch something—a pen, a doorknob—and want to touch it again, caress it, to be sure it was actually there. I smiled more than I usually do, a strained, unfelt smile as I went about my daily routines.

Two service calls, old customers. The van wouldn't start; it was the ignition again. I'd just had it worked on. I got out and went back into the store feeling apathetic. Then, suddenly, I was shouting on the phone at Vince, the service manager at Sky Valley Ford-Mercury. When I put down the receiver of the phone Scott Bisco, my good right arm, was staring at me from across his worktable.

"They wonder why everybody is buying Japanese these days. Twenty-four thousand miles on that van, and it's been in the shop six times."

Bisco reached into a back pocket of his Levi's and tossed me a set of keys. "Take mine. I raked it out the other day."

"Thanks, Scott."

Scott's van was an old orange VW that leaned slightly to the right. Inside it smelled of dogs and gun oil, french fries and burgers, beer and weed and sweaty sin. An old rag rug covered most of the front seat. There was a shoebox on the seat, nearly full of random-size Polaroid snapshots. The lid was half off and I couldn't help seeing the contents. Mostly girls about Bisco's age or younger, showing off their private parts for the photographer, Bisco himself, I supposed. He apparently favored overweight girls with flourishing pubic bushes. Most of the photos appeared to have been taken at night, probably in the back of the van. The eyes of the young girls by flashlight were like the eyes of newly dead animals in the road.

I put the lid on his epicene, trifling trophies. Bisco had two rifle racks mounted in the back. The racks were empty. But there was a .22 automatic in the seat partly under the pornocopia shoebox, not unlike the pistol that, in the hands of Ricky Gene Kindor, had nearly done me in. It looked oily, obscene, useful. I stared at it, but I didn't want to touch it. I had a sensation of coming back to earth with a little jolt; of becoming my old self again. I had survived the shooting. And that was a necessary reminder: regardless of circumstances, I knew I could survive anything.

I was the first one up on Friday morning, and I had hot chocolate ready when Sharissa appeared in the kitchen at six-thirty. Caroline was awake, too; the shower was running in our bathroom.

"Hot chocolate?" Sharissa said, appreciatively. It was a wintertime ritual in our house, but I seldom thought of making the drink during the hot months. I started with a bar of dark bittersweet Belgian chocolate, which I melted in a double boiler, then added milk with two ounces of heavy cream and sugar, but not too much sugar.

"I had a craving," I said. "And I thought you could use an energy boost; you looked a little peaked last night. Do you think you might be overtraining?"

"No, I'm okay. I wanted to push myself hard this week; then I'll taper off a couple of days before the tournament." She sat down at the breakfast counter, hooking her feet behind the tall stool so that the muscles in her honey-colored calves stood out. She tasted the steaming chocolate. "Little stronger than usual, Dad."

"Always takes me a few tries to get the recipe just right. Add a little milk, there's some left in the pan."

"No, it's fine, really. Are you poaching eggs?"

"Almost ready. Toast or English muffin?"

"Half a muffin. Maybe just a bit of egg. Otherwise it's like running with a rock in my stomach."

Sharissa adjusted the terry sweatband she wore at her hairline and drank more of her chocolate. The shower had stopped upstairs. I went to the back steps and hollered,

"Breakfast!" to Caroline. She called back: "Ten minutes!" I took a roll of Canadian bacon from the refrigerator and muffins from the breadbox.

"Where'd you go last night?" Sharissa asked me. "I heard you leave. It must have been after midnight."

I turned and smiled at her. "Chocolate mouth," I said. Then I said, "I needed to go by the store and pick up a new manual that came from the factory. I've been meaning to read the darn thing for a month. You know how something nags and nags at you until you just have to do something about it?"

"Jan Cassiday," Sharissa said grimly, naming her first opponent in the upcoming tournament. Then she gave her head a shake and smiled and crooked her strong right arm, making a fist and showing off her bicep.

Bobby Driscoll rolled up in his brother's Maxicab just as Caroline hurried downstairs in a beige linen suit with big white buttons like Dagwood's. Sharissa, leaving most of her English muffin, slid off the stool and gave her mother a kiss.

Caroline said to me, "Coffee, and that's all I have time for."

"I fixed you a cheese and bacon muffin," I said, "and you're not leaving until you eat it."

"Well, okay," Caroline agreed, not unhappy to be bullied a little. "How do I look?"

"Terrific," Sharissa said, with a little grimace, and pulled some stray hairs from a padded shoulder of Caroline's suit.

"Honey. What's the matter?" Caroline asked her.

"I don't know." Sharissa rubbed her diaphragm in a slow circle. "Feels like something didn't go down right." She sighed and took another sip of chocolate as Bobby came in.

"Hey, Mrs. Walker! Don't see much of you lately."

"Four more days to Primary. Then I get my life back." Caroline nibbled at the muffin sandwich, approved, wolfed down more of it. Sharissa linked an arm with Bobby's, smiling wanly at him.

"Sure you're okay?" I asked her.

"It's nothing. A little cramp. It'll pass. Mom, we're having company for dinner."

"I know. I promise. I'll be here."

"You mean Sergeant Butterball?" Bobby said.

"Butterbaugh, and don't make fun of him. He's a friend. 'Bye, everybody."

Caroline finished her muffin sandwich, licked crumbs from her fingertips, kissed me beside the mouth, and hurried out after Bobby and Sharissa.

"Keep an eye on that right front tire," I cautioned her as the screen door closed.

I had just finished straightening up the kitchen when I heard Bobby's truck in the drive again. I went outside. Bobby hopped out, shrugged, and went around to help Sharissa down from the high seat. Her color was bad. Her eyes looked sick.

"She threw up," Bobby explained, getting an arm gently around her and helping her toward the house.

"I'm gonna be okay," Sharissa protested. "I feel a little cold. I want to lie down."

I said, "We'd better drive you over to—"

"Uh-uh, I'm nauseated, that's all. Maybe I'm stressed. It'll pass."

"I'll stick around," Bobby said worriedly.

"No, go and run, Bob. I—it's like I have something *stuck* here." She placed two fingers under her breastbone. Her lips crimped. "Have to throw up again," she said dully, and lunged into the small bathroom next to the laundry.

"She pushes herself way too hard," I explained to Bobby.

"Yes, sir. That's what I keep telling her. Take a day off once in a while, chill out, you know?"

Sharissa came out of the bathroom with a cold cloth pressed against her head.

"Stomach's not so bad, now my head hurts," she mumbled.

"Want me to help you upstairs?" I asked.

"No, no, I can make it. Dad, my aim was bad in there."

"I'll clean up."

"Sorry. Bobby—"

"I'll be back in an hour, keep you company. If that's okay, Mr. Walker?"

"Sure. I'll stay until—"

"*Both* of you," Sharissa said from the landing on the back stairs, "just go about your business, *please*. I want to lie down for a little while, but it's nothing serious."

After Bobby left I went upstairs and looked in on Sharissa. She was sprawled on her unmade bed, wet cloth over her eyes like a blindfold.

"Baby?"

"Feeling better. Maybe I'll—sleep a little while."

"Have Bobby call me when he gets here."

"Sure thing. Love you, Dad."

It took me less than a minute to swab the floor in the bathroom downstairs. Another minute to change into my mismatched jogging outfit. Nike shirt, Adidas shorts. I put on a baseball cap, a headband and wraparound sunglasses, and went outside to the car.

Six minutes to seven when I pulled out of the driveway. And Bobby had about a six-minute head start on me. But, for a teenager, he was an unusually sedate driver, and of course Bobby's brother would have put several lumps on his head if anything happened to the Maxicab while Bobby was driving it.

I didn't hurry either, on my way out to King Forest. I was familiar with Bobby's jogging routine and I knew where I would catch up to him.

There were no cars in sight when I crossed the Little Chatooga, so I took a few moments to run the window down and throw the prescription bottle of codeine-based cough syrup deep into the slough. It was the codeine in the cough syrup I had mixed with Sharissa's hot chocolate that had caused an immediate allergic reaction. When she was younger she would break out in a rash, along with other, more violent symptoms: extreme shortness of breath, the feeling of something sharp and hard obstructing the diaphragm.

Probably Sharissa had forgotten what brought on those attacks. But I wasn't concerned. I didn't think there would be any questions asked later.

It would have been a risk to leave the car in either of the parking lots at King Forest. About three-quarters of a mile north of the main entrance I came across a boarded-up old general store and parked, out of sight of the state road, behind the ramshackle building. There was a FOR SALE sign on it that could explain my presence if anyone should come around.

I took my small backpack from the truck and put it on. A dump truck filled with tree stumps roared by on the blacktop; then I crossed and entered the woods by way of a creek bottom. All around me roadside kudzu had overgrown the tall trees, turning them into dinosaur and dragon shapes. I followed the shallow winding creek south, jogging when I could. But the light was still dim here and I had to keep an eye out for poisonous snakes, particularly when it was necessary to cross the hulks of rotting trees lying across my path.

After about ten minutes of this I came to a marked trail and then an unpaved service road. So far I hadn't run into anyone, but I heard, before I saw, a jogger laboring uphill toward me, and I stepped off into the cover of understory trees beside the road. The jogger looked like a former football lineman valiantly trying to shed fifty pounds. He was wearing headphones and wiping sweat from his eyes when he went past me.

As soon as he reached a bend in the road I was on my way again.

Four minutes later I arrived at the waterfall above the covered bridge. I made my way carefully down the dripping rocky slope beside the waterfall and stopped twenty yards from the north end of the bridge. I couldn't hear anything except the sound of falling, rushing water. I was breathing too hard: part of it was due to the fact that I was not in peak condition, but the real problem, I realized, was apprehension, or perhaps incipient panic. It was cool and sunless here, and I couldn't stop shuddering.

A group of young church campers came raggedly along the path, urged on by their counselors, one a girl whose wholesome good looks and athleticism made me think of Sharissa. I turned away from them but otherwise didn't try to conceal myself. Seeing the girl gave my spirits a lift. I had better control of my heart rate by the time I turned back to the bridge and the lake simmering in the background. I took out my binoculars and focused on the opposite shore of the lake, on a crowded campground and the jogging path that eventually joined the road that crossed the covered bridge. I picked out several joggers through the early-morning haze and intervening trees.

One of them was Bobby Driscoll, running alone. No other jogger was within a quarter mile of him. I estimated he would reach the bridge in a little more than four minutes.

I was still shuddering. I had hoped to be fully collected, nerveless, for this confrontation, but there were too many variables that now filled me with doubt. My nerves wouldn't improve with waiting. The best course was not to stand around any longer, but to meet Bobby on the run.

I put the binoculars away, beside the stolen pistol in my backpack, and went down to the red clay road, a little slippery in this place from drifting spray. I checked my watch and began jogging uphill through dark green pines. Sunlight would not touch the ground here for another two hours. I cast no shadow. My footprints were among a thousand others, barely discernible. The sound of the waterfall faded. I was alone with my life, my thoughts, in a state of fascination, preoccupied with deeds to come.

B obby?"
His head was down, his flushed weightlifter's neck bulging from effort until I spoke; then he looked up in surprise and broke his stride on the path, less than six feet wide where we were about to meet.

"Mr. Walker?" Bobby stopped then, jogging in place, while I closed the short distance between us. He smiled, puzzled; then his gray eyes flashed in sudden alarm. "Is Sharissa okay?"

"It was just a little stomachache; she'll be fine."

"Oh." The smile returned. The uneven edges of his hair were beaded with sweat. A mosquito buzzed around his glistening forehead and he batted it away. He was two inches taller than me, probably forty pounds heavier. He wasn't wearing enough clothing to conceal any detail of his fine body. I admired the sculpted solidity, appraised the potential danger of him. "I didn't know you were going to run this morning. We could have come together."

"Just an impulse," I said. I pretended to be more winded than I was. "Take a break?"

"Okay." He didn't want to; I had interrupted his routine, but he was gracious about it. "Do you have the time, Mr. Walker?"

"Seven-twenty-one," I said, glancing at my watch.

"I need to finish up and be at the warehouse by eight-thirty. Or my uncle gets all over me for being lazy, you know how that goes."

"Sure. I've got some water, if you want it. And I need to take a leak."

I went off into the woods, hands tingling, blood pumping hard at my temples. After a second or two he followed me, and within a few more seconds we were out of sight of the path. I took my pack off and unzipped a side compartment, tossed a plastic water bottle to Bobby. We came to a shallow dry ravine, littered with stones, in a small clearing. I walked to the edge of the ravine, the pack in my hands. I made almost no sound walking on the thick mat of pine needles. I thought that it was too quiet here. I heard only a few birds, the faint sounds of Bobby drinking from the bottle.

With my back to him I took out the .22 caliber automatic I had stolen from Scott Bisco's orange VW van at a quarter to one this morning, while it was parked behind his girlfriend's apartment house. I dropped the backpack and turned to Bobby with the muzzle of the pistol centered on his chest. We were, I think, about fifteen feet apart.

He didn't know what to make of the pistol. From the look on his face he didn't feel threatened. I was Sharissa's father. On the other hand, I was obviously pointing it at him. He lowered the water bottle, blinking, bit his lip, and thought of something to say.

"Mr. Walker—you should be careful with that."

"I am careful, Bob." I didn't move or change the direction in which I was aiming.

"Oh—is it loaded?"

"Yes, it is."

"Oh." He was blinking again. Now there was tension in his stance, wariness in his eyes. "Sir. I really wish you wouldn't point it at me. You're pointing it at me, you know?"

"I know, Bobby. But I'm not going to shoot you as long

as you continue to look me directly in the eyes, and don't make the slightest attempt to run. If you try that then I will shoot, and I won't miss."

He started to speak, but belated shock cut him off, cost him his voice. He swallowed hard and got it back.

"Sir. Mr. Walker. What—I don't—"

"I'm not enjoying myself, Bobby. I hate doing this, in fact, and I wouldn't be if you hadn't made it necessary."

Silence.

"Look at me, Bob. Don't let your eyes wander again. The next time I'll kill you without warning. You had better know I mean what I say. Look right here at me. Tell me you understand."

"Yes, sir," he said. His throat worked hard and the next moment he started to cry. Tears poured from his eyes and he blinked rapidly, staring at me all the while. His tears made me feel very badly. I hated this, the stupid melodrama. But I had to know.

"—Did I do?" Bobby asked me, forcing his words out through the lockjaw of fear: fear of my bizarre behavior, the warning of unjustified punishment.

Disturbed by his fear, which threatened to release a torrent of my own fears, I was close to trembling again.

"Bobby, I have to know what you've done to Sharissa."

"Wha—Sharissa—?" It had been a couple of years at least since his voice had changed; now it was changing back, to the high tenor of childhood.

"And don't lie. It's your only chance. You must not lie to me. Have you had sex with my daughter?"

His mouth was open. He had a simple, earnest expression, as if I had put him in such a state of terror he couldn't process the question. Then, in a flash of clarity, his shoulders dropped and he cried harder, shaking with grief.

"I love—Sharissa—"

I moved a couple of steps closer to him. I was cold with dismay.

"Have you? You son of a bitch, *answer* me! *Did you fuck Sharissa?*"

My language, deliberately chosen, had the right shock effect. He raised a hand to wipe his streaming eyes. His head swung side to side, slowly. But Bobby continued, as I had warned him, to look straight at me.

"Mr. Walker—"

"Bobby?"

"No, I never—never with Sharissa. No, sir! No. It's true. Oh, God, so help me, don't hurt me, I've never done anything to hurt her!"

"Bobby?"

He couldn't get his breath. It was a panic reaction I hadn't anticipated.

"Take it easy, Bobby." I kept my voice low and neutral in tone. "I guess I believe you. But the trouble is, I've seen the two of you together. Do you understand what I mean?"

"Uh-uh."

"I've seen how you hold her. Your hands were all over her breasts, weren't they?"

"Y-yes, I—but I swear—as Jesus is my Savior—"

"Where else?"

"S-sir?"

"Come on, Bobby. You know what I'm saying. Don't you?"

"Y-yes."

"Okay, then. Maybe you didn't go all the way. But did you masturbate her?"

He couldn't breathe again. I remember hearing that Bobby had been asthmatic as a child. Often the condition is psychosomatic. His face was reddening as he choked. He was holding his throat.

But I couldn't let up on him now.

"Nod your head, Bobby, if you ever went anywhere near Sharissa's vagina during love play."

He shook his head instead. Vehemently, despite the fact that he was suffocating.

I was sorry for him. I wished he could feel as much relief as I felt at that moment. I owned my life again.

"All right," I said. "You'll be okay. Sit down on the ground, Bobby. Catch your breath. You've been very cooperative. And I really appreciate the consideration you've shown my daughter."

He sank to his knees on the turf of pine needles, mouth open, eyes bulging. Then he was able to grab a breath of air. Another. Sucking it in with a terrible sound, the cords in his throat standing out.

I picked up the water bottle and took the lid off, dashed some of it against the side of his face and on the back of his neck. The shock of the water on his humid skin seemed to have a good effect. He was rocking slightly, panting now, a definite improvement. All his attention was focused on the effort to get enough air. He had, temporarily, lost his strength. The strength that threatened me.

I put the .22 caliber handgun down beside my backpack. Of course I had never intended to shoot him. Perhaps I hadn't needed the intimidation the gun represented. I certainly didn't need it now.

In the ravine I found a smooth round geode the size of a large grapefruit, which I was able to palm with one hand. The stone must have weighed seven or eight pounds. I carried it, hand down at my side, back to Bobby, who did not look up. He might not have heard me coming. I had no shadow, but I felt as light as a shadow on my feet.

When I was behind him I reached down with my free hand and stroked the back of his head as if I were soothing a child. He shuddered and moaned something.

"Thank you, Bobby," I said softly, "for not taking her from me."

His scalp was slightly exposed where I had separated the damply matted hair with my fingers. His sweat, welling up along with fear, smelled sharp and rye in the pure morning air. I looked down at the vulnerable strip of white scalp a couple of inches from the base of his skull and then, with sudden intoxicated strength, reached back and slammed the stone down hard. I hit him with a violence that surprised me and took most of my breath away.

Even so I hadn't expected to shatter the bones with a single blow.

Bobby fell forward, sprawling on his face in a spray of blood from his nose. I just stood there, trembling, watching him, the stone poised for a second blow, and quite a lot of time went by before I realized that it wouldn't be necessary. Bobby wasn't going to move ever again.

W̄e had honey-baked ham and escalloped potatoes and green beans for dinner that night, but dinner didn't go well. Caroline was home, but the phone rang every few minutes for her—some emergency or other the volunteers at Claude Gilley's campaign headquarters couldn't or didn't want to deal with. And every time the ringing began Sharissa would fall silent, shifting her eyes toward the kitchen and the nearest telephone, her mouth set in a line that betrayed both worry and anger. Bobby Driscoll had been invited, hadn't showed, apparently didn't have the courtesy to call and let her know he would be late or not there at all. She ate sparingly and paid polite attention to our other invited guest, C.G. Butterbaugh, who gamely did most of the talking and tried his best to ignore all the interruptions and the tension in the air.

Some of his conversation was about genetic codes and the role genetic technology was already playing in scientific detective work, and the possibilities of rewriting history through DNA analysis of the remains of the famous or notorious. But I wasn't much interested in history, or those who made history. History, as someone already had pointed out, was bunk. I would see the little flash of the cross that dangled from Sharissa's left earlobe when she quickly turned her head, and then I would think of the similar cross that Bobby wore, that I stared at while waiting for him to move, but he never moved. Blood had seeped through his hair and darkened, and finally I left him there. Washed in the blood of Jesus, but oh so dead regardless.

On the way back to where I had parked my car I buried the stolen pistol. How long, I wondered, before it would be so much a part of the earth that no one would recognize it for what it had been? A thousand, ten thousand years: Only our genomes, the genetic blueprints of living things, lasted forever.

"Some part of human lives should always be secret," I said to Butterbaugh. "What difference does it make now if Lincoln suffered from Marfan's Syndrome, or Stalin was paranoid, or Handel wrote the 'Messiah' in three weeks on the upswing of a manic-depressive cycle?"

"Well, none, I guess; but once we've conquered the genetic codes, and put computers—better computers than we have now, I'm talking about computers than are small enough to operate inside the human body, even inside a single human cell—put them to work re-engineering flaws that cause disease or mental aberrations, well—don't you think we'd have the possibility of a better world?"

The phone rang; Caroline smiled in apology and started to get up, but Sharissa beat her to it, saying, "Mom, let me this time."

"How do we make a computer that can perform therapeutically inside a single cell?" I asked Butterbaugh.

"Oh, it's coming. Maybe not in my lifetime, although X-ray technology has produced some incredible breakthroughs in computer chip design, but, let's say, in the next fifty years. If you're interested, there was this article in *Scientific American* a couple of months ago, I'll give it to Sharissa when I see her again."

He was watching her in the doorway of the kitchen. Sharissa had her back to us and was talking softly into the phone; I couldn't eavesdrop on both of them at the same time. It was easy to know what was on Butterbaugh's mind, and in his heart, whenever he looked at her.

I thought about it again, for at least the hundredth time that day; but no, I couldn't have walked away and let Bobby live. As long as he was alive then he and Sharissa would find a way to be together. And, as Butterbaugh had pointed out to me following a different situation, it was a case of aggravated assault to point a loaded handgun at someone. Eventually Bobby would have talked about it—to Sharissa, to his parents. Then there would have been hell to pay.

"Immortality," Butterbaugh said. "It's not such a stretch of the imagination that in a hundred years or so we, I mean human beings, may be programmed to live as long as we want—you know, barring accidental death."

"It might become biologically possible to live for centuries," Caroline said. "But what about the psychological burden?"

"Too much of a good thing?" I murmured. "Anyway, I'm sure the Baptists would have a fit, if their parishioners opted for genetic engineering over heaven."

"I'm having enough trouble with this lifetime," Caroline said. Then she looked at me and laughed at my expression and amended, "Well, this *week*, I guess is what I mean." She turned her head sharply and quizzically, as if hearing a knock from a spirit guide, then smiled and caught my eye. "I think I've been luckier than most women."

Sharissa came back to the table looking perplexed.

"That was Mrs. Driscoll. She wanted Bobby to stop by the pharmacy for her on his way home tonight."

"You mean she thought he was here?" Caroline said.

"He didn't go home after work. So Mrs. Driscoll assumed Bobby came for dinner straight from the warehouse. But he wouldn't do that. He needed to have a shower and change clothes."

I got up to pour myself a second cup of coffee. I gave Caroline a kiss on the back of the neck in passing, and she smiled and looked up at me, with that certain light in her pale gingery eyes I was sure no other man had ever seen; and I knew that, despite whatever emergencies might crop up at campaign headquarters, she wouldn't be going back there tonight. I was thankful. I needed her.

"Maybe he's still at the warehouse," Sharissa said. "Excuse me, I'll just call and see if he had to work late."

She called Bobby's uncle, and this time she came away from the telephone somber and a little frightened.

"Bobby didn't go to work today." Sharissa remained standing, gripping the back of her chair. She looked, rather blankly, around the table at all of us. She thought about it. Her voice changed. "He *always* calls. I was sick this morning. But he didn't call me or come back after—"

"You saw Bobby this morning?" Butterbaugh said.

"Well, he comes by most mornings at about ten to seven, and we've been jogging this week out at King Forest. But today I had a stomachache and threw up and couldn't go with him. Daddy?"

"I know, he told us he was coming back after he finished running to see how you were."

"This is not *like* Bobby!" Sharissa said. "To up and disappear for a whole day. I wonder if—if he could have had an accident or something . . ."

"What was he driving?" Butterbaugh asked her.

"Oh, he's had Kevin's Chevy Maxicab most of the summer. That can't be it, somebody would have heard by now—wouldn't they—?"

"I'm sure there's nothing to worry about," Caroline said firmly. "Sharissa, why don't I take the phone off the hook while we all try to have our dessert in peace?"

"No. Bobby might call. And when he does—I'm really gonna let him hear it." She sniffed a couple of times. "I mean, this is so unbelievably *rude* of him!"

"Peach cobbler or cherry swirl cake or vanilla ice cream?" I asked Butterbaugh.

"How about a little of each?" Caroline suggested, smiling.

"Oh—oh," Butterbaugh said, looking guiltily down at his stomach. "Well, maybe—" he glanced at Sharissa. "Maybe I can handle a little of each, if we're going to get that match in later?"

Sharissa looked up slowly, realizing she'd been spoken to.

"Oh, sure. No problem. I have no intention of staying around here the rest of the night waiting for Bobby Driscoll to show up."

Tracker dogs from the Sheriff's department found Bobby, or Bobby's remains, at a quarter past four on Saturday afternoon.

We were all at King Forest—Sharissa, Caroline, and I; Bobby's parents and two sisters—waiting in the lot near the Maxicab Bobby had parked there thirty-six hours earlier, when word came back to us.

Bobby's mother collapsed. Sharissa and the other girls became hysterical. Bobby's father, a big paunchy man I had fished with a couple of times, wept in my arms. It was a very difficult time for us all.

Before and after the funeral, there was a lot of media attention. Nothing we could do but endure it. A murder had been committed. There were no clues, and very little speculation about who might be guilty. Bobby had been well liked by his classmates. Nearly two hundred of them turned out for the service on Tuesday that preceded a private burial.

Tuesday also happened to be Primary Day. Claude Gilley won his party's nomination, which made him a good bet to also win the election in November. Caroline, of course, was unable to take any real satisfaction in his victory, and she stayed away from Claude's celebration. But she couldn't get out of the obligation to accompany Claude to Washington on Thursday to meet with his staff in the nation's capital.

I was left to deal with Sharissa, and her grief.

I decided the best course of action would be for Sharissa to compete in the tennis tournament in Atlanta she'd been preparing so hard for. After conferring with Bobby's parents, who assured her they would not find her participation disrespectful, she agreed.

The tournament was being held on the outdoor courts of the Chattahoochee Tennis Club. Sharissa was making short work of her second-round opponent when Detective Sergeant C.G. Butterbaugh, wearing one of his loud plaid sports coats, slipped into a grandstand seat beside me. He looked at the scoreboard and whistled. The players were taking a break between the first and second sets.

"She looks tired," he said of Sharissa.

"It's emotional more than physical fatigue, I think. But I've never seen her serve so well." I looked at him. "I don't suppose there's anything new?"

"Well, as you know, it's state and not our jurisdiction? But I've got a couple of buddies in the Georgia Bureau of Investigation who keep me up on the case."

"And—?"

He shook his head slightly. "To be honest, unless there's a confession down the road sometime, I don't think we'll ever see a break in this case. It just doesn't look too promising. There's no obvious motive. He was jogging by himself, that we do know; probably decided to take a pee break in the woods, and bang, he got it from behind. Appears to have been spontaneous, not premeditated. A crazy who felt that Bobby was violating his wilderness sanctuary, or something. Bobby's car keys were on him, apparently nothing was taken. The body wasn't moved or molested. It's a reasonable guess that the murder weapon was one of those stones from the ravine near where Bobby was lying. I don't think it'll be found. The offender was a strong guy or very angry, or both. One blow. Bobby never knew what hit him."

"I'd think you would find a footprint—something—"

"No, that turf is spongy with pine needles. Doesn't take much of an impression unless it's soaking wet. And there hasn't been a decent rain up that way for more than a week." He looked at the four o'clock sky overhead, a few small clouds. We were on the shady side of center court, but still there wasn't a breeze stirring.

He mopped his forehead with a pale blue handkerchief and said, "They're going through the computers now, to see if Bobby's murder fits any kind of pattern—location, choice of weapon. Maybe something will turn up after all."

The girls were back on the court for the second set, Sharissa serving. The effort she put into it was explosive. Her opponent, who wore her hair long on top and buzz-cut above the ears, took one step and gave up without offering her racket to the scorching serve.

"Beauty," Butterbaugh said, leaning forward in his seat, lost in admiration, hopeless in his adoration of my daughter.

───────

Sharissa was so used up after her match, she drank a quart of orange juice and went straight to bed when we got home. Caroline had hoped to be back Saturday night, but she was delayed. She didn't have much to say to me on the phone; in fact, she sounded remote, not interested in talking. I assumed Claude Gilley was being a drain on what emotional reserves Caroline had left.

I sat up until after midnight in the kitchen, drinking coffee (regular; we had run out of decaf) and reading *Dombey and Son*, not concentrating well enough to shut out the sounds of the cabinet clock in the front hall. I was fatigued but not very sleepy when I finally put on my pajamas and went to bed. I slept fitfully, and the caffeine in my system prompted excitable, unpleasant dreams.

In one of those dreams the homely Timekeeper in his rumpled black suit took me along a forest path to a clearing which contained a small pyramid perhaps ten feet on a side and twelve feet high, composed of smooth round uncemented stones. I was naked in this dream, coppery from the sun, my bare legs bloodied from the ritual sacrifice. I had a crushing headache from the effects of fasting, but I fell to obediently, taking down stone after stone until I had uncovered the pit with plastered walls that lay beneath the pyramid. I was not shocked or even surprised to find Bobby and Sharissa entombed, side by side in rich burial clothing, hands folded over emptied breasts . . .

I woke up with a start, in a tropic sweat, thunder outside the bedroom windows. I had a rancid odor. Something stirred at the foot of the bed, giving me a moment's prickling fright. But it was Sharissa.

"Daddy? Did I wake you up? I'm sorry. I didn't want to be by myself."

"That's all right, baby."

She curled up again. I got out of bed to get a drink of water in the bathroom. I saw myself in several mirrors, shadowy, my image repeated by lightning. I was fascinated with my faceless self, as if another dream was about to begin. But I'd had enough for one night.

I thought Sharissa had gone to sleep. But as I sat down on the edge of the bed, rubbing my neck, she said in a small bleak voice, "When will I stop thinking it really didn't happen? When will I believe it?"

"It takes time, sweetheart."

"I just have this terrible feeling, everything's going to go wrong now."

"That isn't true," I said, lamely. Then I said, "Could I bring you a glass of milk or something?"

"What was it—bad luck? Is life *that* stupid, and meaningless? I don't want to believe that, but I can't think about anything else! There's this lump in my throat that won't go away. Crying doesn't help. I feel so depressed, wanting to cry and not being able to anymore. Milk? Oh, no thanks."

"What can I do, baby?"

"I don't know." Her voice broke. She breathed shudderingly, sick in her soul. "I love you," she said after a while. "I love Mom. And I loved Bobby. Oh my God. I'm never going to love anyone as much as I loved him."

Neither of us said anything else, and before long her breathing slowed and deepened; after a last quivering sigh I knew she had fallen asleep. I endured a short restless spell, then got up and dressed in old clothes. There was considerable thunder and lightning now, as brilliant and chilling as migraine.

I went outside anyway, and walked, walked around the lake in the rush of wind and the dazzling light. It never rained that night. I cried for Sharissa. I cried for her pain and loss and heartbreak, and finally for her innocence. By the time the sun came up I was able to think about the good times, my daughter year by year as she grew from faerie child in a soap-bubble bath to blessed young woman, and gradually my torment faded. Life, I reminded myself, is not meaningless; nor is it a process ruled by the randomness of events. Life is fate, and fate must be respected, if we are to live sanely and achieve our small purposes. My only regrets were that I could never hope to fully explain this to those whom I loved. To explain myself. To justify what I yet had to do.

On the following Thursday I drove eighty miles to Hartsfield airport to meet Caroline's flight from Washington. The heat wave of the past few days was about to be broken, and with a vengeance: a storm front was moving in from the Gulf coast, and a severe weather watch had been issued for northwest Georgia.

The concourse was crowded, and Delta switched gates at the last minute. By the time I reached the arrival gate the last passengers were deplaning. Caroline must have flown first class. I saw her waiting for me in the smoking area by the check-in counter. She was lighting a cigarette. Her hands were unsteady.

She turned her cheek in a distracted manner when I tried to kiss her. She looked starkly tired in the unflattering light of the concourse.

"How was Washington?" I asked her.

"Humid." I couldn't interpret the look she gave me, yet I knew something was very wrong. "I don't know how anyone could live there during the summer." Suddenly she was chatty: determinedly so, I thought. "But some of us went for a cruise on the Potomac a couple of nights ago. That was fun. You don't mind if I smoke? Just one. I won't smoke in the car."

It was raining when we left the terminal. Caroline said she wanted to drive. She's a better driver than I am, particularly in bad weather, so I let her take the wheel. We headed west on Camp Creek Parkway to I-285. Caroline couldn't, or didn't want to make conversation. It began to rain harder. There was lightning all around us. If she was exhausted, it didn't show in her driving.

I was about to put the radio on, but she stopped me, a hand on my wrist, as if she resented the potential intrusion. I sat back and looked at her.

"What is it, Greg?" Caroline said abruptly. "Is it something so bad you can't let anyone know? Are you a fugitive? Did you kill somebody?"

That startled me; my reaction was to smile.

She looked from me to the lights of a truck looming up through the rain behind us. Her voice was constricted when she spoke again.

"Am I really Mrs. Greg Walker, or—did you have another name once?"

"What have you been up to, Caroline?" I said after a few moments.

"I'm a journalist by trade. So I did what any good journalist would do when—when she thinks the man she loves has lied to her all these years."

A glaring light filled the inside of the Honda. Thunder cracked. Then we rode through the comparative quiet beneath an overpass.

"Go on," I said, my voice louder than either of us expected.

Again the onslaught of gray rain; it was like an ocean turned upside down. I wished she would pull over with other cars beside the expressway lanes to wait it out; but I didn't say anything.

"I checked with the Pentagon first," Caroline said. "There've been dozens of Gregory Walkers in the various services, but no one of your age and description at the time you said you served. There was never a Lieutenant Greg Walker of the Third Transportation Company at Fort Belvoir, Virginia. Anyone can buy an officer's uniform, have papers forged; and phony driver's licenses are so easy to obtain, aren't they—Greg."

"I suppose so."

"I still wasn't—satisfied, so I spent a day and a half in Baltimore. Looking through birth records, checking with the welfare agencies. The date and place of your birth on our marriage certificate checks out okay—but the infant Gregory Walker, whose name you took, died at the age of six weeks. Needless to say you weren't shunted from one foster home to another in your youth. I doubt if you've ever been to Baltimore."

"I've been there," I said.

"For how long?"

"Ten days. Long enough to familiarize myself with the city, and pick up an identity."

"Mother of God!"

"Please don't, Caroline."

Her breath hissed. "I suppose I should be grateful for one thing. Your fingerprints aren't on file with the FBI. You're not on the National Crime Information Center's computers."

"I've never been a criminal. Some occasional indiscretions, misdemeanors. You did a very thorough job. As for gratitude, you ought to be grateful for many things. I've been faithful to you, Caroline. We've had a good marriage. What else do you really need, or want to know?"

"Everything."

"You're going too fast," I cautioned her.

Caroline eased off on the accelerator. I shook my head. "It's just human nature, isn't it? The hardest lesson life offers is learning to leave well enough alone."

"Tell me! I want to know who you are."

"Frederick Sullivan," I said.

"Oh, no! Jesus! I don't believe *that*! The bullet in your head! I think it must have—you've gone completely—you're talking like a—a psychopathic—"

I went on, calmly, "Psychopathic liar? You know better. You've lived with me for eighteen and a half years. I'm a perfectly normal, ordinary human being. Except for one crucial difference. Once every nineteen years I'm required—compelled, if you want to put it that way—to change my identity, my life-style, to become someone completely different from the person I was during my last cycle."

Caroline sounded as if something was caught in her throat. I looked at our speed. We were going seventy, in blinding rain, nearing the interchange with I-75, the way home to Sky Valley. I took a deep breath. There had been some hard years, but I was going to miss the beauty, the orderly pace of life in Sky Valley.

"Do you want me to go on, Caroline? It's an opportunity for me, actually. I've never been able to explain this to any of my wives or lovers. Maybe you'll understand."

"I understand that you—need help, Greg." Her tone was milder, resigned, to the bare-bone facts of what she considered to be my mental illness. I couldn't tell, looking at her reflection in the windshield, if she was crying. There was so much rain streaming down the glass.

"I was married to Roxanne Sullivan. Everything she said was true. Becoming a shitheel named Frederick Sullivan was an experiment in altering my personality, adopting a totally different exterior from that of Barnaby Wilde, who taught fifth-form French at a girls' school in New England during the thirties and forties, and wrote essays for little magazines. But Frederick exhausted me; it wasn't easy to be primitive, even in a raw, primitive place like New Lost River. So I went back to what was closer to my true nature: someone contemplative, religious, of no great importance, just a man who earns a decent living and values his wife, his home, his family. That's the man you married, Caroline. The name doesn't mean anything."

"You're making this up. It's a—like a fantasy that you believe is—"

"Caroline. Since becoming an adult I've aged only a few years in two and a half centuries, and, under normal circumstances, I'm immune to death. I'll continue to live as long as I observe the protocol of the nineteen-year prenatal eclipse cycle that saw me into this world, nearly fifteen cycles ago. These astrophysical cycles were discovered by the Chaldeans in 700 B.C., then passed on to the Maya of Central America when that part of the world was colonized. My cycle as Greg Walker expires next February, when the moon's north node returns to the eclipse degree of February 9, 1713. It didn't expire when I was shot in the head by Ricky Gene Kindor, because almost nothing short of total destruction of my body can kill me. I was gassed in the trenches during World War I. Run through my liver in an *affaire d'honeur* many, many years before that. I've been trampled by wild horses in Australia, fallen from the roof of a six-story building. I mended quickly; all scars disappeared. There is no foreseeable end for me. The solar eclipse cycle into which I was born will continue well into the twenty-third century. I'm not alone, either. I have many brothers and sisters, all of us descended from a single, remarkable progenitor. Men and women totally in control of their destinies. As long as we are willing to pay the small cost involved."

"Insane. Insane. Oh, God. I'm afraid."

She seemed frozen to the steering wheel, guiding us by instinct alone through the deluge. We were still going very fast for the conditions, passing everyone else on the interstate highway.

"Isn't it better to know what you already suspected, Caroline?"

"I wanted to believe—in a miracle. That God saved you. I wanted you—to grow old with me. Oh how I wanted that! But when I couldn't stand to see myself in a mirror anymore, you—you never looked a day older. I tried not to think about that."

"It was an accident of birth, Caroline. I never asked to be immortal. Sometimes—it can be difficult to deal with. Try to help me, by understanding."

"But you don't have to leave, do you, Greg? I'm sorry. I'm really *sorry* I called you a liar. I believe you now. You've been—a wonderful husband, a loving father. Think of us. Think of Sharissa. Stay with us, that's all I ask! Won't you go on being Greg Walker, for our sake?"

"I can't do that, Caroline."

"You were planning to—just walk away, disappear, always leave us wondering—"

"That's the hard part," I admitted.

"And—turn into someone else, marry another woman? But you can't—can't just say you *love me*, and do a horrible, treacherous, despicable thing like that! That isn't love. It's selfish. It's monstrous!"

"Caroline!" I shouted. "Watch—"

I don't know. Maybe if I hadn't tried to grab the wheel, we wouldn't have run into the concrete divider. Caroline had excellent reflexes, even under stress. It was just instinct on my part. But we were going much too fast, and after rebounding from the disintegrating divider the car flipped. We were wearing seat belts and shoulder harnesses, of course. The restraints probably would have saved Caroline's life, but the eighteen-wheeler coming along behind us in the second lane couldn't avoid the sedan in its path. The big transport struck us on the driver's side and tumbled the car off the road, down a long slope and onto an access road.

Thinking back, I don't even remember the impact. What I see in my mind's eye is Caroline's face lit up by the lights behind us. Sometimes I imagine I hear her scream. But I'm human, aren't I? And not immune to guilt.

THE FIRST PART
OF THE
NARRATIVE IS CONCLUDED

The Hotel Itzá Maya, Cobían, Guatemala

A most tragic
end to a fruitful period
of your development,"
Francisco Colon said
to me.

He sipped dense black coffee from a small eggshell china cup. We were at breakfast on the terrace of the Itzá Maya, which he had inherited from his late father. "I hope you were not seriously injured in the accident."

"A dislocated shoulder. I was cut by flying glass. No, nothing serious," I told him. "And your father?"

Francisco gazed momentarily at a man with a tier of birdcages, containing cardinals and keel-billed toucans, which was strapped on the top of his head. Francisco gave directions to the peddler, who then walked, with a graceful swaying gait, down a winding stone path into the tropical gardens of the Colonial-style hotel, where it had been my good fortune to spend several pleasant winters preceding the station of my eclipse cycle.

"Papa passed on peacefully in his sleep at the winter solstice," Francisco said, and turned back to me with a contented smile: contentment for his beloved father, the Timekeeper, and his own, newly elevated position. "He had one hundred twenty-one years." Francisco sipped coffee again, looking frankly at me with obsidian eyes. He was a broad brown man with a neat oval of mustache and beard and long oiled hair which he combed straight back from his forehead. The crook of his prominent nose, his build, were classically Maya.

I glanced at the jade of prestige which he wore on a gold chain around his neck. It was a crudely carved eagle, perhaps as old as two millennia. I could be sure it was the same jade which Francisco's father, and his father's father, who I also counted as a friend, had worn before him.

"Don Santiago's instructions to me before his passing were incomplete," Francisco ventured.

"They were meant to be," I said. In the gardens, among the charming thatched-roof bungalows, which were a recent addition to the Itzá Maya, spider monkeys chattered in their cages and threw rotten fruit at anyone who came too close. On the terrace near us a tethered quetzal spread magnificent wings. The quetzal was the exact blue color of the flawless morning sky. Once you saw them everywhere in the unspoiled Petén region; now they were a rarity. So much had changed here, in a little more than three decades, after timeless centuries.

Francisco lowered his gaze. He was very much like his father, except that he seemed to have too much fondness for vulgar diamond rings. Three of them flashed on his fingers. Don Santiago had been a simpler man.

"I realize that I may not enjoy the longevity of the heirs of Can Ek. Still—whatever extension of my life is available to me will of course be welcome."

"How old are you now?" I asked him.

"I have forty years, sir."

"Then you are barely in the springtime of the long life that will be my gift to you."

His face was immobile, but his chest swelled with relief and happiness. "Thank you, sir."

I looked out over the extensive gardens, to a couple of badly deteriorated pyramids on the lake shore, remnants of a small Maya city of the fourth century A.D. Such sites were common in the region. There was still much to be discovered in the forest of the newly created Maya Biosphere Preserve, and under it. And much that would never be found, as long as the chattels of the Owl and the Harpy, the Timekeepers of the Underworld like Francisco Colon, were faithful to their trust.

"Your time is near?" Francisco asked me, speaking now in the Mayan language as a tourist couple came near our table to take pictures of the rare quetzal.

"On the 9th of February. Fourteen days from now."

"And what will you require?"

"The obsidian knife. The jaguarundi cup. One day soon you will guide me to the stairway of the Golden One, my father Can Ek." At this mention of the father of all immortals, he bowed his head. "So that I may be sure . . ."

Francisco touched his breast over his heart, confirming the sacredness of his knowledge, and his obligation. "I know the way."

"Of course." I smiled at him. There was no reason to remind Francisco that if he was attempting to deceive me as to the rightfulness of his succession, the penalty would be severe. The Itzá Maya would be in the market for a new owner.

Xate palms on the spacious grounds of the hotel—more than half of it new, under Francisco's guidance—rattled in a strong breeze. Francisco glanced at me as if expecting more.

"And—the sacrifice?" he murmured.

"That does not involve you. You will be there only to receive the blood anointment that prolongs your life."

He nodded. "And it is done—in the old way?"

"You know how sharp the knife is. I remove the heart from the breast with a few strokes, at the culmination of the eclipse."

I saw that he was beginning to perspire, although the day was not yet humid.

"The—the matter of the virgin has troubled me. The authorities ask many questions when a local *adolescente* vanishes. Even in my grandfather's day—"

"There were problems in obtaining a virgin. I know. But I resolved that dilemma a long time ago."

Looking again at the gardens, I saw her now on the path leading up to the terrace, coming from our bungalow, her hair the color of a jaguarundi's coat flashing in the sun as she hurried in walk shorts and a shirt of colorful Maya weave toward the hotel. She saw me watching, waved, lengthened her stride, bounded up to the terrace past the appreciative eyes of Francisco Colon and draped her slim tanned arms around my neck. My face was tilted to receive the kiss she gave me on my forehead. I smiled and tingled at her touch, thinking of all the happiness she had brought me, the love in her heart that would live refreshed in me for a thousand years to come.

"Good morning, Daddy," Sharissa said.

August—December, 199—

It is one of those cases where the art of the reasoner should be used rather for the sifting of details than for the acquiring of fresh evidence. The tragedy had been so uncommon, so complete, and of such personal importance to so many people that we are suffering from a plethora of surmise, conjecture, and hypothesis. The difficulty is to detach the framework of fact—of absolute undeniable fact—from the embellishments of theorists and reporters. Then, having established ourselves upon this sound basis, it is our duty to see what inferences may be drawn and what are the special points upon which the whole mystery turns."

I had been a Sherlock Holmes freak for about four months when I copied those lines into one of my notebooks.

I was in the eighth grade. The story was called "Silver Blaze," from *The Memoirs of Sherlock Holmes*, and it was about a stolen thoroughbred and the murder of its trainer. The plot doesn't stick in my mind like the plots of some of my favorites (which I reread when I'm in the mood, and thinking that I can still pull it off, the big career move, maybe become a private investigator working for one of the top criminal lawyers). But I remember clearly the enthusiasm I felt while scribbling those lines down, the "shock of recognition" they talk about in college lit classes. What Holmes had to say to Watson on the train to—(I need to look it up sometime)—what Holmes said summarizes, today, my attitude toward detective work, what little of it I actually get to do as a member of Sky Valley's finest.

"The tragedy has been so uncommon, so complete, and of such personal importance to so many people . . ." That pretty well says it for the way people felt about Bobby Driscoll's murder. What we, I mean the Georgia Bureau of Investigation, weren't suffering from was a plethora of sur-

mise, conjecture, and hypothesis. There just wasn't anything much to go on.

I never officially interrogated Sharissa. It wasn't my case. But I spent more time talking to her about Bobby, about the tragedy, than anyone else. I'm easy to talk to. That's part of being a cop. But there was more to it than that. Friendship. I knew that was the best I could ever make of our relationship, even though we had hit it off right away and you can always dream. And I suppose she saw me as an older brother, someone who had been missing from her life. A guy she could talk seriously to when she felt like it, without having to be concerned that eventually I'd come on to her in a heavy way. Friends, I could live with that. I was thirty-two, and Sharissa was seventeen. Two years, maybe three, I'll probably quit trying to cover up my bald spot.

What she couldn't get out of her craw was the notion that, if he'd been found sooner, Bobby might have survived. I finally convinced her, as gently as I could, that he had stopped breathing only a few minutes after his skull was crushed. And we had a very accurate idea of when that happened. Forensic entomologists know that flies are attracted to faint odors, undetectable by humans, coming from newly dead bodies. They swarm from up to two miles away and immediately begin to lay their eggs inside the nostrils and ears, in the corners of the eyes of the deceased. The eggs hatch on a precise timetable. You can set your watch by them.

But I didn't want Sharissa to think about that: Bobby kneeling in the woods with his shattered head pitched to the ground, blowflies and, later, small animals swarming around.

I found out a lot about Bobby, and his family, from Sharissa. They'd known each other, from church, for years. They started dating in ninth grade. Casually at first, then it became serious. How serious? I didn't know that. I don't think I wanted to know if they'd been lovers. There was something stuck in my craw, too, even if I didn't want to think about it very often. *Maybe, if there's enough time, if I can just hang around long enough . . .*

With Bobby gone, Sharissa wanted to be with me. It was almost as if she were afraid some small lead to his murder would crop up and I'd forget to tell her. She was avid for every crumb of speculation. I felt as if I had to keep coming up with these crumbs, engross her, concentrate her attention on me. Before she surrendered her obsession, outgrew the tragedy, went her own way—to college, to another life, to someone else she eventually would marry.

You get crazy, I guess. In our hearts we're all nineteen, or something like that. I was buddies with girls as beautiful as Sharissa in high school. I had a knack for kidding them, keeping them entertained. Buddies. While I ate my heart out. I wasn't exactly eating my heart out over Sharissa. It was deeper, sadder, more philosophical than that. There was a kind of pleading in her eyes, when we sat and talked—at her house, in a booth at Burger King, on a bench by the public tennis courts next to the high school. *I know you can do something,* she seemed to be telling me. *I know you'll be the one to solve his murder. And I will love you deeply, I will love you forever . . .* that kind of bullshit, which I couldn't get out of my system. Because I wanted it to be exactly the way I was dreaming it. Knowing all the time I didn't have a prayer. I couldn't solve the murder because there was nothing to go on, there never would be short of some offhand confession by a well-traveled homicidal vagrant years down the road. *Oh yeah, yeah, Georgia, young kid, I did that one, too.*

Practically speaking, I couldn't do a thing, and I was experienced enough at police work to understand that, yet . . .

Every waking minute, almost, even when I was supposed to be working on other stuff, I memorized the reports from the GBI and sifted the details, what there were of them. I started getting serious headaches again, and my hair seemed to be falling out faster than usual. *Dumb ass,*

I thought. I didn't like myself, leading Sharissa on—
because that's all it was: as long as I could hem and haw
and pretend that I might possibly be getting somewhere,
she was mine. I neglected my parents. I woke up with
night sweats, gloomy murder on my mind. Thinking, *why*,
and, *there is no why*, and then: *but what if there is?* Right
in plain sight, so obvious nobody can recognize it. *Why
was Bobby killed?* Simple. Because he—

Because he had a secret enemy. Nobody kills that way
for sport. Bobby was condemned and executed, on his
knees, struck down from behind after being judged—
guilty. By someone with a longstanding grudge we hadn't
yet uncovered, or someone—oh yes. *Yes.*

Someone very, very angry with Bobby because Bobby
had Sharissa, and he didn't.

Night sweats. Three A.M. The overhead fan in my bedroom turning, rippling blade shadows on a moonlit wall.
And Collins Gosden Butterbaugh, just tossing and turning,
getting nowhere. Thinking of Sharissa, and was she awake
too, and were the answers there, in her subconscious mind?

B yrd Aycock," Sharissa said. "Then I dated Mel Clark
for a couple of months. Steve Cutrere used to call me.
A lot. I didn't want to go out with him—"

"What's Steve Cutrere like?"

"Oh, he's okay, just sort of cynical and thinks he's cool.
He likes to put everybody down."

"When's the last time you heard from him?"

"I don't know. We talked some at the junior-senior
prom. He was drunk."

"Did he ever proposition you?"

She looked startled, then amused. "Sure, all the time. Not just me. I mean, you don't take Steve seriously, not if you have any brains."

"So what did he say to you?" I asked. I had a cold pack on the muscle in my thigh I'd strained trying to give Sharissa a decent game. We were on the shady side of the country club courts, where Sharissa had invited me to play.

She had another sip of Gatorade. "You don't really want me to tell you."

"Yes, I do."

She scuffed a toe of her sneaker in the pea-gravel border of the courts and shook her head, working up to it. "Oh, he said stuff like, when are we going to eff-you-see-kay." Sharissa made a wry face at this discreet approach to profanity. "I think he just likes talking dirty. Lonnye Sue Mitchell came on to him one time as a joke, and I'm telling you, he didn't know where to put his face."

"Could Cutrere have been jealous of Bobby?"

"Jealous? I wouldn't know. He went out for football once and lasted two days. I don't think he ever dated anybody from our school. I doubt if he and Bobby ever said two words to each other. Why, do you think—"

"Don't know, Sharissa. Have you ever had anonymous phone calls, somebody leaving you suggestive notes, that kind of thing?"

"Well, when I was ten, I had an obscene phone call. I guess that's what *he* thought it was. I thought it was funny. I told him he'd better get Jesus in his life, right away, and hung up." She passed me the bottle of Gatorade, orange, not my favorite. But I drank some anyway. "What are you getting at, C.G.?"

"Somebody who might have had a grudge against Bobby because he was going with the prettiest girl in school—"

"Dee Millican is the prettiest girl in school, like, she is flat-out *gorgeous*. Oh, I see. Somebody who might've had a crush on me and resented Bobby? But, *Lord*, you just don't go around killing—"

Her throat locked; she took the towel from around her

neck and buried her face. "Can't believe that," she said, her voice so muffled I barely understood her.

"I have to ask these questions, Sharissa. And more questions, until something clicks. I'm not trying to punish you."

"I know." She dropped the towel in her lap, took a long discouraged breath, and changed the subject. "Your leg still paining you?"

"Not so much."

"Want to quit?"

"Am I a quitter?"

"No, you're not."

We looked at each other for a few moments.

Sharissa murmured, "That's just one of the fine things about you I don't think many people have had the chance to appreciate. Why didn't you ever get married, C.G.?"

"Well, wait a minute. Don't rush me."

"You mean to tell me you never got that serious about somebody?"

"Oh, I don't know about that."

"So you did get serious once?"

"Twice."

"Did you live with them?"

"One of them."

"Didn't work out, huh?"

"She was a philosophy major at Cal State Los Angeles. Talk about not being able to communicate with someone."

"Ever go with a girl here in town?"

"Seem to be spending most of my time with you."

"Begged that question, C.G."

"Her name's Tricia. Assistant head teller at the Wachovia downtown. We still have coffee once in a while."

"You're gonna get married some day, C.G.," Sharissa said, as if she'd detected a flaw in my confidence. There were plenty of them, God knows.

"And have short, dumpy kids with bowed legs? No, thanks."

"Marry a tall, beautiful girl, then it's fifty-fifty."

"Beautiful girls don't marry guys who look like me."

Great, now I was beginning to whine. I wished we could just play tennis.

"Shoot they don't, all the time; and looks don't have a thing to do with it. After you get to know somebody."

She wasn't teasing me, but I must have had a cynical expression.

Sharissa elbowed me for emphasis and said, "Sometimes I get the feeling you don't place enough value on yourself. And I've had the urge to say something. So I finally said it, that's all."

She stood and draped her towel over my head and observed with a melancholy amusement, "that cute little bare spot's gonna get sunburnt, C.G." Then she bent down and kissed me on the forehead, lightly, but damn it was a kiss, and went away looking more melancholy than ever, saying, "I'm gonna work on that hitch in my serve while you recuperate."

Some days are too good to ever allow them to end—in memory, or in my dreams.

After a lot of tennis that long afternoon I drove Sharissa home. Caroline was in Washington, Greg was in Atlanta attending a seminar for RCA dealers in the Southeast. He wouldn't be back until late. At the door we said good-bye, and then, having opened the door on an empty house, Sharissa called me back.

"I'll fix us something to eat, if that's okay."

It was okay. I knew by the look in her eyes that it wasn't my company so much as the fact that she didn't want to be alone.

Tuna melts on English muffins, a salad, lemonade—we

ate on the deck with the sun going down, and then it was full dark with a yellow three-quarter moon rising and occasional flashes of blue light from the bug zapper by the sliding doors. I did a lot of talking. I made Sharissa laugh. I felt as if I were back in high school, entertaining the prom queen until her boyfriend showed up from football practice to take her out. I felt a little ridiculous and sad, too, but the night wore on and I couldn't stop talking. Sharissa stared at me, smiling, with her gaze that was eating up my heart.

We went in, finally, and Sharissa went upstairs to her room while I scraped paper plates into the Disposall and rinsed out the lemonade glasses. I had made up my mind to let myself out while she was still upstairs, but when I closed the dishwasher and turned around she was standing on the last step to the kitchen, looking as if she were walking in her sleep except for a tear track down one cheek, a tear about to fall from the line of her jaw. That was what I looked at—not the rest of her face, her eyes, her body, but that single tear about to fall.

"Hold me," she said.

I'm sure she said it. Maybe she didn't have to speak at all. But I don't think about it very often; there are memories you don't want to risk by examining them too closely, too often. Not even in your dreams.

A little more than twenty-four hours after we played tennis for the last time that summer, Sharissa's mother was dead.

I was filling in for Ed Hagood on the three-to-eleven when the call came in from the Georgia State Patrol in

Marietta, relayed from one of the troopers at the scene of the accident. Greg and Caroline Walker had been seriously injured in a crash on I-75 north, and were being transported to Kennestone Hospital. No word on the extent of their injuries, but apparently Greg was no worse off than LOC times two—conscious and coherent. He had asked GSP to get in touch with me.

I had about thirty minutes to go on the shift; Lieutenant Neidermeyer released me and I drove immediately to the Burger King across from Gatewood Mall, where I knew she would be closing up. Rain had started about ten o'clock, and it was really coming down hard. My glasses were wet and they fogged up right away when I walked into the King.

There were no customers. Sharissa was back in the kitchen. The assistant manager brought me coffee, and Sharissa.

She didn't say anything when I told her. She just sagged in the booth and looked as if she couldn't catch her breath. Her nails bit into my right fist.

"I don't know how bad it is," I said. "I'll patch through to Kennestone as soon as we're rolling."

She didn't let go of me until we were in the car. Then she muffled a scream with her hands, slumping in the seat. I put my arms around her.

"We don't deserve this!" she moaned. "No more. No more! I can't—really can't—"

There was a lot of lightning, every few seconds, and thunder that shook us to the bone; I held on, and she screamed it out of her system, then sat there shuddering, her skin appearing pale blue by the naked light of the sky. I turned up the heat and rubbed Sharissa's cold hands.

"They're not dead," she whimpered. "They're not. God's not so unfair."

"We need to get going."

It was a miserable night for driving, on any kind of road. I wondered what had happened to Greg and Caroline.

"Your mother just came back from Washington, didn't she?"

"Y-yes."

"I'll see what I can find out. We should be at the hospital in forty minutes."

I learned via the phone in my car that Caroline was in surgery. Greg's injuries apparently were less serious. Nobody would tell me about Caroline's condition.

Beside me in the seat Sharissa tried to pray. About all she could manage, over and over, was a heartbroken "Please, God." My own heart was breaking, too, to see her suffering like this. I would never have said anything, but I was afraid it was going to be bad news once we reached the hospital.

We were rolling south, as fast as I dared to go, through the rainstorm pushing north, and finally, a couple of miles below Cartersville, we ran out of it.

About the time the rain slackened to a light patter on the windshield, I had my first uneasy thought about Greg Walker. My thought was: *He has too much luck.* No more to it than that. But like I say, it made me uneasy in a way I couldn't define. On the other hand, I didn't know the extent of his injuries. So I put it out of my mind until the moment I saw him at the hospital, an arm in a sling, cuts on his chin and one cheekbone, and found out that Caroline had died just a few minutes before we got there, of massive internal injuries.

Too much luck, I thought again, almost as if I resented him. Because Sharissa was suffering, and Greg—well, to give him the benefit, he seemed to be in a daze, in that state where you can't release your feelings, can't begin to grieve.

They had to sedate Sharissa, find a bed for her in the outpatient clinic. I wandered around the hospital and finally found one of the troopers who had covered the accident having coffee in the canteen. He let me look at his report. Caroline driving, a little too much speed on a wet highway. Hit the divider, lost control. And a truck behind her.

"Was she conscious when you got there?" I asked the trooper. His name was Brooker. There were some Brookers on my mother's side, but I didn't think we were related; his people were all from down around Eufala, Alabama.

"LOC times one," he said, med-tech shorthand for "Level of Consciousness." "She didn't respond when I asked her name. She couldn't tell me anything about the accident."

"Didn't have anything to say at all?"

"Oh, a few words. Blood kept coming to her lips. I just held her hand, the one I could reach, while we waited for the fire department to cut her out of that mess."

"Could you make sense out of what you heard?"

He paused to light a cigarette. "Greg. Kept saying his name, over and over. Looking right at me. " 'Greg—not Greg.' "

"Oh."

"We'd already pulled him out of the wreck. I told her he was okay, he was going to be just fine."

"That must have been some comfort to her," I said sympathetically.

"I don't know. Probably she didn't understand, because she kept saying the same thing, over and over."

"Greg—not Greg. Did she say anything else?"

He shook his head. "Well, I didn't pay close attention. You know, it was pissing rain and there was a lot going on, we just wanted to get her out of there and into the hospital, although when you've seen enough of the real bad ones, you get a sixth sense for who's going to make it."

I leaned back enough to stay out of the smoke curling from his cigarette, so I wouldn't have a coughing fit.

"She did ask for somebody . . . might have been family, or a minister. I didn't catch the name right off. They were putting her on a gurney then."

"Sharissa? That's her daughter."

"No, don't believe that was it. Maybe one of the medics heard what she said. If it's important."

I couldn't say that it was. Brooker was working a four-to-midnight and had to get the unit back to GSP on 41, a couple of miles from the hospital. I returned to outpatient and looked in on Greg Walker and Sharissa in the cubicle where she was lying down.

A chaplain was with them. He spoke in low tones. I looked at Sharissa's glazed face and at the back of Greg's bent head. There was nothing I could do; it was no time to intrude. Caroline's father and mother and other family members were en route. Greg, I recalled, from some casual conversation or other, was an orphan.

The sky was clearing and the moon was visible when I walked out of Emergency. In the covered driveway the medical technicians who had responded to the accident call were straightening up in the back of their truck. I walked over to them and identified myself.

"I wonder if she said anything on the way?" I asked one of the team, a gum-chewing redhead named Kristy McIlwaine.

"Oh, she was muttering some. Nothing coherent," McIlwaine said.

"Low sick?"

"Well, I didn't think with her vitals we'd get her to the door, and then traffic was a fuckin' nightmare, as you can rightly imagine. But she'd rally."

"One of the troopers said she asked for somebody. Maybe her husband?"

"The one they transported in the patrol car? What's his Christian name?"

"Greg."

"No, that wasn't what she was saying." McIlwaine called to her partner, who was in the front seat making a log entry. "You recall her talking out loud, Witt?"

"Yeah, she did a time or two."

"Know what name she was saying?"

"Let me think on it. *Van*, something. She was breathing real ragged. Didn't she say *Rick*, too? I believe she did. Rick, Van. Those her kids' names? That's about all I heard out of her."

"Well, thanks," I said. I had my notebook out, force of habit. I jotted the two names down. Then I stood there, looking at what I had written in the sodium vapor light of the covered driveway.

Van
Rick

It didn't mean anything to me. I put the notebook away.

Some people were crossing the street from one of the parking lots. Two of them elderly, both with white hair cut almost identically, walking slowly but resisting the solicitations of the younger members of the family. I heard their footsteps, saw the tears on her cheeks as they came closer to the light. Caroline's mother and father, I assumed. They didn't know me, and I had no reason to introduce myself. I left Sharissa and her family to their grief and drove back to Sky Valley, feeling leaden and defeated, although I couldn't name just what it was I had lost.

The service for Caroline Walker, at First Iconium Baptist, was crowded. She was from a large family, and, according to Sharissa, she'd kept up with nearly everyone who had been a friend during her school days. Senator Claude Gilley delivered the eulogy. The burial was private.

A week after Caroline's funeral, Sharissa went back to school for her senior year. I heard from her less often. She would call to see if I knew of any progress in Bobby Driscoll's case. From her tone of voice it was obvious she was having a tough haul recovering from the double tragedy. A couple of times I said we ought to get together for a match, and she said, without enthusiasm, Fine, but I don't think I can this week, and I said, Fine, well, we'll make it another day. By the middle of October, I guess it was, she stopped calling.

We both worked downtown, so I saw Greg Walker occasionally. He looked thinner to me. There wasn't much trace of the shooting accident that had almost cost him his life three months ago. We exchanged a few words in passing. He was polite enough, but that was it. When I asked about Sharissa all he said was, She's a very brave girl.

My mother had another stroke, came back from it but not all the way. I figured one more, with luck she would go peacefully. She was seventy-three. I took ten days off from work, did some repairs around the house, raked leaves. I thought about Sharissa more than was good for me. I went over every word of every conversation I'd had with her. A specialist I went to gave me some expensive prescriptions for stuff that was supposed to retard hair loss. I didn't notice any difference. Maybe I was pulling it out in my sleep.

When I got back to work there was, among other notes on my desk, the phone number of an administrator at the North Georgia Mental Health Center. *Re Roxanne Sullivan.* I'd almost forgotten about her. I called the hospital, talked to a woman named Wilkins. Mrs. Sullivan's liver was no longer functioning, and she was comatose. Wilkins said that probably she wouldn't last out the week.

"I was wondering if you'd managed to locate her daughter, or perhaps her husband."

"No, ma'am. Nothing's ever come back from the Canadian authorities." I had the case file in front of me. Husband Frederick Sullivan, daughter Bonnie. Whereabouts unknown.

"Thank you, sergeant. I'll begin work on the forms for state burial."

"Did she ever come out of it?" I asked, doodling on my notepad.

"Let's see—she was in a condition of tonic immobility when admitted, I believe . . . no. Neither of her doctors noted any progress whatsoever during her stay here. It's possible her poor physical condition had something to do with her persistent catatonia."

"Sorry we couldn't be more help," I said.

After I hung up I sat and thought for a few minutes about the night Mrs. Frederick Sullivan showed up at the Ovenbird to claim Greg Walker as her long-missing husband. He'd had an interesting summer, to say the least. Near-tragedy, farce-tragedy, real-tragedy . . . I looked at my notepaid, and then it just leaped out at me. I picked up my pen, an old Waterman my father had used during his years as headmaster of Tarleton Day School, and nearly broke off the point underscoring two parts of her name.

Mrs. Frede*rick* Sulli*van*

Then I thumbed through my notebook to the night Caroline Walker had been killed on I-75, and saw that I'd remembered correctly; they were the words I had written after talking to the med techs at Kennestone Hospital. *Rick, Van. Those her kids' names?*

No. But maybe what Caroline had been trying to say was, *Frederick Sullivan.*

Why?

Because Frederick Sullivan was on her mind. Because—just possibly—he was the other passenger in the car with her at the time of the accident.

Greg—not Greg. Not Greg. *Is* not Greg!

Nice going, Holmes, I thought; but I have to admit I was dazzled by this surmise, conjecture, hypothesis, whatever the hell it was—so much that I hit my knee hard against the desk when I stood up suddenly.

A cup of black coffee sobered me, and then I didn't have much time to think about the—call it a cockeyed notion—for the rest of the day. Crack cocaine was all over the county this fall, a plague in some of the schools. We were making a lot of busts, and that meant additional court time for the arresting officers. Most of the youthful offenders, so called, were being shipped off to a work-camp in Coweth to give them the opportunity to think about what the hell they were doing with their lives.

After a tough day and a meat loaf dinner that didn't set too well on my jumpy stomach, I went back to the office about nine o'clock. I was beginning to feel a little foolish, but I pulled the file on Roxanne Sullivan again, and signed out everything we had in the evidence room.

It didn't make much of a pile on my desk. Letters and photographs and documents, the pistol she'd threatened Greg Walker with—an old nickel-plated Baretta, obviously secondhand—and a small envelope containing the gold locket we'd found in the parking lot outside the Ovenbird Restaurant.

I studied all of the documentation again, trying to make it work.

Frederick Sullivan. According to the marriage certificate, he was thirty-five years old when he married Roxanne in September of 1954. There was a faded post-wedding photograph of the grinning bride and groom, taken by an amateur with a cheap camera. Too much contrast. Hard to make out what Frederick really looked like. A year later, he and his wife opened a cocktail lounge in New Lost River, British Columbia. They operated the lounge for eighteen years. Until Frederick abruptly took off, accompanied by their adopted daughter Bonnie. That was in 1973. The war in Vietnam was winding down. I was thirteen years old. The two of them disappeared, apparently without a trace, and Mrs. Roxanne Sullivan lost enough of her marbles to warrant confinement in a mental hospital.

In 1973, if the birth date recorded on his marriage certificate was legitimate, Frederick Sullivan was fifty-four years old. His present age, if still living, was about seventy-three. That would make him one year older than my father, who walked with two canes after a hip-joint replacement, and who had maybe forty percent of his hearing left.

Some people age faster than others. But nobody at the

age of seventy-three was as fit as Greg Walker, particularly after surviving a bullet to the brain.

Bullshit, Holmes, said Dr. Watson. *There is no earthly way Frederick Sullivan could be—*

I was tired and annoyed. Annoyed at being nagged by the stubborn feeling that something was very, very wrong. I dropped a couple of Alka-Seltzer in a glass of Evian and drank it slowly and stared out the bullpen windows at the Civil War statue a block away on the square. Made of bronze, and built to last. A hundred, two hundred years, unless a tree fell on him ... but we were all flesh and blood: the body, except for irreplaceable brain cells, renewing itself about every six weeks. Always with a difference, each copy of the original cell-blueprint a little fuzzier until, after fifty years or so, you had to look hard to see whatever trace of the boy remained in the old man ... to each of us there is a season, and so forth. My father would know the exact quotation. Greg Walker might know, too; he read his Bible and went to church. He had raised a fine daughter and was true to his wife, as far as anyone knew. Worked hard, kept himself in shape, made no waves in his community. People liked him, but who really knew him? All I knew about Greg Walker was, he had a lot of luck. And a woman named Roxanne Sullivan had been convinced he was her husband. She had married a man who, as far as we had been able to find out, had no background. None.

And Greg Walker ... wasn't he an orphan?

I had picked up Roxanne Sullivan's locket. Wasn't really conscious of running the chain through my fingers as I let my mind wander. The locket had a very well-concealed catch. I had opened the locket once before, but had forgotten how. Little things like tricky metal watchbands defeat me. I'd never been able to solve Rubik's Cube, either. But there was something inside I needed.

After I repacked the evidence carton and returned it, I headed home. The locket was in a pocket of my jacket.

My mother always had been a light sleeper. The last

stroke hadn't changed her habits. She couldn't get out of bed without help any more, but her hands were as deft as ever. Ten seconds after I handed her the locket, she had it open. She looked at me, smiling, and then at the snippet of hair inside.

"Whose?" she said.

"I'm almost afraid to find out," I told her.

I didn't have an excuse for visiting Greg and Sharissa, but I paid a call anyway, two nights later, when I knew she would be off from Burger King.

Sharissa was doing her homework at the kitchen table when I drove up. She let me in by way of the back door.

"Hi! What's new?" She looked sharply and hopefully at me.

"Nothing about Bobby, I'm afraid."

She accepted that with a thinning of her lips and a tight shrug. Sharissa had lost weight, and the hollows of her eyes were dark bronze from fatigue or stress.

"I need to talk to Greg about a couple of things," I said. "That old case—the woman at the Ovenbird?" Before she could be alarmed, I added, "it's routine. Mrs. Sullivan's never going to be a threat to anyone."

"Dad's in the den. Could I get you something, C.G.?"

"Apple cider?"

"I'll bring it to you."

The pocket doors to the den were half open. I saw Greg inside, in his favorite chair, head to one side, eyes closed. His Bible was in his lap. I knocked. He gave a little start.

"Sharissa?"

"No, it's me, Butterbaugh. Mind if I—?"

"Come on in, C.G. Must have dozed off." He marked his place in the Bible and stood, shook my hand. "Keeping busy?"

"We could use some extra help. Frankly, we've been swamped."

"This drug problem?"

"And everything that goes with it. Burglaries, stickups, two drive-by shootings in the West End last week. They're shooting at us, too. Two-time losers for crack cocaine possession get life in this state, can't do much worse if you kill a cop while you're at it. Thirty-seven thousands deaths by guns in this country last year, while the pro-gun lobbyists invoke the sanctity of the Second Amendment. Bullshit. It was a good idea once, now it's just a bad law."

He shook his head wearily. "You read about all the drugs, and you think, well, it's a ghetto problem. Big cities. But here in Sky Valley . . . *our* high school? I'm glad Sharissa will finish her course requirements in January. And it's pretty well helped us make up our minds."

"About what?" I glanced at the doorway as Sharissa came in with two glasses of cold cider.

"Dad, thought you might like a drink."

"Thanks, honey. How's the paper coming?"

"I'm going to lick it tonight, or else." She looked at me with a wan smile. "C.G., if you'll excuse me—"

"Sure. Get back to work."

I settled down on the brass-studded green leather sofa, facing Greg. He picked up his Bible again and sat back holding it unopened in his lap.

"You said you'd made a decision about something—?" I prompted him.

"Oh. Well, Sharissa and I have been meeting with the group at our church that sponsors our missionaries in the field, and the more we talked about it, the more it seemed like something we really want to do. Sharissa's very enthusiastic. I think it's just what she needs. Of course Caroline's parents were horrified—"

"You're going to become missionaries?"

"Oh, it's not something permanent—" He smiled at me, as dead earnest as I'd ever seen him. "At least not for Sharissa. A year, at the most, then we want her to go on to college. They'll hold her scholarship for her, but if they don't, well—Caroline's life insurance policy. It paid double if she was doing work-related travel, I didn't know about that. So there's—plenty of money, you see."

I nodded and drank half of my cider. He stroked the black buckram binding of his Bible, lightly, not looking at me, eyes softly unfocused, smiling slightly.

"It'll be especially good for me," he said. "I need to—detach myself. From my life here. And do a Service. Something lasting for the Lord."

"Where do you plan to go?"

"Oh, Central America. Not sure which country yet. We'll be assigned wherever the Mission Board feels we can be most useful. Of course we'll be working with experienced career missionaries." He cleared his throat, looked at his glass of cider but didn't touch it. "It'll do us a lot of good," he said hopefully.

Greg didn't say anything else for at least a minute. I listened to the ticking of the mantel clock. I heard, from the kitchen, Sharissa ripping out a page of notebook paper, crumpling it. She got up, walked around, sat down again, banging the legs of her chair on the plank floor.

"We're putting the house on the market," Greg said.

"You are?"

"I've arranged a bank loan for Scott Bisco. He's worked for me three and a half years. He'll be taking over the business."

"Sounds as if you don't plan on coming back, Greg."

He looked slowly around the paneled den. "I don't know. But I think—it would be very hard for us to come back—to this house."

I finished my cider. Before I put the glass down he said, "You can have mine, if you want it."

I drank his cider, too. Greg said, "The girl across the

street—Erica Lashley—she and two of her friends were arrested for possession of narcotics. Thank God none of that has ever touched Sharissa."

"She's too fine a person. All credit to you and your—"

"Did you want to see me about something tonight, C.G.?"

"Oh. I did have some news. I hope it's not unpleasant for you, my bringing this up? Do you remember Mrs. Sullivan?"

His smile was slightly twisted. "Will I ever forget?"

"It certainly was a unique experience. Anyway, she's— her liver failed, and it seems to be a matter of days."

He just looked at me, thoughtfully. "I'll say a prayer for her."

The telephone rang. Greg looked at it as if trying to think of a good reason not to answer it. Decided to answer.

"Oh, hello, Adrienne." He leaned against a bookcase, rubbing his head, suppressing impatience. "Doing as well as can be expected. I took your suggestion and called Jean Maxwell. I know, it's a terrible real estate market, but I've made up my mind. Jean's listing the house at one sixty-nine. No, we're not including the furniture. Would you like to talk to Sharissa?"

From the kitchen Sharissa called, "Tell Grammer I'll call her back when this stupid paper's done!"

Greg couldn't get off the phone. He looked at me and shrugged. I got up and glanced around the den, wandered out into the hall. Greg was still talking, with great forbearance, to Caroline's mother. I walked up the stairs, casually, just having a look around.

The master bedroom door was open. A lamp was on by the bed. A framed photograph of Caroline Walker, probably taken when she was in her twenties, graced the bedside table. There was a small black bow pinned to one corner of the frame. I looked at her portrait for a few moments, feeling both sad and a little ridiculous for having intruded to this extent. The tentative way Greg moved,

carried himself, the tone of his voice—there was no denying that Greg Walker was in a painful state of mourning.
But I had a theory to test, ridiculous or not. I went into the
bathroom, closing the door behind me.

The bathroom was large enough for separate walk-in
closets, an alcove for a makeup table. Filigreed gold-
colored tray with cosmetics on it, a woman's spiky hairbrushes—nothing of Caroline Walker's had been disturbed.
Greg's part of the bathroom was almost as neatly maintained. Beside the basin there was a folded hand towel
with military-style hairbrushes and a comb on it. The cap
was on the toothpaste tube, which was rolled up from the
bottom. Greg was neat, conservative, methodical, a man
who thought before he spoke, and he took good care of
his smallest possessions, or his necessities. But he hadn't
cleaned his hairbrush for several days.

I took a small Ziploc sandwich bag from my coat pocket
and pulled a few strands of hair from between the bush
bristles, sealed them in the bag. Then I used the toilet.

When I came out of the bathroom, the toilet flushing
behind me, Greg was standing in the hall doorway,
watching me.

"All that cider," I said. "Hope you don't mind my using
your bathroom."

"No."

He stepped aside for me, and followed me downstairs.

"Central America," I said. "That won't be dangerous,
will it? I mean, for somebody like Sharissa."

"There's always some danger in primitive places. Particularly where the governments are unstable. Guatemala,
for instance. But the spiritual rewards certainly outweigh
the risks."

I wasn't so sure, but then I wasn't big on religion either.

Greg paused in the foyer, a hand on the front door handle, obviously wanting to let me out. I could see a part of
the kitchen past the dining room, Sharissa hunched over
the table where she was writing. Staring at the back of her
head, I felt pleasantly paralyzed, thinking of the closeness

we had enjoyed not so long ago, and craving her attention now. I could easily have stayed all evening, watching over Sharissa, if time—and her father—had been that accommodating.

"See you, Sharissa," I called.

"Come for dinner some night," she said, not turning around.

"You bet," I said, but it hadn't been much of an invitation. I looked at Greg and held out my hand. "Hope to see you before you go. When will that be?"

"January. After Sharissa finishes her exams." For a couple of moments there was something in his eyes that might have been curiosity or speculation. "There's nothing else about the Sullivan woman?"

"How do you mean?"

"Did she—well, I wonder if she ever admitted that she'd made a mistake, imagining that I was—"

"No. From what I've been told, she went into a coma without saying a word to anybody. By the way—"

"Yes?"

"You don't happen to remember what it was you said to her, just before—the gears in her head froze up."

Greg frowned. "It wasn't anything I *said*. I explained this, didn't I? I rolled back my sleeve and showed her my right forearm. Her husband—Frederick—had a bad scar there, from a sawmill accident. When she saw that I was—unscarred—she reached for me, and then—as soon as she touched me, I could almost feel the vitality, the—desperation—that had driven her so far, draining out of her. All that was left was the terrible kind of panic that leaves you hung up in a void. You can't hear, see, feel, reason." He shuddered slightly. "I was like that—not right away, but a week or so after Caroline was killed. I mean I felt it coming on, like a massive shock to the nervous system. I read Psalms. Again and again. Until it passed, and the danger was over."

I stepped out to the veranda. He didn't come outside with me. In the yellow light beside the door I studied his smooth, apparently unblemished forehead. It seemed to me there'd been a trace of scars there from the accidental GSW, the last time I'd seen him. But he nodded and smiled good-bye and closed the door before I could be sure.

O ne of the guys I work with had to take emergency leave and go up to Kentucky where his mother was suffering from Alzheimer's and his father had been hospitalized with a bleeding ulcer. He sold me a pair of Hawks tickets he wouldn't be able to use and I called a buddy of mine from high school days, a bachelor like me. We met outside the Omni on Friday night. The Bulls were in town, a sure sellout.

We had great seats, mid-court, six rows up. I bought Dan a beer and one for myself. There was plenty of time to get caught up before the game started. Dan was a microbiologist. He worked for one of the country's larger biotech companies over in Norcross, on stuff he was usually not allowed to talk about. They also did some of the more difficult trace evidence analysis for the Georgia Bureau of Investigation.

The Bulls blew the Hawks out; afterward we had ribeyes at Bone's. I paid. Dan was impressed with my generosity.

"I need something done," I told him. "I'm working on it unofficially, and I can't go through channels?"

He nodded, and I got out my hair samples: hair that I suspected was from the head of one Frederick Sullivan, whereabouts unknown, and the hair I'd removed from Greg Walker's brush at his home three nights ago. He looked the samples over without taking them from the Ziploc bags.

I said, "The sample marked 'A' is at least twenty years old, maybe older than that. The other is very recent. I think it's the same man. But I need a DNA match to prove it."

He lit a cigarette and moved the baggies around, shaking one of them, studying the hair samples.

"Don't think we can do it."

"You guys are supposed to be miracle workers. What was that you were telling me, getting a match from as little as forty sperm? That's not enough to show up on the head of a pin."

"Okay, but this is different. DNA-coding works best with blood and tissue samples. Exhibit A here, this lock of hair has been cut. Unlikely we'll find an intact follicle. We need DNA from follicle tissue, not the hair shaft. Probably the best we can do is establish that the same class characteristics exist between the two samples of hair."

"Which doesn't rule out coincidence."

"I'm afraid not. If A and B are the same guy, can you tell me what you want him for?" I must have looked tense. "Complicated business?"

"Well, if B is the same as A, he should be in his seventies now, and he doesn't look a day over forty-five. His worst crime may be bigamy. He would have abandoned a wife in Canada almost twenty years ago, changed his identity, remarried here in Georgia, raised a daughter. Can't blame the guy for wanting to change, I met his first wife. But what bothers me, aside from the sheer improbability of his not aging visibly over a period of twenty years, is the fact that A had a teenage daughter with him when he left Canada. Now, if it was me and I wanted to change my name and my life and settle down a long way from Canada, then I don't think I'd want to take my daughter with me. Not without a good reason. Was A afraid the girl would be abused by her mother? Was that one of the reasons for splitting in the first place, to protect the girl? If so, what happened to her? Has he been in touch with her, all these years? No answers. I don't have anything to go on. But cop sense tell me something is really wrong here. And I'll tell you another thing—how about a second bottle of that Sicilian red?"

We stayed late over the wine. And I tried to lay everything out for Dan's analytical mind, all the jagged pieces that wouldn't, no matter how I arranged them, make a coherent picture.

"B is planning a big change in his life right now. Kind of an eerie similarity in pattern? I don't mean he's going to disappear, change his name—but he and his daughter, they're leaving for Central America in January to act as lay missionaries for the Baptist church. His wife was killed in an accident on I-75 in August, and—I didn't tell you about that."

"No."

"She died maybe an hour later from massive internal injuries. B was in the car, too. Dislocated shoulder, that was the extent of his injuries."

"Lucky man."

"Lucky? Less than two months earlier, he survived a gunshot wound to the head. Survived, hell. He came back so quickly it was like he shrugged it off."

"I can see why you're—fascinated with him."

"You mean obsessed. Call it what it is. Daniel, I don't want him to leave town. I just don't want him to leave Sky Valley with Sha—with his daughter, until I know a hell of a lot more about him."

Dan looked at the hair samples again. "I'll see what I can do. But—if B is not who he's claimed to be all these years, then there has to be a phony paper trail, doesn't there? Can't you nail him that way?"

"I can't conduct the kind of investigation you're talking about without suitable grounds. He's not charged with anything, he's not a suspect in an open case. It's more difficult to pull off now, but twenty years ago there was no trick to establishing an ID that would pass all but an FBI security clearance check."

We drank some more in silence. The Dago red made me sweat, and I was slightly manic. And I talked too much, finally.

"Bonnie. Sharissa. Both girls about the same age. Where's Bonnie now? And why does he want to take Sharissa away? She could enroll in college, come January. But he wants her to go with him. What the hell am I—"

I stopped, but I didn't have to fill in blanks for Dan. After a while he said, "A girl named Lourdes came to work for us, three—almost four years ago. She was from Costa Rica, but she went to school in the States. Little bitty thing. Black hair to her waist, and these incredible turquoise eyes. Nineteen years old. I couldn't even talk to Lourdes, I was that crazy about her. A year ago she got married, to an anthropology professor at Emory. But that didn't change anything. I can't get interested in another girl. You know how you meet someone and that's it, she's perfect?" I nodded, glumly. Dan said, sad but adamant, "There'll never be another girl like Lourdes." Daniel is six-three, bones like soda straws. Thick glasses. Women pay more attention to a discarded sofa on the street than they do to men like us.

It was our fate, and we drank silently to it, and I drove home, mostly sober, worrying, more than a little bathetic. *Who is your father, Sharissa?* For her sake, I had to find out. Without arousing Greg's curiosity and maybe his suspicion of me.

That struck me as being particularly important. There was something about Greg Walker that was closed, guarded, even dangerous.

For the next couple of weeks I was busy, and on overtime, as part of an enforcement team playing tag with drug dealers. The game goes like this: we bust a dealer, and he's "it." Then it's one-to-fourteen unless he cooperates and hands us his supplier. We tag that one, who then becomes "it," gradually moving up the chain of informants, hoping for a big coup: a major regional distributor. But when you run into a dealer who's stubborn or stupid or scared to woof, the game ends, and you start over.

I was enjoying a day off, too pooped to do anything but drink beer and watch a not-very-interesting NFL game, when Daniel called.

"The hair thing?" he said. "Pretty much the way I told you it would go. No DNA match possible."

I yawned. My father was sitting by the fire, talking to the cat in his lap. My mother had gone to bed. "Thanks for trying, Dan."

"I did turn up something interesting."

I sat up straighter and put the TV on mute. "What?"

"Well, it was obviously a lock of hair trimmed by scissors, but a small curved pair, like manicure scissors. Maybe his wife snipped his hair for a keepsake while he was sleeping. Used little sharp pointed scissors."

"So?"

"She drew some blood, apparently. Nipped an ear, or something. Tiny little drop. He might not even have felt it. I sorted through all the hairs in the sample, four hundred eighty-four by actual count. Three of them were stuck together with what I thought might be dried blood. So I did a leuco-malachite test. It was human blood, all right."

"You should have been a po-lice, Daniel."

"Not with my sensitive digestion. Anyway, not to make all of this overly technical, with degraded material like dried blood we go through a process called a polymerase chain reaction to amplify the fragments of DNA from the blood cells. That gives us the so-called DNA blueprint. We match it with the DNA we took from cells in subject B's hair follicles. The result was a high level of specificity."

My skin was prickling. "How high?"

"Well, you know, a lot of baloney has been written about the statistical probabilities of DNA matching. It's not an exact science. There hasn't been enough research on population frequencies, for one thing. Small homogeneous population groups can yield a high number of matches, as many as two out of five."

"But in our case—" I interrupted.

"—That wouldn't be relevant. And three of us concurred on the reading. So—ruling out the possibility of identical twins, A and B are the same man. Hope this does you some good. I'll put the autorads in the mail first thing tomorrow, along with the standard forensic report."

I thanked Dan and hung up. My head was seething. I stared at the gas log flames until both Blacky the one-eyed cat and my father felt the drawing power of my gaze and looked around at me. I went into the kitchen then and mixed myself a sour mash and soda.

So that was it. Frederick Sullivan and Greg Walker, one and the same. And now that I knew, what was I supposed to do with the information? Mrs. Roxanne Sullivan had passed away, unmourned, on the twenty-second of November. Frederick Sullivan was not wanted for anything, I knew that much. Did Greg Walker have someone else's birth certificate? Probably. Did he have a criminal record? Not in Sky Valley, where he'd made his home for the past eighteen—almost nineteen—years. He was an imposter who had lived a decent, hard-working life. Unlike Frederick Sullivan. He'd attended church regularly, joined the usual merchants' civic clubs, raised a daughter, made no waves.

Would Sharissa care that her father had been someone else in Canada?

What would be the point of telling her?

Well, Holmes. The facts are most remarkable and dramatic. But their meaning is, I confess, damnably obscure.

I had another sour mash, not much soda this time.

Uncanny, I thought. That was the word that summed up my feelings about Greg Walker. He had demonstrated remarkable powers of recovery from devastating injuries. And in twenty years or more he showed little or no signs of aging. From photos I had seen, evidence of his true age based on Roxanne Sullivan's testimony, he was an exceptionally robust seventy-three. Or older. I had heard of hard-working peasants in favorable environments in remote places of the earth who lived on goat cheese or yogurt or something, and who achieved very long, active lifespans. Biologically Greg Walker might be a genetic rarity, but if that's all he was, then it was no business of mine.

But my cop sense wouldn't allow me to leave it alone. There was still a loose end that bothered me. Her name was Bonnie Sullivan. I wanted to know where she was, what had happened to her. Only her father could tell me that.

It took me a while to accept what I had to do. Simple enough. You want answers, you ask questions. And I had a real itch to discover what Greg Walker would say when I confronted him with the fact that I knew he was Frederick Sullivan.

In a way I was cornering him. Challenging his plausibility. He had been consistently plausible since the day I'd met him at the hospital. It's a trait all complex psychopathic personalities have in common. They are the world's best liars. And some of them are killers. I decided I wasn't going to take any chances with Greg Walker.

By then it was five days before Christmas. When I tried to call the Walker house to invite Greg to lunch, I found out the phone had been disconnected. Greg had already left Sky Valley, taking Sharissa with him.

FOUR

Cobían, Guatemala

I have a new friend, I think. Her name is Veronica. She goes everywhere I go. She walks with a slight limp and carries an Uzi semiautomatic rifle.

Dad thinks it's necessary. There has been renewed antigovernment guerrilla activity in this part of Guatemala, although nobody seems to make much of it. Last night we heard gunfire again, a lot of shooting; it went on sporadically for five or six minutes across Lake Petén-Itzá from the hotel. Also we heard rumors that some tourists were detained on the main road to the ruins by the FAR—the armed rebel forces. All the rebels stole was some gasoline, which is sometimes hard to come by up here. Nobody got hurt.

Anyway, Veronica is a first cousin to the man who operates the Itzá Maya, Mr. Colon. She's short, about five-three, but otherwise doesn't resemble most of the Maya girls you see in Cobían, who run to chubby and are shy but good-natured. They smile a lot. Veronica never smiles. Not that she's disagreeable. And the spiderweb of scars on the right side of her face doesn't really detract from her looks. I didn't know until today how she got the scars. Didn't know she spoke more than a few words of English, either, although I thought it was a good bet she understood more English than she was willing to let on about. I found out she spent two years in a Catholic girls' college in California (Mount San Antonio). Also, surprise, she's older than she looks, about twenty-eight, and was married. Her husband had something to do with the government; he was killed by the FAR three years ago. That gave us something in common to talk about, once Veronica decided it was worth talking to me at all. And I found that I really did want to talk about Bobby, because the hurt just won't go away.

But that came later, much later. I need to say something first about what happened in Kan Petén when Daddy and I visited the site this morning. Because I don't understand why he acted the way he did. I've never known him to be rude to anybody. And never in my life has he said anything to so completely humiliate me in front of other people—total strangers! I can understand him being protective, we've both been through so much heartache the past few months. I'm *trying* to understand. But he seems tense and on edge since we came to Guatemala. I thought the change was what we both needed. As for the gang of guerrillas we hear about, but haven't seen—I guess he's just nervous because of me. I *am* glad he arranged for Veronica to hang out with me, although I felt foolish at first, going into town with her and her Uzi, the way everybody stared, and kind of snickered behind our backs. *Gringa.* I took three years of Spanish in school, but I didn't learn how many ways you could say that word and make it sound so unpleasant.

This is the so-called dry season in the northern Guatemala rain forest, which means it doesn't rain enough to close the unpaved roads in the area—that includes almost all of the roads outside of Cobían. A few years ago during the "wet" season (summer), they had *sixteen feet* of rainfall! But because of all the tourists who come to see the ruins in winter, the government maintains a good paved road to Kan Petén, and the trip from our hotel overlooking the lake takes only about forty minutes.

We traveled to the ruins in Veronica's Land Cruiser. Myself, Dad, Veronica, and her stepbrother, Benito, who also works at the hotel. Benito brought along a 12-shot, 12-guage shotgun with a pistol grip that he carried on a sling across one shoulder. He always kept at least one hand on the gun, and seemed really proud of it. In contrast to Veronica, Benito, who I think is about sixteen and still goes to school, liked trying out his English on us. He is a few inches taller than Veronica and twice as wide, very muscular.

The morning was dry and cloudless, but, as always since we arrived, there was a haze of smoke in the air to the east, toward Belize. We could smell the smoke as we drove northeast to Kan Petén.

"Burning, every day, the forest," Benito said. "To make graze for cattle, no? Very bad. Also trees cutting, every day. For wood. ¿Cómo se dice? Muebles—"

"Furniture."

"Yes. Make Furniture for U.S., I think. So many trees gone. One million hectares."

We stopped in a village for gas. Dad had his morning headache: he said he was probably drinking too much of the rich Guatemalan coffee they serve at the hotel. He went into a *farmacia*. I walked across the plaza to take some pictures of the church, which was yellow and green and pink, the colors wearing off in places, and the school building next door.

Some boys at recess were playing basketball and started showing off for me, or the camera, grinning over their shoulders. A couple of the daring ones came toward us, giving each other little shoves, and spoke to Benito. One of the boys was wearing a straw hat with a tall crown and a blue band with a four-pointed star pattern that was almost like the hat Benito wore. They were in awe of the Striker shotgun. He let them have a closer look at it. They discussed the damage it could do, and one of the boys made shotgun noises. Then the boy with the hat like Benito's spoke to him for a long time about something that sounded serious. I don't think he was speaking Spanish; it must have been the Itzá dialect.

Benito didn't say much, but he gave each of the boys a coin and they walked away.

Benito looked at me. "He is Porfilio, a cousin. Saying there was killing in another village not very far from here, two nights ago. Soldiers look for rebels hiding there." He shrugged. "Always fighting here, long time." He shrugged again. "The government does not care for us."

"Are the Maya rebels?"

"Maybe. Because we are Indians. Lowest people, long time. Most of us make no problems. Only live here, in our towns. Very poor."

"Your cousin Francisco isn't poor. He owns the hotel."

"Oh, yes." Benito tapped his breastbone with his fingertips. "He is a man of the *cofradía*. This is like—especial man, especial to God, a—protector of the old ways of Maya. Such a man is respected everywhere: *un hombre de privilegio,* always from father to son. *¿Usted conoce?"*

Dad was calling us from across the plaza. I took a couple of pictures of a huge ceiba tree that was surrounded by a sort of ramshackle gazebo, and some boulder-size heads, stone faces with big eyes but no pupils that Benito said were gods of rain and wind. The day was getting warmer. Benito stopped at a stall on one side of the plaza and bought me a straw hat with a tall crown, like his. He wouldn't let me pay him back.

"Look what Benito gave me," I said, pulling the brim of the hat down over my eyes, the way Benito wore his. Veronica gave him a look that implied he had a crush on me, and drove away from the *gasolina.* We both ignored her. *"¿Muy guapo, no?"* I said to Daddy.

Dad smiled. "Looks good on you. Is that what *guapo* means?"

"It means handsome, and you'd better start learning some Spanish."

"Tomorrow," he said. He still had that deep line between his eyebrows, which meant the headache was still bothering him, or else he was worried about something, like being stopped on the road at gunpoint. I think he would have been happier just to hang around the hotel until the Randalls, who were in charge of the mission team at Usumucinta, drove up to get us on Saturday. But I had nagged and made a pest of myself, so here we were on the way to Kan Petén. Which, according to what I'd been reading, was one of the most incredible sights in Central America.

But at first glance Kan Petén was a disappointment. "Disneyland," Daddy said disgustedly. There were small hotels and cafés and souvenir shops for a kilometer or so leading to the gravel parking lots, then more shops and stalls and cages filled with birds and animals—most of them threatened or endangered species, if I understood Veronica's mumbled Spanish correctly. I saw a sorry-looking quetzal (but still the most beautiful color of any bird, except flamingos), a sleeping golden anteater, and a margay, which looks like an oversized spotted housecat. We walked a long way up a wooded hill, seeing the rugged tops of some pyramids, and stelae along the path, all of them worn down and partly covered with lichen.

It was humid in the forest we walked through. For a few minutes we were out of sight of any buildings. We came to a series of waterfalls and a pool some tourists on a guided tour were throwing coins into, and up another long gradual rise with the trees beginning to thin out and suddenly there it was, the Great Plaza and the pyramids of Kan Petén! Even if you don't know anything about archeology, and I don't know much, you have to be impressed.

Kan Petén had been discovered a hundred fifty years ago, almost nine centuries after it was abandoned. Only parts of it had been dug out of the forest so far. According to my guidebook, Kan Petén covered fifty square miles; more than a thousand years ago the city, or city-state, had been home to as many as sixty thousand Maya. Now, except for all the damages that time (and probably acid rain) had done to the stonework, the North and Central Acropolis of the Great Plaza still resembled what they must have been when Kan Petén was the center of one of the great Maya cultures.

The only modern additions to the site were an air-conditioned museum and souvenir shop and a cafeteria, each with a thatched roof, and a large official-looking building in a cleared area several hundred meters east of the Great Plaza. There was a helicopter landing pad beside this building. A big helicopter circled overhead and landed as we crossed the plaza to climb the temple that stood beside a reservoir. Three men and a couple of women got out. All of them wore muddy boots and jeans and khaki shirts. Two of the men were wearing guns, and one of them, the tallest of the group, had on an Indiana Jones-style hat. It was almost like a movie. They unloaded a few crates and canvas bags of tools and carried them into the building.

Archeologists, Benito explained, and he pointed south, where the helicopter had come from.

"Working at another site, 50 kilometers from here. No roads. Many *ciudades* like this one, no one finds them all yet."

Temple Two was as high as a twenty-story building, with steps that went up at an angle of about fifty degrees. Of the restored pyramids it was the least dangerous to climb, but signs in four languages warned of missteps. The way to do it was to climb at a lean, sometimes using the steps above for handholds. I played indoor tennis until the day we left Sky Valley, but halfway up the temple I started feeling all those steps in my calves. Veronica and

Benito climbed stoically and methodically up the front of the temple, as if they'd done it dozens of times. Daddy was below me at arm's length, ready to catch me if I stumbled. He wasn't having any trouble with the climb, but he was breathing hard.

He needed to sit down when we reached the top. I sat beside him and squeezed his hand.

"Beautiful," he murmured, looking around. Beads of sweat were clinging to the rims of his sunglasses where they touched his cheeks. They looked like tears. I wanted to wipe them away, but he turned his head, looking east. "They came three thousand years ago, nobody knows from where. Their culture survived six times longer than the Roman Empire. They had an accurate calendar, predicted eclipses, built great cities—and this temple we're sitting on—with a few simple tools."

"And then the Spaniards showed up."

"It wasn't the Spaniards who destroyed Classic Maya civilization. Most of it had vanished by the end of the tenth century. Six hundred years later the Spaniards mopped up what was left around here, and farther north along the coast of Yucatán—a mixture of Toltec and Maya society."

"Didn't know you were a Maya scholar," I teased him.

"Oh—I wasn't sleepy last night, so I rummaged around in one of those books you brought along."

"Does anyone know what happened to the Classic Maya civilization?"

"Yes," Veronica said, and I looked up at her, startled. Then I smiled, encouragingly, I think. She didn't change expression but she went on, in English, "One man can destroy what thousands have built, if he have the power. Probably it happen here. At least Glen think so."

"Glen who?" I asked.

She nodded toward the helicopter pad. "You saw him. The one with the hat. His name is Glen Hazen. From Vanderbilt University. The site they are working at Dos Pilas have a tomb twelve hundred years old. They find a king in the tomb, but they also find writings that may esplain how Classic Maya civilization collapse in less than a century."

"Vanderbilt? That's where I'm going to college when I get back."

"Small wurl," Veronica said with a shrug. "If you would like to meet him, maybe he talk to you more about this."

Which is how I met Glen Hazen, in the busy cafeteria at Kan Petén.

He's tall, probably six-six, with crinkly red hair and a reddish brown mustache. He greeted Veronica with a kiss on the cheek, but near enough to her lips to give me the impression they might be more than just casual friends; although her expression was still sort of frozen, the pupils of her eyes looked, all of a sudden, bigger. Just a little "simmer" to the dark chocolate. Glen's brown eyes pop slightly, like a Sendak goblin's eyes, but in spite of that he isn't bad-looking. His hands were red and swollen from conga fly bites. "Archeology seems like a glamorous profession," he said. "Until you learn that basically what you are is lunch for a lot of exotic bugs." It seemed as if better than half of the cafeteria crowd were archeologists, from all over the world; and they all knew each other. There was a lot of cross-talk and loud talk, greetings flying back and forth across the room.

Veronica and I sat on either side of Glen, and I had to lean close to him to catch what he was saying.

"Our theory has it that Maya civilization died when their rules of warfare changed," Glen said. "Mayas always had a taste for blood and conquest, which certainly doesn't

make them all that different from the run of human beings, but instead of fielding great armies and systemati-
cally reducing the population, their early conflicts were
ceremonial in nature, ritual enactments between elite
groups. A ruler from a city like Kan Petén—Speaking-
Serpent, for instance—would capture the king or a high-
ranking member of the nobility from, say, Tikal or
Caracol. Then Speaking-Serpent would torture his rival,
keeping him just on the edge of death for months or even
years, thereby enhancing his own stature with his subjects,
and the gods. And while this was going on, the ordinary
people would go about their business, most of them farming small plots of ground cleared from the forest. They
practiced crop rotation, which was a necessity. Topsoil in
a rain forest ecosystem is thin, and the heavy rains constantly leach out nutrients."

"But the rules changed, you said."

"One of our neighborhood kings—we don't know his
name yet, we just call him Ruler Two from Dos Pilas—
began to covet not only high-born captives, but his neighbors' land. To take it, and hold on to it, he needed the
equivalent of a Roman legion or two. In order to resist his
armies, rival city-states raised their own armies. The era of
the siege began in Central America. Cities built walls and
moats—we have good examples of this kind of construction, and the changes in warfare, at Dos Pilas—and the
scattered plots of farmland had to be moved inside the
walls, to prevent total destruction by roving armies."

"So they wore out the soil in a few years," I said, "and
then they all—"

"Starve to death," Veronica said, making a motion
across her throat with the edge of her hand. "All but a few
survivors, who hide out in the forest. Like peasants during
the Dark Ages in Europe."

"If you'd like to see something really unusual," Glen
said to me, "I'm flying down to Machaquilá in a couple of
days. Some of the people from the University of Texas
camp have located a cave and cenote that was probably

used for ritual sacrifice twelve centuries ago. It's supposed to be a more important find than Naj Tunich—"

"I don't think so," Daddy said, with a smile, kind of a thin smile. "I don't trust helicopters. Didn't you all lose one last month?"

"A copter did crash near Topoxte, but it wasn't our group. Some Danish anthropologists who chartered an old Huey from the Guatemalan Air Force. We've got a new Bell we leased from an oil company—"

"Still don't like the idea," Daddy said. "Sorry, Sharissa."

"*Dad*. It's fascinating; when will I ever get another chance to—"

"I heard the helicopter was shot down by rebels, and there is no way I'll allow you to—"

"Dad, *chill*. Don't you think you're being overprotective?"

Sometimes you just pop off and say the wrong thing without thinking. I probably sounded antagonistic, but I was excited. A helicopter trip to ruins in the jungle—I really wanted to go and if Glen thought there was any danger I'm sure he wouldn't have invited me. I know I wasn't trying very hard to understand Daddy's point of view. Mom was gone; I was all he had left. He had a good reason to be worried.

Dad stared at me for a few seconds, as if he couldn't believe I was the daughter he'd raised.

Glen said, not trying to be too persuasive, "Promise to take good care of Sharissa, sir."

Dad shook his head, not angrily but as if he had too much on his mind and this wasn't worth arguing about. To me he said, "Time to go." He looked back at Glen. "Nice meeting you, Hazen."

Glen nodded, then smiled at me and shrugged slightly, and I made a last try. "Dad, I know I'll be all right—"

"*You* don't know anything," he said bitterly. He might as well have reached across the table and slapped me, hard. I was stunned, and then I did the most stupid thing imaginable, I started to cry. It wasn't a big deal, I didn't make a fool of myself, some tears just spilled out. I had thought that was over with, my heart clenching up and tears coming out of nowhere. He was a little surprised, but it was a hostile kind of surprise; he didn't say anything else to me, he just looked grim and walked away. That was the really humiliating part. He might have said something conciliatory, at least tried to make it look better, but there I was in front of strangers with tears running down my cheeks.

Veronica looked at his back. Her expression is usually hard to read but she seemed astonished and puzzled. Benito was fiddling with his shotgun, not meeting anyone's eyes. Then Glen did something nice; touched my shoulder and said, "Hope I see you again. Where're you staying, Sharissa?"

I tried to tell him but my throat was raw and dry.

"Itzá Maya," Veronica said. Then I heard Daddy again. His voice was loud, but he wasn't calling to me.

"You've made a mistake!"

He sounded so agitated that I was scared suddenly, afraid he might really be losing it after five months of grieving. I saw him by the cafeteria door, looking down at a man in a wheelchair who was more or less blocking Daddy's way. The man was large from the waist up, fat bulging out of his short-sleeve shirt in a few places. His legs were as short and useless-looking as those of a ventriloquist's dummy. He had a triple-chinned face red as roses. He was smiling broadly. His teeth were so big and white and obviously false it looked as if someone had tiled his mouth.

There was a lull in the loud hum of conversation in the cafeteria, otherwise I probably wouldn't have been able to hear what he said to Daddy.

"Oh, no, I don't think so." He sounded Scandinavian. "I'm not so good with names always, but faces, those I don't forget." He had offered up a hand to Daddy. "Nils Lagerfeld. Uppsala University. And we met before, here at

Kan Petén—yes, I'm certain of it—almost twenty years ago. Your lovely daughter was with you."

"I've never been here before." Dad looked around, searching for me, I think, and gestured. "That's my daughter, over there. She hasn't been here before either. Now if you wouldn't mind—Veronica! Sharissa! What's holding you up? I said we're going!"

The man in the wheelchair peered at me, and didn't seem convinced he was mistaken. "Another daughter? Oh, yes, lovely. But let me refresh your memory. I can recall almost word-for-word our conversation about the dynasty of Smoking-Squirrel. You were extremely well informed for a layman, and I am sure your name will come back to me—"

"Just get out of my way, you old fool," Daddy said. This time he wasn't loud, but his voice made my heart skip and the man in the wheelchair stopped smiling. Without hesitating he backed his chair out of Daddy's way and Daddy stalked out. The man in the wheelchair looked around at his colleagues at a nearby table, threw up his hands and made a face. They laughed.

Veronica said in my ear, " *Vámanos*, Sharissa."

"He's not like this," I said to Glen. I had to bite my lip, hard. I was desperate to explain. "My mother died a few months ago, and Daddy—well, he's been holding it in too much, I think, we both have."

"I'm sorry, Sharissa. Listen, it's no problem, really. Why don't I give you a call later?"

"I hope you will," I said, and followed Veronica and Benito to the door.

The man in the wheelchair gave me a friendly glance as we went by. He was saying to his friends, "Have you ever known me to make a mistake about someone? Names, yes, I forget names! But I have been coming to Ken Petén forty years, I could look it up in my diary. The day we spoke. Remarkable, he looks just the same after so many years, not like us, old—"

"Excuse me," I said.

He looked over his shoulder at me again. "Yes?"

"That was my father, and I'd like to apologize—"

He stared, then turned his chair with a quick stroke of one hand on the right wheel, still staring as if he were trying to compose what he was going to write in his diary tonight, about me.

"Then you *are* a sister—or perhaps, half-sister of the girl I remember?" He smiled encouragingly, but I must have looked awfully blank. "Hmm. She was blond, not tall as you but with larger cheekbones, such a lovely humorous mouth and—yes, gray eyes?"

He was asking me if he had described her accurately. "I don't have a sister," I said. "I only wanted to—"

Veronica's hand was on my arm, fingers sliding to the soft place inside the elbow. She pressed hard with two fingers, not pinching, but her grip was painful. I shot a look at her. Her expression wasn't hostile; she looked sad and sort of remote. She smiled politely and said, to me and to the others, "*¿Por favor?*"

Then Veronica took me away from the man in the wheelchair. It was obvious I was being led like a donkey out the door. One humiliation after another, but I didn't know what else I should say to him. And the crazy thought hit me, like the sun through the glass as the door swung open: *What if it was true?*

Daddy was walking fast. He was already across the plaza, not waiting for us. I put my sunglasses on. I felt as if what I'd eaten for lunch, some rice with red peppers and chicken, wasn't going to stay in place for long. I was dizzy from the thick, wet heat, and apprehensive.

He was waiting in the Land Cruiser when we got there. He was reading his pocket New Testament and had a handkerchief in one hand, to blot the perspiration on his forehead and throat. I got in, leaving space between us, and looked again at what I could see of Kan Petén from the parking lot.

"Were you talking to that nut?" Daddy asked me, not looking up from his page.

"What? I don't think he's a nut! I can't *talk* to people? What is the matter with—"

He glanced at me, looking pained, and misunderstood.

"You have to be careful who you talk to down here. There are legitimate archeologists, and a lot of fakes, adventurers, criminal trash. Who knows what some of them are capable of. You're a beautiful girl, Sharissa, and—you've been more or less sheltered, is what I'm saying. We're not rich, but we could be taken for rich, That's all I'm trying to say—"

"You're not *saying* anything! You mean you're afraid I might be kidnapped?"

He nodded. His mouth was tense in an expression of apology, but I wouldn't let him touch me. My arm still hurt from Veronica's grip. She drove away. I looked back and felt as if there was something coming after me, something black and cold from the old tombs. The sun seemed to grow darker. It was probably nausea. I yelled at Veronica and when she pulled over to the side of the narrow road I got out and sprayed my lunch around.

The rest of the afternoon I stayed in our bungalow at the hotel, flat on my back and with a cold cloth on my head, rinsed in water from a plastic ice bucket. Whenever I dozed off my legs or arms would give a jerk, which woke me up. I felt hollow and headachy and awful, very PMS but even murkier than that. Worst of all, I felt so alone. A call to Grammer and Grampa might have cheered me up, but I didn't know what to say to them: I'd been so gung ho about coming down here, and now I wished I could get on a plane and fly home—for a little while, anyway.

We'd been gone since before Christmas—celebrated the holidays on a cruise ship. I understood why Daddy hadn't wanted to stay in Sky Valley. It was a big family thing at Christmas, Mom's family, and he was suffering so much he couldn't face them all. I thought I felt the same way. He was fine on the cruise, making an effort for both of us. We gave each other a lot of hugs and smiled too much, I guess, and kept busy with aerobics and swimming and shuffleboard.

After Christmas there were the seminars and training programs for our mission, which were held at a big camp near Caracas, Venezuela. I tried to be careful about what I ate but got a parasite anyway. Daddy seemed to be having a hard time keeping up his spirits, even though he still assured me he was fine and that the mission was the right thing to do. He stared at me sometimes in a way that made me feel so sad for him; other times he just wanted to hold my hand.

Daddy came into my room a couple of times during the afternoon to see how I was getting along. Maybe he wanted to hold my hand again, work up an apology for the way he'd treated me. But I was still mad and pretended to be asleep. Then I didn't hear him around our bungalow for a couple of hours.

I had Chilly-Willy, my lifelong stuffed penguin, with me, but I was past the age where I could talk to him without feeling self-conscious. I listened to the macaws and howler monkeys in cages on the grounds, and their noise made me more and more edgy. The tennis courts were full, the sounds of rackets stroking balls more soothing than the wildlife. I thought about good old C.G. Butterball, which is what Bobby had called him. I certainly owed him a letter. Probably should have phoned to say good-bye, but once I had permission to leave school early, it was a hectic three days getting ready to go. He had such a crush on me. Really a sweet guy. I got melancholy thinking about C.G., as if I missed him. Maybe I did. It was easy to miss everything about home, because everything was so different, and strange, in Guatemala. As strange as the fat archeologist in the wheelchair, greeting Daddy like an old friend.

Maybe that's all he was, a nut, saying I had a sister with blond hair and gray eyes. But I couldn't believe anything was wrong with him. Some men can make you cringe with a glance, you know exactly what's on their minds, but I hadn't minded him staring at me. I felt appreciated. He seemed like somebody I could talk to, wanted to talk to, before Veronica dragged me away with her version of the Spock pinch.

I needed to get up and go to the bathroom. It was almost dark outside, the sky an incredible deep blue shade. The bungalow had screens and we burned mosquito coils in every room, but still I had a couple of more bites near one of my bubbies. I had learned to dab Merthiolate on every bite; a little sweat and they itched like crazy, and scratching bred infection. Both of my breasts and my bottom were freckled with the orangey stuff.

When I came out buttoning my shorts Veronica was in the living room of the bungalow turning on a lamp. She wore her usual boring paramilitary stuff, but with a bright Maya neck scarf for accent. She had propped her Uzi upright on a cushion in a highbacked rattan chair. She sat in an identical chair a few feet away with her hands on her knees. She had a way of being so still that it seemed unnatural.

"I don't want any company right now," I said crossly, and went back into my bedroom to look for my hairbrush.

"Your father say I should stay with you. So I stay."

"Where is he?"

"I doan know."

"He went somewhere without telling me?" I complained, crosser than ever.

"Would you like something to eat, there is cold chicken in the fridge, some plátanos fritas."

"I'm not hungry."

"Do you have the runs?"

" *No.* Sort of." I found my hairbrush under Chilly-Willy in a tangle of bedclothes and went back to the living room. "I took some Lomotil. I'm not really sick. It's just when I get nervous."

Veronica nodded, sat back in the creaking chair, stared at the ceiling fan, and closed her eyes for a few seconds. Instantly she looked as if she'd fallen into a trance.

I sat on the edge of the couch opposite her.

"You're sure Daddy didn't tell you where he was going?"

She opened her eyes. The blades of the fan were turning about half as fast as an airplane propeller, humming almost too softly to hear.

"He'll be back."

Something hit one of the window louvers outside, a soft thud. I reacted; when I looked at Veronica again she was half way to the window, moving quickly in spite of her limp, the Uzi in her hands.

"If you're going to shoot something, make it one of those damn monkeys," I said. I was in a really bad mood, swearing like that.

"The howlers are protected here. They are becoming extinct." She peered through the louvers from the side of the window, then adjusted them.

I had a cramp. I fell back on the couch with my hair half-brushed, my knees up.

"It was probably a bat," Veronica said.

"Could you leave the louvers open? I like looking at the moon. It's almost full."

"Yes, in three days." She cranked the louvers again, a little farther apart. "There is an eclipse this month." She glanced at me, then limped across the room to the refrigerator.

"What happened to your foot?" I asked her.

"It became infected when I was a child. They almost cut

it off." She took a can of Sprite from the refrigerator. "Would you like one?"

"Yes. Thank you."

Veronica brought me the Sprite, and I sat up again. Her hands smelled as if she'd been cleaning her rifle. But her nails were clean, and so was her hair. She started back to her chair but I said, making an effort to be pleasant, "No, why don't you sit with me."

She hesitated, then parked her Uzi where it would be handy in case a vampire bat flew in to the bungalow. I'd heard they had them down here.

"Veronica," I said, "do you honestly think anything's going to happen to me?"

"You doan know this country. Or what war is like. We have war since I am a little girl. Maybe nothing happen here. My cousin Francisco now wears the Bird of Omen, the jade harpy. But anyway I am esposed to stay with you, and that's what I am doing."

"How did you get those scars on your face, did someone shoot you?"

"At me," she corrected. "I didn't run fast enough. So part of a wall, a mortar destroyed it, splinters struck me in the face. My husband was not as fortunate. He was cut deeply, here." She put a finger across the jugular in her throat, then jerked it away savagely, with a hard, desperate expression.

"I'm sorry."

"Well, I doan want to talk about it."

Silence. I drank some of my Sprite, and she drank a little of hers. Bubbles went up my nose and I giggled, and she looked at me as if I were stupid.

"Do we just sit here and not say anything to each other? That gets on my nerves."

"Then you will have to go to the toilet again, I suppose."

"Oh, the hell with you, Veronica." I had never said anything like that to anybody. "I don't know who you think you are or where you get off with your superior attitude.

No, I don't know your country and I've never been shot at, so I guess that means I haven't lived, which makes me a child in your eyes."

Her expression didn't change until she swallowed, then she looked bunched and bitter around the mouth; a familiar expression which I'd seen on the faces of two maiden aunts of my mother's who lived together in their shacky old house in Austell, Georgia, for thirty years without saying a word to each other: it was a screwed-up mouth that really savored resentment. I wondered if Veronica has just singled me out to dislike, or if her resentment covered all *gringas*.

"Yes, I think you are a child; and no I doan think you have lived."

"Well, you just listen." I was doing it again, flooding with tears, but I could still talk. "My boyfriend was killed. I mean murdered. One hundred thirty-two days ago. No reason. Somebody smashed his head in with a rock while he was out jogging. He would've been co-captain of the football team. And—I'll never know *who*, or *why*. My mother—" I had to stop for breath. Each breath was hot and hurting, like something jagged moving in my chest. "My mother died a week later in a car crash. I never got to say good-bye to her! *Both* of them! Everybody says, be strong—but I'll never get over this. You want to know something else? God is *not* good. It's a—a *joke* that I'm down here to be a missionary because—I don't believe in His mercy anymore, I've lost faith."

Veronica crossed herself automatically, then caught both my hands and held them. I would've had to fight her to get away, but I didn't have the strength.

"Don't hurt me!" I sobbed. "Don't ever try to hurt me again!"

"No, no, Sharissa! I doan want to hurt you! I only want to protect you. Believe me. I am afraid for you."

I was trembling and so emotionally conked that what she had said didn't sink in right away. Then, while she was holding me, not letting me pull my hands free, something passed between us—I don't know how to describe it. But I began to calm down. We looked at each other and it was as if we'd changed into the other's skin; a sisterly kind of thing. I felt friendship, concern.

"What do you mean, Veronica? What's the matter?"

"This place—I wish you were not here—such a bad time—"

"You said the guerillas wouldn't attack the hotel!"

"No. That is not what I mean." Now she wanted to let me go, but I was the one who clung to her. Veronica's eyes narrowed as if she were in pain, and I couldn't see her pupils, only whites. The scars on her cheeks stood out, as white as her eyes. "It is something else. Not only superstition—more than that, I am sure. In three days, the eclipse. Like before, when the Marquise—I doan know how to esplain. *Por favor,* let me go!"

I couldn't hold her any longer anyway. She got up, snatched the Uzi, and started for the bungalow door.

"I think—I should look around outside."

"Veronica, wait. What do you mean? What about the eclipse?"

She looked back, confused.

"My cousin ask me to be with you—few days only, he said. A favor to him."

"I know that. Till the Randalls drive up from Usumucinta."

"Saturday they will be coming."

"Yes."

"One day before the eclipse."

"So what?"

Veronica shook me off and was through the door and across the little porch before I could blink. It seemed to me that she was running away. I scrambled off the bed and slipped into *huaraches.*

She let me catch up to her on the stone walk that made a figure-eight around the bungalows in the torchlit garden. There was no need, that I could tell, for her to do any patrolling; the hotel employed armed guards, and it was a quiet evening. So far. I looked at the rising moon, nearly full, pale orange with shades of pale crater blue—amazing how close it seemed in the clear black sky. Close enough to give me goose bumps. Eclipses were supposed to be unlucky, or something. I'd never seen one back home in Sky Valley.

We walked together past a waterfall. A chilly breeze was rattling the palm fronds. My goose bumps began to feel like pebbles. I wished I had brought a sweater with me.

"Are you afraid of eclipses?" I asked Veronica.

"It is foolish to be frightened of fate. I am Catholic, but—I know it is the movements of the lights and planets that rule our lives. The stations of the eclipse cycles are especially important in Maya numerology and calendars."

"What's an eclipse c-cycle?"

"The sun and the moon joining—or opposing each other—at a time and place in the heavens that can be mathematically determined for centuries in advance. The solar and lunar eclipses that occur nineteen or twenty years apart have been occasions of renewal, or defeat. Birth or bloodshed. The Popol Vuh, our sacred text, says that the wurl has been created, then destroyed, many times. The gods of the cosmos desire beings who will honor their greatness. They have so far made us out of mud, and wood, and maize in their efforts to perfect us. Now we are flesh and blood. Better, but still we are not perfect. We do not honor them correctly; we worship ourselves instead. So there must be another time of destruction."

I was shuddering again. "I guess I know what you m-mean by that. But I don't hate God. And he knows. He knows my heart just goes dead when I think about what happened to Bobby."

"I understand your grief. My husband work for the government, but he was not of the military. An agronomist. Why did they fire on our harmless little van? Because of the license plate only. We were 'of the government.' For their atrocity I despise the guerillas. I fight against them. Fighting, killing, for so long. But the eclipse can bring bad things—ancient things—worse than the fighting. That is why I think it is bad for you to be here. I doan say this to anyone else. But I say to you, *leave*, Sharissa. Do not be in Cobían at the station of the eclipse. It may be difficult for me later, because they will know what I have done. But I will help you to go."

"Veronica, look, I'm sorry, you're—you aren't making any sense."

"How can I say more clearly, there may be great danger for you here!"

"If *I'm* not safe, then Daddy—"

"You doan need to worry about him. Only yourself, for a little while. After that—"

We passed a tall cylindrical cage filled with blue and orange parrots. They were restless as we went by them.

"After that, what?"

She shrugged off my question and asked, "Has he been a good father to you?"

"The best. I love him."

"Of course. Otherwise you would not follow him, trust him—"

"I trust Daddy with my—"

Veronica rubbed her head in agitation. "*Claro*. Then how can I think—how could such a terrible thing be possible? But I know, I know, I know what I saw! The Marquise—" She began speaking then in Mayan, her head back; she was staring at the moon with animal eyes. I was afraid of her, in the night, speaking in a frenzy to the moon, but I moved closer, because I had to find out what she was carrying on about.

Suddenly she stopped, and snapped her head toward me.

"But I am so stupid! Because I never ask you—"

"Ask me what?"

"How old are you, Sharissa?"

"I'll be eighteen in June. I'm Gemini. What d-does that have to do with—"

"Answer one more question, then maybe I can go away and not bother you again."

I was trembling so badly she must have thought I was shaking my head *no*.

"*Querida,* try to understand me. This friend of yours, the one you say was murdered—"

"B-Bobby."

"You were his lover?"

I was filled with shock and then despair, thinking of the relationship Bobby and I would never have. Wishing that we had, just once, made love all the way. My eyes were burning. How could she ask such a question? Didn't she realize how much it hurt me?

"You must answer," Veronica insisted. "If not that friend, was there someone else?"

"There was only Bobby. And we never—oh, God!"

She knew I was going to run, and she stepped into me, hooking an arm inside of mine, pressing her fingers so that the pain went streaking from elbow to wrist.

"Are you a virgin, Sharissa? Tell me!"

"Yes!"

I put my free hand against her breast and shoved, hard. Veronica let me go, reached down and caught the chunky gold crucifix she wore on a chain around her neck. She pressed the crucifix to her lips. It had tiny rubies on it, representing Christ's wounds, and his tears.

"*¡Ay Dios!*"

Behind us, a howler monkey roared. It wasn't much, they all sound like someone with bad asthma gasping for breath, but I jumped about a foot.

"What's the matter with you! What difference does it make if I'm a—if I never—"

I had nerve ends dangling everywhere. Veronica sat down slowly on a stone bench, still clutching the crucifix, cherishing it, her fist on her breast. Behind her there was a garden enclosure with stelae inside, some badly worn carved columns up to ten feet high. I could make out faces on two of them. Stern brows, cruel mouths. Faces of the Maya. Kings who had lived almost fifteen hundred years ago. Veronica's face was so still and cold in the moonlight she could've been carved in stone herself. Crucifixes, eclipses, old stones. Superstitions. *Ancient things.* The world created, and destroyed. Death. Rebirth. My nerves were bad and my heart was beating so hard it hurt me. Flesh and blood, flesh and blood, we are not perfect. Only virgins are perfect, or supposed to be.

I sat down beside Veronica, crossed my arms to try to stop shuddering. After a while I felt her hand on my shoulder near my neck, not to make a prisoner of me, but for comfort.

"Veronica, can't you tell me what has you so upset?"

"I talk too much already. It is so hard to speak . . . what I know to be true, what I think is possible . . . but I am not a crazy person, even though there is much I have difficulty to esplain. So that you will believe me."

"I'll try to believe you, but you've got me so confused—"

"You are not Maya, so—that is a difficulty also. Matters of blood, *knowing* that which cannot be put into words. I am Catholic, but I understand that what is now a thing of horror was once a part of the natural order, ordained, demanded by the gods. Ritual bloodletting."

I stiffened. She stroked me. "Yes, it still goes on, in the hidden sacred places, but I only hear of such ceremonies, I have never seen one."

"Human sacrifice?"

"No, I am speaking of self-mutilation. But there was a time—as recently as a hundred years ago—when adolescent boys and girls disappear suddenly from the neighborhood of Cobían. For some evil purpose, perhaps. I have no knowledge of those times. I have only one story to tell, the truth that I know—the story of the Colon family, and the Hotel Itzá Maya. If you listen, and if you believe, then you must decide for yourself if the danger to you is real."

"C-couldn't we go in? It's so chilly."

"No. Be patient a little while. We're alone here. No one can hear us."

Veronica turned her eyes to the hotel, three stories of tall glowing windows on the hill three hundred yards from the heart of the garden. We heard footsteps on the stone path, a murmur of voices—some guests out for a stroll before bedtime—but no one came close to where we sat by the stelae and tree stones.

I am from one of the poorer branches of a prosperous family," Veronica began. "My father was a lawyer and civil servant. He died when I was very young, barely knowing him. He left debts which were cleared up by my uncle Santiago Golon. My mother was educated woman, but she could not make a living for us—myself, my sister Miriam, who was four years older than I. After a while we came to Cobián, where my mother was given suitable employment as clerk, here at the Itzá Maya. I was ten years old. We lived in a house that has since been removed for more tennis courts. It was a small house, but with nice furniture. Miriam and I shared a room.

"My uncle was not only a provider, he took a real interest in us. He was as close to a father as I had, although when we are coming here I am certain he was at least one hundred years old."

Veronica looked at me for a reaction. I didn't have one, except to shrug.

She said sharply, "In this part of the wurl that is almost twice the life expectancy for any of us. Those who survive infancy, I mean. Not much better than the Middle Ages of

Europe, if you know history. There is still too much disease, not enough food for all. So my uncle was exception, no? Have one hundred years, but a brittle old man, half blind and deaf, sleep eighteen hours a day? That is what you think? Listen. Don Santiago would play tennis every day, one, two hours in the hot sun. He was married once only, but he had *many* women, and who knows how many children by his women; even Francisco doan know. Santiago Jesús de Córdoba Colon took care of them all. And when he die last year, I swear to you he had *two* mistresses, one who was nineteen years, and pregnant by him. He went peacefully in his sleep. He must have been one hundred twenty years old when he die. What a man. Like his father before him, who lived as long, or longer, perhaps, and was the founder of the Itzá Maya Hotel in the year 1827."

"I didn't know the hotel was that old. It looks—"

"Very modern now. With air-condition. And always, the best food and drink. Equal to a five-star hotel of Europe, in spite of its isolation. The hotel was modeled after the Colonial buildings in the old capital, Antigua Guatemala. Built at no small cost, in this wilderness. Even the Spanish avoided the jungle north of the lake. In all of the nineteenth and the early twentieth century, there was nothing here but Peténeco farming villages. The Maya *adoratorios* and temples had all been destroyed by their overlords. Then the loggers began to trickle in for the mahogany and sapodilla wood of the forest, and a few large landholders settled here. Yet . . . the Itzá from the beginning was a favorite of people who can afford it, and who in the old days could make the long and difficult journey, by ship and then on horseback, from the port of British Honduras, what is now Belize City. They would come, from the capitals of six continents, even when there was nothing much to see. Before the discovery of Kan Petén. In the rainy season, a handful still came. Not merely difficult but a real hardship, even for people with much money. I have seen their names in the old registration books that are stored in the hurricane cellar. Who would want to come here in the rainy season? Unless—"

"Unless what?" I asked her finally. She seemed to be in another mini-trance.

"They had to come," Veronica muttered. "No other explanation is possible."

"Why would anybody have to come here if they didn't want to?"

"Because here is a center of the Maya religion; or what remains of the religion, those rituals and observances now in the keeping of the *cofradía*, wearers of the sacred jade of prestige. Men destined to live long and prosper in their calling, like Francisco, Don Santiago's successor."

"Do your people still practice the old religion?"

"Many do."

"Does that mean the guests who've been coming to the hotel all these years are descendants of Maya?"

"Oh, no. But a few, that I believe is possible. By the end of the seventeenth century the exalted ones, ancestors of the truly great people of our society, were nearly all gone. Killed, driven away, by their conquerors. But I think some escape—maybe, if they were young women of royal blood, by becoming wives or mistresses of Spanish lords. Women who had great powers, necessary to their survival. Who sometimes bore special childrens with similar powers. Those children they would instruct in secret: passing on the mysteries that sustain our culture for two thousand years. They are the ones who find their way back, again and again, to Kan Petén."

Someone appeared on the path from behind a clump of tropical broom, scaring off a couple of the peacock-like turkeys that roamed the hotel grounds. Veronica tensed until she recognized him; one of the night patrol. He was carrying a stubby machine gun on a sling. He paused to light a cigarette. Then he waved at us and walked away on his rounds

Veronica had turned and was looking at one of the stelae in the fenced area behind us.

"Don Santiago could read the stelae, as easily as one reads a newspaper. He was a humble man, of less than average size, dressed always in a black suit and white shirt, but so powerful in prestige I have seen other powerful men of our country tremble in his presence. No one wronged him and lived. No one. Not even my sister Miriam. Who, I am sure, he loved even more than me."

Her cold, flat tone shocked me as much as her words.

"Veronica—"

She made a sound, part sob, part inhalation, a wounded sound.

"Afterward he had all pictures of her destroyed. We were forbidden to speak her name. We bore her disgrace like a brand from a hot iron that could never heal. But although I burn for her I still love my sister. Because I know I would have done what Miriam did."

I couldn't say anything. But my heart was jumping again.

"I am no beauty. My sister—even when she is fourteen, the year we are coming to Itzá Maya, men of means stare, they fall in love, they would have paid anything to possess Miriam. How can I describe her? A small face, almost catlike, with very large eyes. Of course her body was perfect. And she had a quality that was more than virginal, she glowed with paleness, the purity of a young saint. She was shy but not backward, she seemed to have been born with a sense of calm, the conviction all of us seek that we are worthy. Thoughtful, pious, a treasure; someone who could never offend. Yet she compromised the prestige of Don Santiago. And without a qualm he had her killed." She drew a long, shuddering breath. "There are . . . evils in this wurl no one can hope to understand."

"Veronica, what did Miriam *do*?"

Her smile was one of the saddest I've ever seen.

"She had the bad fortune to fall in love."

With a guest at the hotel?"

Veronica nodded. But for a few moments she seemed

so despondent I didn't think she was going to continue. Then she lifted her head.

"He was a guest. His name was Gerard. That is all I ever know about him, his name, his age. Sixteen, one year older than Miriam when . . . they come in the spring to Itzá Maya, just before the rainy season, in the month of another eclipse."

"Sixteen? And Miriam had a crush on him?"

" 'Crush'? If you want to say it like that, okay. And Juliet's feelings for Romeo, a passing fancy, you think? *No.* She was not a stupid flirty girl. Her feelings were deep and true. His, the same. I know they could not help themselves. It was their fate."

"Was your uncle . . . jealous of that boy? Was it one of those things?"

"Oh, no, it was not sexual jealousy. Nothing as simple as that. And I am certain Gerard was not the lover of the woman with whom he lived, his . . . guardian. She was the Marquise de Rochaude—a strange, beautiful woman, very rich, and a widow. I think they were not lovers because, although she was affectionate with Gerard, it was like the affection one has for a pet, something sleek and gorgeous but kept on a leash so that it cannot stray. She and Don Santiago appeared to be old friends. It is possible that she had traveled to Cobían many times in the past. I do not know her age. But I heard her speak in the Itzá tongue when they thought no one was listening. They argued. I had never heard anyone speak sharply to my uncle. I was amazed. He was firm with her. He would be accommodating, he said, within reason, but she could not have everything she demanded. I didn't know at the time what they were arguing about. Soon it became clear.

"The Marquise, like so many guests of the Itzá Maya, was fascinated with Miriam. She could not take her eyes off my sister. They were hungry eyes. I said that she was strange. Uninterested in the manliness of her young traveling companion, but Miriam . . . enflamed her. She gave my sister gifts—small gifts at first, a silk mantilla, a ring with semiprecious stones. She invited Miriam to dinner. It was just the three of them, for appearance's sake, no doubt. But that was her big mistake. Once Miriam and Gerard had spent an hour together, there was no keeping them apart. *Ay Dios*. Sixteen, fifteen . . . two young virgins. But not for long, such was their passion for each other."

"Did Miriam tell you?"

"She didn't have to. We shared a room. The look in her eyes, dazed from lovemaking, a crumpled handkerchief with a little blood on it, Miriam's blood . . . I knew. I was scared for her, scared of that woman. 'You better not see him again,' I said. Miriam just look at me, with love and pity. No fear. 'I have to,' she said."

Veronica was quiet, slumped, barely breathing until the tears began running down her cheeks. I was jittery and cold from sitting on the stone bench. I got up and thought I saw, about a hundred feet away, someone watching us from behind a screen of lianas and orchids cascading from the thick limbs of a mahogany tree. He was barely visible by the torchlight of a tall brazier on the path. On the short side, portly. I saw a glint of light that could have been reflected from one of the lenses of his glasses. I looked away, blinking, and back again, but this time I didn't see anyone there. There were no footsteps on the flagged path. Little to hear except for the metallic background noise of tree frogs. Even the spider and howler monkeys were silent in their cages.

"*Did* she see him again?"

"They ran away together. I doan know how Gerard persuade my sister to accompany him. I think he was desperate himself. Afraid of what the Marquise would do to him, once she knew of their affair. But she did nothing. She was not able to. She died, a few hours following the culmination of the eclipse. She died in a convulsion that snapped the joints of her bones, a terrible thing. I have not forgotten her screams, and her curses.

"Don Santiago closed the hotel immediately. He sent

the other guests away. He called for my mother, and spoke to her. She never told me what he said, once she was able to speak at all. But she was in shock. She prayed for three days at the Basilica Iluminada. By then . . . their clothing had been discovered next to the cenote at Río Pasión. A popular place for lovers. In the past the cenote was often used for sacrifices. The water is deep there. But their naked bodies, joined at the wrists by a heavy ceremonial chain of gold, had risen to the surface."

"They committed suicide?"

"Never! They were murdered. Probably they were forced to take poison. Even today, if their bodies were removed from the unmarked crypts where they lit, it could be proven by scientific analysis. Once they were dead, or dying, they were thrown into the cenote. The chain that bound them together was very old, made of links fashioned in the likeness of the harpy eagle. I had seen it before, among the ancient treasures in the vault of the hotel. It belonged to Don Santiago. The chain joining their wrists on their journey through Eternity was his signature, acknowledgment of retribution for the wrong done to him by Miriam."

"I still don't get it, Veronica. Why did the Marquise die? What happened to her?"

"Her death throes began with the passing of the eclipse. That is all I can tell you. And I believe Gerard was a virgin when he came here. No way to prove that, of course. But once he and Miriam became lovers, he was no longer of value to the Marquise. And perhaps by the time she learned of his . . . disloyalty, it was too late for her to find another virgin to take his place."

"What's this?" Daddy said. "Girl talk?"

Neither of us had heard him coming. Veronica's head jerked up and around. He looked from her face to mine, smiling quizically, then walked closer and bent to kiss my forehead.

"Hi, Daddy."

"You're cold. Don't you think you should come in?"

"I . . . guess so. Where've you been?"

"Veronica didn't tell you? Francisco and I had a chess game going. Oh, I was able to get through to Usumucinta tonight on the missionary band. Had a nice chat with Reg and Cora Randall. Everything's set for Saturday."

"That's good." I said vaguely. He smelled like cigar smoke. I knew Daddy never smoked, so it must have been one of Francisco's cigars. The lingering strong odor made me feel queasy, and I was having a hard time pulling myself back from the grip of Veronica's lurid story. My first thoughts were that it was totally unbelievable, but there was no denying *she* believed everything she'd told me. How old had Veronica been at the time? Ten, eleven years old? Maybe over the years the facts of her sister's tragic death had become mixed up with a lot of superstition. I didn't think she was just putting me on, passing some boring time by finding out how gullible I was.

Daddy held out a hand and I took it; he pulled me to my feet.

"How about a couple of sets of tennis?" he asked me. "One of the courts was available when I came by them."

"Sure." He hadn't wanted to play me for a long time. On the court I carried Daddy as much as I could, but it was male pride or something. This would be like old times. I put an arm around him.

Veronica got up slowly. "I should go back to the hotel, then. To see if Francisco needs me."

"Can we go to town in the morning?" I asked.

"It will depend on your father's wishes," Veronica said formally, looking at him.

"We'll make tomorrow's plans tomorrow," he said vaguely.

Veronica nodded, lowered her eyes, picked up her Uzi, and walked quickly toward the hotel.

Daddy and I headed for our bungalow. He seemed more relaxed to me than he had for several days. And I was happy; tennis always had been the best therapy for whatever was wrong with me emotionally.

"What were you two talking about?" he asked.

"Oh—Veronica was in some kind of mood. I think she must be one of those people who are affected by the full moon, you know? I mean, she seemed really fatalistic tonight, neurotic, whatever. But I can't blame her, she's had such an unhappy life. Her father died before she got to know him very well, and her husband was killed. Her sister died too, it was like some sort of bizarre suicide pact. Veronica blames her death on their great-uncle, and there's a lot of other totally spooky stuff she—"

"Spooky stuff?"

"Well, she's Maya as well as Catholic. How superstitious can you get?" I shrugged. "What she was telling me sounded at least half made up. There was this Marquise who came to the hotel years ago, with a boy who wasn't her son—you really want to hear about it?"

Daddy shook his head and smiled. "No, thanks. What did you do with the tennis gear, honey?"

We ran up the steps together and went inside the bungalow. I missed the white message envelope lying on the floor inside the screen. Daddy paused to pick it up. I went into my bedroom and pulled the duffel with our rackets and balls out of the wardrobe, put on a sweater and headband. I felt, for the first time in a while, warm and secure. I didn't want to think about the last hour I'd spent with Veronica; her warning. So I didn't think about it, but still it stayed with me, keeping me a little off balance and annoyed, like a pesky mosquito buzzing around.

When I went out to the living room of the bungalow Daddy was staring at the white message card with an expression I'd never seen before.

"Daddy?"

He looked at me slowly, but not as if he recognized me. His face was stiff with outrage. I don't think he was breathing. Then his chest moved, a surge as if he were packing in air, and he trembled, once.

"What is that? Did something happen to—let me see!"

"No. It's—okay. There's nothing—I don't want you to read this." He crushed the card in his fist. "Damn fool—someone must have the idea I'm the merry widower."

"Why can't I see it? What does it say?"

He breathed out slowly, still trying to control himself. "Sorry, honey. One of the female guests in the hotel thought I might be in the mood for a—a specific invitation to join her tonight."

"Specific? You mean—"

"I'm sure you get the point."

"Why, *Daddy*. Well—it's nothing to get insulted about, you're—you're a very good-looking man."

"Thanks. But it *is* something to get insulted about, the way she put it."

"And you're not going to let me read her note," I teased him. "What's her name? Now I'm curious."

"No name. Just an initial. And her room number, of course." He shook his head as if he needed to clear it, and smiled wryly.

"Probably won't be the last time," I said. "Better get used to it."

"I guess I'm a little old-fashioned. If the day ever comes . . ."

This time when he shook his head, he looked so sad I

could've cried for him, but it wasn't something either of us needed just then.

"Hey, hurry and change before that court's gone."

"Oh—sure. Be with you in a minute, Sharissa." He went into his bedroom and closed the door. I went outside and practiced some strokes on the walk, waiting for him.

Daddy didn't have much to say as we walked toward the bright lights of the tennis courts. I decided to take the risk and talk about something that was going to nag me anyway, now that the subject had been half-raised.

"Dad—it's probably too soon, but I know, as much as we both miss Mom, that one of these days—you'll want to get married again."

He sighed. "I haven't even thought about it."

"But it's perfectly natural to want—I'm going to college in the fall, and then—well, we each have our own lives to live, in spite of everything. What I mean to say is, you shouldn't consider not marrying again just because you have the idea I wouldn't approve. Dad, I want you to be *happy*. That's what I want more than anything."

He seemed to stumble on the path, then just stopped and looked at me. Such a helpless, devastated look that I wanted to take his face in my hands and kiss him. At that moment I understood perfectly the impulsive mystery woman who'd invited him to her room tonight. The truth was, I'd had some pretty confused feelings about Dad for a while. The school psychologist I'd talked to said it was normal, under the circumstances. My protective, not sexual, instincts were taking over. So she said. But there on the path in the tropical garden in a place far away from what I had known all my life as home I had the sweet scary feeling that it would be so easy, if I wanted, to go to Daddy while he slept tonight, and lie down beside him and hold him in my arms, and—

Scary; then I flushed and felt sick and ashamed of myself. I turned and ran the rest of the way to the tennis courts. I was snapping balls against the backstop hard enough to hurt my elbow by the time Daddy got there.

It would have been insulting to play him left-handed, but his game was in poor shape and he seemed to be just going through the motions anyway, smiling gamely at me when he missed an easy one. I wondered if he was thinking of the woman in the hotel, waiting hopefully for him. What was she like? I tried to recall some of the women I'd seen around the Itzá Maya, none of them young, a few working hard to try to disguise the fact. Except for Veronica and a couple of the women on the staff, nobody even close to my age was staying there.

I nearly turned Daddy inside out with a topspin backhand drive, and he sprawled against the net, losing his grip on his racket.

"Sorry!" I called.

He got up slowly, grimacing. His left knee was scraped. "Now that . . . was a dirty trick to play on your old man."

"You know how I am. Can't afford to lose my competitive edge."

"I'm feeling a little run down. Not that I'm making an excuse, but—"

I leaned over the net and kissed his moist cheek. "Can we get something to eat? I tossed lunch and missed dinner, and I feel kind of hollow."

"You go ahead. I'll take a shower, if they've got the hot water going, and relax with a book."

"Remember, you promised you're gonna learn some Spanish."

"First thing tomorrow, I'll get started."

I gave him a doubtful look and put our rackets away. Daddy carried the gear back to our bungalow. I watched him walking down the stepped path of the garden. The fathers of most of my friends, some of them only in their late thirties, were already in the going-to-pot stage, but Dad would never let it happen to him. He had too much pride in himself. He looked terrific, in spite of everything that had happened in the past eight months . . . that twinge returned, not half as powerful as what I'd felt an hour ago in the garden, not nearly what it had been like with Bobby those couple of times when I was sure I was going to forget all about good old-fashioned integrity and common sense; still, it was obvious enough to upset me. The little-girl-crush-on-her-father feeling, together with an overwhelming sense of loneliness and loss. Just the two of us left—and God forgive me for even thinking about my father in that way.

As I watched him out of sight I had the disturbing feeling that someone was watching *me*, staring a hole in my back. I turned and looked toward the windows and balconies facing the courts enclosure. No one else was playing now, and I was alone with the bugs swarming at the level of the brilliant lights.

When I walked through the gate in the chainlink fence the court lights and, closer to the hotel, the poolside lights, began to go out, leaving a brief afterglow, a light-storm floating in front of my eyes. Off to one side of the afterglow cloud I noticed someone, a man, leaning against the railing of a balcony on the third and top floor of the Itzá Maya. The underwater lights of the pool were still on, and the glow from the slightly breeze-roughened surface of the water was reflected against the white stucco side wall of the hotel. The man on the balcony stood out against the whiteness in his Maya-print shirt. For a second or two I wondered if, or where, I'd seen him before. He wore glasses, I could tell that much, and seemed to have a beard, but it was such a light color it was hard to be sure. I couldn't read the shape of his head because of the dark-colored baseball cap he had on.

I walked toward the hotel, glanced up again. He was about a hundred yards away, and now he had turned toward me, holding something bulky up to his face; probably a camera with a long lens attachment. Taking my picture? I didn't know what results he would get, although even with the court lights off behind me the moon was high and bright enough to give definition to the grounds. I cast a faint shadow.

I guess I didn't want my picture taken without knowing

who he was. I'd been having a problem with the little toe on my right foot, a rubbing that might turn into a blister. I stopped to take my sock off and retie the shoe, and when I started walking again he wasn't on his balcony anymore.

There were a lot of people in the Itzá Maya's open-air lobby, mostly men; everybody wore name tags. A gathering of some sort seemed to be breaking up. I recognized a few faces from the cafeteria at Kan Petén. And it wasn't hard to spot Glen Hazen. All that red hair, and at six-six a head taller than the other men milling around the lobby. He was on the telephone opposite the reception desk, his back to me. I thought about going over to say hello, but I was still embarrassed by what had taken place at lunch, so I went the other way, to the coffee shop that was still open. The hamburgers there were okay, and I had one with a Coke.

"Thought I noticed you out there in the lobby," Glen Hazen said.

I looked up. He was wearing a name tag with the legend PETEXBATUN REGIONAL ARCHEOLOGICAL PROJECT.

"Hi," I said.

"Hi. Okay if I sit down for a few minutes? Maybe I've got time for a burger." He checked his watch. "Drinks at ten-thirty, some VIPs from the National Endowment of the Humanities. Our project sugar daddies."

"What's going on?" I asked him.

"Convention. Mostly it's an excuse to get together with our Guatemalan colleagues, some of the diplomatic people, and the local bureaucrats who suffer our presence here. Unfortunately, we have to be away from camp a few days. Hope the rebels don't raid us and make off with our generators while we're gone. Not that the government troops don't do their share of thieving. It can be hard to tell who the bad guys are in Guatemala, and even the guards we pay aren't all that reliable."

"I guess my dad was right. You do live dangerously down here."

Glen ordered what I was having, and helped himself to a couple of my french fries, which I wasn't eating anyway. Not on a touchy stomach.

"Yeah, I admit his concern is well placed. It's just that we get used to it. There's a big Guatemalan army base near us, at Las Pozas, and the rebels hit them all the time. We've heard firefights but haven't seen any, and this is my third year at our dig. I guess we don't get on the wrong side of any factions. Also Dos Pilas is probably the most significant dig, I mean one that has a real theoretical edge, in the last fifty years of MesoAmerican studies. Am I boring you? Most people your age are bored by archeology. How old are you, anyway?"

"I'll be eighteen in June. I never knew much about archeology, but I'm not bored. What do you mean by a 'theoretical edge'?"

"Oh, well, see, it has to do with the central cultural mystery: what happened, and where did they go? Societies rise and fall, of course, but the Maya society was at least a thousand years old, the population numbered in the hundreds of thousands, and within a few decades it simply dissolved. The Spanish missionaries left us with almost nothing in Maya literature—three or four books—and the monumental carvings which they didn't know about or couldn't destroy. Dos Pilas is rich in carvings as well as walls and defensive systems. So we believe the definitive theory of what went wrong, environmentally, will come from our discoveries."

"Siege warfare equals starvation, isn't that what you were telling me today?"

He nodded, looking at me in approval, and I had to smile.

"I'm not an airhead. I was listening."

Glen nodded again.

"The significance, of course, goes beyond political greed. The causal order of the collapse of societies has been the same throughout history. Short-term strategies and goals. Everybody's interested in today, not tomorrow—here in El Petén, in the Amazon, Borneo, Madagascar, there's a classic ecological disaster, and last but not least, the U.S. We're besieged by population problems in many areas, and societies are notorious for ignoring the environment in favor of short-term, wealth-now, self-destructive policies. Let the next generation worry about the consequences. With this sort of political foundation, castles will crumble and kingdoms will fall. Probably what we're seeing in the world today is a mirror image of the Maya dissolution; and also a last-chance scenario."

He turned in his chair, both ways. "Hey, what happened to that hamburger?"

"You just ordered it five minutes ago." My expression must have been glum. When he looked at me again he seemed startled.

"Didn't mean to carry on that way. You okay?"

"Sure. Want the rest of these french fries?"

"Thanks." Glen waved to a couple who had come into the coffee shop and were looking for a vacant table. I was glad they didn't come over. "Tom and Rita Hawkins. University of Texas. Our big rivals down this way. Along with Tulane. Rita's one of the best glyph readers in the world. A very few have the gift. It's enough to make you believe in reincarnation."

"Speaking of reincarnation—" Veronica crossed my mind then, and a second later I shuddered; I was wearing a tennis sweater but they kept the temperature way too cold in the coffee shop. Glen was smiling at me, waiting. I smiled back and shrugged. "Oh, nothing. How long have you known Veronica?"

"Met her two years ago. A few months after her husband was killed. Did you know about that?" I nodded. "Then she came to Nashville for a few weeks to have some reconstructive plastic surgery done at the University Hospital. Pete Clausen, one of the best in the south, did the work. I recommended him to 'Nica. While she was recuperating, we went out a few times. So what's the association? Veronica and reincarnation?"

"Well—maybe I don't want to say anything if you two are, uh, real tight."

"I'm not sleeping with her. I don't think she can handle a serious relationship right now. You've got me curious."

"It's just that—something really upset her tonight. She was rambling on about—not reincarnation, but astrology and Maya sacrifice and eclipse cycles, and she said I was in danger, being here before an eclipse. Because I'm young and I'm a—oops."

"A what?"

I looked down, then looked him in the eye.

"Virgin."

Glen didn't smirk or have a witty comeback. He just looked puzzled.

"That's—a little out of character, for 'Nica. I mean, she doesn't talk all that much, about anything."

"Did she ever mention a sister to you?"

"Didn't know she had one. I only know Benito, but they aren't blood kin. He's the son of her mother's second husband."

I told him the story Veronica had told me. I must have told it pretty well. His hamburger came, but he didn't touch it or take his eyes off me.

"So her uncle Santiago had both kids thrown into a cenote, after—what was it supposedly happened to the Marquise?"

"She died. A horrible death. Veronica's uncle, she says, closed the hotel immediately."

"Died of what? A stroke, in a fit of rage? Because the boy—who wasn't her son—ran off with Miriam?"

"Convulsions, not a stroke."

"If the old man closed the hotel, maybe she had something catchable. Cholera, yellow fever, who knows."

"You think that's it? And it didn't have anything to do with—"

"With the moon and star-crossed lovers? What do *you* think?"

"Star-crossed *virgin* lovers," I said. Then I laughed. And shuddered again.

Glen decided to eat. Between mouthfuls he said, "Well, I've always found Veronica to be level-headed. More than a little enigmatic, but not neurotic."

"I don't think she was putting on an act. She really believes all that stuff. She was—scary."

He frowned slightly. "Where is she now?"

"I don't know," I said. "Doesn't Veronica live at the hotel?"

"Close by. Most of the help here live on the street where that half-finished time-share condo is moldering away. Maybe I'll run by tonight after the cocktail, see how she is."

"Are you worried about her?"

"No. Nothing like that. I'll just say hello."

"When are you going back to—what's it called?"

"Dos Pilas. Day after tomorrow."

I was glad he wasn't leaving right away. "Are you in the hotel?"

"Can't afford the Itzá Maya on our grant. We're thirty miles from town, on the northwest shore of the lake—the part without crocodiles. It's called the Parador Libertad. The restaurant's decent, if you're not doing anything for lunch tomorrow? Your dad doesn't want you in a helicopter, but maybe he wouldn't object to a boat ride or a tour of the Biotopo."

"Dad's mellowed out. He really has. I'd love to."

"Terrific! I'll pick you up about eleven-thirty in the minibus." He looked at his watch and abandoned his hamburger. "Got to run. I'm assigned to Congresswoman

Delaney tonight, from the great state of I-forget-where. She thinks the way you solve questions of human rights abuse is to get in the faces of certain Guatemalan government officials and talk to them as if they were not particularly bright housepets."

"Good luck," I said, wishing he'd invite me to go along. All I had to look forward to was some sleepless hours and an Anne Rice horror novel I didn't want to read right now—not after Veronica and the grim spooky spell she had cast that was still making me uneasy.

The lobby was less crowded when I left the coffee shop. On the mezzanine of the hotel there was a shimmer of cymbals and a woman with a husky voice was singing a sad love song in the terrace lounge. On my way outside I ran into Francisco Colon coming out of his office. He looked preoccupied, but he smiled at me.

"Good evening, Miss Walker."

"Who won?" I asked him.

He glanced down at a sheaf of faxes in his hands, then over his shoulder, as if waiting for someone, then back at me.

"Who won—?"

"The chess game."

Francisco shook his head, looking blank. "I don't play—" He looked back again; a stocky woman in a pin-striped gray suit had come out of the office. She was an assistant manager. He said something to her so fast I couldn't catch any of it, then remembered me standing there, handed the faxes to the woman, stared at me for a few moments as if he dimly remembered I had spoken.

Then he brightened. "Not very good chess," he said. "If you'll excuse me—we are so busy tonight—"

I left the hotel, wondering about the look he'd given me. He had started to say, "I don't play chess." I was sure of that. Then he changed it, as if he knew he ought to. I didn't think it was all that important, but it bothered me a little—that Daddy had said he was playing chess with the man, when he wasn't. I couldn't think of any reason why he'd make up a lie to explain where he'd been. Maybe he had visited a woman after all, and she had sent him a pornographic love note. Which would account perfectly for the expression on his face . . .

There was a security guard outside our bungalow, not one I remembered seeing before. He nodded and smiled at me. I went up the steps and inside.

"I'm back."

Daddy didn't answer. For some reason I'd had the feeling he wasn't going to be there. His Bible was open on the seat of a rattan chair in the living room. I looked around, but he hadn't left me a note. I went outside and called to the security guard from the porch: "Have you seen my father?" He smiled as if he didn't understand my Spanish. I repeated it. *"¿Has visto mi padre?"* This time he shook his head.

Nothing to do but wash my hair and watch satellite TV. The water was lukewarm and my hairdryer wasn't doing well on the converted voltage. In a few days I wouldn't be able to use a hairdryer at all. I hoped the Randalls would be okay; walking with the Spirit was one thing, but I'd met missionaries who were so churchy you couldn't tell a joke around them, or wear a Guns 'n Roses T-shirt. The hotel's dish brought in stations from Denver and Los Angeles, ESPN and HBO. Ice hockey and western movies. I turned the set off, picked up Daddy's Bible and glanced at the chapters he had been reading. Like most of the pages in his Bible, they were marked up, passages underscored with different colors of Hi-Liter. I couldn't remember a day when I hadn't seen him take advantage of a few minutes to sit down and read, to meditate.

"Does a spring send forth fresh water and bitter from the same opening? Can a fig tree, my brethren, bear olives, or a grapevine bear figs?" I wondered what was on his mind tonight, what solace he was looking for; but I was miffed that he'd suddenly taken off again without telling me.

It rained for a while. Dad came back about midnight. I was finishing a letter to Grammer and Grampa. He looked dead-tired, hollow-eyed, but he smiled.

"Still up?"

"Not sleepy. I wish you'd let me know when—"

"Oh—I went to church."

"Catholic church? That's all there is here except for the Charismatics, and I know how you feel about them."

"Didn't matter. I just—sat there for a while. The candles, shadows, incense, the Stations of the Cross, voices murmuring everywhere, it was—exalted, in a way I couldn't explain. I took a taxi into town. I mean to say something to you, but you were with that red-haired archeologist in the coffee shop, so I—what was his name again?"

"Glen Hazen. It wasn't a date, I just ran into him. He invited me to lunch tomorrow, at a place called the Parador Libertad. If it's okay."

"I don't know, Sharissa. Look, I don't want you to feel suffocated here, but there was an incident outside of Cobían tonight, government troops blockading the road—"

"Not again," I said dismally. He watched me for a few moments, sympathetically I thought, or maybe he was just too tired to argue. He sighed and nodded.

"If you've already accepted, then I suppose—but not just the two of you, I want Francisco to send somebody along. And you're to be back before dark."

"*Not* Veronica, please. Because it *is* a date, and I think Veronica and Glen used to have something going, although he didn't want to tell me."

"Okay."

"Thanks, Dad." I got up from the writing desk to hug him. He took his hands from the pockets of his safari jacket and held me. He bit his lip suddenly. "What's the matter?" I said.

"Want to hear something dumb?" He showed me his right hand, which looked swollen across the knuckles. He couldn't flex it very well. "I slipped in the shower, whacked myself against one of the handles."

"Put ice on it," I said authoritatively. I'd had more than my share of sports injuries, between tennis and volleyball. "Twenty minutes on, twenty minutes off. That'll take the swelling down. But you might have broken one of your knuckles."

"No, I don't think so. I mean, I know what that feels like, I did break a knuckle once, on the other hand. Ice is a good idea. And a couple of those painkillers I bought this morning." He glanced at the photos I'd been sorting through to send home. "Give the folks my best," he said.

"I'll wrap some ice in a towel for you."

"Thanks, baby."

He went into his room to lie down. When I had chipped enough ice out of the small trays to give him some relief I found him stretched out on top of the bed, eyes closed, already asleep. He trembled when I put the wrapping of ice on his sore hand; there were tremors in his eyelids, too. I sat beside him and held his other hand. He muttered something. There were the usual rustlings of palm rats in the thick mat of the pitched roof overhead, sounds that had kept me awake most of the first two nights we spent at the Itzá Maya. But the rats were shy and harmless. After a while his shallow breathing became deep and slow. I kissed his hand and cheek and went to my own room, and said my prayers there. Prayers for my mother and for Bob, that I always hoped they would hear. Then one for Daddy—I prayed that his suffering would end, and he would find peace for his mind and soul in Usumucinta.

I didn't have much peace myself—at least while I was sleeping. My dreams were cluttered and strange, sometimes terrible.

I also dreamed that I was with Bobby, and we were making love in the family room of my house. Not all the way, but close. All the lights were on. I knew Mom and Dad were in the kitchen, talking. They didn't seem to realize what was going on, or did they? But I didn't want Bobby to stop what he was doing. That was the good part of the dream. Holding Bobby again, kissing him. Between my legs he felt like a warm plum. Pushing, pushing, but I was wearing underpants and it wouldn't go in. His heartbeat was drumlike, powerful. His pain, his ecstasy, had me in a frenzy of my own. Then he stopped, all of a sudden. There was no more family room, comfortable couch, it was all dark and unfamiliar, a starlit landscape of ruins. We were lying naked on hard ground. In place of his heartbeat I heard the howler monkey gasping, like the last breaths of a dying man.

I held Bob in my arms, my thighs were trembling from the effort, I knew he was dead. His face was composed, like the faces of tree stones, but the back of his head was a crushed egg. I woke up tingling, as if I'd been playing with electricity in a lab experiment. Hearing voices. Mom and Dad, like it had always been, talking in the kitchen late at night. I heard my name, but I didn't understand what they were saying about me. When I moved my legs my underpants were wet and clinging along the labia. I thought I'd peed a little while I was asleep, like sometimes happened when I was three years old. But this was a different wetness, and I felt turned on, not disgusted with myself. When I touched with my fingers where I'd imagined Bobby's plum had been, it was slick as bath oil and I twitched all over. I pulled my pants down below my knees with one hand, then rubbed lightly the flesh-pea between my index finger and thumb, and quicker and harder with my thighs open wide and the next thing I knew it was like having a heart attack and going over a waterfall at the same time. Or a series of waterfalls. I was swamped by the sensation, breathless but safe from drowning. And I thought, *Shouldn't have. But I don't care.*

As I lay there, the voices continued in conversation, and I thought I recognized the language: Mayan, different from Spanish, filled with explosive *k*'s and *ch* sounds. I didn't recognize the speakers. Didn't matter. My heartbeat was almost back to normal, but my belly burned, my breasts were hot around the nipples. It was a lot of sensation to have to sort out, and cope with. When I could move I took my pants off and dried myself between the legs with them, then got up to look for a clean pair to put on.

The louvered door to my room was open an inch. I looked out and saw Dad on the daybed with his back to me, and Francisco Colon in one of the wicker chairs, leaning forward, hands on his knees, frowning, speaking in Mayan. My father listening, then answering, and I thought, what is this, the middle of the night, he's having a language lesson?

"Daddy?" I said, behind the door.

He turned, startled. "Sharissa? Did we wake you up?" Francisco rose from his chair.

"No. It's all right. What're you—"

"Learning to ask directions. I thought it might come in handy. Sorry if we were bothering you."

"I should go," Francisco said.

"I'll walk out with you. Can I get you something, Sharissa? A drink of water?"

"No, thanks. I'm going back to bed." I was feeling light-headed, disoriented, and I thought, *Wow, if that's what an orgasm does to you—*

Thirty seconds later I was huddled under the sheet, shivering, biting my lip, so sad and depressed I was almost choking. Thinking about Daddy asking directions in Mayan, only it hadn't sounded like a question, more of a command. But I didn't know the language, so how could I tell? I didn't know a lot of things. I only knew I was in love with a dead boy and afraid I would never never get over him.

That was my big problem: in grieving for Bobby I was really feeling sorry for myself. Concentrating on the self made me a poor excuse for a Christian. I was denying the Spirit, shutting Jesus out of my life, which was not going to get any better without Him.

I slept better than I had in weeks, woke up early and went jogging. At breakfast I asked Daddy about his language lesson. He smiled and said Francisco was trying to teach him a few words of the Kekchi Indian dialect, one of thirty-five Mayan languages. The mission we were assigned to ministered to a large Kekchi population.

Mr. Colon was a busy man, as he had said, and his hotel was full, but he seemed to have a lot of time to be with Dad. In fact, he treated both of us like royalty, providing security on and off the hotel grounds. I hadn't given much thought to these arrangements, but I knew that all the weeks we'd spent away from home had to be costing Dad a lot of money. Which was something he'd always been cautious about. Half of the insurance money had gone into a trust fund for me. Ten percent of the remainder he'd given to the church, which was not paying any of our expenses to and from Usumucinta.

"We're a long way from being broke, honey," he explained when I sounded worried about it. "I took a little money out of the business when I sold to Bisco, and there's the savings we had, some equity in the house. With conservative investments, inflation way down, I—we could live for a long time just on the income."

"What are you going to do, Dad?"

"Do?" He looked a little startled.

"Somehow I don't see you spending the rest of your life as a missionary."

"Oh—you mean, what am I going to do with myself after—?" He looked away from me. From where we sat on the terrace the moon was still visible but dissolving like a wafer in the pale blue of the brightening sky. "Haven't got that far yet in my thinking. I have faith that—something will come along."

Francisco Colon had come up with two men in a red Jeep to keep Glen and me company. At least they weren't riding with us. I didn't know what kind of guns they had with them, and didn't want to know. Both men wore guayaberas and dark glasses and looked, I guess, businesslike. In a way I missed Veronica.

"Didn't have time to go by and see her," Glen explained as we drove around the south shore of the lake on our way to the Parador Liberdad. The red Jeep stayed about a hundred feet behind us. The road was narrow but paved, and there was more traffic than yesterday: it was a market day in Cobían. Glen looked back at the two men riding shotgun for us. He called them Heckle and Jeckel.

"Your father must be a man of considerable influence. Is he in politics?"

"No."

Glen smiled. "Then you have to be a movie star. Have I seen any of your pictures?"

"Oh, come on. I told you—he just worries about me."

"I wish I could tell you who the bad guys are down here, but I'm not sure myself. We've lost cameras and a couple of wallets, but I've never heard of anyone being kidnapped, and fortunately they don't hunt archeologists for pleasure or profit. It wouldn't be hard. This time of year I think we outnumber the locals in the Petexbatun." He yawned. "Sorry. Stayed up to three o'clock this morning."

"With that congresswoman?" He nodded. "What's she like?"

"Well—" he said, guardedly.

"Did she put a move on you?"

"You're talking about a pillar of our democratic society. Yes, she did."

"But you—"

"Fast on my feet when I need to be."

"What other sports do you play?"

He smiled and leaned on his horn to discourage a minibus that was trying to edge onto the pavement ahead. The Jeep pulled closer behind us.

"You know something, I really like you. Too bad I'm old enough to be—"

"My older brother. I'll be eighteen in June. And I'm going to Vanderbilt next fall."

"Good choice. Where're you spending the next few months?"

I told him. He said, "Usumucinta's maybe seven minutes by helicopter from Dos Pilas—"

"You're kidding!"

"And a bad day's drive on roads that disappear come May. I'll figure something out, since we don't have a helicopter on a regular basis."

"You mean you'll come and see me? How old are you, brother?"

"Twenty-nine last Thursday."

"I guess the mustache makes you seem older."

Glen was easy to talk to, to kid around with, and not pretentious for someone who had already published a book while he was still a graduate student of anthropology, which apparently had a lot to do with archeology. I couldn't be sure, because Glen talked so fast about a lot of subjects—ethnohistory, zoology, university politics (which he claimed was a branch of zoology), skydiving—that I wasn't able to ask a lot of questions. Usually I was laughing. He'd been born in Princeton, New Jersey, where his father was an Episcopalian minister ("I come from a long line of De-Caf Catholics," Glen said) and his mother taught prep school mathematics. He admitted that he was not much of a teacher himself.

"Grubbing away in old tombs with a two-by-four holding up the ceiling may seem like a strange way to spend your life," he said while we were having lunch. "But I never liked school. Who was it said, 'Brilliance in the young is most easily cured by a dose of compulsory education'? Maybe I did. Anyway, I was lucky enough to be born with a mind that operates intuitively and rejects the formulaic, and I managed to fall in with teachers who had the patience or the foresight to indulge me. Like the Chair of my department at Vandy. Too few of those around. The ranks of college professors should be thinned every so often, like a herd of deer too large for the food supply."

The restaurant at the Parador was built out over a cove of the lake; it felt like being in a large treehouse, with the forest of the biotopo just behind the lodge building. Glen knew the menu by heart. He said the venison was safe but if I was feeling adventurous I should try a dish of *tepezcuintele*. After I made him admit that *tepezcuintele* was a species of jungle rat, I had the venison.

The walls of the restaurant were slabs of untreated mahogany, and there were a couple of uncaged toucans in the rafters. We were at a table away from the toucans and close to the water. There was a swimming beach below the campground next to the Parador, and a boat dock.

Heckle and Jeckel sat at a table near the entrance. Each of them had a beer and one of them read a newspaper. They didn't seem to be paying attention to us, and after a while I forgot about them.

Glen showed me dozens of pictures of Dos Pilas. "We're just getting started, actually. Already we have evidence that Dos Pilas was to Central America, in terms of territorial expansion, what Britain was to the world in the nineteenth century. But so much of it is still completely covered by forest it'll be years before we have a restored site to compare with—"

"Glen? Hi." It was an urgent-sounding greeting. We both looked up. I recognized the woman from the coffee shop of the Itzá Maya, an archeologist from Texas. Her hair was short and going gray and she wore a paisley bandana around her neck. Glen introduced us, but she barely glanced at me.

"Guess you've heard the news," Rita Hawkins said. Her lips were thin anyway, but she was pressing them together so tightly from tension they disappeared. Glen shook his head warily. Rita took a deep breath. "Dr. Lagerfeld was killed last night. In his field office at Kan."

"Good Lord." They stared at each other for a few seconds. "Does anyone know—"

"It must have been terrorists. His office was torn apart, as if they were looking for something to sell."

"How—"

"He was struck in the back of the head with a machete. Poor man. Totally helpless in his wheelchair, a wanton act of murder and nothing more."

I knew who it was then—the man from Sweden I'd talked to in the cafeteria at Kan Petén, the one who was so sure I had a sister.

Rita said, "I'm trying to locate as many of us as I can. We're getting together at Kan at four o'clock. I mean, I'm sick about Nils, but this could be the start of something we've been hoping would never happen. And the government troops won't be of much use to us, they already have their hands full in the Petexbatun."

"I'll see you there," Glen promised.

Rita gave me a wan smile and hustled out of the restaurant past Heckle and Jeckel, who didn't look at her. One of them was still reading his newspaper, and the other was dealing out cards for a single-handed game. Each time he laid one down, with a little flourish, sunlight glittered on what looked like a gold Rolex wristwatch.

Neither of us wanted any more of our lunch. Glen clenched his hands and said, "I don't understand it. Maybe if he'd tried to resist them—but we all know better than to do something stupid like that. There's never been a killing like this down here. What a loss. Nils was one of the top men in our field."

I thought of the friendly man in the wheelchair, how he'd looked me over in the cafeteria with his quizzical smile—*in the back of the head with a machete.* And for no reason an image of Bobby came into my mind: struck down from behind, *in the back of the head with a rock.* And I felt sick inside, hating all cowards and murderers who destroyed good people for no reason.

Glen said, "You okay?"

"I'm sorry."

"I know. Let's get out of here, go for a walk."

I told Glen a lot about myself that afternoon, as we wandered along the paths of the nature preserve near the Parador. It was a comfort to me; and he could listen as well as he could talk. I liked looking at him too, that shock of red hair and the reddish-brown mustache he'd probably have been better off without; but I suppose he wanted to look more mature. After a while it was time for Glen to put his arm around me, and he did. I just leaned against him, feeling secure for a change and almost happy, no longer needing to say anything. Before I knew it the afternoon was half gone and he drove me back to the hotel.

"I don't know where I'll be; just somewhere near Usumucinta. It's a medical mission, there's a clinic for the Indians and *campesinos.*"

"I'll find you," he said.

He kissed me on the cheek so that it wasn't just a vague promise, but a promise to keep; then I watched him drive away from the Ixtá Maya. And for the next twenty-four hours or so I was busy getting ready to move us down to Usumucinta, preparing myself for what good I might be able to accomplish there.

The Randalls turned out to be big, blond, cheerful people who had met while they were students at Mercer University. They'd been missionaries since Cora Randall got her MD degree from Emory twenty-six years ago. Cora said they had raised three children in the field—the Cameroons, Boliva, and Guatemala, where they had established the Usumucinta mission eleven years ago. Naturally they carried a lot of pictures with them.

"Pete's a lawyer in Cincinnati," Mr. Randall said, showing us a towheaded kid in a breechclout, "and Reg—Reg junior—is in his second year of med school in Birmingham."

"Reg is the lawyer," Cora said, gently correcting him.

"Oh, that's right," Reg Randall said. He was so walleyed he made me think of aquariums. He blinked a lot and looked as if he were having trouble waking up, although it was eleven o'clock in the morning. "Polly, Polly's going for her DCE. Where's that again, Mother?"

"Oral Roberts University."

Reg Randall blinked and blinked at me. It seemed to be uncontrollable. "You're a very pretty girl, chérie." Cora smiled, a little sadly, not needing to say anything. I assumed she'd explain later what his problem was.

We all posed for more pictures in front of the Ixtá Maya. I wondered where Veronica was. I'd left word with Francisco that I wanted to say good-bye, but she didn't show up and finally we had to be on our way, in the Randalls' old Land Rover.

Cora drove. " 'Mine eyes fail from looking up,' " Reg explained, and seemed content to sit in back with Daddy, where he did most of the talking. Sometimes he lapsed into the Kekchi Indian dialect, and Cora would look back over her shoulder and shout, "Stick to English, hon!" I don't think Daddy cared. He was very tense.

We drove south on roads that quickly went from bad to awful, a jumping, jolting ride at less than thirty miles an hour. The right-hand seat was barely padded, and Cora bounced obstinately over rocks I would have tried to drive around. There was slash-and-burn devastation for miles on either side of the road, and a couple of shacky villages with the smell of smoldering garbage everywhere. We met only a few other vehicles and some *campesinos* walking a mule or a small herd of runty goats. After about an hour we came to an area where the forest was still untouched, and filled with mist near a murky river. It wasn't much cooler, but there was some relief from the sun.

"Guess you wonder what you've got yourself into?" Cora said, the sun flashing off the lenses of her round glasses when she turned her head toward me.

"Sort of."

"Does the sight of blood bother you?"

How much blood? I thought. "Oh, not really."

"That's good. Mostly we deal with abscesses, breech births, rotten teeth, but the aftermath of a good machete fight or a chainsaw accident can be unnerving until you get used to the sight."

I swallowed hard. Cora began singing a hymn I hadn't heard since I was in the children's choir at First Iconium: "Kum Ba Yah." She smiled at me encouragingly; I joined in, then looked back at Daddy, who was holding his bowed head with one hand.

Cora hit the brakes while I was still half-turned in the seat, not holding on too tightly with my right hand. The swerving stop banged me against the dashboard, hurting my ribs. I looked around. There was a bridge ahead and a Jeep painted in camouflage shades of green blocked access to the bridge. I saw a couple of government soldiers, or maybe rebels, lounging against the back of the Jeep with assault rifles in their hands, and two more men sitting in the front seats.

"No problem," Cora said. But she was frowning. "This goes on all the time."

"How do you know who they—"

"Sometimes you don't. They're probably okay. Just stay put and let me do the talking."

Cora came to a complete stop fifty feet behind the Jeep. The two government soldiers, if that's what they were—they looked authentic, in forage caps and boots and baggy pants—sauntered toward us.

"Patrol," Cora said. She looked a little more at ease. "There've been a couple of bridges blown down this way."

The two men were young, at least one of them about Benito's age, and both wore mirror sunglasses. Cora greeted them in Spanish, asking them if it was okay to proceed, we were missionaries, etc. They took their time looking us over without commenting. One of them also looked into the back of the Land Rover, and tried to see under the tarp-covered roofrack, where our luggage and some boxes of medical supplies were stored.

They spoke to each other; the one on Cora's side motioned with his head. They wanted us to get out.

"What's going on?" Dad asked. "I don't like this."

"It isn't anything," Cora said softly, and smiled at the one she'd been talking to. She didn't budge, and gave him a rapid-fire argument. He listened gravely, shook his head a couple of times. Cora ran out of arguments.

"We have to get out," she said, "while they poke around. Don't worry, there's no chance we'll be molested."

I wished she hadn't put it that way. I couldn't swallow at all. Cora put a hand on my forearm, reassuringly. I glanced at Daddy, who I thought was about to have a heart attack. He looked white around the mouth. It was very quiet on the road, except for birds back in the forest. I could smell the strong smoke of the dark-colored cigarettes the men in the Jeep were smoking. They hadn't paid much attention to us. One of them laughed and flicked his cigarette into the creek. He was wearing a gold wristwatch, shaped like one of the pricier Rolexes, which reflected the sun. There's something about the way gold gleams in bright sunlight; I didn't think it was a cheap knockoff.

Cora saw it, too. She was frowning again.

They lined us up on the side of the road. Reg Randall said with a little smile, " 'Therefore be patient, brethren, until the coming of the Lord.' " Daddy held his tongue and fretted. The youngest soldier, the clean-cut one who reminded me of Benito, smiled at me.

"¿Cómo se llama?" I asked him. He shrugged and glanced at the other, who told him curtly to unlash the tarp. The boy took out a knife.

"Let me," Cora said, and moved toward the Land Rover. I guess she had tied the expert-looking knots.

The older of the two soldiers lowered his rifle, one like Veronica's beloved Uzi but with blotches of corrosion, pointing it at her.

Cora's face clouded with indignation and she said something on the order of, "That won't be necessary." Then she turned toward the Jeep and shouted, *"¡Jefe! ¡Misioneros! ¿Podemos proceder en paz?"*

The one with the gold watch turned his head slowly and looked at us. For a few moments I was sure I'd seen him before, without the officer's cap—but with the gold Rolex—and I flashed back to the restaurant at the Parador Libertad, lunch with Glen Hazen, Heckle and Jeckel at a table by the door passing the time, Jeckel dealing himself cards, a fancy Rolex on his wrist. I stared at his face, but I couldn't be sure, and it was so farfetched anyway.

The one in charge gave a signal; the soldier with the knife started slashing through tarp cord while Cora glowered.

Reg Randall said, " 'Do not be afraid, nor be dismayed, for the Lord your God is with you wherever you go.' "

Cora said, "Shut up, Reg."

"Obviously we have a problem here," Dad said.

I had to go to the bathroom.

Both men got out of the Jeep and came toward us, as if they had all day to kill. The two soldiers started pulling down luggage and boxes and stacking them in the road. One of the leaders reached into the Land Rover and pulled the keys from the ignition.

"Hey!" Cora fumed, her temper snapping. She took a couple of long strides toward him. With the bale of keys in his fist, the man turned and hit her in the face.

Cora fell down and there was blood all over, from a broken nose, from cuts around one eye where a lens of her glasses had shattered. Reg Randall wailed, a high-pitched sound that startled me just as shock had begun to turn me to stone.

Then Daddy grabbed me by the arm, almost yanking me off my feet.

"Run!"

He half-dragged me off the road and through a low ditch. The forest was a few feet away. I have good balance, but Daddy was strong and pulling too hard. I stumbled and sprawled, Daddy losing his grip on me as one of their automatic weapons went off. Bullets spattered through the palm growth above my head like hard raindrops. I heard Daddy grunt, and looked around as I was getting to my feet. He was motionless, dark with his back to the sun, one hand extended toward me. His mouth was open in surprise.

"Run," he said again, his voice choked. He sat down hard, still looking surprised. Behind him, on the road, I saw rifles aimed at us. They had stopped firing. I grabbed Daddy's hand, but I couldn't pull him up.

One of them shouted an order; I knew they would be coming for us. Dad was shot, I knew that, too. I could've stayed there shaking from terror while they came to get me, or I could run. There was no deliberate choice involved. I don't think my mind was working at all. I'd been an athlete all my life. The ball was over the net, and my feet moved instinctively.

It wasn't as dense and dark as the high forest that surrounded Kan Petén. A lot of sunlight penetrated the low canopy. The first thing I ran into was spiderwebs, which felt as thick as fiberglass. It would have made me hysterical if I'd had the breath for screaming. Then vines and more vines, blooming with purple and white flowers that attracted a cloud of butterflies. The air was filled with flying things, some as big as rhinoceros beetles, others so small they could only be seen in mistlike swarms. I was wearing jeans and a long-sleeved shirt of tough cotton and bush boots that gave me some protection from stinging bristles and thorns as I thrashed my way across rotted logs and stumbled onto a path, like a deer trail back home.

I didn't know if they were following me: blood was pounding too loud in my ears for me to hear anything.

After a couple of hundred yards or so I calmed down enough to realize I might be circling instead of going deeper into the forest. I had turned my ankle, which forced me to go slower. I stopped and held my breath so I could hear better. I didn't hear voices, only trickling water, cicadas humming, birds that sang and hawks that screamed. Almost like human beings screaming. What was happening back there on the road? If they had killed my father—

I couldn't think about that; it would paralyze me. For now I was probably safe, if I didn't get bitten by something other than the bottle flies that were making me miserable. I remembered hearing that fer-de-lance vipers liked to sun themselves on jungle paths, looking like stripes of shade until you stepped on them. I had to think about how to get back to the road, then find help. My throat was burning up from bile; some little midges were flocking around my eyes, getting in my nostrils when I tried to breathe. It was better when I started moving again, toward the sun. As long as I continued in that direction, I thought I would probably reach the road eventually.

Before long I came across the stream I'd been hearing. The water was muddy, which might mean a Milpa field nearby, or even a village. How many miles? I heard monkeys but didn't see them. Then, from a distance, came the unmistakable sound of a church bell at noon.

I stood there wiping tears with the cuff of my sleeve, smearing my cheeks, looking upstream where I would have to go to get help. If it wasn't too far, then maybe—

The cabbage thicket behind me swished dryly; my spine almost jumped through the back of my neck.

"Here you are," Daddy said.

I stared at him as he came toward me. He was sweat-stained but not bloody. Smiling.

"Oh my God!"

"You led us quite a chase. I forgot you were in such good shape."

"Daddy—you—how—"

There was something in his hand the size of a pocket calculator, but with an antenna about a foot long. I heard a low-pitched beeping. He telescoped the antenna and dropped the gadget into a cargo pocket of his bush jacket as two more men in Army fatigues came out of the brush behind him.

"Look out!"

He turned casually, then looked back at me, still smiling. Ear to ear. Strange. A false-face kind of smile. His chest was heaving.

"They're on my side."

"What—do you mean—the Randalls—"

"They'll be okay, although Cora's eye—"

He made a sympathetic clucking sound. I saw the flash of a gold watch band as one of the men batted at an insect on his pock-marked cheek.

"She move in a way I no 'speck," he said. "And I no pool my punch in time. Or I only knock her out a little while."

"Let's do this quickly, Jaquez," Daddy said. "And get her out of here."

The blood drained from my head so fast, drained to my feet, that I had the sensation of sinking into the ground. My skin was turning cold, and colors faded even as the sun blazed and blinded. Daddy was gone; he had simply vanished, somewhere. The young soldier who had reminded me of Benito took an olive-green canister like a shaving cream bomb from his rucksack and handed it to a man I didn't know, along with a cotton pad. I went for a slow-motion, numbed walk. The two men came toward me. I knew I should try to run, but I had no feeling anywhere except in my heart, which I thought was going to explode from pounding. They each seized an arm, pinning me rigidly between them. A muscle in my shoulder cramped; I screamed from pain, and screaming drained all of my strength.

The man I didn't know looked up from what he was doing. The sun off his dark glasses went to my eyes like needles. His own eyes were wide-awake in that darkness, touched with fiery red.

I realized them what it was all about. *I* had done this. Called up the devil with thoughts of lying with my father. Called him with an act of masturbation. I had sinned. *I belonged to the devil.*

The man I didn't know soaked the cotton pad in something cold and fuming from the canister. Came up to me, the way figures move in a dream. Sweat ran down his cheeks. I saw myself naked and lustful in the mirrors of his glasses. I tried to move my head so I wouldn't have to look. But the horror, the sheer horror had locked me up tighter than the chains of hell.

Tooth-gleam. The ecstatic smile. False. False-face. Devil!

"Daddddyyy—!" But he was gone, had vanished, I had no father.

The man I didn't know pressed the cotton pad over my nose. Already it was nearly dark inside my head. When I was forced to breathe, it got darker still. Dark and deep and silent, except for the faraway voice of he who knew my sins—

Saying:

"Good-bye, darling."

BUTTERBAUGH'S NOTEBOOKS

FIVE

December–February, 199-

No, I never
warmed up to that man.
Although I made a sincere
effort, I always believed
that sooner or later he'd
bring heartache to my
daughter.

B ut this—this is ungodly!"

Adrienne Crowder's face had darkened, and I could clearly see the pulse of the carotid artery in her neck. Living with infirm parents for the past couple of years had made me unusually sensitive to the frailties of old people, and I worried about a possible stroke. On the other hand, she was a whiskey drinker—George Dickel—and she looked pretty tough to me, in spite of her age. I waited, in the sunny family room of the Crowder home on Tchula Road, and didn't say anything else. For the most part I was relieved, because I had come this far on risky business, and obviously she had accepted my story.

Dudgeon gave her a mild coughing fit, and the cough she soothed with another sip of Tennessee whiskey, which she drank straight. She looked toward the windows at the extensive gardens and orchard—the property included at least six acres. Some workmen were pruning big crape myrtles near a pond edged in December ice. The late afternoon light had the golden intensity you find in this part of the country on cloudless winter days.

When she looked at me again my spine tingled the way it had when she'd first opened the door to me: they were Sharissa's eyes, an even lighter shade of amber than the half ounce of the Dickel that was left in her crystal glass. Her hair, white but thick for her age, was cut straight across her forehead, bangs that nearly met the unplucked line of eyebrows.

"So the man was a bigamist—all the years he lived with Caroline. And what does that make my granddaughter?" Her face wrinkled in an expression of disgust and pity. She leaned forward on the settee in front of the partly draped windows; her hand trembled when she touched the folder of photographs, the DNA documentation I'd brought with me. She exhaled and I had a whiff of her breath, which convinced me, along with the thickened heavily veined whites of her eyes, that she wasn't just drinking to keep me company, it was a daily necessity. She looked up at me sharply. "Cheat, liar, opportunist—but this isn't all you know about him."

I shook my head. "All anyone knows about Sullivan is there. Everything else is speculation on my part. I've spent a lot of time thinking about—why don't we just call him Greg?"

"There are better names I can think of. Oh, all right." She paused, studying me grimly, and with a certain calculation. I was as much a stranger to her as the man who had called himself her son-in-law. "I suppose you've come here because there's nothing the police can do."

"That's one reason."

"What do you know about—*Greg*—that you suspect, but can't prove?"

I hesitated. She drew herself up tightly, fists in her lap, and said, "Does my granddaughter have anything to fear from this—prize son of a bitch?"

"I can't be sure, Mrs. Crowder. Obviously he's not your average human being."

"I should say not! *My* age. And he was married to—I had better not ever lay eyes on him again, that's all I can tell you! I was a crack shot when I was younger. My father taught me. Dove, quail, we never missed a season. The guns are still there, in the armoire. And I don't neglect them."

"Mrs. Crowder?"

She wrenched her attention back to me. For a few moments she trembled, and looked dismayed. "My God. If anything should happen to Sharissa! You don't suppose—he is *that* kind of man?"

"No. If he was sexually obsessed with Sharissa, it probably would've surfaced before now. I had a talk with Dr. Jesse Fernando—the neurosurgeon who operated when Greg was shot? I leveled with him, showed him what I had. And he told me something they discovered about Greg. He has an extremely rare gene, or combination of genes, that could contribute to unusual longevity. It's possible that Greg's history goes farther back than his identity as Frederick Sullivan. No way to trace it, of course, no matter how much time or money you had to spend."

"My granddaughter is coming home! If I have to go and fetch her myself."

"Do you know where she is?"

"At the moment, on a cruise ship." She pondered this dilemma, and looked to me for help.

"Suppose you catch up to them. Then you try to convince Sharissa her father hasn't exactly been a paragon, way back when. The fact is, she loves him for who he is now, what he's always meant to her. I think from what I know of Sharissa that she's a stout-hearted kid, but there's a limit to the emotional shocks any of us can absorb in a short period of time. You have to consider her breaking point. First Bobby, then her mother. Then you're attempting to take her father away—even her name. A question of identity—potentially that's more devastating to Sharissa than coming to terms with Caroline's death. And just how well is she coping right now?"

"I had a postcard yesterday. From some island in the Caribbean. She sounded as if she were all right." Mrs.

Crowder shook her head glumly. "Yes, yes, I see what you mean. Open one can of worms, there's another can inside."

"Are they planning to come back to Sky Valley after the cruise?"

"Oh, no. They're going to do missionary work. Some Third World village—Guatemala, I think. Why he couldn't let Sharissa finish the school year baffles me. She had completed her requirements to graduate, of course, but she's missing all the activities, the fun of graduation . . ."

Mrs. Crowder looked at the bottle of sippin' whiskey, and steeled herself against its allure. "Oh, well. No use pretending she might have enjoyed those things after so much tragedy. Maybe she's better off away from here, even though she's with *him*."

"I don't think so," I said.

She frowned. "It won't be for much longer. With your permission I'll turn this information over to Fitz—our attorney. He will find a way to deal with this man; get him out of our lives forever, while sparing my granddaughter as much heartache as possible."

"I think Greg may save you the trouble by turning into somebody else. After all, he's done it before."

"Wouldn't *that* be a blessing."

"The big question is, what happens to Sharissa?"

"Well—in time—surely she will get over—"

"Mrs. Crowder, I could use this much more of the Dickel's." I held my thumb and forefinger an inch apart.

"Surely." She poured whiskey into the glass I held out to her, not looking at me; but there was trouble in her eyes, in the deep lines of her forehead. She gave in and poured one for herself. "All right," she said shrewdly, "what haven't you told me yet?"

I took an eight-by-ten enlargement of an old photo from the envelope I deliberately hadn't opened until now, and gave it to her. She stared at it, feeling around on the coffee table for her reading glasses.

" *Him* again? And—who is this girl he's with?"

"Her name is—was, Bonnie. Frederick and Roxanne Sullivan's adopted daughter. She left Canada with Frederick a few months before he reappeared, in this country, as Greg Walker. I was able to find out that the two of them were issued Canadian passports a few days before they—as far as anyone can determine—vanished. They didn't need passports to go to the States. Sullivan must have had a particular destination in mind. Europe? Mexico? South America? A country in which he was unknown and could change his identity, leave Frederick Sullivan behind him. But where?"

"Does it matter?"

"I think so. If he also left Bonnie behind, which he almost certainly had to do. Remember, he was about to become someone else. A totally new person, judging from what I know about Sullivan. I lie awake nights wondering about this. Why did he take Bonnie with him, if his plan was to change, not only his identity, but his personality? Would've been simpler just to leave her in Canada. It's almost as if he was compelled, for some reason I don't understand, to take the girl along. She was only sixteen. Was he indifferent enough to abandon someone that young in a foreign country? Or did something happen to her?"

Adrienne Crowder didn't say anything. But the pulse in her throat was visible again, and she didn't take her eyes from my face.

"Was he—a murderer? Did he commit some other crime that forced him to leave Canada?"

"Not that I've been able to learn."

"Then—if he had no logical reason to change his identity—"

"His reasoning was illogical. To you and to me, that is."

"You're saying that—he might be insane."

"We know that Greg is a biological rarity. Sawmill accidents and gunshot wounds apparently leave no permanent marks on him. He may also be a psychological rarity, someone whose motives are beyond our understanding."

She bowed her head for a long moment. "You have succeeded in frightening me, Sergeant Butterbaugh."

"I'm sorry. I scare myself sometimes, because I'm obsessed by him."

"Greg," she pointed out, "has not disappeared. Hi intentions are quite clear."

"So far. But is there a pattern in his behavior, an obscure timetable he's following? How long did he know your daughter before they were married?"

"Less than three months. The wedding was in October, as I recall. Yes. They would have celebrated their eighteenth anniversary a few weeks ago."

"Frederick Sullivan was married for eighteen years. Then, for whatever reason, he got up and left. Eighteen years and a bit, and now Greg is gone, too. With Sharissa."

"But they are going to Guatemala! They arrive there at the end of January, after attending seminars for lay mission work. Sharissa stays in very close touch with us." She wagged a finger at me, not lecturing, but as if she needed to reassure herself with a display of authority. "I see coincidence, not pattern, in his behavior."

A middle-aged LPN looked into the family room from the hall, and Adrienne Crowder glanced at her.

"Yes, Maria?"

"Mr. Crowder was asking for you."

"Tell him I'll be a few more minutes. Has he had his bath?"

"Yes, ma'am."

The nurse went upstairs and Adrienne Crowder looked vague and distracted for a few moments, absently stroking her chin with the back of one hand. The long-necked Abyssinian cat that had occupied the center of the mantel like a piece of bric-à-brac stirred suddenly and began washing with half-closed eyes. It was warm in the room; there was a gas-log fire going and the midafternoon sun fell directly on the large picture window.

"Barr is making progress," she told me. "Certainly he's better off at home than he would be in a hospital."

"Cancer, you said?"

She nodded. "They discovered the tumor shortly after— after the funeral. Barr and Caroline were very close. I didn't enjoy that sort of relationship with her, unfortunately. She was never good at accepting my advice and I was, I suppose, too ruthless in applying it. But all I ever said when she told me she wanted to marry—Greg—was, 'Wait a little longer, Caroline. Be very sure.'" Her hardbitten mouth set itself in a line of bitter dismay; then her attention wandered again, from the unchangeable past. "I believe it was Barr's grief that set the thing off. A little time bomb, ticking away in some obscure gland for who knows how many years." Her head went from side to side, as if she were subconsciously miming the mortal ticking she seemed to be hearing in the otherwise quiet house. Then, for the first time since I'd met her, she smiled, and I recognized a fleeting ghost of Sharissa again. "But from the beginning Sharissa and I understood each other so well."

"Mrs. Crowder, suppose I could prove that when Frederick Sullivan left Canada with Bonnie, he went to Guatemala."

"And what would *that* prove?"

"That he is on a timetable, acting in accord with some deep-seated psychological, maybe pathological need. Tell me this: were they assigned to Guatemala by the Baptist Mission Board, or was it Greg's choice?"

"I—I don't know. As a lay missionary, I believe he could select the area where he wanted to do his service. I can find out, with a phone call to a friend who's a member of the board."

"If Greg did choose Guatemala, then I think I'm going to have to go there."

"You suspect—"

"That he may be planning to change his identity again.

But that's not what I care about. I care most about Sharissa."

"Sergeant Butterbaugh, do you have any knowledge whatsoever that would lead you to believe Sharissa might be in danger?"

I was so long in answering she began to fidget, not concealing her displeasure with me.

"No," I admitted. "There's nothing. Nothing. She's his daughter, after all. Sharissa loves him, and if he's capable of loving anything or anyone, Greg must love her. This is where I—run into a big blank wall."

Adrienne Crowder nodded, almost as if she'd lost interest in the discussion, and in me. Then she surprised me by saying, "So you came to tell me that you'd like to get Sharissa away from him, by such means as you think necessary. Until, legally, I can make sure he's never allowed to go within a mile of her again. Or until I've bought him off, and facilitated his—next change of identity. I'm convinced this must be done. I must also speak my mind and say I have grave doubts that you're the man for the job."

"Well, you see . . . I'm in love with Sharissa, Mrs. Crowder."

That made her smile again, but not as if she were delighted. "Oh. So there's an imperative, if not proficiency."

"I've been a cop for a while, Mrs. Crowder. I've managed to handle myself well enough in places like South Central Los Angeles. I wouldn't delude myself that Sharissa loves me or ever will, but I think she's learned to trust, maybe even depend on me, through some rough times this year."

She gestured, palms up. "I'm very grateful for all you've had to tell me. I am impressed with the care you've taken not to go beyond the facts. And I very much share your concern for Sharissa. No matter what manner of man he may be, and I have never come across anyone remotely as loathsome, obviously Greg has destroyed any hope of a continuing relationship with his daughter. It can't be permitted. I want her home, with me, as soon as possible. I know there are men I can hire—"

"The right people won't touch it, Mrs. Crowder. The wrong people could cause a hell of a lot of damage, trying to get Sharissa away from her father and out of a foreign country. No matter if Greg's marriage to Caroline was not legitimate, in the eyes of any court he is still Sharissa's father and her legal guardian, until she's eighteen. Your husband is sick, and you can't leave him now. I'm the only one who has a chance to pull this off, to get Sharissa home in the shortest possible time. To do that I'll have to deal with Greg in some way."

"But you have no plan."

"I have an idea of how to go about it."

"I suppose you will need my—financial help?"

"I've got a VISA card and nine hundred dollars in the bank. I'll have to take an unpaid leave of absence from the Sky Valley police department. I don't know how long I'll be away. Both of my parents are infirm, and caring for them is a big expense."

She said, noncommittal as a banker, "Do you have a figure in mind?"

I took a folded sheet of paper from my inside jacket pocket and handed it to her. She put her reading glasses on and went over my estimates with a cold eye. As usual, when I didn't have anything else to do, I took off my grandfather's Hamilton watch and wound it, a ritual that I found soothing, although it couldn't compare with a couple of Tums and a glass of Dr Pepper. I waited to be humbled, or dismissed, but she nodded instead, adopting me without exactly approving.

"I believe I can manage this, Sergeant Butterbaugh. What other help can I give you?"

"Their itinerary. You said they expected to be in Guatemala by the end of January?"

Adrienne Crowder carried my estimate of expenses to an antique secretary, returned with a checkbook and a copy of an itinerary prepared for Greg and Sharissa Walker by a local travel agent.

"They'll be arriving in a place called Cobían on the twenty-fourth. The hotel is the Itzá Maya. Certainly Greg made no effort to conceal his travel arrangements."

"He wouldn't want to give anyone here cause for concern. And if he decides to change his plans at the last minute, it wouldn't be any problem. He has plenty of money, I think."

"Caroline was insured for two hundred thousand dollars."

"And they had thirty percent equity in the house. By the way, he took out a loan against that equity three days before they left Sky Valley. Adding joint savings with Caroline to his other reserves, Greg had a total of $1,200 in checking at Wachovia and $260,000 in a no-load European government bond fund with Schwab. His taxes are up to date. He's paying for their trip with credit cards."

"How do you know all that?"

"Equifax. Greg Walker will continue to live in their computers, with gold-plated credit, long after there is no more Greg Walker. One of the ironies of the Information Age. They know everything about him, except who he really is."

Which, if course, was my major problem. Once Adrienne Crowder's check cleared, I made arrangements with a couple of cousins I knew to be reliable, paying them to live in and look after my parents. I sorted through my options. Finally I made plans to fly to Guatemala, without any certainty that Greg would show up there. By then Adrienne had talked with Sharissa in Venezuela, where she was having problems with a stomach virus at the training seminar. I was itching to go to Venezuela, but there was no way I could position myself in a rural area to keep an eye on both of them without letting Greg know he was under surveillance.

I made a phone call and learned that the Itzá Maya was a resort-style hotel and, in midwinter, nearly booked solid. A visa for Guatemala was available from American Airlines. I also needed a passport, but that had to wait until my beard grew out. I drove to Atlanta to be fitted for a hairpiece and to pick up a new camera, the Nikon N6006 with additional lenses. So much for eyes; for extra ears I visited a shop on the sixth floor of an office building near Lenox Square. No name on the door, just a tasteful brass plate and three script initials. It was a candy store for paranoid business executives and professional snoops who wanted the latest in ultrasensitive listening and recording devices, packaged to be undetectable, even to Customs officials.

With the addition of long-wear contact lenses, I was all set.

When I saw my passport photos I didn't know myself; I doubted if either Greg or Sharissa would recognize me, if we happened to pass by in the lobby of the Itzá Maya. Truthfully, I thought the added hair and cropped beard were major improvements in my looks. After leaving my job I'd had extra time to work out at the Y, and the pounds that had accumulated while I was sitting at a desk most of the time were gone. I had almost forgotten what it was like to have a flat stomach.

A new, bolder, more capable-looking me: the transformation gave me an insight into the seductive pleasure of becoming someone else. My passport still read *C.G. Butterbaugh*, but I couldn't find him in the mirror. I felt reckless and eager, overconfident. It was all acting-out and maybe I needed the courage a disguise lent me, because my common sense told me to be very, very careful: the temporary jolt of pleasure I'd felt could be a serious addiction for Greg Walker. And addicts reacted viscerally whenever they were threatened with a loss of whatever it was that turned them on.

On the eighteenth of January I flew to Miami and from there to Guatemala City, laid over in a hotel near the airport, and then caught a feeder flight north to Cobían at seven-thirty the next morning. The plane, a retread 737, must have felt heavy to the pilot, because he didn't seem to gain much altitude. We skimmed over dark-green forested hills half obscured by fog and haze, close enough to get a good look at some king-sized vultures floating above the treetops. There were small plots of farmland in the forest basins, occasional villages, and very few roads. The Latin businessman sitting next to me spent all fifty minutes in the air saying his rosary. I assumed he'd been on this flight before.

The airport at Cobían was new: it was about the size of a high school gymnasium, with a mezzanine at one end and a solarium roof in the shape of a pyramid. For some reason we had to go through Customs and Immigration again. I had two carry-on bags with me, all currency and traveler's checks in a money belt.

Inside the airport and on the perimeter there were government soldiers, too many of them kids, like gang members I'd known in South Central L.A., carrying the same kind of fire power but wearing military fatigues instead of home-boy colors. A Humvee and an armored weapons carrier were parked behind a heavily sandbagged guard post beside the airport exit. Our aid dollars at work, I assumed, to protect what passed for democracy in Guatemala.

There was a van going to the Itzá, but it was full of German tourists and a delegation from Amnesty International—several middle-aged women with crow's feet and pinned-back hairdos—by the time I got to it, so I let a taxi driver hustle me. He had a battered old pea-green V-8 Chevrolet that looked as if it had been rolled a couple of times, and hammered back into shape with a two-by-four. The hood was as rumpled as an unmade bed.

I found out why his car looked the way it did: He was

the driver-ed equivalent of a dyslexic. I had a stress head-ache by the time we reached the hotel, which was on a broad low hill facing the south shore of Lake Petén-Itzá, a few kilometers from Cobián. And my mind had been rac-ing for days. I understood why Sherlock Holmes needed a touch of the needle now and then. In my room, which overlooked a complex of tennis courts and a jungle gar-den with ten bungalows half-hidden beneath the trees, I took Tylenol and ate some dried fruit to kick my blood sugar back to a normal level. The faint dizziness went away after a tepid shower. I put on walk shorts and toured the hotel grounds.

So I had some time to wait before Greg and Sharissa ar-rived. Assuming they would show up at all. But I had a hunch as I looked around, a hunch certified by a persis-tent buzz at the nape of the neck, that on arrival I may have crossed paths with the real Frederick Sullivan. A trail grown so faint no bloodhound could pick it up. Much of the Itzá Maya looked as if it had been built during the last dozen years, but there was an older, smaller, cloisterlike building behind the wing in which I was quartered on the third floor. Most of the windows were shuttered; flowering vines grew on the stained outer walls of thick square stones. On the ground floor there was some construction work going on, at a slow pace. Scaffolding in the inner courtyard, cement mixers, dust in the air.

I had listed myself on my passport as a "corporate travel advisor." I carried embossed business cards testify-ing to my eminence in my fictitious occupation. I also had a dummy magazine cover that I took with me to the mez-zanine office of the woman in charge of promotions for the Itzá Maya. Her name was Carlotta. She was attentive and helpful, and spoke pretty good English.

"As far as we're concerned," I said, "Central America has been seriously neglected as a setting for the small but important high-end business conference."

"I could not agree more, Mr. Butterboss."

"We're looking for destination resorts with unique attractions in the vicinity, luxurious accommodations for up to two hundred executives and their wives. The resorts must be near an airport that has the capacity for the largest business jet flying today."

She looked at the cover for the proposed boutique magazine. "Work on the runway at Cobían International Airport is due for completion in early May. It will then be possible to fly directly to the Petén from the United Estates. And of course this region is second to none in historic signification. Folk festivals, ah, and the grandeur of the ruins! Always there is much to see and do."

I frowned. "There's no golf course, which I'm afraid is a drawback."

So she got out all the plans and renderings for the 18–hole "Jack Neekloss championship course" they were going to build on adjoining land.

"What I'd like to do," I said, "is prepare a comprehensive report on the Itzá Maya for our newsletter subscribers, then follow up with a photo spread in, let's say, the upcoming fall issue of our magazine."

"Whatever I can do to help you—"

"I had a couple of ideas for the report I'm going to write. Some background on the origins of the hotel."

"I know is hard to believe, but the original building, which now has begun to renovate, dates back to 1827."

I nodded enthusiastically. "That's exactly the sort of thing I need."

"The hotel has been in the Colon family since that time. Our president, Francisco Colon, is the grandson of the founder."

"Grandson? Only three generations since the early nineteenth century? That's almost—two hundred years."

"*Claro.* They are very long livers, the Colons. Don Santiago, who die only last year, have one hundred twenty-one years when he pass away. His father before him, more than a hundred years, I believe."

I made a note of that. "I wonder if I could look through the registrations, you know, going back twenty or thirty years, to see if there are any famous names who stayed here."

"No problem. The film director once upon a time, I think it was John Hooston, start to film a movie here. That was before I was born, but my mother tole me the story. Anyway, the moneys was not guaranteed, or something, so they all go back to Hollywood."

"Mind if I get a crack at those registrations today?"

"Well, for ten years now, everything is on computer. Before that, like, file cards, I think. And a long time ago, big ledger books. They have not done so well, you know, because of humidity and *cucarachas* in the old days. But everything is stored now in air-condition room downstairs. Why don't we go now, I will introduce you to Señor Colon, and arrange a place for you to do your work."

Francisco Colon was a stocky, dark-complected man who wore a pink guayabera and three diamond rings. He was so soft-spoken and polite it was easy to overlook how alert his eyes were. He had television monitors built into a paneled wall of his office. Twelve color screens that gave him one or more angles on every public place in the Itzá Maya. He welcomed me to his hotel, told me his entire staff was at my disposal, and set me up in a small unused office lined with deep bookshelves and card-catalogue files, each drawer labeled by year.

I pulled 1973 and went to work. It took me less than ten minutes, and there it was: January 26. *Frederick Sullivan. Bonnie Sullivan. New Lost River, British Columbia.* Canadian passport numbers. Two rooms, adjoining.

Although it was what I'd been hoping for, I needed a little time to believe what I was reading. My pulses were really jumping.

Then I unfolded a sample of Greg Walker's handwriting which Adrienne Crowder had provided, and compared the signatures. My father had been an amateur graphologist all of his life, and when I was thirteen, about the same time I discovered Sherlock Holmes and became infatuated with detective work, I learned a little about handwriting analysis.

There were two points of comparison on the signatures which even someone who had no interest in the subject could isolate without difficulty. Large, stand-alone capital letters (a vigorous slash representing both the crossbar of the *G* and the top of the *F* in Frederick) and a tendency to squeeze the loops of *e*'s until they all but disappeared. Psychologically this expressed a huge ego bound by a need for secrecy.

An older-model Xerox machine occupied a corner of the windowless office. I copied the Sullivan registration card, one for me, one for my father, who could work up a really impressive personality profile from signatures alone, and put the file drawer back.

At that point my mind wandered, into a reverie that was almost like a trance. I'm not sure how long it lasted. The hairs on the back of my neck sizzled in a pleasurable, sensual way. I saw, in the smallest detail, an old post-wedding photograph taken in New Lost River, British Columbia. Of course I was familiar with every detail: I was a photographer myself, and I'd thoroughly studied the groom's youthful, shadowy face. Now, as I meditated on the remembered photo, these numbers appeared across his face, bold as a billboard: *1954.*

And I thought, *If there is no so such person as Greg Walker, then who is to say Frederick Sullivan was the real thing?*

The sizzle of intuition, the sense of ghosts swarming behind a facade of lies and superficial plausibilities, prompted me to take a few steps to another file cabinet. Registration cards for the Itzá Maya, 1954.

I began again with January, and a couple of minutes later there it was, jumping out at me, the tell-tale capital letters and the loopless *e*, but the name this time was *Barnaby Wilde*, address *188 Post Oak, Prichard, New Hampshire.* In residence from January 22 until February 10, 1954.

Accompanied by his daughter Naomi.

Copy for me, copy for my father.

Now I was trembling, inside and out, from amazement and trepidation. *And if Barnaby Wilde was not the real thing—*

I looked for a file drawer labeled *1935*.

There wasn't one. I had to start going through the ledgers, which were large and musty, so much so I needed to hold a handkerchief over my nose with one hand, or else have a sneezing fit, while I laboriously leafed through them. And they all had a lot of stuck-together pages. Excited as I was, my mouth dry and my lower lip sore from biting it. (I wondered if Holmes ever had had tongue ulcers, from sucking on his pipeful of shag tobacco in those hours of intense concentration before the answers gleamed suddenly like gold in chaff-piles of mundane facts.) But Sherlock Holmes never had been the real thing, either, even if I did need to have him around sometimes, the way I'd needed my teddy bear when I was four.

The name appeared on the day of January 19, 1935. *Robert Canfield, Bartstown, Rhodesia.*

And under that, in her own hand: *Cynthia Canfield.* Who, I assumed, was not his wife, but another daughter. Like the others, she had occupied a separate room at the Ixtá Maya.

I couldn't Xerox the oversized page, but I made a note of the names and the address of a town that had probably been off the map for a while, or hadn't existed since Rhodesia became Zimbabwe.

Carlotta looked in on me while I was bringing another long-unopened ledger to the small desk.

"Would you like something to drink, Mr. Butterboss?"

I ordered a beer, and kept going, back nineteen years at a time. January 30, 1916. *Eben Edward Porter, New South Wales, Australia.* Two minor children had accompanied Mr. Porter to Guatemala: *Ellen* and *Joseph*.

In 1897, the January sojourner was *Emile de Louquier* of Avignon, France. But de Louquier either had come alone, or with a companion who had a different last name.

1897! Almost one hundred years ago. If the handwriting

analysis I planned to have done confirmed it, then Greg Walker, the man I was dealing with, had been returning to Guatemala at least once every nineteen years, always in the latter half of January. Assuming Emile de Louquier had been an adult, then Greg Walker was at least one hundred twenty years old.

I couldn't quite bring myself to call this conclusion sheer insanity. I didn't know enough to account for anything yet.

The beer helped my parched throat, but I wasn't able to sort through more old ledgers just then. Allergies had me feeling weak and as tired as death. My eyes were hurting; I took out the contacts and put my glasses on. I planned to come back with another camera, for photographing documents, in a day or two. Every link of the chain I had put together begged for a conclusion that was not credible; for an explanation that leaped over reason into a fog of the supernatural. A nice soupy Victorian fog that Holmes might have relished; but I didn't want any part of it. Because there had to be things in that fog that would make my flesh creep.

Y"ou're from a very unusual family," I said to Francisco Colon.

He was slicing a crescent of melon into small chunks, rind and all, and didn't look up. "Unusual?" he said politely.

"I was told that both your father and grandfather lived to be well past a hundred."

"Oh, I see." He ate two bites of melon and then he did look at me, without expression. "Yes, it is true. A few of the men of our family have been blessed with good health, and they have lived long."

"Only the men?"

He thought about that, and nodded. "It seems to be so. My own mother died of complications from a miscarriage, when she was only thirty-four. My grandfather married, oh, many times. Seven, eight wives. Most bore him children who did not survive for long. Even though he was a privileged man, a landowner, this place—" he looked around from the terrace of the Itzá Maya, where we were having our lunch—"the Petén Department, was primitive and poor, with little or no health care until very recently. My people, especially, have suffered."

"The Maya?"

"Yes. Although my family, we are descendants of priests who build the great cities of the Petén. So we have, how should I say it, enjoy many benefits of this kinship." He touched a jade carving, a bird of some kind, that he wore on a gold chain around his neck. "Have you visited?"

"You mean Kan Petén? No, not yet." With my father's old Waterman fountain pen I made a couple of notes on the legal pad beside my plate. "That's a real interesting angle, Señor Colon."

"Angle—? How do you mean?"

"Your ancestors were builders—temples, pyramids— and you've built all of this, in the last twelve years. The new wing of the hotel, the gardens—"

"Well—" He smiled, for the first time we'd sat down to eat. "I have more of an interest in business than my father. For many years he welcome only select guests, entertaining them as you would entertain in your own home. What they pay was small compensation for the attention he lavished on them. I think you see what I mean. So the Itzá Maya was not so much a business to him. Confidentially, it did not make money." He gestured ruefully, as if this was a patriarchal sin that still kept him awake nights. "Every year was necessary to sell some important asset to balance the books, to afford the luxuries the hotel provided its clientele. A piece of rare jewelry from a king's tomb, a few hectares of good land."

He shrugged and finished his melon; almost immediately a waiter whisked the plate away, and another waiter served avocado soup. A third appeared with a bottle of white wine. Señor Colon nodded after a glance at the label, and the wine was poured, pale gold in the sunlight that checkered the table through the latticework of a palm umbrella.

"I think you will like this, a Clos Blanc de Vougeot I choose myself. Three times a year I travel to Europe, study the business of the finest hotels, call on former guests, visit vineyards. I am happy to say that after nearly twenty years of effort, the Itzá is on a paying basis, and our creditworthiness is second to none."

I lifted my glass of wine. "To your continuing good fortune and long life."

"Salud."

"Delicious," I said. "So you personally keep up with former guests of the hotel?"

"A few. Old friends of my father's. During the past year, there were those I wished to notify myself of his passing."

"I wonder if you have any photos of your father and grandfather I could run in my newsletter?"

"Certainly, if you would be so kind as to return them."

"I'm curious about why your grandfather decided to build a hotel here. Of course you never knew him—"

"He died before the beginning of this century."

"Wasn't much here, I mean, in the way of tourist attractions?"

"The lake, the forest. The ruins, all hidden after centuries of abandonment. There was nothing that one could dignify by calling it a road."

"Then why build a hotel in such a location?"

Francisco Colon had noticed something, a small chip on the side of the shallow soup plate. He signaled with a sharp turning of his head, and a waiter came quickly. Señor Colon raked him with a barrage of Spanish; the soup plate was taken away. He looked back at me, thoughtfully.

"Why did he build here? For religious reasons."

"Oh. I don't think I understand."

"I am not speaking of worship, as such. Nowadays we are Catholic. But there are traditions of the great Maya civilization one wishes not to lose, if one is at all conscious of his heritage. Traditions that are preserved by certain *cofradías*—there is no exact translation. Brotherhood, fraternity—more sacred than that, although no formal priesthood exists. Men of respect and learning, who pass on the traditions to their sons."

"Like yourself. How many sons do you have?"

"Oh, I have not married. Time for that later."

"You must expect to live as long as your father," I said.

"Perhaps." Another plate of soup was set in front of him. He had a couple of spoonsful. "You seem more interested in this matter of, what is the English—longevity?"

"Everyone's interested in living as long as they can. Staying healthy while they're at it. Did the Maya usually live long lives?"

"No more than other peoples. Probably they live less than average, because of the hard life."

"Do the privileged have longer lives? I wonder. How about some of your father's friends—the ones you said you visited? Were some of them as old as he was?"

He was so long in answering, intent on his soup plate, that I thought he might have discovered another flaw there. "No. I don't believe so. Not nearly as old as my father."

"That's surprising. Your friends tend to be your own age, don't they?"

"I haven't thought about it. I have many acquaintances, but few friends. You make friends through hobbies, clubs, and so forth. But I have little time for those things." He glanced at his wristwatch, a simple Piaget with a black face that looked expensive. "I'm afraid I must go— another appointment, a particularly bothersome Department official I am forced to deal with from time to time. I am delighted to have had this opportunity to become acquainted with you. Perhaps I might have a look at the article you're preparing before it is published?"

"No problem, Señor Colon."

"Enjoy your good wine and this fine day." He nodded formally to me as he rose to go. *"Esta en su casa."*

I wasn't a wine drinker, but the stuff seemed smooth enough. A glass of wine and a little of the spicy avocado soup was about all I could handle. My stomach hadn't been dependable since I'd arrived in Guatemala. Maybe if I had been on vacation I might have enjoyed myself more. The ambience was satisfying—a well-run hotel, a terrace that was shielded from the heat of the early-afternoon sun, which made the humidity a little easier to take. But my beard itched and I had heat rash where I couldn't get at it in a public place, and I'd slept poorly in a foreign country. Exotic birds, monkeys, a weight of centuries in the dense atmosphere beside a timeless lake—even when I did fall asleep, I dreamed I was awake. Also I was pretending to be somebody else, which shouldn't have bothered me. But I couldn't adjust, because each day brought me to a new level, or depth, of disorientation. An hour ago I had traced Greg Walker back to the year 1840 in the old ledgers of Don Santiago Colon's remote guest house. I had photographed all of the ledger entries in that familiar handwriting with a dependable old Minox camera. The kind they had been using in spy movies since World War II. Then lunch, with a man who complacently looked forward to a lifespan of more than a hundred years. That would leave him, maybe, a few decades or even a full century short of Greg Walker's record—

On the other hand, Greg might not be the record-holder. All I had to do was spend a few more days culling the registration cards and books, looking for other signature traits that would match up (at nineteen-year intervals?), going back to the beginning of the Itzá Maya. But I didn't have the fortitude. I don't think I wanted to know. Greg Walker was enough for me to cope with, in and out of my imagination.

I looked around at the lunch crowd: every table was full. A few Americans, from what I overheard of their conversations; Europeans, Latin businessmen, local officials, a table of nuns in pale blue dresses. The Itzá Maya had become the most popular meeting place in the region, according to Francisco Colon. But it wasn't a health resort. There were no curative waters, nothing that promised an extension of your life in exchange for a few nights in residence. Greg Walker, in all of his identities, had never stayed for longer than two weeks.

I sipped some wine and stared at the lake and the remnants of a two-thousand-year-old civilization on the near shore. Crude pyramid shapes, hazy through thin drifting smoke that was sometimes visible all day on the horizon. The smoke created spectacular red sunsets every night.

He had a compelling reason for coming here, to what was still a remote part of Guatemala, sometimes accompanied by minor children. The terrace was a recent improvement, so nineteen years ago Greg had sat somewhere else with Bonnie Sullivan, probably in the flagged courtyard of the old hotel. Talking about—what? What did he say to her?

Time for me to become someone else, Bonnie.

Okay, why? Why not go on being good old Frederick Sullivan, someplace other than New Lost River. Was he afraid Roxanne would track him down? Was he sexually involved with his own adopted daughter? But there had been other adolescent children with him during his sojourns—a son as well as daughters. If I knew anything about Greg Walker, I knew he had never compromised Sharissa. No, it just wasn't part of his pattern.

They came, Greg and his alter egos and his children: they stayed for up to two weeks, they left.

He left.

He left, and became another person.

Either the children left with him, and became other persons too, or—

They didn't leave.

The grinding began again, at a level below my heart, in

the diaphragm, the grinding feeling that I needed to throw up. I tasted soured wine.

But that made no sense—to bring adolescents here, abandon them or even kill them. Serial killing was one of the possibilities I'd considered. But I'd never read about a serial killer with a methodology remotely like that. Many of them were wanderers, but they acted much more frequently and compulsively. Greg hadn't always come with a daughter or a son. In 1840, as *Junius Halthorpe of Alexandria, Egypt*, a British subject, he had been the only registered guest during the month of January. There was a possibility he had come with servants, who might not have been registered. I didn't know what sort of man Junius Halthorpe had been, or what he did for a living. He might've been able to afford a family of servants, including a young maid or two; maybe someone like Sharissa whom he was particularly fond of . . .

I almost sobbed out loud, from one of the unexpected knifings of grief that had become more frequent as I looked into Greg Walker's astounding past. I had to push a wadded napkin against my mouth, thinking about her, remembering how long it had been since I'd seen Sharissa. It was more than just my obsession, which I'd learned to live with: I felt that if I didn't see her face soon, if I couldn't be reassured that she was still alive, I would go crazy.

I woke up on the morning of January 25, after another long night of itching and sweating and medication and whiskey on top of the allergy pills, woke up hearing her voice.

I got out of bed in my shorts and went groggily to the balcony doors, which were open. The sun had been up for an hour; the light was strong and it was already hot. I put my prescription sunglasses on.

"Out!" Sharissa called to someone.

I opened the screen but stayed inside the room. She was on the third of four AsPhlex tennis courts, her opponent a dark bow-legged man with silver hair—the resident tennis pro, who had once been a member of the Mexican Davis Cup team. I'd played him a couple of times since arriving. He still had power and more shots than I could cope with, when he was able to get to the ball, but arthritis in both knees had slowed him down.

I only glanced at the tennis pro. For the next fifteen minutes, while I scratched the rash that had spread to my testicles in spite of daily applications of Desenex, I stared at Sharissa; I drank her in: the quick, smooth, gliding steps I knew so well, the fierce two-handed returns, the pleased abrupt toss of her head when she smacked one by the pro. He'd been really good in his time and she couldn't beat him, but she played him even while I watched. I wished I could have cheered; I fantasized Sharissa looking up and seeing me—her astonishment, her pleasure. Her big grin.

Hey, Butterbaugh! Where the heck did you come from?

But all she would have seen was a half-naked guy with an unfamiliar beard and a hairpiece and a woody in his shorts, scratched up while he was trying to kill the maddening itch.

It was the fiery rash that finally drove me into the shower. And there my fantasies continued . . . to a climax that only partly calmed me down.

By the time I was dressed Sharissa had left the courts. The pro was giving a lesson to a couple of women with weak backhands. The terrace had begun to fill up for breakfast. Sharissa wasn't there; probably she'd gone to her room for a shower of her own. But I saw Greg.

He was sitting at a table next to the low stone wall

around the terrace. Francisco Colon was with him, drinking coffee, listening intently, nodding occasionally. I say occasionally, because I watched them for nearly half an hour, part of the time through a long lens while I took some pictures, and during the half hour his lips seldom moved and his eyes almost never left Greg's face.

Greg Walker was not just another tourist stopping at the Itzá Maya Hotel. He had been, for the better part of two centuries, an honored guest there. And I was sure Francisco Colon knew that—not only did he know Greg's history, but also his purpose in returning once again.

So much for the facts. Facts presupposed some sort of logic, but everything I had learned in the past few days was tormentingly illogical. I had to make myself better informed.

S oon I saw Sharissa again, taking a long flight of steps two at a time. Greg turned as she reached their table, her long arms embracing him from behind. She had acquired a deep tan on their Christmas cruise of the Caribbean, and afterward at the camp meeting in Venezuela. She looked thinner to me. But she seemed to be in an upbeat mood after all that exercise with the tennis pro. She kissed Greg on the forehead. A proper little smooch, but it chilled me. I took the picture anyway, as Greg welcomed his daughter to breakfast with an affectionate smile.

They were staying in bungalow nine in the gardens. I spent most of the day deciding how to get the listening devices into their bungalow.

The staff of the Itzá Maya were accustomed to seeing me all over the place with cameras. Hotel security was heavy because of the hit-and-run activities of government troops and a concentration of FAR guerrillas in the vicinity. I had heard gunfire, way off somewhere, automatic weapons that may have included fifty- and sixty-caliber machine guns, and twice in the night there had been brief mortar barrages. It was common to see helicopter gunships zipping low over the lake in pairs. But I suppose word had gone out that I was okay with management. Nobody paid attention to my movements around the hotel and grounds, even in areas considered off-limits to guests, like the kitchen and the construction zones.

I decided the best way was just to walk in, as if I were staying in the bungalow myself; which I did while Greg and Sharissa were at dinner the next night.

The locks on the bungalow doors weren't much; I could've taught any eleven-year-old kid how to pick one in under two minutes. But they hadn't bothered to lock the door behind them. The garden was surrounded by a dense hedge that grew berries in clusters and long, sharp thorns. It was impenetrable from outside the hotel's perimeter. Anyone trying to hack through the nine-foot hedge with a machete also would need to wear a suit of armor.

Three small units, each about the size of two Alka-Seltzer tablets combined. Power cell, transmitter, a hair-thin antenna, microphone the diameter of the lead in a number two pencil. Three separate ultra-high frequencies. A useful life of six to seven days. Range, up to four hundred feet. My room, on the third floor facing the gardens and with a clear view of bungalow nine, was about two-thirds of that distance.

In the tropic heat, the sticking power of chewing gum worked well. I popped a snooper under the table beside Sharissa's bed, another in Greg's room, a third in a wall-mounted light fixture in the living room, away from the hum of the small refrigerator and the sink in the kitchen area. Walked out with a smile and a wave and a "good night" for the benefit of anyone who might have observed me in passing, went back to my own room, sat on the edge of the bed in the dark with the receiver, which was also a Sony Walkman CD player if I happened to be in the mood to listen to Waylon or Hank Junior, and waited.

Quarter past nine, footsteps. The screen door slapping shut. Damn! And Sharissa's voice, as clear as if she were sitting on the bed next to me.

"How about a few hands of gin?"

"Shouldn't you call the folks?"

"It's two hours' difference. They'll both be asleep."

"I forgot. Okay, gin it is."

Two thousand dollars well spent, I thought. I'd been avid since their arrival to be as close as possible to Sharissa. But there was no way I could follow her everywhere she went. Now that we were all here, I had yet to figure out how I was going to get Sharissa on a plane for home without running into some major opposition from Greg. But for now I could lay back and hear her anywhere in the bungalow. The microelectronic ear I'd planted under her nighttable even picked up, when she left the bathroom door ajar, some familiar, intimate sounds.

And I was with her that night, all night, through her prayers, through whispers as she read passages from the Bible half aloud, through every restless movement she had in her sleep. Twice she spoke, sharply, disturbed in her dreams.

"I want a flower," she said. And, later, "The dog's all wet, Mom!"

Greg, in his room, snored. If his own dreams bothered him, he had nothing to say about them.

The next thing I knew, Greg and Sharissa had a couple of bodyguards.

One of them was a young woman who wore combat boots and a photographer's vest and carried an Uzi. The other one was a kid, but he was impressively armed, too. The names were Veronica and Benito; Francisco Colon was their uncle. I assumed he had supplied the guards at Greg's request.

Nothing much happened for a few days.

Sharissa swam in the pool and played tennis with the hotel pro. She read, on the porch of the bungalow, or took trips into Cobían with Veronica. Greg spent a lot of time with Francisco, usually in his office at the hotel. I found out, at my nightly listening post, when Greg and Sharissa planned to leave for the Baptist Mission down-country.

Their sightseeing trip to Kan Petén was planned a couple of days in advance, so I had no trouble following them up to the site on one of the scheduled minibus tours.

I'd been aware of Greg's growing tension. He wore shades almost all of the time, even at night, as if his eyes had become abnormally sensitive to light. Twice he'd growled at Sharissa for no good reason. "You're so jumpy!" she complained. Yes, he was. And keeping a very close eye on his daughter. When he wasn't with Sharissa, Veronica kept her company. As if Greg wanted to know what Sharissa was up to every minute. She complained about that, too. Some days Sharissa seemed bored and sad. Once, late at night, she woke up sobbing.

She cried in the cafeteria at Kan Petén too, because of something her father had said to her, which I didn't catch. The room was crowded and noisy. I was sharing a corner table with some tourists from Belgium, who carried as much camera gear as I did. We looked like a photography club.

Then Greg walked out, or almost walked out. He was stopped by a man with pathetically foreshortened legs in a wheelchair. The greeting was friendly, but Greg looked snakebit.

"You've made a mistake!"

It was obvious to me that the man knew Greg—or was it Fred Sullivan?—from somewhere.

"Nils Lagerfield. Uppsala University. We met before, here at Kan Petén—almost twenty years ago. Your lovely daughter was with you."

I had the autofocus Nikon around my neck with the lens cap off, and a few moments with nobody in the way; I snapped several pictures unobtrusively, from chest level, without looking through the hundred-milimeter-lens.

Then it was over; Greg stalked out of the cafeteria and, watching him, aware of a tautly concealed fury, I knew there was only one way to play this from now on: take advantage of his insecurity. Lean on Greg, and lean on him hard. Throw everything I knew or thought I knew in his face, pin him into a corner, take Sharissa and run like hell before he could react.

To get away with what I was planning, I thought I might need to recruit some help.

When the man from Uppsala University left the cafeteria with a couple of his colleagues, I followed them outside. Greg and Sharissa and their bodyguards apparently had left the site. Lagerfeld was having a leisurely argument with the friend who pushed his wheelchair along the walk to the museum building. He used a lot of hand motions when he talked, and looked as if he was enjoying himself.

They all went into one of the offices located behind the exhibition wing. I stayed outside in the sun near the helicopter landing pad, and took a few pictures of the Bell copter with pyramids in the backgrounds. It was hot, and sweat aggravated the heat rash on the back of my neck.

"There's some stuff the Kekchi use for that," a voice said behind me. "It stinks to heaven, but your skin clears right up."

I looked at the tall red-headed archeologist Sharissa had been talking to in the cafeteria. "I'll pay anything," I said woefully.

He laughed. "I might have some in my kit. Let me take a look. Is that the new Nikon you've got there?"

"I couldn't part with it," I said. "I'll just have to go on scratching."

He laughed again. "No charge to a fellow sufferer. With my complexion, I get eaten up by everything. Mosquitoes, bottle-ass flies, Azteca ants. Where're you from, Georgia?"

"Little place called Sky Valley."

"I think I know where that is. Between Chattanooga and Atlanta? I live in Nashville when I'm not in places like this. Glen Hazen."

"C.G. Butterbaugh."

He opened a door of the tinny-looking flying machine. There was a corporate logo on the door. BAYOU TECHE OIL. The rotors that drooped above us didn't fill me with confidence in the essential airworthiness of helicopters. Up close, they looked even more dangerous than they did in the air.

"You a professional photographer, C.G.?" he asked, as he rooted around in a gym bag, hunched awkwardly half inside the copter. There were seats for six, and luggage room, but it rocked with his every movement. The whirly things got to going real fast, then it just lifted straight up off the ground . . . no, thanks. "Not with *National Geographic*, are you?"

"I wish. No, I've won some juried shows, but I still have my amateur standing. Are you in the family oil business?"

"I'm an archeologist. Vanderbilt University. We leased the copter for a couple of months from an alumnus. He's back home in Louisiana trying to raise more money. In spite of the political situation, there's a lot of oil prospecting going on in the Petén. This baby's loaded with electronics. It even has forward-looking infrared, don't ask me why."

He backed out and closed the door. He had what looked like an old blue Vicks VapoRub jar in the palm of his considerable hand, covered with a piece of aluminum foil that was held down by a rubber band.

"Try this. Probably it'll sting at first, then your skin cools off."

I took off the rubber band and foil, and reacted.

"Yeah, well, the smell's a tradeoff for comfort. Throw some aftershave on top, and you'll probably still be able to get a date."

I dipped a couple of fingers into a grayish-looking mess, in consistency somewhere between mayonnaise and petroleum jelly. Rubbed it across the back of my neck.

"Indians bleed it from some root or other. It's like thin milk at first, then turns to jelly."

"Maybe there's money in it, for a couple of sharp entrepreneurs." I ruined a good handkerchief cleaning my fingers; but the smell lingered. Like rotting potatoes, mixed with a corrosive. "Do you know how to fly this thing?" I said, putting my hand on the helicopter. I yanked it back. The afternoon sun had turned the metal skin hot as a stove top.

"Sure. My brother's a West Pointer. He flew gunships in Vietnam, until he lost a leg. Kyle had me soloing when I was fifteen."

"Are you working at Kan Petén?"

"No, our dig's down at Dos Pilas. I'm here for a few days, then back to work until the rains set in."

"Nice talking to you, Glen. Here's your goop."

"You're welcome to what's left, I have more."

I thanked him and walked over to the offices, where the overhanging roof provided a little shade. The name NILS LAGERFELD was on one of the doors. I knocked a couple of times.

"Come," he said, sounding irritable.

I opened the door. The room inside was filled with crude shelves piled high with broken pieces of pottery. An old air conditioner in one window dripped on the concrete floor. He was seated in his wheelchair behind a long table, red of face and sweating under high-intensity lamps, handling more pieces of pottery laid out on a shallow square of wire mesh.

"Yes? What is it?"

I closed the door. "May I ask you a couple of questions, Dr. Lagerfeld?"

"Questions?"

"It's about the man you were talking to in the cafeteria—the one who said you'd mistaken him for somebody else."

"Oh, him. So?"

I held out my folder with badge and photo ID. He was wearing a pair of glasses with magnifying lenses attached. He raised the glasses to the crown of his head.

"What is this? Police?" He looked up at me. "Where do you come from?"

"Sky Valley, Georgia. Near Atlanta."

"Oh, yes. Georgia. 'The Peach State.' I was there once, for a lecture. At the Institute of Technology. You are interested in this man I spoke to? What has he done, that you come so far?"

"The worst thing I can say about him is that he was a bigamist; but the wives I know of aren't alive to complain."

Lagerfeld heard the nuances in that statement that I hoped would intrigue him.

"What is his name?"

"He's had several names. When he was here, nineteen years ago—" Lagerfeld's eyebrows rose slightly as I confirmed his memory for faces, "—he was using the name Frederick Sullivan."

"Sullivan." He repeated it to himself a couple of times, and shook his head. "No, I don't remember names. But I would have made notes of our meeting, as we spent several hours together one afternoon. He was very knowledgeable about Maya culture, for someone not in the profession. Almost like a genius, a genius manqué."

"Do you think you could identify a picture of his daughter? Her name was Bonnie."

"Yes, I think so. You have picture with you?"

"No. When would it be convenient?"

Lagerfeld shrugged. "I am here, every day. And often until late at night." He looked slowly around his workroom and office. "What we know of these marvelous people, only a fraction. What I have learned in my lifetime, a much smaller fraction. And I have lived very much longer than I was given, as a child. You see that I am in a wheelchair. 'Archeology?' they said. 'It is a profession for the able-bodied. What can you hope to contribute?' My strengths, I said. Patience, passion, scholarship, inspiration. Eh? But who knows where I would have gone, what discoveries I might have made, with a sound body."

He fell silent, staring, not at me, but at something from the past that made him uneasy. Suddenly he snapped out of it, wheeled his chair around, came to an old steel filing cabinet, rusting away in places, and yanked open a drawer. Well-worn file folders inside, tied with black ribbons. He searched for a few moments, yanked out a file and opened it.

"Knowledgeable," he muttered, and I barely heard him over the noise the air conditioner was making, "but a braggart. We both had too much to drink that day—still, I remember—yes, yes, this is it!"

He read through some dog-eared, handwritten pages as if he'd forgotten I existed, twisting his lower lip between the thumb and index finger of one hand, then turned the wheelchair again with a chuckle.

"I had forgotten some of this. His scholarship, which impressed me, and his—flights of fancy, which I remember amused me greatly. But I held my tongue. One could tell, drunk or sober, he was not a man to be ridiculed."

"Sullivan?"

"What name does he have now?"

"Greg Walker."

"You know him personally?"

"Yes."

"Describe him in one word."

"Dangerous," I said, not needing to think about it.

"Ah. The trait persists, along with his remarkable, perhaps unique, youthfulness. He appears untouched by time. Apparently I misjudged him, at our first meeting. He claimed, then, to have access to some talisman of eternal life . . . it is coming back to me now. 'An elixir?' I said. Oh, we were quite drunk. But I am never *too* drunk, understand. To listen, observe, remember. He sat back, glowering at me. He tapped his chest with a finger. 'This heart,' he said, 'will continue beating when you are dust. This hand—' he held it over the center of the table, and made a fist, '—will never lose its strength.' Then he opened his fist and turned his hand over, palms up. 'Look,' he said. 'Each line is a lifetime; and there are more lines than you can count.' It was true. His palm was as finely meshed as the screen on this table.

"Well, I said that he was a braggart. I played along. 'But you haven't told me to what you owe this gift of immortality.' He looked at me with a certain contempt that was gradually replaced by an expression of—forbearance. There was salt on the table in the *comedor* where we had whiled away the afternoon. He spread the salt across the table and wetted it with beer; then he drew in it with a fingertip. 'Can you read these glyphs?' he asked me. I could not. They were not like anything I had seen on the lintels or hieroglyphic stairs of Kan Petén or other sites in the vicinity."

Lagerfeld handed me a sheet of paper covered with glyphs.

"I drew these, with a ballpoint pen on the palm of my left hand, when he got up to visit the WC.

"I cannot read them today," he admitted. "Nevertheless, I strongly believe the glyphs are part of a written language that either predates the Mayan language, or existed concurrently with it. When Sullivan saw that I was puzzled, and frustrated, he laughed and said, 'The priests have always had a language of their own. The Catholic Mass was in Latin for nearly two thousand years, wasn't it? Okay, the quatrefoil signifies an opening in the earth. That much you know, I am sure.' He was toying with me, as an adept will mock the clumsy efforts of the novitiate. Then he pointed to other glyphs ... I don't remember which ones, but they represented, he claimed, Three Descents, the Great Star shining, the Lesser Star occluded, and the River of Blood.

" 'The River of Blood,' he said, 'is the river of eternal life.' "

"And you don't think he was making all of this up?" I said to Lagerfeld.

"If he was, then he was mixing fact and fiction in a rather dazzling display of virtuosity. He read texts, from photographs, the keys to which had only recently been discovered. He had a knowledge of the Dresden Codex eclipse tables that was virtually encyclopedic."

"There are all kinds of madmen," I said. "But I guess this one is in a class by himself. Did he give you any hint that he'd been here before?"

"No. May I see that again, please? Now that my curiosity is—"

He took back the page of glyphs, turned it in a couple of directions, then put the paper on the table where we could both see it, and placed a finger beneath one of the glyphs.

"This is familiar. Allowing for discrepancies from the haste with which I reproduced the glyphs, I've seen this one worn on the clothing of victims of blood sacrifice."

"Human sacrifice? I thought only the Aztecs—"

"No, no. The Maya routinely offered the bodies of captives to the Vision-Serpent and other gods. The usual method·was through ritual decapitation, but there were other ways, as ingenious as any bloody-minded priest could conceive."

"Why?"

"Their purpose? Religious propitiation, to enjoy the favor of the gods. To make themselves stronger in the eyes of their peers."

"Or with the notion that to take someone else's life would help them to live longer?"

"If so, all their efforts were in vain. If we know anything about the Maya, we know that for all their privilege most of the royals had normal life spans. Often they did not live as long as the average citizen because of the exhausting rituals of self-inflicted blood-letting. Or they were unlucky enough to be taken prisoner by a rival."

"Getting back to Sullivan. Did he say anything that would give you the impression he might have been so caught up in Maya lore and religion that he'd done some bloodletting himself?"

Lagerfeld shook his head slowly. "No. That would be . . . grotesque, would it not?"

"More like fatal for someone."

"What? Do you really believe this man may be a homicidal maniac?"

"I hope not. Jesus, how I hope it isn't true. Because if it is, then I can be reasonably sure most of his victims have been his own children."

Once I spoke what had been on my mind for a while, I knew the waiting game was over. Now it was time for me to do something about Greg Walker.

"It is a formidable difficulty, and I fear that you ask too much when you ask me to solve it. The past and present are within the field of my inquiry, but what a man may do in the future is a hard question to answer."

My mentor again, replying to a question of Dr. Watson's in *Hound of the Baskervilles*. Wishful thinking that I had even one-tenth of Sherlock Holmes's (or his author's) cleverness. I knew that I wasn't clever at all. My basic virtues were curiosity, skepticism, and thoroughness. Might as well add a fourth virtue: I was no quitter. For all the good that was going to do me, because what I was up against had me goddamned scared. No, that didn't go deep enough: I felt the kind of elemental panic a timid child feels in the dark, in an unfamiliar place. I could remember every scene of every movie that had terrified me when I was a boy, and the aftermath: the sick headaches, the queasy stomach. I had learned to be relatively fearless, as a cop in uncontrollable situations, by concentrating very hard on the results to be achieved. And by shutting down my imagination. The more vivid the imagination, the less control you have over your nerves or emotions at crunch time. Greg Walker had a certain power over me because, one, I didn't understand him, and two, I didn't know how he would react when threatened.

At least temporarily, I had to take those advantages away from him. Establish, in his mind, my own power, even if most of it was a deception. Get him off balance and keep him there, but not to the point of desperation.

And stay cool, Butterbaugh.

Thanks to the miracle goop Glen Hazen had given to me, my assortment of skin irritations was diminishing. For most of the afternoon I tried to relax in my room at the Itzá Maya, having an occasional cautious nip from a quart of sour mash I'd brought with me to Guatemala. And Sharissa was alone in the bungalow a couple of hundred feet away, trying to nap. From time to time I tuned in on her while I decided how to word the message I was going to send to her father. I had already settled on the best place for us to have our meeting.

I wanted to stun him when I played my opening card. But I didn't want him to cut and run, with Sharissa, to another, even remoter place. It encouraged me to think that probably he needed to be here, in Cobían, that for some reason he couldn't leave right now. We all seemed to be hostages to events taking shape in a calculating but seriously bent mind.

Toward evening I napped with the headset on. Greg had been there for a while, and left. I was awakened by another voice: Veronica's.

"It was probably a bat."

And Sharissa:

"Could you leave the louvers open? I like looking at the moon. It's almost full."

"Yes, in three days. There is an eclipse this month."

I took off the headset, yawned, got up to go to the bathroom. Then I put on pants and a shirt. It was dark now. I saw the rising moon and heard voices from the terrace; the kitchen staff was getting the nightly buffet ready. Quarter past eight. I picked up the headset again.

"—Something else. Not only superstition—more than that, I'm sure. In three days, the eclipse. Like before, when the Marquise—I doan know how to esplain—por favor, let me go!"

I don't know what had spooked Veronica, but she had my full attention. And Sharissa's.

"What do you mean? What about the eclipse?"

"My cousin ask me to be with you—few days only, he said. A favor to him."

"I know that. Till the Randalls drive up from Usumucinta."

"Saturday they will be coming."

"Yes."

"One day before the eclipse."

"So what?"

Veronica had nothing more to say. I heard the screen door bang shut.

My binoculars were handy. I picked them up and went outside on the balcony, focused on bungalow nine. I saw Veronica, dressed as always like a woman soldier in a high-fashion ad, walking away fast. Then Sharissa came bounding out of the bungalow and took off after her. I lost both of them behind a huge ceiba tree that was thickly hung with lianas.

With everyone out of the bungalow, it seemed like an ideal time to leave my message for Greg.

During the afternoon I had done a cut-and-paste job from headlines in a Spanish-language newspaper. Big black letters that read: I KNOW ABOUT BONNIE SULLIVAN. Then, underneath, the invitation, if he wanted to think of it as that: MEET ME TOMORROW 9 P.M. BASILICA ILUMINATA.

I inserted the message card into one of the hotel's envelopes, on which I had printed *Personal—Greg Walker*, and put it in a cargo pocket of my vest. Then I hurried down to the garden. I didn't know how soon Sharissa would be going back to the bungalow. It didn't matter to me if she found the message before Greg did. Probably she would obey the *personal* request, but regardless I knew she would be sure to show it to him.

As usual there were a couple of guards on the perimeter of the garden; I recognized both and they knew me. *Buenas noches. Buenas noches,* guys. They paid no attention as I strolled on to the bungalows, past a cage of howler monkeys and another cage like a wrought-iron tower of Babel, filled with scarlet macaws, parrots, and toucans.

I went up the steps to number nine in no particular hurry and slipped my envelope under the screen door. As I was leaving I heard Veronica's voice—*¡Ay Dios!*—from another part of the garden; then nothing more. But my curiosity was stimulated. It was obvious she was agitated tonight, and I thought it might be worthwhile to find out why.

A t a few minutes before nine I was back in my room, dictating everything I'd overheard in the garden— Veronica's story about the old Don and the star-crossed virgin lovers who, Veronica claimed, had been murdered for their transgressions.

". . . It was too late for her to find another virgin to take his place."

I had been so involved in eavesdropping, trying to get closer and closer to the two of them without attracting their attention—although Sharissa had glanced my way once when I was on the move and, I'm sure, had seen me—that with a little bad luck Greg Walker and I would've bumped into each other. But I had just moved as much into the dark and as far off the path as possible, standing very still between two small feather-duster palms. And his eyes were on Sharissa anyway, as she sat shivering on a stone bench.

"Girl talk?"

Veronica went by me first, close enough that I could see into the bore of her Uzi, her scarred face gleaming in the moonlight. But her eyes were fixed straight ahead. If I was a bloodhound, I probably would've been able to smell the fear streaming off her. She was followed by Greg and Sharissa, who had an arm around his waist. Her head was on his shoulder.

". . . Veronica was in some kind of mood. I think she must be one of those people who are affected by the full moon, you know?"

Meaning she thought Veronica might be two bricks shy of a load. That wouldn't have surprised me, either. But I wanted to have a conversation with her myself, just to be sure. The moon was nearly full over the lake and an eclipse was due—of the moon, or the sun, I had no idea which. Eclipses seemed to have something to do with the death of virgins, at least in Veronica's fatalistic visions. The craziness was compounding faster than I could keep track of it. *". . . another virgin to take his place."* Take his place for what? Ritual slaughter?

Veronica might have been getting to that when Greg interrupted. It was the part of her story I needed to hear now.

Five after nine. Dinner was now being served on the terrace. Greg and Sharissa, by themselves in the courts enclosure, were playing tennis. I watched them for a few minutes, wondering how Greg had reacted to the note I'd left in their bungalow. I was beginning to have symptoms from going without food for too long. I went back inside and called room service.

While I waited on a chicken sandwich, fries, coffee, and *crème brûlée*, I made an effort to locate Veronica.

I knew that her last name was Nespral, and that her husband had been killed in a minor skirmish involving the rebels. Nowadays she worked for her cousin Francisco. Maybe she lived in the hotel.

The hotel telephone operator told me she didn't. I was reluctant to ask her any more questions about Veronica, because hotel operators were incorrigible gossips. There were other ways to track her down.

A waiter came with my order. I ate my sandwich standing up at the sliding door to the balcony, watching Greg and Sharissa wind up their tennis match. He went back downhill to the bungalow, and she stood, all alone, watching him. Something about the way she looked on the brick-red court in her white shorts and sweater, a little-girl pose with hands loosely clasped below her back, leaning on her left foot—I grabbed a light meter and decided that, with a 250mm lens on my camera and ASA 2000 color negative, I'd get some interesting portraits. I put on my dark blue Braves cap and went outside on the balcony.

I took a couple of shots; then Sharissa turned and walked out of the courts enclosure. At the same time the lights went off. She was looking up, in my direction. I didn't have enough film speed for moonlight only—4000 ASA black-and-white would have given me some grainy but interesting closeups, that starkly pretty face, her hair swept back—but I took one more with what I already had in the Nikon, then went back inside

Seventeen going on eighteen, but she had always seemed more mature than that. And, as usually happened when I saw her unawares, watched her from a distance, I had to think hard about something else to get my heart to behave.

After coffee and dessert I loaded up my vest pockets with film of different speeds and an auxiliary flash unit, packed away my minicorder and extra cassettes, and went downstairs to the lobby, which was crowded with people wearing name tags, groups of well-dressed older people who had the kind of formidable assurance that only wealth and political dominance can give you in a place where ninety-five percent of the population is poor and hostile. The women with hairdos like spun glass, the men with jowls heavy as ticks ready to pop from overfeeding. I also heard a lot of American spoken. They were partying it up pretty good in the mezzanine club called Bahía, and the coffee shop was doing a lot of business. I saw a couple of familiar faces inside when I went by: the red-headed archeologist Glen Hazen, at a table with Sharissa. He was helping himself to her fries and talking with the kind of animated earnestness some guys adopt when they want to make a big impression.

My new friend Achille wasn't at his post by the bell captain's desk, so I waited for him. I had been laying some good tips on Achille for a week, in case I might need him for something important eventually. He was a half-Haitian Carib from Guatemala's Créole coast, the color of burnt toast. He wore an eyepatch, was loosely hung together, walked with a prance, smiled happily, and was hell with the ladies who worked at the Itzá Maya. He was just the man to understand my own lovelorn condition, all alone in the sensual tropics like I was.

"Boss! Taking manny more peeksures today?"

"Many pictures, Achille. Looks like the hotel is jumping tonight."

"She jomping for sure. When you tink I see *my* peeksures?"

"Day after tomorrow, that's what they told me at the photo shop in town."

I saw, past Achille and some women in high-fashion cocktail dresses, Greg Walker on the move. He was wearing dark glasses and not looking in my direction as he threaded his way through the traffic in the lobby with an expression that could be called ominous. He went to the door of the manager's office beside the reception desk and let himself in without knocking. His attitude was that of a man who owned the place, or at least some important part of it. I felt the pulses in my throat and my temples thumping.

Achille was distracted and about to veer off in response to a signal from one of his boys. Also the phone on his desk had been ringing for a full minute.

"Achille, maybe you could help me with a little something?"

I had his full attention. He smiled. "Ya boss! I am only too 'oppy."

"There's this woman I met. I think she's related to the owner of the Itzá Maya—"

"Mon, I am knowing exactly who you mean! Her name Veronica, she?"

"That's the one. We had this little conversation a couple of days ago, and I think we hit it off. At least I hope we—"

"*Claro!* She plenty *guapa* womans, even wit de face, you know?" He scratched quickly at one cheek with his hand like a claw, indicating scars. "But there sometink 'bout she—I no have de word in English, *apartada* we say." He gestured, boxing Veronica with his hands. Making smaller and smaller boxes.

"Yeah, I think I understand. I heard that she's a recent widow. But the point is, I'd like to get to know her better, only I haven't seen her lately; and I don't have any idea how to get in touch—" I sighed in frustration.

"Yes, yes!" Achille gestured again, like a genie about to fulfill my heart's desire. He whipped around to the computer terminal on his desk, danced his fingers over the keyboard, peered at the screen and smiled again, broadly.

" *¡No problema!* You see?"

I looked past him at the screen. Veronica Nespral. Telephone number, address, a hotel ID code beside her name. Achille had snatched up a pad and was jotting it all down. He tore off the sheet with a flourish.

"All yours, mon. *¡Buena suerte!* De woman like to have she peeksure taken. It very flattering way to, what you say, 'come on to she.' "

"I don't know my way around Cobián. Where do I find—"

"No problem! Behind dis hotel. *Ruta Tres Altares.* You are going one kilometer, *entonces izquierda.* Den two houses only. No number. De house, she blue color I tink. *Con permiso,* boss, I must answer dis crazy phone. *¡Buenas noches, Botones!*"

I slipped a folded twenty-quetzale note under his other hand, made my way through the lobby and past the entrance fountain. More people were arriving outside. The night was still cooling off. I heard a helicopter, and saw lightning in the distance, illuminating some dirty-looking clouds. But the moon was still visible.

Probably it wasn't in my best interests to go walking down an unlighted country road with a lot of valuable camera equipment. Maybe, I thought, I should wait and see her in the morning. But I was restless.

In the tropics rain doesn't begin with a gentle pattering of drops through the trees. One second I was dry, the

next I was scrambling for cover, as if I had suddenly
walked under a waterfall. I'd come about half a kilometer.
The bright lights surrounding the hotel were obscured as
I tried to stay dry next to the trunk of one of the mahogany trees that grew shoulder to shoulder along the graveled road. There was no wind, so the rain fell straight
down, most of it sluicing off the canopy overhead to run
in rivers down either side of the road. I was damp but not
drenched. Lightning flared, but not in my vicinity. The
flashlight I'd brought had enough beam to allow me to
pick my way over exposed humps of roots from tree to
tree.

I came to a chainlink fence topped with concertina
wire, all of it rusted. The fence enclosed a construction
site, six open floors of poured concrete. Past the uncom-
pleted building there were rows of small one-story houses
with tile roofs, heavily barred windows and gated car-
ports. The protected cars were VW bugs or dilapidated
Detroit models, all of them two or three decades old.
There were some yellow outside lights, but the metal window louvers of the houses were tightly closed. Everybody
had at least one dog, and the dogs were all barking up
against the gates as I dodged from tree to tree. But nobody in the modest homes was curious enough to look
out.

The rain was still heavy when I came to an intersection
with some commercial buildings not unlike the houses
nearby; a few were two stories high, with metal awnings
over upstairs porches. There were cars parked haphaz-
ardly in front of a café, where I saw the only signs of life
in the neighborhood, and heard music. A *rockola* was
playing Paul Simon's "Graceland." Next to the café were a
Laundromat, a beauty shop, and a grocery. Then the
buildings petered out, and there was nothing to see but a
few isolated lights shining through the rain.

I had run out of big trees. The landscape along the road
that angled left off the main road featured cedar and
broom and small varieties of palm. I was disoriented, and

wondered if that was the way Achille had meant for me to go. *Izquierda,* he said. "Left." But I didn't see any houses by the fading flashes of lightning.

I waited ten minutes under the storefront awning of the *peluquería,* until the rain stopped, and then I slogged down the hump of the secondary road, which had just enough gravel mixed with the mud to give me some footing. The flashlight kept me out of some bad potholes. Then the road took a turn and went downhill. I made out lights and rooftops, off to the left in a thick grove of trees. Two crude log bridges spanned a ditch. I passed the first house, which was closer to the road, and seemed deserted. The second house wasn't visible through the trees. But I saw the taillights of a car parked in there among the cedars.

Across the bridge the drive was paved with concrete blocks thinly covered by run-off mud from the wooded slopes. The rain had erased most of the tracks made by whatever vehicles had passed that way recently. I walked up the drive. It started raining again, with a whoosh. The canopy of cedar boughs above the driveway didn't keep me from being soaked this time.

Shielded floodlights at the corners of the house glared through the deluge. It was a blue house. The car parked in the drive was a dark-colored Mercedes, blue or black. The headlights were on. Somebody was behind the wheel, smoking. The gates of the carport stood open. There was a Toyota Land Cruiser parked inside. Next to the Land Cruiser a husky black dog with the mixed look of Mastiff and Rottweiler was lying very still on the terrazzo floor. It was raining hard enough so that the junkyard dog might not have been aware of me. I probably could've walked all the way up to the gates without being noticed by the dog, or by the driver of the Mercedes. I was sick of the rain running down the back of my neck. But I stopped and turned my flashlight off.

Probably just in time to avoid being spotted by the two men who came quickly out the front door of the house

and crossed the small porch connected to the carport and
breezeway.

The porch lights were off. I didn't recognize them until
they moved into the perimeter of a floodlight below the
carport roof and paused there, one of them swinging the
heavy iron gates shut. Francisco Colon. Greg Walker
watched him, not offering to help. From the way he was
rubbing his right fist with his left hand, he had hurt it.

Francisco closed the padlock on the gate and they hurried through the rain to jump into the Mercedes. That was
when I left the driveway and scrambled up a slick em-
bankment, grabbing at anything that grew there to keep
from sliding backwards, hauled myself up to a thick
clump of broom and watched while the Mercedes turned
around and drove by me toward the road. The Mercedes
was a diesel, and it left a noxious spoor that was quickly
washed out by the rain.

I turned my flashlight on and picked my way through
tangles of vine to the clearing around the house. Some cedar trees had been carelessly chainsawed, leaving uneven
stumps everywhere. There were stone pots filled with
plants and twig baskets of bromeliads and orchids hanging the length of the carport inside the pierced-concrete
outer wall. With my flashlight I could tell that the mixed-
breed dog had lost some blood, but he stirred slightly on
the terrazzo floor when I rattled the bars of the padlocked
gate. I didn't know if he'd been shot or bludgeoned.

There was no point in wasting time yelling for Veronica
Nespral. If they'd half-killed her guard dog to keep him
out of the way, they hadn't been very nice to Veronica either.

I needed to find a way inside, but the small house was
like a fortress. I went out into the rain again and circled
beneath the overhanging tile roof. The louvers of the first
four windows I came to were closed. Screens covered
them, then jailhouse bars bolted to concrete. In the walled
backyard, thickly planted with banana trees and bamboo,
there was a *casita*. But the metal door was padlocked too,

no way I could break in to look for tools. A porch with pierced concrete walls ran the length of the house in back. A croton hedge, waist-high, surrounded the porch. There was a broken downspout at one corner of the porch, creating a narrow waterfall off the roof. The flood-light was out.

I worked my way close to a wall of the porch and flashed the light around inside. I saw a washer and dryer, an ironing board, a plastic basket of clothing turned up-side down, a broken broom handle on the floor, Veronica sprawled facedown. She was wearing bikini underpants and a bra. The soles of her feet were dirty. Her back was livid and welted from the beating she'd suffered. I couldn't tell what the rest of her looked like. I couldn't be sure that she was still alive.

She didn't respond when I called to her. The rain cas-cading off the roof a few feet away from me made a lot of noise on the paving stones that encircled the house. I went down on my hands and knees to dig up one of the flat rectangles of cast concrete. It was about eighteen inches by twenty-four inches, and heavy. I put the flash-light in an oblong opening of the concrete wall, aiming it at one of the appliances inside. The bounce light off the enameled side of the dryer gleamed on the back of Veron-ica's head. Then I maneuvered the paving block under the waterfall from the roof. Water poured onto it, and was di-verted through another opening in the pierced wall.

I had to experiment to get the angle just right. The rain was cold, and I was trembling. I kept the diverted stream of water aimed at Veronica's bare welted back for much too long a time, getting no response at all.

"Wake up, damn it! Wake up, Veronica!"

I thought I saw a shudder pass through her body; then one hand closed in a slow convulsion, and she gasped. I put the slab of concrete down and turned the beam of the flashlight on her face, calling her name.

It took her a while to drag herself into a sitting position. She was shivering uncontrollably, moaning. Some blood ran in a trickle from one corner of her mouth. Her eyes were closed.

"My name is Butterbaugh! I'm a detective. I want to help you, Veronica! You have to get up. Don't lie down again." I splashed around to the padlocked porch gate and rattled it. "Let me in! I'm here to help you!"

"No más," she protested, in a weak voice, then groaned more loudly. *"Dios mío! Estoy suffriendo! Ay, ay!"*

"I'm not going to hurt you! Please let me in, so I can get you to a doctor!"

She groped blindly along the floor, teeth chattering. She moved on hands and knees, very slowly, toward me. Bright blood dripped from her open mouth. I think she was following the beam of the flashlight on the terrazzo floor to the gate. When she got there, she pulled herself up, hand over hand, breathing harshly. Her eyes were barely open. I don't know if she saw me or not. I was afraid she would lose her grip and fall down hard. I didn't know what was causing the internal bleeding. If she was lucky, it was only a broken rib. But she could die from shock if I didn't get some help for her right away.

Her face was only a few inches below mine as she clung gamely to the bars, mumbling in Spanish, breath hissing through her teeth between expletives.

"The key," I said. "Can you get the key?"

"Kill them," she said in English. "K-k-kill them both."

"The *key*, Veronica."

She opened her eyes wider and stared at me. *"¿Quién es?"*

I said my name again.

"You are friend—of Kiki?"

"Yes," I said, "sure I am. The gate, Veronica. Can you unlock the gate?"

"Unlock these gate," she repeated thickly. *"Sí, momentito."*

She let go of the bars, one hand, then the other, turned toward the kitchen door. Hunched over, shuffling, she made it to the metal door, leaned on it for several moments, breathing with a raspy, sobbing sound. Then she turned the knob and slipped inside. I heard her fumbling in the dark. The flourescent lights went on. After another long wait she reappeared, clutching a ring of keys. Shuffled back to the gate.

Blood from her mouth was smeared across one cheek. Tears ran through the blood. They hadn't touched her face. There was no way to know yet how much damage had been done to soft tissue and vital organs. Her thighs and hips were striped with ugly welts.

Sagged against the gate, shaking badly, she fumbled with the keys and managed to get the right one into the big padlock. I opened the gate carefully, reaching around to get a grip on her so she wouldn't fall. She screamed twice while I was trying to lift her in my arms. She wasn't very big but she was slippery from the dousing, and tremors made her hard to hold.

She kept saying "Kiki," over and over, as if she were delirious. That small, slow trickle of fresh blood persisted at one corner of her mouth. Light from the tiled kitchen was reflected off the white walls of a dining and living room, guiding me through the house to her bedroom. I put her gently on the canopied bed and turned on a lamp with a pink bulb in it. She lay in a fetal position, shuddering while I covered her with a comforter from the closet.

In the bathroom I soaked wash cloths in water as hot as either of us could stand and packed her body with them. The bra was drenched and I unsnapped it, took it off. She was about half-conscious, and didn't seem particularly aware of me.

"Bastards," she said. "Bastards!"

"Why did they do it, Veronica?" I asked her, but either she couldn't hear me, or she didn't have the strength to answer.

Once I had her chills under control, I looked for something she could wear. There were a couple of Filá jogging outfits of a crinkly lightweight material hanging in the closet. She was going *"Ay, ay, ay"* on the bed, moving torturously under the comforter, trying to find a bearable position to ease the pain. I discarded the tepid cloths from her nearly naked body, talking soothingly to her while trying to get her to sit up. I wiped blood and froth from her lips again. Her eyes opened; although she was shrouded in pain she had a few moments of lucidity. She touched the dark nipple of a small bare breast and focused starkly on me.

"What are you . . . doing to me?"

"Getting you dressed. You need to see a doctor."

"*¿Habla español?*"

"No, I don't speak Spanish. My name is Butterbaugh. I'm a detective, from the States. Try to put this on, Veronica."

"*¡Dios, Dios, Dios!*"

"I know it hurts. He probably broke a couple of ribs. How many times did they hit you?"

"They . . . no. Him only."

"Greg Walker?"

"Yes. He said, 'These bitch should be killed,' but Francisco, he saying no, she learn her lesson. 'Doan you learn, Veronica?' Pig!"

"Learn what?"

But I'd lost her again. Her face squeezed tight and she quivered from a deep electrifying pain. I zipped up the jogging jacket and lowered her head to a pillow. Her underpants were wet, too. I found a pair of scissors in a drawer of the table beside her bed and cut them off, then worked the jogging pants up over the broom-handle welts on her legs. At least a dozen of them, more on her back. Then, not satisfied with the extent of the punishment, he'd used his fists. There were swollen bruises everywhere, lumps the size of turkey eggs.

"Bad man," she said, gasping. "These Walker. Very bad man."

"I agree. He'll get what's coming to him."

"Next time . . . I see him, I will have a gun."

"Why did he do this to you?"

"Say . . . I talk too much to Sharissa. I did not know before if . . . if he was one of *them*. But I know it now. An' he will destroy his own daughter, so his life may go on and on."

"How? What does killing his own child have to do with prolonging his life?"

"It only happen . . . if he shed the blood of a virgin, *un adolescente,* at the right time . . . during eclipse of the sun or moon. It is . . . an old, old ritual. The anointing power of virgin blood, taken from a still-beating heart."

"Bullshit," I said, but I was livid from shock. "I don't know why he's as old as he is, or what keeps him looking the way he does. But if he's been sacrificing kids to justify his mania, then he's nothing but a psychotic murderer."

"And how . . . do you explain all the others, who are just like Walker?"

She was calm now, lying very still under the comforter, but taking shallow breaths, her eyes opening, closing. The blood had stopped welling at the corner of her mouth. I was the one who was shaking. Everything I had on was soaked.

"I don't know about that! I don't care about . . . others. It's a lot of goddamned superstition. If he killed Bonnie Sullivan in one of his rituals, then I'll do my best to nail him for it. But nothing like that is going to happen to Sharissa, you hear me!"

"What . . . can you do, Detective? Can you kill him? Not simply kill him, but . . . cut off his head?"

"Jesus! What are you saying?"

"Walker . . . is too strong for you. Too cunning. The power of the *cofradía* protect him. Growing up, I am hearing many things. Whispers of ancient secrets. The secret of the Timekeeper. Don Santiago, my uncle . . . was a Timekeeper. Chattel of the owl and harpy. A society of these peoples who can live long, very long, as they desire, and if they are careful . . . not to make themselves known to ordinary human beings. Above all, taking care not to lose their heads. There is no ritual that can restore life to the headless. Even so, they are sacred beings, descended from priests of Maya. Now I think the new Timekeeper is

Francisco. From father to son, no? He is sworn to protect the immortals. I am . . . tired, *amigo mío*. And the pain is very strong."

"I'll take you to the hospital."

"Hospital no good here. Too many sick people, I will catch something awful and die. There is a *clínica*, run by a friend, Dr. Arturo Gúzman. Francisco may . . . change his mind about me. Thinking I am a risk to him, and the *cofradía*. I will be safe for a little while at Arturo's. It was there my husband and I were taken, after . . ."

Tears were flowing again, and she whimpered. I held her hand.

"You are cold from the rain," she said. "Take time to change now. In the next room, clothing of Enrique's. Some of his things . . . may fit you."

Kiki, Kiki—it was her late husband's pet name she'd been saying on the porch. The clothes she was talking about were in an old steamer trunk, a lot of rugged mail-order stuff from Bauer and Bean, everything washed, ironed, and packed away. I guessed that Enrique Nespral had been a few inches taller than me, and big through the chest. I stripped to the skin, put on clean socks and khaki walk shorts, a short-sleeved shirt, and a roomy bush jacket. The Nike running shoes were surprisingly small and pinched my toes, but at least they were dry.

In a drawer of the trunk there were two loaded handguns in woven leather holsters, a Firestar automatic and a Cobra .357 Magnum revolver. I'd never been partial to automatics, even with the extra capacity. I put the Cobra, holster and all, into an inside pocket of the bush jacket.

Veronica wouldn't let me carry her outside to the Land Cruiser. She forced herself to walk. Little sliding steps in *huaraches*, leaning on me for support.

When she saw the dog stretched out on the carport floor she groaned in anguish. "Zorro!" He looked at her, quivering, but made no attempt to get up. He had a gash on his head behind one ear from a blow that might have damaged his brain. Or maybe he only had a bad headache.

"Arturo will send someone to look after him," Veronica said. "Leave the lights and lock everything behind us."

The rain had stopped. I backed the Land Cruiser outside and closed the gates. Veronica slumped in the front seat beside me, head bowed, suffering as silently as she could, giving directions in a monotone. I drove down a lot of unfamiliar roads, through a couple of villages, going around the swampy west shore of the lake, then heading north on higher ground.

"There were guns in the trunk," Veronica said. She held her head up, staring through the dirty windshield. "I forgot to tell you."

"I saw them."

"Did you take one?"

"The Cobra."

"Are you good with a gun?"

"Yeah, on a target range."

"Can you shoot Walker if you have to?"

"I'm not going to shoot him," I said. "I'm not going to cut his head off, either. I told you, I only care about Sharissa."

"But you took the gun anyway. That was so you will feel brave?"

I didn't answer her. I thought about it, and I still didn't have an answer.

"You will kill him," she said. "When the time comes." It wasn't a request, it was a pronouncement.

A few minutes later I passed through the open gates of a small *hacienda* at the end of a rocky village road and next to a church and orphanage.

The *clínica* had double-barred glass doors off a spacious tiled veranda. I rang a few times. A man came down the central hall and looked out. He was wearing a robe and slippers. He had a very obvious glass eye, and a suspicious manner.

"It's Veronica Nespral," I told him through the door. "She's been badly hurt. My name's Butterbaugh." I held up my shield and identification for him to look at. He nodded and unlocked the door.

"So? What's a redneck cop doing in this neck of the woods? You on vacation?"

"No. Veronica's in the truck."

"Can she walk?"

"I think it'll take both of us to get her up these steps."

He followed me out. "Veronica? What the hell happened to you?"

"Hi, Arturo. You meet my friend? What was your name again, Buzzerball?" She couldn't hold her head up for more than a couple of seconds. Her speech was slurring. I was scared for her.

"Yeah, Buzzerball. She got beat up pretty bad, doctor."

"Okay, let's get her inside."

We carried Veronica between us, fireman's carry, to a treatment room of the clinic. She kept saying, "Kiki, Kiki," and moaning. "No, it hurts. ¡Dios mío, give me something!"

Arturo Gúzman took off his robe and put on a white jacket after we placed Veronica on the table. He must have rung for help when I wasn't looking; a sleepy-looking young man showed up in the doorway, glanced around and put on another jacket hanging behind the door. Arturo spoke rapidly to him in Spanish. Then he looked around at me.

"You could wait in the office across the hall."

Veronica said, not opening her eyes. "He see everything I have already. We are practically engaged."

Arturo said, "That's nice. Maybe you're hungry, Butterbaugh. Or help yourself to coffee in the kitchen."

I took the hint. As I was leaving Veronica cried out and said, "They broke my ribs, 'Turo!"

"You let me be the *médico* here, *cara mía*. Relax now, we're just gonna give you a little something to take the edge off."

I poured myself some coffee in the kitchen, and added several lumps of sugar. I had a stress headache. I took a look around while I sipped the coffee. The *clínica* was scrupulously clean. There were four treatment rooms and an operating room, up-to-date X-ray equipment, an infirmary with six beds, four of them occupied by children. A night nurse was on duty; she was reading a Spanish fashion magazine by the light of a gooseneck lamp. I wandered back to Gúzman's office. The lack of an accent was explained by the diplomas on one wall—prep school in Los Angeles, UCLA for college and med school. He'd done his residency in internal medicine at St. John's Hospital, Santa Monica. There were pictures of his wife and kids on his desk. She was a California blonde with long legs, posing with her arms around a surfboard.

After about forty-five minutes in the treatment room and X-ray, Gúzman and his assistant wheeled Veronica, sedated, into a private room next to the small infirmary. They were giving her IV fluids, two bags of it. Gúzman left instructions with the nurse and came out, put a hand between my shoulder blades and guided me back to his office. He was about my height, stocky, with heavy eyebrows, a sensual Latin nose and a chin cleft that probably drove women nuts.

He closed the door and took out a pack of American cigarettes.

"Yeah, I'm one of those doctors who still smoke. But only three a day." We both looked at the ash tray on his desk. At least a dozen filter-tip ends were there, snitching to his conscience. He sat on the edge of the desk and pushed the ashtray behind him, held out the pack to me.

I shook my head. He lit up and inhaled. He had unkempt curly hair and sunken, darkly circled eyes. The glass eye put his gaze a bit off-center, but it was nothing that detracted from his wounded-Romantic looks. He studied me thoroughly while he took a few more drags.

"So what kind of trouble is she in?"

I had been thinking about how much of an explanation I was going to give him. I stalled by saying, "How much did Veronica tell you?"

"Nothing. From the looks of her, I'd say they worked her over with a pole or stick, then got in a few bare-knuckle licks, which did her ribs in. A lung was nicked. Her spleen is okay, but her diaphragm has a tear. Kidneys, I'm not sure yet. No indication of rape. Do you know who they were?"

"Her cousin Francisco." He winced, and vented smoke through his nostrils. "He was there, I suppose he sanctioned the beating, but he didn't participate, she says. It was a man named Walker, Greg Walker, from my hometown of Sky Valley. What are the chances we can get him locked up while the local police investigate this?"

"Investigate? You're kidding me. If Francisco had her beaten, she won't rat on him. It would bring dishonor to the family. I don't know how long you've been in the Petén, but it's like the Old West around here. There are laws, and there are prohibitions, and then there's Francisco Colon and the *cofradía*; they're the final authority when something is going down. The local magistrates, on those occasions when the government allows the judicial system to function, would look the other way, even if Veronica dies. The situation doesn't exist for them."

"Yeah, I thought so," I said dispiritedly.

"Don't make a mistake about my loyalties. 'Nica and my wife are good friends. What's your reason for getting involved? Do you know Veronica from somewhere?"

"I know Greg Walker."

He smoked, watching me, and neither of us said anything. Then he reached into his pocket for another cigarette, glancing at the photos on his desk.

"Barbara's away doing a year of residency at Cedars

Sinai," he said. "The kids are all in boarding school. Gets damned lonely around here."

"You're both doctors?"

"Well, Barb came to medicine late. She was a sorority chick at SC when I married her. Family went crazy, Barb married a spick, and all that. Old Pasadena family, groves or something. I come from original Spanish land-grant people, late eighteenth century. Half of the Santa Clarita Valley still belongs to some of us."

"You're a long way from home."

"This *is* home, Butterbaugh. Came here for six months on a WHO grant to complete a research project, and never left. That was twenty-three years ago. When the kids got old enough, Barb told me she wanted to be a doctor, too. Until then she'd concentrated on fund-raising for health-care facilities all over Central America. Fifteen million dollars. I said, sure. Go for it. What about this Walker? You want him for something?"

"I'd like to put him away. But I can't prove what I suspect."

Gúzman waited, and yawned. "That's all you want to tell me?"

"You saw the damage he did to Veronica. I think it would be better if you didn't know any more about him."

"Or his relationship with Francisco Colon?"

"That, too. By the way, did you know Francisco's father, Don Santiago?"

"I met him. I wasn't his doctor. I don't think he ever needed a doctor. He was . . . one of the most remarkable men I've heard of or read about."

"Because he lived to be a hundred twenty?"

"It's not medically impossible to live that long, or even to retain a certain amount of mobility at such an age. But the Don played a mean game of tennis. And he was still ready and able to hell around with the ladyfolk."

"How do you account for that kind of longevity?"

"Obviously it's a matter of cell replication and elasticity, which requires an abundance of an enzyme called superoxide dismutase—the enzyme neutralizes free radicals in the body. He had a hereditary endowment the rest of us can only wish for."

"Do you think it's medically possible for a man to stay in his prime for a hundred fifty years?"

Gúzman looked at me with kindly contempt. "A biologist friend of mine at Cal Irvine selectively bred fruit flies until he came up with a group with a life expectancy, in fly time, equal to one hundred fifty years. That kind of selective breeding with humans is way off in the future somewhere. What are you worried about, Butterbaugh? You can't be much over thirty. Relax and enjoy your normal three score and ten."

There was something hard in my throat that I was having trouble swallowing. And something heavy in an inside pocket of my borrowed jacket, a reminder of just how soon it could be over for me, if I made a wrong move in the next twenty-four hours.

"I hope I'll be able to do that," I said to Gúzman.

Gúzman's assistant, a med-tech named Cuellar, drove me back to Veronica's place in her Land Cruiser. It was two in the morning. I had him ease into the driveway with only the parking lights on. There were no other visitors at the moment, but the dog was gone from the floor of the carport. I got out with my flashlight. The carport was empty and locked up. So someone had come back, disposed of Zorro in some manner, and probably looked around inside. They might have decided that Veronica had come to and driven herself to the hospital. On the other hand, whoever it was could have been sharp enough to conclude from the wet clothing I'd left hanging on the back of the door in the other bedroom that a) a friend had arrived, probably on foot in the rain, and b) had seen enough to be a potential problem. I hadn't left anything in the pockets of the wet clothes to identify me, but still I was beginning to feel insecure.

On the way back to the hotel I scribbled a note to Gúzman expressing concern for Veronica's future safety and gave it to Cuellar. Then I had him drop me at the foot of the drive to the hotel, and walked to the entrance from there: I didn't want anyone seeing me arrive in Veronica's Toyota.

By then it was three in the morning. I tuned in to bungalow nine and heard nothing but the sounds of sleepers. I put the headset aside and changed into my own clothes. There were iron-on tags with Enrique Nespral's name on them in everything of his I'd borrowed. I rolled shirt, jacket, and shorts up tight and put them, along with the too-small sneakers, into a hotel laundry bag, zipped the bag into one of the compartments of my Samsonite hang-up. I tried to get some sleep then, because I had a good idea of what the next thirty-six hours would be like. But all I could see when I closed my eyes was Veronica's small nude battered body. Gúzman had taped her like a mummy and shot her full of antibiotics, but the internal and psychological damage would heal slowly, if at all.

Greg Walker's violence toward her suggested a man at the edge of his control. But in my dreams he just laughed at me, as I fired round after round from the Colt Cobra into his forehead . . . the bullets falling away like swatted flies. *Don't hurt my daddy,* Sharissa screamed. *Don't hurt my daddy!*

Oh, kid. I'm so sorry. How am I going to get you out of this?

I checked out of the Itzá Maya at seven the next morning, and took the hotel's shuttle van to the airport. There I stored most of my luggage, keeping a leather carry-on case that would fit beneath the seat. Then I went to the TAPSA counter and bought two tickets on Saturday morning's flight to Guatemala City, connecting with a flight to Houston at two in the afternoon. I sent a telegram to Adrienne Crowder with instructions for her to follow, had a few bites of *huevos rancheros* and a sticky bun for breakfast in the airport coffee shop, and rented a car from the local Hertz affiliate.

The rental was a stick-shift Ford with sixty thousand miles on it. No air conditioning. The windshield had a long diagonal crack on the right side, and the last renter had smoked a lot of cheap cigars. I needed two shots of nasal spray before I could breathe at all.

The road to Kan Petén was half a mile north of the airport. I arrived at the ruins about eight-thirty, just before they opened for the day, left all but my cameras and a manila envelope at the *Inspectoría*, and took the long walk uphill through cool misty woods to the visitors' center. The Bell helicopter was still on the pad next to the museum wing where Nils Lagerfeld had his workroom and office. I hoped he would be in this early.

He was, and he wasn't.

He didn't answer when I knocked. The door was unlocked and not tightly closed, which I found out when I tried to use it for backing to write a note to him. The door swung inward a few inches. Inside there was wholesale devastation: shelving tipped over, file drawers emptied. He sat in the midst of it all in his wheelchair, withdrawn and silent, his chins on his chest, hands lying palms-up in his lap. Sunlight grazed the back of his head, disturbing the flies drawn to all the blood. I heard them buzzing in the dusty gloom. I shut the door slowly and carefully, as if I didn't want to wake him up. I walked away from the building and crumpled the note I had begun to write, then shifted the envelope containing an enlarged photo of Bonnie Sullivan with her father from one sweaty arm to the other.

I knew what I should do, but I had no qualms about putting distance between myself and the body of Nils Lagerfeld. I saw only a few early-bird tourists on their way to the pyramids, heading away from me, chattering obliviously. I wanted badly to know a lot of things about Lagerfeld's death that a few minutes' observation might have told me, and I already had information which would be valuable to the investigators who would be showing up eventually. I wondered how long they would hold Greg Walker, based on what I could tell them.

For a little while I was tempted to raise the alarm. But I knew the government cops would hold me a lot longer than Greg, once Francisco Colon's influence came into play. In the meantime I would probably lose track of Sharissa forever.

I didn't know if Greg had killed Lagerfeld and ransacked his files, or merely suggested that it be done. It wasn't important how it had happened, his motive was clear. Now I was the only one in the neighborhood who could connect Greg Walker to Bonnie Sullivan, presumed missing and probably long dead by her father's hand.

I inspected three hotels in and near Cobían before deciding on the Petén Grande, three blocks from the *zócalo* and the Colonial-style basilica to which I had invited Greg Walker at nine o'clock. It was the feast day of some locally prominent saint, the church bells were ringing hourly, and the trees in the plaza in front of the basilica were decorated with strings of lights and paper bunting.

The entrance to the Petén Grande was off an unpaved street, through double wooden doors of a size you might expect to find in a German castle. The doors were set within a thick masonry wall twelve feet high. There was a pleasant courtyard with a fountain behind the wall, with the usual bird and monkey cages. A good breeze came off the lake and through the lobby of the hotel. There was an elevator that went as high as the third floor. I was on the fourth and top floor, overlooking the lake. Double room with telephone, balcony, private bath, a ceiling fan and an electric fan on the lacquered rattan dresser, twenty dollars a day in season. There were two good locks on the door, but still I didn't want to leave anything valuable behind when I went out again.

I had the number of Gúzman's clinic on a card he'd given me. I got a woman who didn't speak English and then, after a lengthy delay, Gúzman himself.

" 'Nica's as good as could be expected. Give me a week and I may be cautiously optimistic. She's asleep now, but maybe you could see her for a few minutes this afternoon. Want to make it three o'clock?"

After talking to Gúzman, I went for a walk, stopping at the photo store in town, which, like most of the other shops, was open. Apparently the minor-league Saint's Day wasn't significant enough to interfere with business. I picked up the pictures I'd shot of Achille, the bell captain of the Itzá Maya, and some of the other people who worked there. I had intended to mail them to Achille, but the post office was closed for the day, so I added them to the collection of stuff I was carrying around with me and crossed the *zócalo* to the steps of the modified basilica: Spanish-Colonial style, four towers instead of two. The steps were crowded with people. Kids and old women were hawking religious souvenirs and bunches of flowers, paintings of the honored saint on everything from paper fans to china plates. There was a lot of activity inside the basilica as well, although no mass was in progress.

The size of the sanctuary surprised me. I was interested in finding a location where I could watch, without being conspicuous, the main entrance to the basilica. There were side doors as well, but no one was using them. They might have been locked. On each side of the high altar, where offerings of flowers rose to the nailed and bloodied feet of Christ, there were tower chapels, or grottoes; one of them included a stone tomb. The altar was well lighted, but the nave was not. Very little daylight passed through the high, narrow, stained-glass windows. Votive candles burned in pyramidal rows in two locations, in holders of smoked ruby glass. There were four confessionals, and vividly enameled statues in Easter-egg colors at each Station of the Cross.

I sat near the left-side aisle while I looked around. Several penitents went past me down the rough stone aisle on their knees, praying or weeping aloud. Our concerns were different, but I felt a pained affinity. The voices of other worshippers scattered in pews down by the altar added to the echoing din.

After a few minutes the dust and aromatic smoke had me coughing. I left without having made up my mind about anything that related to my meeting with Greg. If he showed up. But I didn't see how he could afford not to.

A little before three I found my way back to the village of Las Figuras, where Dr. Gúzman had his clinic. By daylight it wasn't a bad-looking place, with a central park and basketball court shaded by old ceiba trees, a couple of modest hotels and some ruins nearby, on a small bluff above a shallow bay that looked like a waterfowl refuge. There were a lot of boats in the muddy water below the village. It was a good afternoon for boating, breezy, not too humid. On a day like this I could understand why Gúzman had been persuaded to stay.

His own home was on the walled grounds of the clinic, in a grove of trees a couple of hundred feet away from the larger building. There were gardeners with machetes on the grounds. Two teenage boys and a blond girl were working with tools under the hood of a 4WD Suzuki in the driveway beside the stucco house, arguing like siblings about the nature of the problem. Gúzman supervised, a bottle of beer in one hand. When he saw me pull up he sauntered over, wearing threadbare jean shorts and a Lakers jersey.

"Kids are home from school for a week," he said. "No emergencies until the feast-day boozing gets out of hand later tonight, so I took the afternoon off. 'Nica had a couple of visitors from the hotel. Don't look so worried, I vetted them before I let them in." He made a gesture with the beer bottle, directing my attention to a couple of compact young men, bare to the waist, pruning a sprawling purple bougainvillea next to the clinic.

"These are my guys. Very deft with their big knives. I took your note seriously."

"How did anyone know she was here?"

"Veronica asked me to call a friend, have her bring some clothes and personal stuff. Said she could be trusted."

The blond girl was dancing around on bare feet, fists up, offering to punch out one of her brothers.

"Don't hit him in the nose, 'Cesca!" Gúzman yelled. "I can't do any more with it if it gets broken again!" He beamed at me. "Just like her mother," he said. "Barb taught them all how to box. I'm the nonviolent type. So what's going to happen, Butterbaugh? You mixing into something local?"

"With luck I'll be out of here in less than two days. I don't think I've stirred up anything yet. I'm taking Greg Walker's daughter with me. I have every reason to believe she's in real danger if I don't get her out of Guatemala."

"Sounds a lot like kidnapping," he said edgily.

"No. Sharissa knows me well, and I think she trusts me. I'm doing this with the full knowledge and cooperation of her grandmother."

"What kind of danger?"

"Veronica thinks Greg Walker may be planning to offer his daughter as a ritual sacrifice to some old god or other. He may have done this in the past." I opened one of the envelopes I had with me, slid out the photo of Frederick and Bonnie Sullivan. "This was the daughter he had with him when he visited Cobían nineteen years ago. By the way, speaking of lucky gene selection, he looks today just like he did in this photo."

"Only now he goes by the name of Walker. Why did he beat up 'Nica?"

"She tried to warn Sharissa. She believes there've been cases of human sacrifice in this area, in recent times. It's a local mania, drenched in superstition, who knows how it ever got started: a few people who claim to be descended from the elite Maya have been fortunate to live well past the average life span, and they attribute it to something supernatural like bathing in the blood of a virgin. The Hotel Itzá Maya and its owners apparently have figured into the cult bloodletting, going back to the hotel's beginnings."

"How come I never heard anything about this?"

"It wouldn't be a public spectacle. The people who are participating in these ritual acts are delusional, but still they must recognize the fact that they're committing murder."

"Assuming there's some truth in what you're talking about, could 'Nica be mixed up in it?"

"I don't even know Veronica. We didn't have the chance to talk much last night. What do you think?"

"What I know about Veronica is that she has suffered. Her husband was killed, two years ago. She loved him very much. There are people who handle tragedy or crisis better than others. It has to do with one or two enzymes in the brain. Barb has been a friend to 'Nica, but Barb's been away at med school. I don't know who her other close friends are, or if she has any. Maybe she stays to herself too much, and broods. Goes without sleep. The need for sleep is more psychological that physiological. Deprive susceptible individuals of sleep for a few days, it's amazing how quickly they become delusional, even psychotic."

"How has she been acting today? Depressed?"

"I wouldn't say depressed. Subdued. That's from trauma, and the medication. She hasn't had much to say about what happened to her."

"Could I see her now?"

"Yeah, I guess so. But only for a few minutes, and I'll

be there too. It looks as if I have a small stake in this business. I've worked in the Petén for twenty-three years. I give one day a week to the public hospital in Cobían, and three days a month I do the flying-doctor bit. I suppose you'd say I've established a certain rapport with the departmental bureaucracy, but if I cross the wrong people, like Francisco Colon, I'd be deported in a day. So far I haven't done anything but treat an injured woman. Beating up women isn't considered to be a crime in Third World countries, so I'm not looking to be interrogated. As long as I'm treating 'Nica, she's protected. Once she leaves, I can't help her. I have no interest in you, one way or another. You understand? Good. Let's go in."

One visitor from the Itzá Maya was an older woman who worked in the business office. She wore thick glasses and had bleached her hair to a rusty orange shade. Her name was Encarnación. Veronica's other visitor was the night bell captain, Achille, who greeted me enthusiastically outside the private room where Veronica was recuperating. Off duty he wore primary colors and gold chains.

"Boss!" Achille had never made much of an attempt to get my name straight. "What a terrible ting! But you de one who finding she, yes?"

I nodded. Encarnación said anxiously, "Did you see them? These terrible robbers who beat her?"

"I didn't see a thing."

"Poor Veronica. All her life, she is so unlocky."

"But she not killed," Achille said. "We must be thankful."

I had his photographs with me, and took them out of the envelope. While they were exclaiming over Achille's likeness I wound my watch. Gúzman let himself into Veronica's room, closing the door behind him.

"Boss, for what I owe you dese wonderful peeksures?"

"They're a gift, Achille."

"I must do something for you! Very fine old watch you have, for sure, but need winding, always. I get you a wonderful Rolex, mon, de greatest watch in de whole wurl. Never need to wind. It not exactly a Rolex, you understand, but even de Rolex people have difficulty to tell. Two hundred fifty quetzales."

"Thanks, Achille. But this one has sentimental value."

"You like dese gold chain? Stupendous value! I have a place to buy."

"Maybe later, Achille. I need to talk to Veronica now."

He shook my hand and Encarnación kissed my cheek, and they left.

I heard Veronica's voice when I knocked. She was more or less sitting up in the hospital bed, at an angle of thirty degrees. Apparently Encarnación had brought her a nightgown and a satin bed jacket with a Mandarin collar. Her hair was brushed. Her dark eyes had a high shine to them, and the tracery of scars, like part of the skeleton of a leaf, was prominent on her right cheekbone. She still had IVs taped to one wrist.

"Hello," she said. "You are the one who save my life. I doan remember your name."

"Butterbaugh."

"For sure. Buzzerball. Now . . . it comes back to me. How are you today, Buzzerball?"

"Okay."

"Tell me, Buzzerball. What were you doing at my house last night?"

Gúzman leaned against the wall next to the single small window in the room, arms folded, taking us both in.

"I'm a detective," I said. "From Greg and Sharissa Walker's home town. Remember? We talked about him on the way over here."

She closed her eyes. "Oh, yes. And you—you are trying to protect Sharissa?"

"At her grandmother's request. I don't have any official status. Greg Walker isn't a suspect in a criminal case. If we were in Georgia, I could lock him up for assault. It might be possible to do that here, in spite of what Dr. Gúzman thinks. Which would make my job a little easier."

Veronica was silent for a while. Then she looked at me as if from the end of a tunnel and said, "Nobody hit me.

It was raining. The floor was slippery. I was doing the laundry. Ooops. I fall and hurt myself."

I looked at Gúzman and said, "You two have time to fix this up before I came in here?"

He shook his head, looking speculatively at Veronica. Then he spoke to her in Spanish, softly. She smiled a bitter smile and didn't reply. He seemed concerned, glancing at me as if I were getting on his nerves just by existing.

I said, my tone angrier than it should have been, "You're lucky Walker didn't put a bullet in your head. He's probably done worse, to others." I couldn't tell from her unwinking eyes if she was depressed, hostile, or merely indifferent. Then I realized Greg must have let her live out of deference to Francisco, who he would trust to keep her in line from now on.

"I'm going to take Sharissa home," I said to Veronica. "It's all I can do, but I think I can accomplish that much."

"Good for you, Buzzerball."

"Can you tell me why you think Walker planned to kill his own daughter in a ritual sacrifice?"

Veronica turned her head on the pillow, grimacing.

"I have always . . . heard things. About the sacred beings, and . . . their sacrifice of virgins. Then this man Walker come with his daughter, before the eclipse. He is . . . he seem to be . . . especial friend of Francisco. Who is all but on his knees to Greg Walker. This is not like Francisco. But it was the way of his father, too, when . . . others came to the hotel, from around the wurl. Always with an *adolescente*, who they treat like a prize calf. You understand? Is it superstition, my imagination, is it that I am crazy for a long time? Maybe. What do you think, Arturo?"

He didn't say what he thought.

I said, "A man named Nils Lagerfeld, a Swedish archeologist, remembered Walker from the time he was here before. Made notes of their conversations. Walker, or Sullivan as he was calling himself then, had an encyclopedic knowledge of Maya lore. He could read glyphs. He bragged about living many lifetimes. I saw the notes myself, but they're probably missing now. Lagerfeld was killed in his office, last night or early this morning."

Gúzman made a dismal whistling sound through his teeth.

"I don't have evidence that Walker murdered Lagerfeld, or had it done. But his circumstances make him the logical suspect. If he is guilty, I should know soon."

"How?" Veronica said.

"I'm meeting him tonight."

She frowned. "Alone?"

"No, in a very public place. The Basilica of the Iluminata."

"You must be careful anyhow. Very careful."

"Don't doubt it for a minute."

Gúzman came unstuck from the wall. "You have first-hand knowledge of a motive for Lagerfeld's murder," he said to me. "What are you planning to do with that information?"

"Once I have Sharissa out of the country, I'll send my notes and some photographs to the Swedish embassy in Guatemala City and let them approach the local authorities. They'll push it a lot farther than I ever could."

"Meanwhile," Veronica said, "Greg Walker will leave the country."

"He might get away," I admitted. "I've said before, Sharissa—"

"Is your only concern. *Claro*. But it seems a shame. One can only hope he will suffer the fate of the Marquise."

"Who?" Gúzman asked her.

She smiled wearily. "That is a story for another day, 'Turo. But now . . . I am finding it hard to talk and breathe at the same time. *¿Permiso?*"

She seemed to have fallen asleep even as we were going out the door. We walked toward the clinic's foyer. In a treatment room Gúzman's med-tech assistant was taking care of the split bloody knee of a kid from the orphanage. Gúzman detoured to give the tearful boy a pat on the head, and rejoined me on the veranda.

"Let's say we arranged for you to call me after midnight tonight, but that call doesn't come. In fact, nobody hears from you again. Which would be a shame, naturally, but those things happen when you play detective."

"I am a detective," I reminded him.

"You're a fish out of water in this country. A big shiny carp."

"I'll be taking very good care of myself."

"But—"

"I thought you didn't want to be involved."

"I could manage a few things anonymously."

His kids were playing keep-away with a garden hose on the lawn near his house; they seemed to be having a hell of a good time while they got soaking wet. The spray from the hose created brief effervescent rainbows in the summery air. I felt some interior tremors, a sense of remorse, as if I had been persuaded that I'd failed already. I had set up this confrontation with Greg Walker as deliberately as I knew how. But I wasn't at all convinced I was good enough to win my own game. Gúzman had reminded me: there were only two kinds of fish in the sea. Sharks, and food for the sharks.

"One A.M.," I told him. "If I don't call you by then, all the information for the embassy will be in an envelope taped to the back of the first confessional on your left in the basilica."

I was an hour early for my appointment. A Mass was in progress, and the nave was nearly full, with standees in the small atrium. I felt comfortable and not too conspicuous in the crowd of worshipers. The amplified voice of one of the three priests on the altar created a sepulchral echo above the murmuring sea of responses. The confessionals were doing good business while the Mass was said. Small flames of candles flickered in shadowy places. Pockmarked plaster saints with rosy cheeks stared at one another across the bent backs of the dutiful and the penitent.

Unable to stand in one place for the duration of the Mass, I maneuvered slowly through the doorway to the nave and toward the left-side aisle. For the second time in forty-eight hours, I almost ran right into Greg Walker.

He was standing, flanked by but a head taller than a family group of dark-faced local people, near the aisle, with his face turned away from the altar and toward another family group: Joseph, Mary, and the infant Jesus. The Virgin's feet were bare, bone-white and nearly toeless, probably from repeated fondlings and kisses.

Greg was wearing tinted glasses, as if the glow from the altar at the front of the nave was like the incandescence of a blast furnace to him. He also had on the bush jacket I'd seen him in every day since he came to Cobían. It was humid in the basilica, and there was a sheen of perspiration on his highlighted profile.

I came up to him on the other side. A little girl wearing an embroidered white dress and a tiara glanced at me and moved closer to her mother, giving me room. I jabbed the muzzle of the revolver I had taken from Veronica Nespral's house against the small of Greg's back. The revolver was in my left hand. There was nobody between me and a font of holy water standing against the wall.

"Kneel down," I said, "while we talk."

He stiffened, but didn't move. "What's that?"

"Colt Cobra. It won't make much noise going off like this. It *will* go off if you try to turn around."

He hesitated a couple of moments, thinking things over. "C.G.? Is that you?"

"Yes, it's me. Get down on your knees."

"I thought I recognized . . . what's this all about?"

"Maybe I can't kill you," I said, "but I'll bet a shot-up

liver will put you under the weather for a few days. Now *get down.*"

"All right," he said, and dropped slowly to his knees in front of the statues. I followed him all the way with the muzzle of the revolver pressed against him.

"Give me a hand back here," I said. "Thumb up."

He put his left hand behind his back, and I snapped my cuffs on the exposed wrist. Prodded him with the pistol to offer up the other hand. I cuffed the wrists together. He drew a sharp breath. They were a good pair of handcuffs, nickled case-hardened steel, with a two-inch-wide hinge instead of the usual chain separating the cuffs. It allowed for no movement of the hands at all.

"Break a knuckle beating up on Veronica Nespral?" asked him.

"Am I under arrest?" He sounded exasperated and inconvenienced, but not angry. "I haven't committed any crime. And I'm sure you don't have jurisdiction—"

"I'm just giving myself a high comfort level while we talk," I said.

I put the revolver back in my pocket and changed my position, on one knee beside him where I could watch his face. He seemed composed, in spite of the awkwardness of the restraint. It was dark enough near the floor so that anyone looking our way probably wouldn't notice that he was handcuffed.

"The Virgin has blue eyes," he said. "I've visited the basilica quite a few times; it's odd that I never noticed before."

"How many times have you been in Cobían? I could only trace you back to 1840."

"Oh, I see." His head dipped, as if he were hiding a slight rueful smile. Except for the gloss of humidity on his tanned skin, he was so damned at ease he was making me nervous. "I suppose I never gave you credit for being such a good detective. Even when I had warnings that you might have been alert to something. What was it?"

"Too many coincidences. That, and a hair sample

Roxanne Sullivan carried with her in her locket. I have an exact DNA match, no room for doubt."

He nodded thoughtfully, but not as if he cared anything about DNA matching.

"C.G.? I'm uncomfortable like this. Isn't there somewhere else we can talk?"

"No."

"I'm willing to answer whatever questions you may have. It really can't do me any harm."

"What happened to Bonnie?"

"She died."

"In Guatemala?"

"Yes. There was a cholera outbreak shortly after we arrived. It's a matter of public record."

"Where did you bury her?"

"In a mass grave, near the village of Matapalos."

"How about your other children? Naomi. Cynthia. Ellen. Joseph. What mass graves are they buried in?"

An unexpectedly wide smile, that seemed remorseless to me. Otherwise he was calm, invulnerable, looking up at the face of Mary. The light above the heads of the statues made iridescent pools on the bronze lenses of his glasses. His fingers flexed behind his back, as if he were trying to find something to anchor himself to.

"They weren't all my children. Cynthia was my wife. We came to Cobían on our wedding trip. Let's see, that was—"

I had a sudden throatful of nausea. "How old was she?"

"Seventeen. Her eyes were blue. The blue of the Virgin. I loved Cynthia very much. It was an ideal platonic relationship. Unfortunately, we couldn't remain together for as long as I would've liked."

"Did you kill her, Greg?"

No great change came over him. I once sat in on the interrogation of a murder suspect who had denied guilt consistently and rationally for three days; then, between drags on his umpteenth cigarette, he tamely admitted chopping up a couple of preschoolers in his toolshed. Bells rang on the basilica altar: once, twice, thrice. The bells seemed to signal to Greg that it was time to move on, to a more meaningful level of confession. *Did you kill her, Greg?*

"Yes."

"All of them?"

"I don't deny it."

"Bonnie, too?"

He altered his story. "She had taken sick. The cholera. It was a bad time to come to Guatemala. But since I didn't have any choice—I was able to spare her a terrible death."

"How did you kill them?"

"Humanely. I promise you that." As if he were satisfying a condition for my approval and compassion. "The act of killing is a cruel thing. But they were all my dear ones— they died blessed in me."

"You're insane, Greg. I hope you realize that. And that it's time to stop."

He looked at me, for the first time since kneeling in that shadowy corner of the basilica. His eyes were unseeable, the light having vanished like spirits from the lenses of his glasses. And something else was gone too: the pretense, despite my rough handling of him, that we were like two casual acquaintances who had run into each other between flights at an airport far from home. Making small talk about bloody crimes. There was a tone of emotion in his voice when he spoke again.

"You simply don't *understand*. But how could you hope to? I've had a fortunate existence. I'm superior to all but a handful of men on earth. That is a fact, not lunacy. My father, who was renamed by the Spaniards Don José Pablo Canek, recognized, soon after I was born, that I was one of the immortals. He brought me here when I was seven, to be instructed by the Timekeeper. There is nothing impure about the ritual. It is an honor to those we choose to assist us. They are exalted by our gods."

"Your gods exist only in your own mind. And it stops *now*, you hear that?"

He shook his head to silence me, then cocked his head

toward the altar, where the Eucharist was being celebrated.

"*The body of Christ,*" he murmured. "*The blood of
Christ.* In all ritual we find renewal. Spiritual, physical. A
timeless thing, of sublime meaning and beauty. The Sacred Heart is the lodestone, the great seed of life. You
shouldn't be afraid of what you don't understand. Why
don't you take off these handcuffs now? They don't give
you any power over me, not in this place. And I don't
mean you any harm."

"Somebody else will take them off," I said, "when
Sharissa and I are well on our way out of here."

It was reckless of me; he jerked his head in a display of
nerves and passion that emphasized the danger in him.

"Oh, no. You've made a mistake, C.G. You can't take
Sharissa away from me."

I had the Colt out again, where he could see it. I
wanted to stick it in his ear. "Let's go," I said. "On your
feet."

I pulled him up with my right hand, yanking on the
sturdy hinge that connected the bands of steel around his
wrists. It is guaranteed to be very painful. He reacted to
the pain by arching his back. Then he threw his weight
against me, just as I shifted my own weight back onto my
right foot, and was slightly unbalanced for half a second.

His move staggered me. He couldn't do anything with
his hands, but he pivoted and drove the top of his head
into my breastbone. I went sprawling into the midst of
worshippers kneeling nearby. A woman screamed as I
rolled over her. Greg came after me, trying to kick my
balls off. I caught the kick on my thigh instead, scrambled,
was eye-to-eye with a terrified little boy, pushed myself to
my feet and lunged for Greg. I clubbed him in the side of
the head with the Cobra. A lot of people were screaming
now. The blow to the head bloodied Greg's ear and sent
him reeling toward the aisle. I was hobbled by the kick
and slowed by worshippers cowering on the floor as I
went after him.

"¡Policía!" I shouted, pushing my way through what was turning into a panic-stricken crowd, trying to get my hands on Greg. But he was shouting too, in a language that wasn't Spanish, his voice rising hysterically, like a demagogue's. He turned to look at me, tinted glasses askew on his face, one brown bloodshot eye like that of a stampeding bull, trampling, screaming. A plaster saint rocked on its pedestal as bodies jostled against it. I stepped blindly on someone lying facedown in the narrow aisle. People were rising in the pews, looking at us in horror, staring at me with the shiny gun in my hand. Some of the Maya faces were angry, not horrified, as Greg continued his retreat, gaining a little on me, pressing backwards down the aisle, still shouting above the uproar of shrieks and lamentations.

"¡Policía, policía!" But I couldn't reach my shield, I was too tightly packed in with a lot of people who were suddenly acting very hostile. Toward me, not Greg.

Somebody grabbed the gun, a dangerous thing to do; at the same time I was pummeled from behind. I had to let go of the Cobra or have a couple of fingers or my wrist broken. I took a fist in the ribs and one in the kidneys and realized I was in serious trouble. Then it was just fists, fists, and feet as I went down and tried to assume the correct position to protect my vitals. I was too stunned to be afraid, even though I knew I was in danger of being beaten to death by a mob. None of it seemed very real to me. I must have been in shock. I wasn't interested in Greg anymore.

I don't know when they stopped kicking me and started smothering me with the weight of their bodies. I was on my side in the aisle with my head against a pew, and there wasn't much air to breathe down there on the stones. I felt like I had as a kid when I was gang-tackled in football, all the other kids deciding to have fun by piling on Butterbaugh. It was my punishment for being gullible enough to think they were going to let me run with the ball. I felt close to tears, even as I slowly suffocated.

I was never going to score the winning touchdown. And Sharissa stood off in a fog on the sidelines, smiling sadly before she turned away.

Church bells were ringing. They sounded distant, and alarming. It was the last thing I remember about the Basilica of the Iluminata.

———

Lights; but unsteady lights, as if I were peering with blurred eyes at a night sky that contained only two widely separated galaxies. At least I was able to breathe again.

A lungful choked me; it tasted like cement dust. I coughed until something jetted up and spilled down my bearded chin. A sour, almost bitter liquid. I coughed some more. By then my heart was beating wildly. I couldn't feel my hands or feet. I seemed to be numb in a lot of places, but damp in the crotch.

The coughing brought pain. Lord, it was a lot of pain! As if my body had been twisted into an unnatural shape, then pressed in a vise. Sharp pains in my lower back. An aching neck. A mouthful of cement and puke.

I had the bright idea to call for help.

As soon as I tried that, one of the galaxies that had been shimmering at the edge of my field of vision sharpened and swung closer; it seemed to smack me in the side of the face like a comet.

The blow sent a few more stars shooting through the darkness out there. The light stayed close to my head, dangling, swinging slowly in a circle. It assumed the shape of a bulb in a cage. A workman's utility light. The glare made my eyes water. I heard voices: low, indistinct.

They were speaking Spanish. I heard other sounds, that I couldn't identify: one was a rhythmic scraping, metal against metal.

I was sitting down. Concrete floor. Legs stretched out. I was wired at the ankles. My hands were in my lap, I discovered, also wired together. My back was against something solid, a wall with uncomfortable horizontal ridges. I blinked a few times to try to clear my eyes and saw someone moving through the periphery of the bright bulb swaying near my head. He wore dusty paratrooper boots and military-style jungle camouflage pants.

"What's . . . going on?" I said.

The other side of my face was struck—an open-handed slap. His hand was hard. I yelped.

"Don't do that," Greg Walker said. His voice came from somewhere else; he wasn't the one who had hit me.

The boots moved away. The scraping, slopping sounds continued. I identified the odor of wet cement. More conversation in Spanish. Someone lit a cigarillo. I saw his face briefly. Swarthy, pockmarked, two unshaved chins, and a scar straight down the center of his forehead. Smoke drifted my way.

"I'm allergic," I said, just to be saying something.

Footsteps. They echoed slightly. I had the impression we were in a large unfinished room somewhere. There were concrete block walls on either side of me. I seemed to be sitting in a three-sided alcove about six feet deep.

Greg Walker showed up in the light, holding the manila envelope I had taken with me to the basilica. The envelope had contained photos of him with his daughter Bonnie Sullivan, with Francisco Colon in conversation on the terrace of the hotel, with Nils Lagerfeld in the cafeteria at Kan Petén. Copies of the DNA autorads. All of my notes on the investigation, including Lagerfeld's statements, unfortunately not signed by the late archeologist.

Greg had taken off the tinted glasses. There was a cut on his right ear that had dried, but the ear was red and puffed from being struck by my revolver.

"How did you manage it?" I asked him. "Those people in the basilica . . . wanted to kill me."

"Most of them were Maya," he said. "And you have green eyes."

"More hazel than green, except when I wear . . . contacts."

"For the Maya, green eyes are a sign of evil. I told them you had been possessed by a demon, but God would protect them if they drove the demon from your body. If there had been any stones handy, they would have stoned you to death." He was looking at me with an expression of mild regret. "I'm really sorry about all of this," he said. I think he was referring to the contents of the envelope, which he replaced.

"There's copies everywhere," I said. "Adrienne Crowder knows everything I know."

He nodded, acknowledging that I was a prudent and cautious guy, then said, "Well, that doesn't really matter, C.G. None of this information will do anyone any good. Another 48 hours, and I won't be here."

"Where will you be?"

Greg smiled and shook his head.

"More blood on your hands?"

He looked perplexed by the implication of butchery. "You just don't understand. How deeply I loved them all. Sharissa has been a wonderful part of my life."

"Spare me." I tried to clear my throat. "I'll get you, Greg. No matter where you run . . . we both know you'll be running in a circle. If it takes nineteen years, when you come back here I'll be waiting for you."

"Yes, you will be here," he said without irony. "And long forgotten."

That clarified one thing. I was being walled up here instead of dumped in a ditch with my heart cut out, because unexplained disappearances tended to lessen the urgency and thoroughness of follow-up investigations. *Whatever happened to C.G. Butterbaugh? Maybe he went native or something, down there in the tropics.* Gone without a trace. And who would really care, other than my aging parents? Adrienne Crowder would probably believe I'd been bought off by Greg.

I tried to get up then. I was able to lift my butt off the floor, but I couldn't get my balance on wired-together feet. Dizziness from the surge of activity toppled me. I don't remember hitting anything; I must have blacked out for a little while. When I came to I was seated again, but this time there was baling wire around my neck, fastened to what felt like an eyebolt in the wall behind me. Someone had plastered my mouth with filament tape.

The worklight was still on, and a couple of men were crouched at my feet, busily slapping cement onto concrete blocks with trowels.

Either Greg had left, or he was standing, godlike, in the dark void, watching me being walled up in the alcove. The wall which the workmen were building in front of me had risen to three courses of block. Just behind them the man in jump boots and jungle fatigues was smoking another cigarillo, looking impassively at me. He had a flashy gold Rolex on one wrist.

The other two worked quickly. Slather on cement with twists of the wrist, gently knock the block into place. How long did it take cement to dry? I tried to get my feet up to kick at the wall, but I was inches short, and the baling wire cut into my throat. Strangling was an unpleasant way to die. Better to stay calm and try to think. Be rational and objective. Count my blessings. I was still alive, that was something, wasn't it?

Hell no it wasn't, and the panic center in my brain was shooting off fireballs. Breathing was already a chore. I raised my hands from my lap, attempting to get at tape across my mouth. They had thought of that, too. A thinner wire I hadn't noticed ran from my wrists to the wire that bound my ankles tightly together.

The man with the dark-toned cigarillo frowned, and put a hand on a shoulder of one of the workmen.

They moved out of his way, and took a break. He

stepped over the low wall and crouched in front of me, cigarillo in one corner of his mouth. He picked up my hands and pushed back the left sleeve of my jacket, then unstrapped my wristwatch and looked it over.

"Ees old one, no? But valuable." He put the Hamilton watch in a pocket of his own jacket.

I felt indignation stronger than my fear of dying. Maybe he sensed that. As he was stepping out of my little cell, or tomb, he stopped and grinned at me. Then he sat on the low wall, reached out and put the nicotine-yellowed thumb and forefinger of his right hand on either side of my nostrils. He pinched firmly. I held what breath I'd been able to collect for what seemed like a very long time, looking into his bloodshot eyes. He smoked with his other hand and studied me intently, with a continuing hint of amusement, until I passed out again.

Dreams, or visions, of drowning. Rising through depths of black water toward a wavering light. Unable to reach it, or to breathe. Then breaking the surface and gasping, hearing scrapes and sharp metallic strokes on concrete. Seeing the worklight through a hole in the wall only half a cement block square. Then the light disappearing as the last block is snugged into place in the wall and cemented there. A final tamping sound in utter darkness. Then nothing but my own harsh breathing through clogged nostrils, I was dragging in air with enough force to pop a blood vessel, but it wasn't ever enough.

Don't panic don't panic goddammit no-no-no—

Ankles wired together. Wrists wired together, and to the ankles. Baling wire around the neck. No lateral movement. Hands spread about six inches, but so what? Mouth sealed shut, if I get nauseated again, will drown in my own vomit. How much air? A few hours, a day's worth? Did they leave any little chinks or spaces through which air could seep? Holmes and Watson at least two weeks away by hansom cab. Good work, Butterbaugh. You asshole.

Feeling weak. Low blood sugar. Hard to concentrate. But I'll get out. I'm going to get out. For Sharissa's sake, I must get out. I'll think of something.

Just as soon as I take a little nap.

B uzzerball?"
 Heavy, muffled pounding sounds. There was a lot
of pain in my chest. My lungs felt as if they were pressed
flat. When I tried to breathe, it was like drawing air
through closely packed cotton wadding. In fact, I couldn't
breathe at all. My throat was bulging, I was about to swallow my tongue.

Pieces of broken concrete block showered over me as
a light pierced my eyes. Then there was air, and my lungs
swelled. The shaft of light was cut off for a few moments.
I heard voices speaking Spanish. The sledgehammer
pounding started again, and the jagged hole in the wall
got bigger with each stroke. Pieces of broken block fell all
over me. There was a lot of dust in the precious air I was
dragging in. I had to keep my eyes closed so I wouldn't
be blinded by flying bits of concrete.

When the pounding stopped I blinked a few times and
saw a lanky dark man grinning in at me.

"Ya boss!"

Another face shimmered under the light, and became
more distinct.

Veronica Nespral said, "Next time pay a little more, and
they give you a suite."

Very funny. Achille reached in through the five-foot
hole he had made in the wall, touched my face with his
fingers, then ripped off the layers of filament tape, along
with a considerable patch of mustache. Then it felt as if
my upper lip had been blowtorched.

He retreated and ducked out of sight; there were clink-
ing sounds, as if he was rummaging in a tool bag.

"How . . . did you find me?" I asked Veronica. It was the voice of an old, old man. My throat was sore from dehydration.

"Momentito," she said. Her face was stiff and her eyes looked as if she were carrying a load of painkiller. Achille reappeared with wire cutters and leaned in to snip away. He was sweating from his exertions. But my skin was dry; I couldn't sweat.

Even when I was free of the wall and could move my tingling hands and leaden feet, I barely had the strength to get to my knees. I coughed hard enough to uproot a lung. My head throbbed and my heart was racing.

Achille handed me a liter can of tepid pineapple juice. I sipped some of it. The tingling in my hands had turned to needles of pain as circulation improved.

"Come on," Veronica snapped at me. "Get going, Buzzerball. There is a whole lot of shit in the fan, and we doan have much time."

". . . Time is it?" I wheezed, trying to crawl through the break in the wall with Achille's assistance.

"Cinco menos quatro." Four forty-five. My brain was as sluggish as my reflexes. I drank more of the juice with shaking hands.

"You mean it's . . . almost morning?"

She shook her head slightly. Every movement seemed to cost her something. "Not morning. *Tardes*. Saturday afternoon, Buzzerball."

" *Saturday?* Jesus. You're saying . . . I was in there for almost two days?"

I had climbed out of the improvised tomb, trembling all over, wobbly and disoriented. I couldn't stand without Achille's support. Veronica stared at me in dismay.

"You won't be any good to me like this," she complained.

"Oh, sorry. Just give me a goddamn minute here, and I'll be . . . leaping over tall buildings."

I shook Achille off and groped my way along the wall, away from the worklight he had rigged. Then I opened my pants with stiff fingers and pissed on the floor. There wasn't much of it, and the stream was discolored with rusty blood. My kidneys hurt like hell. Thirty-eight, maybe forty hours in that hole. I should have been dead. I didn't smell dead, but I didn't smell very good, either.

I walked a dozen steps back to Veronica and Achille without losing my balance. The pineapple juice was beginning to do me some good, elevating my blood sugar.

Achille had shouldered his canvas bag of tools. Veronica was carrying her Uzi rifle, or one just like it, on a sling. She also had a revolver in her shoulder holster, a Lady Smith .38, and a machete strapped to her side. I wondered just what action she was ready for.

"Where are we?" I asked her.

"Itzá Maya. The old part of the hotel they are restoring."

I nodded. "So how——"

Veronica reached into a pocket of her flak vest and pulled out my Hamilton Piping Rock watch. Achille flashed a grin.

"Jaquez," he said. "I see him in hotel lobby, wearing Rolex on one wrist, dese one on de other wrist. Jaquez collect manny watches, he known for dat. But I see dese old-time watch dat I know I am see someplace else, and I go, 'Yes!' to myself. I am afraid for you, mon, tink you must be in croc's belly. Jaquez known for dat also. But I go right away to *clínica*. Veronica get up from her bed wit' manny curses and come to your rescue."

I said to Veronica, "You still couldn't have known——"

"Jaquez told me," Veronica said. "Come on, let's get out of here, we are late already. Glen is waiting for us at Kan Petén."

"I need a shower and a change of clothes."

"There is no time for bathing. *Move it,* Buzzerball."

We moved it. I gritted my teeth and got down two flights of steps without groaning aloud. I knew Veronica was in trouble too, from her deliberate pace, but otherwise she didn't show any distress. There was a resolve in her face that impressed and worried me.

"How did you get Jaquez to tell you what they'd done with me?"

"It was no problem. I shot him a couple times first, so he could be certain I had serious business to discuss."

I looked at her in amazement, thinking it was a joke. But I'd been close enough to the muzzle of her rifle to know it had been fired recently. I had been told that the Maya who remained in this land after twenty centuries were a tranquil and submissive people. Maybe Veronica was a throwback to the notoriously combative Itzá soldiers, who had been the last of the Maya to surrender to the Spanish. Or maybe she was a little crazy.

Her Land Cruiser was parked on a service road behind a neat hedge of heliconia, a few yards behind the old hotel building. There was a kid wearing a straw hat with a tall banded crown behind the wheel. It was late afternoon, all right. The brightness stunned me. Temperature in the eighties and unseasonably humid, but I still couldn't sweat.

"Get in back," Veronica said to me. "I brought more of Kiki's clothes. Change while we are driving."

She turned and spoke in Spanish to Achille, who protested whatever it was she had said. She shook her head firmly and finally his shoulders slumped. He glanced at me, and I nodded my thanks for the rescue. Then Achille walked away from us.

Veronica got into the Land Cruiser. "This is my brother, Benito," she said. "Benito, you are meeting the famous Buzzerball."

The kid offered me his hand to shake. "Why did you send Achille away?" I asked Veronica.

"He has no part of this. I do not want him to get hurt."

"What about your brother?"

"I will look after him." She popped the top on another can of fruit juice and handed it to me. It was pink and heavily sweet. I drank it off as Benito drove down the road away from the hotel grounds.

I stripped to the skin. The shorts were bloody in front.

I could only hope the stomping I'd absorbed in the basilica hadn't finished off one of my kidneys for good.

Veronica gave Benito some instructions, then turned and looked me over, deliberately, but with little expression while I pulled on fresh boxers, triple-stitched duck pants I had to roll up six inches at the cuffs, and a well-worn denim workshirt. In the bottom of the duffel she'd brought along was a quart of rum and another of her husband's pistols: the 9-mm Firestar, Spanish-made but a pretty good handgun, with nice balance and, I remembered, both range and accuracy—two-inch groupings at twenty-five yards.

"You have balls like a bull," Veronica observed. "When you get some common sense, you might be a man to take a chance on."

"Thanks a lot."

"But you have green eyes. No Maya woman would marry a man with green eyes." She smiled, as if to assure me that she didn't buy that particular superstition. "You are not sweating yet. Drink some rum."

I wasn't sweating, but the headache had dulled down acceptably. I took the cap off the rum and drank a little, passed her the bottle. Veronica had a good long pull, enough to unfocus her eyes for a few moments.

"I am not going to ask you how you fucked up. I am not even interested, *claro*? But there is no more room for fuck-up."

"Don't worry about me. Why are we going to Kan Petén?"

Benito swerved to pass a minibus on the lane-and-a-half road, then swerved again to miss a pothole. Veronica gave him a tongue-lashing. He grinned through most of it.

"The helicopter is at Kan Petén," she said. "We will need it tonight, I think. Glen will fly us where we must go."

"Where's that?"

"First we are stopping at the hacienda of my cousin Francisco."

"Is Greg Walker there?"

"I doan know. I hope so."

"Wait a minute. *Saturday*. On Saturday they were driving to the church mission at Usumucinta."

"They did not get there. Jaquez and other men employed by Francisco intercepted them at a roadblock. It was made to look as if guerrillas kidnapped Greg and Sharissa. That, of course, was not the real purpose. They are sposed to disappear, without a trace. A few hours from now Greg will kill Sharissa in a blood sacrifice."

"A few hours!"

"The sacrifice is timed to the eclipse, I know that much. The eclipse comes about half-past eleven tonight. Maybe we have enough time to save her. Finding the place of sacrifice will be the problem. I have this feeling that it is hidden in the jungle of what is now the biosphere. An old temple, restored and protected. There are many such temples, but they are as good as invisible beneath the canopy of the forest. Even so, our only chance to get there in time is by helicopter, before the sun sets. After dark, probably it will be hopeless."

We were heading northeast. I looked back at the sun, low in the western sky. An hour and a half, maybe two hours of daylight left.

"Does Francisco know where to find the place of sacrifice?"

"Of course. He is the Timekeeper now. And Greg Walker, who I think has been there many times, and could find the way by himself."

"What if neither of them is at the hacienda?"

She shrugged. "Then it is hopeless. We will not be able to stop this terrible thing from happening."

"Dammit, stop saying it's hopeless!"

Her mouth was turned down, her eyes half-closed in an expression of sorrowful resignation.

"Even if we find Francisco at his hacienda, it may do us no good. I believe he will be willing to die rather than betray his trust. He will suffer great pain, and never speak. Maya are accustomed to pain."

"You made Jaquez talk."

"Him?" Her eyes flicked to one side, contemptuously. "A mestizo. Too much white blood, he have no guts." She gave a deliberate pause. "Francisco is proud, tough, stubborn. I will have to kill him. To leave him alive would do him great dishonor. You see, I do not think of him as a bad man."

We didn't encounter northbound traffic at this time of day; there was nothing at the end of the paved road except Kan Petén, which closed at five-thirty.

Glen Hazen was waiting for us at the edge of the parking lot near the *Inspectoría*. I don't know how much Veronica had told him about Sharissa, but I think she was relieved to see Hazen there.

She turned and looked hard at me.

"Listen. I have been a complete liar to Glen. He thinks that Sharissa and her father were in the biosphere, exploring some little ruins nobody know about, and that she was injured in a fall. He likes Sharissa very much, so he is willing to fly us to the hacienda. To go that far, Glen will be in no danger. When we reach the hacienda, then we are on our own. I esplain you to be a doctor who is a friend of 'Turo Gúzman, visiting in the Petén. Benito, he is doing some hunting tomorrow."

"I met Hazen," I said. "I didn't tell him anything about myself."

"You agree we keep peddling this crock of shit? Because I doan want to involve Glen more than is necessary."

"Okay," I said. I was still feeling rocky, and I didn't have my wits about me, letting Veronica be in charge. Maybe she halfway knew what she was doing, but the government also had helicopters in the vicinity, and what we needed now was soldiers, some sort of authorization to go raiding the *hacienda* of her cousin.

Which might take only two or three days to secure, provided we could get anyone to believe what we were telling them.

Benito came to a skidding stop in the gravel parking lot and we got out of the Land Cruiser. Veronica moved carefully with all of her weaponry and a backpack. Her eyes were slitted from the pain of unmended ribs. It was amazing that she was up and around at all. I had a panicky heartbeat.

Glen Hazen looked at me, remembered, and smiled. "Here's the man from Sky Valley, Georgia."

"Go Dawgs," I said.

Hazen glanced at Veronica, who managed a smile, and at Benito, who was carrying a pistol-grip shotgun and wearing a bandolier loaded with shells. It was an awesome weapon he didn't seem well suited for.

"Hell of a shotgun," Hazen said, thinking the same thing. "What are you hunting up that way, some kind of booger bear?"

Benito shrugged. Hazen took the Uzi and backpack from Veronica and kissed her cheek. "You feeling okay?"

"Sure."

"We're gassed and ready." To me he said, "How bad off is Sharissa?"

"I don't know," I said truthfully, then made something up. "We didn't have much of a phone connection. It may be a broken leg."

"Seats come right out of the coptor to make room for her. Damn shame, I hope she's going to be all right. How far do we have to go?"

"I will show you on the chart," Veronica said.

We walked as fast as she was able through the shady patch of forest between the road and the site. The sun was below the peaks of the highest group of pyramids when we reached the Bell helicopter.

I hadn't seen any of the electronics the aircraft was stocked with on my first visit to Kan Petén; one seat of seven had already been removed to make room for some of it. Electromagnetic mapping equipment, a computer, other compact technology with small monitors that I couldn't identify.

The LongRanger III helicopter rocked as we all settled down, and my stomach sank almost as low as my confidence. I harnessed myself into a bucket seat behind the pilot and put on a headset. Benito was beside me, and Veronica sat up front with Hazen. His hands were already busy preparing for the mission of mercy. There were numerous switches on the two control levers, one at Hazen's left hand and one between his knees. He also had a couple of pedals and foot switches to operate. It looked very complicated to me.

The high-speed starter motor came to life with a shrill whine. The rotors began turning and the turbine caught. A sweet warm smell of kerosene seeped into the cabin. With an increase in pitch we lifted off, so smoothly the sensation was like falling up to the sky. Beside me Benito grinned with pleasure.

I was flying into the sunset with a wounded bird and a kid and Sharissa's life in the balance. I put a hand on the automatic in the duffel I'd brought along, which gave me no answers as to what I was up against, but offered a small measure of satisfaction.

The sprawl of Kan Petén behind us was much larger than I had thought it would be. There were many plazas, each with its group of buildings, quarry pools like molten metal in the fading sunlight, the massive stair-step pyramids in colors from greenish-gray to pink and orange-red, probably different shades of lichen that still clung to the worn stones. And a lot more of the city-state was partly visible in areas still not fully reclaimed from the surrounding forest. How many people had lived in Kan Petén in the days of its greatest glory? It seemed so deserted now. They were all gone, and much of their civilization was a mystery. It couldn't all have been warfare and bloody ritual, obedience to demanding gods. And what god was Greg Walker seeking to honor by offering the heart of his daughter?

I didn't know if he was a phantom or a freak or a man-god himself, from a culture long extinguished. But I had stopped thinking of Greg as a human being. He was only something evil that needed to be destroyed, and the realization both sickened and excited me.

"Some of Kan Petén has been there since 200 B.C.," Glen Hazen said. "But it's more fragile than it looks. We have to fly in and out from the south, otherwise the vibrations could cause structural damage to the buildings."

Veronica had opened a map and was consulting with Hazen, pointing here and there with a forefinger. He seemed to know where she wanted to go, and made a course correction that in a few minutes had us cruising along the north shore of Petén-Itzá at five hundred feet. The damned thing really went fast. We passed a flight of red and blue macaws over a shady brown lagoon. The sun was burning low on the horizon, reddening in the nightly curtain of haze. There was also smoke from cookfires in isolated lakeside villages below, *cayucos* clustered like matchsticks on the shore in front of the huts.

West of the lake and the town of Las Figuras, the virgin forest resumed, broken here and there by cleared plots on which the Indians grew corn for two or three years, until the thin soil gave out. There was a single dirt road connecting timber camps, a couple of farm settlements within more extensive slash-and-burn acreage, and swampland in a basin dominated by a couple of oil drilling rigs. The land rose to a series of low hills, two of which had been extensively cleared. North of the hills was a dark lake much smaller than Petén-Itzá. The rust-red sun shed no more light, and darkness spread like a tide across the immense canopy of unbroken forest beyond the lake.

On the dusky hillsides I saw cattle, and the buildings of a large *hacienda* that overlooked the lake. Some had zinc roofs and one building, the main house, had four tile roofs with the flat crowns of pyramids. The house was surrounded by a gleaming white wall. There was a satellite dish behind the house, then a landing strip equipped with lights and what looked like a VOR-TACAN cone in a protective enclosure. Parked on a graveled apron in front of a corrugated metal hanger were single- and twin-engined planes.

"That is the *hacienda*," Veronica said.

"Nice layout," Hazen said. "Why did they build it forty klicks from Cobían?"

"Don Santiago owned this land. Almost as far as you can see in any direction from the hill. So I think there must be an important temple not too far away. But hidden and protected for many centuries."

"Ruins? I'd like to have a look. Is that where Sharissa and her father were exploring?"

"I doan know for sure," Veronica said. "Glen, you must set down close to the house. Leave the engine running. In case it is an emergency and there is no time to lose."

From her backpack Veronica took a multicolored serape with a complex diamond pattern and put it on, then draped her head with a long blue shawl. The shoulder holster and the lady's pearl-handled pistol she wore were covered. I took the Firestar automatic from the duffel between my feet and checked the load, then tucked it inside my belt, under the long-sleeved shirt, where it was still about as obvious as an iguana sitting on my shoulder. But I wasn't going anywhere without it.

As the helicopter banked into the wind and flew toward the apron end of the runway, a couple of men in denim workclothes and baseball caps came out of a stable and looked up. Veronica waved, and they waved back.

"The tall one," Veronica said, "is Emano, Francisco's foreman."

Having recognized her, the two men went back into the stable. Floodlights illuminated the outside of the house. Veronica spoke to Benito in Mayan as we touched down; he nodded. He was holding his shotgun across his lap. I had seen a couple like it on the streets of L.A. It was accurately called the Streetsweeper; wound up to full automatic, it fired twelve loads in three seconds, enough to blow the hinges off hell.

Veronica looked at me as if she were trying to decide if I was going to be reliable.

"Let's go," I said, scowling.

We got out of the helicopter; the rotors were on idle. The chill in the hilltop air surprised me. We walked the fifty yards to the house, past a pen filled with ocellated turkeys, which had tails almost as colorful as peacocks. From somewhere else I heard dogs with deep voices, tolling our arrival. Hounds. Nobody came out to greet us. Veronica paused and rang the bronze bell suspended over a high wooden gate in the freshly painted concrete wall.

Before long a pregnant maid who looked to be about fourteen years old answered the bell.

They knew each other. The maid shook her head when asked about Francisco. Veronica asked her several more questions. The maid nodded, gestured, shook her head, shrugged a couple of times, smiled apologetically.

Veronica turned and walked away from the gate, her face stony.

"What is it? What's going on?"

"¡Cho! They have left already. About five o'clock. Francisco and Greg Walker, together in Francisco's big pickup truck."

"Together? What about Sharissa? Wasn't she with them?"

"Juana says no, there was no girl when they come here by airplane, early this afternoon."

"What the hell!" I pulled at her arm to stop her, and she inhaled painfully. "What do you mean? Sharissa's not here? How can you be sure? Aren't we going to search the house?"

"No. Please let go of me. Juana is truthful. But if she did not see Sharissa, it does not mean she wasn't here. Unconscious maybe, hidden—I doan know! The fact is, they are gone, and we cannot find them now."

"We have to find them!"

"Look!" Grimacing, Veronica swept a hand toward the dark blue sky, the darker canopy of jungle, not a light showing for miles. "That is the biosphere out there. How big? Like another country. They left while there was still light to see. Even if we had something powerful to drive, and could find the track they use to go deep into the forest, we cannot get there in time. You have never seen anything like this forest at night. It is a darkness that swallows light. There is no chance to find them out there, none."

"Has to be a chance. Understand? It's only six-thirty. There's another truck—" I pointed to a pickup down by a cattle chute. "We'll borrow that one!"

She shook her head. "No, my friend. That truck would fall apart on a jungle track. Only good for farm roads; it does not have four-wheel drive. We would only strand ourselves."

I saw Glen Hazen get out of the helicopter. "What's wrong?" he called. "Where's Sharissa?"

There were tears on Veronica's face. She wiped them away with a weary hand, and shuddered in the wind that blew across the hilltop.

I looked away from her and shielded my eyes against the glare of floodlights, facing the rising moon. It was full and looked startlingly close in the black sky. A blind man could have detected that huge moon by the prickling of his skin. It had a ruddy color, as if it glowed from the reflected heat of the no-longer-visible sun.

Heat—

"Oh, Jesus!" I shouted.

Hazen crunched closer on the gravel walk to the house. "Isn't she here?"

"No," I said. "Sharissa's out *there*, and we have to go get her. Come on!"

They both looked at me as if I were babbling.

"Greg and Francisco left about five," I said to Veronica. "It's six-thirty now. Probably they wanted to get where they were going before dark. So the site must be less than a ninety-minute drive from here—over a terrible road. How many kilometers could they cover in ninety minutes? Fifty? They could be even closer to us than *that*. Come on, damn it, get back in the helicopter, I know how we can find them!"

Even with the helicopter's landing lights blazing, it was a tricky business flying low over miles of tropical forest after sunset. The immediate danger was running into an unexpectedly tall banak or ironwood tree, jutting dozens of feet higher than the surrounding canopy, like an unlighted radio tower. The ride was unpredictably bumpy, depending on the density of the cooling air above the canopy. If the rotor disk lost its cushion of air, for any number of reasons, the helicopter would turn into an eight-hundred-thousand-dollar anvil and plunge straight down. There was also the possibility that we would overfly a rebel camp in this wilderness, and be fired on.

Hazen had confidence in his flying ability, but he wasn't in a good mood.

"I don't understand why you lied to me," he said to Veronica.

"Time," she said wearily. "Only because of the time."

"Human sacrifice? *Virgin* sacrifice? What *is* this shit—it's his own daughter!"

"You're an archeologist," she scolded him. "How many temples have you explored in this country? Once the stones of the *adoratorios* dripped with blood, offered in exchange for power. You think this has all changed, we are too civilized now? Human nature does not change. The ultimate power one has over another human being is in the shedding of his blood. How much more powerful is the man who sacrifices the beauty of one he truly loves in honor of his god? Is it not in the Bible? Is Greg Walker a common murderer, or is he a king of a lost people?"

I said, "He claimed his father was someone named Don José Canek, or something like that." I didn't look up or otherwise take my eyes off the FLIR screen, which was about the size of a laptop computer. Forward-looking Infrared. It scanned the area we were searching north of the lake, penetrating the thick canopy of leaves below. On the grid-marked screen appeared a tiny glowworm for anything larger than a jungle rat that gave off heat. I had a lot of glowworms that could have represented anything from jaguars to nocturnal feeders like the kinkajou or ordinary deer, but so far I hadn't come up with anything human-sized, or the glow representing the heat from a truck's hard-working engine.

"Can Ek," Hazen said, correcting my pronunciation. "The name means 'Serpent-Twenty-Star.' He was the last ruler by that name of the Itzá Maya dynasty of Tayasal, the centers of which were grouped around Lake Petén-Itzá. They were big on human sacrifice. Lord Can Ek himself cut out the hearts of Dominican friars who came to Tayasal to convert him to Catholicism. Eventually the Spaniards conquered Tayasal and Can Ek. A Franciscan priest named Avendaño studied the sacred Katun prophecies and was able to convince Can Ek that the Maya world was coming to an end on March 13, 1697. Avendaño described Can Ek as being very different from other Maya: he was tall, handsome, much lighter in complexion. He baptized Can Ek, gave him his Christian name, and took him back to Spain. Where, I understand, he enjoyed a long life and many wives and mistresses. Anything yet?"

Benito was shielding his eyes from the copter lights and staring down at the canopy. "There is the river again," he said. We had flown back and forth across it, a needlelike gleam appearing momentarily in the blanketing darkness.

Hazen said, "I hope you realize that even if we locate the truck, there's no place to set down through the trees."

"We doan know that for sure," Veronica said. "Because a temple will mean a village nearby. Probably it will be on water—the river, or a small lake."

"Why?" I asked her. The helicopter shuddered and dropped sideways unexpectedly; the drop was only twenty feet or so, but I held my breath.

"Why a village? The temple is a sacred site, visited by outsiders for many centuries. Then it must be maintained, and the approach to the temple kept clear. That is no easy job in the midst of a jungle. There must be caretakers, who need shelter and cleared land to grow food. In the museum of Kan Petén there are pictures of great pyramids so covered with earth and vegetation that many people walked past them before they were excavated, never knowing what they were. An entire city, three thousand buildings, fifty square miles, smothered by the forest!"

That wasn't encouraging. My eyes and neck muscles were aching; I hadn't changed my disposable contacts for several days. Focusing on the small glowworm-filled screen for something I could put a name to was a severe strain. I had lost track of the time. When would we run low on fuel, and have to turn back? I didn't want to ask that question.

Hazen had come up with the exact time of the lunar eclipse—when the earth's shadow crossed the face of the moon—from an ephemeris stored in the helicopter's navigational computer. Eleven-forty-eight P.M.

Hazen made a course correction, and we entered another quadrant. Veronica was using binoculars to scan the monotonous canopy. and I was still glued to the screen, blinking and rubbing my forehead to try to ease the pain. How long did it take a truck's engine to cool off, after running for an hour, maybe an hour and a half? Would I be able to recognize the shape of a man on a thirteen-inch video screen? Was anyone down there, or were we far off the track, wandering blindly into nowhere despite all the electronic gear on board?

Then something, a slightly larger glowworm than the rest, as the helicopter's nose swung a few degrees northeast. I used the trackball to isolate the signature, then with a keystroke produced the coordinates on-screen. I read them off to Hazen.

"I want to have a closer look at this," I told him.

"Could it be the truck?"

"Too soon to tell. But it's bigger than an animal, unless it's a whale."

We flew toward the signature on my screen, which was now about six klicks away.

"Right on course. Can you get lower?"

"Maybe it's not the best idea to fly directly over it. Whatever the hell it may be. Veronica?"

"No, nothing yet," she said, looking through the binoculars.

Vague shapes had begun to appear, and cluster, around the larger glowworm on my screen.

"It's hot!" I yelled. "We've definitely found something."

We were close enough so that I could see that the smaller glowworms were in motion, as if in response to the almighty racket of the helicopter coming in over thick canopy.

"Could be people. Around a campfire, maybe."

"Oh-oh."

Veronica said, "I see a couple of lights. It might be a village. Yes, look at all the cohune palms, that is a sure sign—turn your searchlight on, Glen."

I looked up from the screen and covered my eyes momentarily, hoping to wipe out the afterimage, then pressed my nose against the window just as the trees fifty feet below thinned out and we did a fast climbing turn over a clearing illuminated by the lights mounted on the nose and under the fuselage of the LongRanger. Hazen wasn't taking any chances on us being riddled by automatic weapons. I had a glimpse of the truck we'd been looking for, parked on a smooth white plaza that might have been paved with stone, some steep thatched roofs arranged in a compound, and several half-naked kids near the front end of the truck, staring up at us.

"That was Francisco's truck," Veronica said calmly. "And this is the village I thought we'd find. Glen, go around again and land."

"Taking a big chance—"

"No, I doan believe any harm will come to us here. The temple is in another place. There is a ceremony tonight, so the temple will be guarded. But the village should be nearly deserted."

We circled, and came in slowly over the treetops. The plaza below was about the size of a softball field, with the river at one end divided into several shallow streams by sandbars in this season of low rainfall. Curious kids scattered in the wash from the rotors. They wore breechclouts, or ankle-length skirts of white cloth.

We took an elevator approach to the plaza, and did some bouncing on wind gusts. Hazen made three attempts before setting us down with a jolt on the heels of the skids. He swore under his breath. We were fifty feet from the truck, a big muddied Maxicab. Near the river, fishnets that glowed like pale moths in the moonlight had been hung from poles to dry. Downriver from the village there was a pigpen that looked predator-proof, with fencing of sharpened outslanting poles. Along the banks the huge trees spread gray roots that looked like the carcasses of prehistoric beasts. Dugout canoes were tethered to a stone quay.

Hazen shut down the helicopter and we sat inside for a couple of minutes looking around the plaza, which was now deserted. Dogs were barking, but not showing themselves. Apparently there had been a recent feast. Mahogany tables grouped around a firepit were covered with clay dishes, pots, and calabashes. The remains of a couple of deer were suspended on spits over the still-smoking coals of the firepit. Maybe it had been the coals lining the pit, which was about six feet by ten feet, that I had picked up on the thermal imager, and not the truck's engine.

Situated around the plaza were dozens of simple thatched huts made from roughhewn weathered poles. Each had a doorspace, but no windows. On the west side of the plaza were larger buildings, made of stone, with some walls covered in plaster and painted over with glyphs. But the buildings were too small to be temples. Storehouses, probably. Around the perimeter, large, perforated clay pots on pedestals glowed like jack-o'-lanterns at Halloween. They must have been lined with pyrites, or some other reflectant material.

"Well, I guess they know we're here," I said.

The bugs knew we were there, as soon as we got out of the helicopter. Veronica handed out spray cans of Off, and gave me a Maya scarf to cover my neck.

From a distance came the sounds of drumming, and what might have been primitive wood or shell instruments. The music was mournful and eerie. There was a February chill in the air. A wind along the river swayed the crowns of the high trees.

"Do you have any flares?" Veronica asked Hazen. He nodded. "Bring them with you."

"¿Á donde va?" Benito said to her.

"To find the temple. You stay here. Don't let anyone come close to the helicopter."

He looked disappointed, but not afraid to remain by himself. Veronica smiled slightly and kissed him, as if she were kissing him good-bye. I shuddered, feeling like a target in this open space. Veronica glanced at the automatic in my hand, cocked but not locked, and shrugged at my tension.

"No one will be in the village but the very old, the very young, and the sick."

I wanted her to be right, but I didn't put the pistol away. I walked across the plaza to the pickup truck and looked inside. There was a strong odor of cigar smoke, a couple of crushed Coke cans on the floorboard. The keys were in the ignition. On the narrow bench seat in back I saw a crumpled blanket, and, on the floor, a pair of desert boots. I looked at one of them. Size seven. They might have belonged to Sharissa. If so, maybe they had carried her to wherever they were going. I hoped that meant she was drugged, and not hurt.

"Yes, she was brought here," Veronica said behind me. "This is the place of her destiny. And mine also."

I looked at her. Her joined hands were against her chin, in an attitude of prayerful resignation. The drumming, the mournful lowing of horns, gave me gooseflesh.

"Veronica, stop the bullshit and let's get going."

Glen Hazen was shining the halogen beam of his light around the plaza. The captive peccaries were disturbed; so were spider monkeys in a large cage suspended from the branch of a tree. They expressed their annoyance by squirting streams of urine through the bars. The eyes of a shambling armadillo glowed redly for a moment at the edge of the plaza.

"God Almighty," Hazen said. "We've traveled back in time."

"They live here as they lived five hundred years ago," Veronica agreed. "They fish and farm and hunt the old ways, without guns or iron plows or machetes. They live peacefully. At least they did before tonight."

She turned and limped toward the huts lining one side of the plaza.

"What were you cussing at 'Nica for?" Hazen asked me. He was wearing a revolver in a belt holster, two half-gallon bags of water in a shoulder yoke, and a backpack he had crammed with some things from the helicopter, including a first-aid kit.

"I think she's going bush on us," I said. "Maybe we should search the huts."

He aimed his light in Veronica's direction. I saw children, wearing shell necklaces and stripes of red and yellow paint on their bodies, withdraw into shadows. The invisible dogs were still barking. An old woman with an infant wrapped in a shawl looked out at us from a doorway.

"Not yet. Let's see what 'Nica's up to."

Veronica made some sounds like tongue-clicks, and waited at the edge of the plaza to be acknowledged. After a few seconds she was answered. She approached one of the huts; a fire was flickering on the floor inside. An old man appeared, stooped and with half his right arm missing. He was wearing a headdress like an upside-down pot, a beaded breastplate, and a belt of colorful feathers— decorated like an old vet left behind while younger men marched off to war.

She spoke to him for a couple of minutes, raising her hands to the sky to emphasize a point. It was hard to tell if he was hostile, but he obviously wasn't dangerous. He shook his head several times; each time his protest, or denial, seemed weaker. Finally he answered her. Veronica nodded, and came back to us, pausing to reach up painfully and take a lantern from one of the pedestals.

"He was a sorcerer," she explained, "but he lost part of his arm to the bite of a coral snake, and also his powers. Now his sons are the priests of the temple. The language here is Yucatec, not Itzá, and the idiom is old, I had difficulty to understand him. We're going this way, I think about a twenty-minute walk. Follow me."

Veronica had taken a dozen steps when a stone was thrown from shadows. She shied, and it missed her. But the abrupt sideways motion caused her to cry out. I heard, like an echo, a wailing sound, a lamentation, from the hut of the old sorcerer. More stones came at us, without much force behind them.

Veronica said tautly, "By the way, we will not be welcome there. You can stay behind with Benito, if you wish."

"Wouldn't want to miss anything," Hazen said, glancing wryly at me.

I fell in behind Veronica as we passed between two of the large buildings. Jaguar pelts had been attached to the walls. Just behind the buildings the forest loomed, but there was a paved path, only about a yard wide, winding off between trees deformed by the embrace of strangler vines thicker than my arm. She had been right about the depths of darkness inside the forest. One lantern, two flashlight beams attracting swarms of insects, the big hardshell kamikaze type, and still I felt as if I were walking blindly into the throat of something that would consume me. Beetles with sticky legs got hung up in the hair of my forearms, adding to the spooky discomfort.

On either side of the path vegetation and vines had been hacked neatly and vertically to a height of about twelve feet, where the overarching branches were woven together almost impenetrably. The path, of unmortared loaf-sized blocks, was slightly humped to allow for runoff. The stones had been recently scraped clean of lichen.

Veronica stopped suddenly, then reached down slowly and picked up a piece of black glass.

"Part of an obsidian blade," Hazen muttered. "Razor-sharp."

"There may be other shards," Veronica said. "Be careful where you step, they will slice through the sole of a boot."

There were a few lizards on the winding forest path,

but no litter. Each step might have taken us closer to the monotonous drums and low tones of primitive wood-winds, but as the minutes went by I couldn't be sure we were making progress. I wished I could see the moon overhead. The night was still cooling, and I had a bout of chills as the path crossed a wide swampy area on crude wooden footbridges. Then the path sloped upward, and we left the swamp behind.

I thought I smelled smoke. Veronica was moving more slowly, her limp more pronounced. She seemed to be dragging herself along. We stopped for water. When she raised one of the flexible water bottles to her lips, I saw a thread of fresh blood on her chin.

"You've done enough," I told her. "Go back now, while you still can."

"It makes no difference. I will not leave here alive to-night. But there is still a chance for you and Glen. And Sharissa." She wiped her mouth, looking at us with exhausted eyes. "*Vámanos.* I think we are almost to the top of this hill."

Before long firelight was visible through the spaces between thinned-out trees. As we approached, the flickering light became the flames of a fire made from the trunks and branches of whole trees; we could feel the heat a hundred yards away. The fire was blazing near the center of a plaza twice the size of the one in the village. The wind carried a torrent of sparks high above the big trees growing inside the plaza's perimeter. We saw dancers, moving elaborately, slowly exchanging one posture for another, silhouetted against the flames. But the most remarkable sights were the temples at either end of the plaza. They had stairstep terraces, with smaller structures mounted on each terrace, and one very long central staircase rising at a forty-five-degree angle to the topmost terrace, which was nearly at treetop level. Stone carvings capped the pyramids: a crouching jaguar, a serpent with a human, a kingly head like some versions I'd seen on tree-stones at Kan Petén. The figures were realistically painted.

The eyes of the spotted cat, fixed on the celebrants in the plaza below, glinted like jade dinner plates in firelight reflected from the underside of the forest canopy.

We reached the edge of an I-shaped ballcourt with seating on both sides. Veronica set her lantern aside and warned us to turn the flashlights off. We didn't need them anyway; the fire, and torches shaped like ebony wine goblets with long stems, provided plenty of light.

"What do you make of this?" I said to Hazen, who had taken a Leica with a zoom lens from his backpack.

"The most amazing goddamned thing I've ever seen. Early Classic design; there are similar temples at Tikal and Rio Azul, but not so elaborate. And nothing this well preserved anywhere."

"Flash that camera," Veronica said, "and you will have your throat cut in no time."

"Not using a flash; but I have to get some pictures." The look on his face was ecstatic. His hands were trembling; he seemed afraid that it was a mirage, or a hallucination, and was about to disappear. "They must have spent weeks plastering and painting to get ready for tonight."

I looked around us. The trees at the edge of the plaza were thickly hung with lianas, a screen behind which we were as inconspicuous as shadows. And the Maya may have been under the influence of their strange, three- and four-note music for hours. I could understand why; the beat of drums, the doleful woodwinds, was painfully seductive. It appealed to a primitive part of me I had never been aware of. It influenced my emotions, and made it difficult to think coherently.

Veronica licked her bloody lips and jostled me. "Snap out of it, Buzzerball."

"Right. Okay." Hazen had edged off closer to the plaza for a better angle on the jaguar temple. "What do we do now?" I asked her.

She almost laughed, but it turned into a grimace.

"It might only take us another day or two to explore inside these temple."

"Are they hollow?"

"Many rooms inside. It is a very sacred place where they will offer their sacrifice. Which means that the sacrificial altar must be in a place known only to the Time-keeper, and the immortals."

Nobody is immortal, I wanted to say. I looked at my watch. It had stopped. I had forgotten to wind it after Veronica gave it back to me.

"How much time do we have?"

"Until the silence. When the music, the dancing stop. And everyone waits for the immortal one to reappear, to bless them."

"After Sharissa is dead."

"This is what I think. But I do not know for sure." She looked unsteady on her feet. I put an arm around her.

"You need to sit down for a little while."

"Then I may not get up again." Veronica looked shyly away from me, as if she'd shared a secret, and I had reacted badly to it. "Doan worry so much. I am not buying the farm yet." She asked me to help her off with the back-pack and to take out the binoculars. She scanned the plaza, then concentrated her study on the jaguar temple which, I thought, faced west. But I had no orientation after our walk through pitch-black forest, and what sky I could see was filled with flying sparks, not stars.

"Glen," Veronica said softly, "come here."

He clicked off another couple of shots, then came back to us.

Veronica handed him the binoculars. Then she leaned against me, and clutched my hand. I felt flattered, and scared. The sudden violent motion of avoiding the stone had torn something inside; it was making her bleed. She had to have a doctor, and soon. Sharissa, now Veronica—I couldn't let either of them die, but I felt frustrated and helpless.

"The temple of the Vision-Serpent is a tomb, I think," she said to Hazen.

He looked it over. "Uh-huh. I don't know who he was.

'Most holy lord'—there's a cartouche for *ch'ul ahou*, the animal form."

"They would not perform a ritual sacrifice to prolong life in an old tomb. So it is the other temple, the *ch'ul na* of the Lord *Balam*, where we should find them."

"Is there a back door?" I said, trying to lighten the prevailing mood.

Glen Hazen had turned the binoculars on the jaguar temple.

"No back doors in Maya temples. The major house is the one at the top of the central staircase. In their religion, the pyramid represents a mountain; the way into the mountain is always through the mouth of a monster. All those carvings around the doorway of the *ch'ul na* represent aspects of the monster of the sacred mountain that rises from the forest of tree stones on the plaza."

My heart was beating very fast. "So that's where we have to go?"

He lowered the binoculars slowly, nodded. "We've come to the tough part. It's by invitation only."

Veronica said, "Inside the doorway is the Otherwurl—a place of the, the—"

"Supernatural," Hazen said.

"Yes. The temple complex may be only fifteen hundred years old. But the temple site, where the power from ritual sacrifice accumulates, that is maybe another thousand years, who knows how old? And the power of time and space, concentrated there in lines of magnetic force, all the cosmic energy of the gods who pass back and forth through that doorway from *Xibalba*, the Otherwurl, might be enough to destroy us as soon as we leave our wurl . . . to enter theirs."

"That's nuts!" I said. The pressure of ceremonial drums, at my temples, against my chest, had me dizzy and half-sick from anxiety. My eyes dripped tears. "If Sharissa's in that *ch'ul* place, that's where I'm going!"

"Well, I cannot go with you," Veronica said faintly. "Not

because I am afraid, Buzzerball. But because, all of a sudden, it is too many steps for me."

She began to cough, spraying a fist with blood, and slumped against me; I lowered her to the ground.

"God, what's wrong?" Hazen said, his normally popped eyes wider, and frightened.

"She took a beating a couple of days ago. Something's—I'm not sure, a punctured lung, maybe that's all it is. Can you carry her back to the helicopter?"

"Yes. What about you?"

"The truck's there. I'll drive it out. You fly her to Dr. Gúzman's clinic in Las Figuras."

"Man, you can't hope to pull this off on your own!"

"I'm not superstitious," I said impatiently. "Look, I'm going to get as close to the temple as I can without attracting attention. Then I'll need a diversion."

"Flares," Veronica murmured. "We will shoot them . . . in the sky above the *Wacah Chan* . . . the Wurl Tree in the center of the plaza." She pointed to a sculpted column, larger than other treestones, around which the Maya had been performing their unhurried three-step dance, stylized as a minuet. She looked up at me, with a thin-lipped smile. Then she wiped a hand across her mouth, reached out and painted my forehead with her blood. I don't know if it was a gesture to give me courage, or an endearment, a moment of ritual we had no name for yet.

"Buzzerball?"

"Yes."

"Take off your clothes, all of them. And take my . . . Uzi rifle with you. Hold it like you would a sacred object. I guarantee . . . they will think you are a god." She looked ingenuously at me. "Or at least a monster, one they know nothing about. That will be your protection, until you reach the sacrificial altar. Of course . . . Don Francisco, Greg Walker, they will recognize you. Then you are . . . truly on your own."

I stared at her. I had to laugh. She wanted to laugh too, but couldn't stand the stress on whatever was hurting her.

"Green-eyed monster from the Otherworld," I said. I could still feel the touch of her fingers on my forehead, the warmth of her blood. I began to strip, flinging off my shirt and unbuckling the belt of the too-big duck trousers that had belonged to her late husband.

"A god among gods," she said, admiringly, I thought.

"I'll see you back at the copter. No more talk about dying, Veronica."

"Call me . . . 'Nica."

I pulled off the duck trousers, then my undershorts and shoes. I wasn't wearing anything but my Hamilton watch—I guess I was a little superstitious, after all—and 'Nica's Maya scarf. I was shaking, more from a kick of adrenaline than fear. "Leave me a flashlight," I said to Hazen. I reached down and took the Uzi from 'Nica's hands. I'd seen plenty of them; they were one of the weapons of choice on the streets of South Central Los Angeles.

"Okay," I said, dancing up and down to stay warm, hopefully to keep the adrenaline pumping.

Glen Hazen nodded. He had taken the flare pistol from his backpack, and loaded it.

"Run like hell," he advised me, grinning.

By then I was choking with laughter. Hazen busted out laughing, too. And 'Nica, 'Nica was doubled over, from pain or amusement or both.

"One thing is for sure . . . ," I said, "nothing . . . this fucking weird will ever happen to me, the rest of my life."

I had the Firestar automatic in my left hand. Laughter had turned to hiccups, and I was burning up too much precious energy. I turned away from them, focusing through blurred lenses on the oblong windowless building at the top of the pyramid, crowned with a crouching jaguar. Lord *Balam*, they called him. I pumped myself up a little more by imagining he was waiting for me. It was all games and rituals, and I was half-drunk with a frenzy that had been trying to possess me from the morning I got off the plane from Guatemala City. And now there was no more time to lose.

I was at the base of the huge pyramid when the first flare whistled and burst over the center of the plaza, painting the neatly plastered stonework a hot pink shade.

I scrambled up twenty feet to the first terrace, then turned to look out over the plaza. The three-note music had stopped abruptly, leaving a void in which my heart thumped madly. There was a rippling of consternation among the Maya, some shrill outcries. They were all wearing their best costumes, and costume jewelry. Some of them had turned to Lord *Balam* for an explanation of the starburst above their heads.

What they saw was the hairy monster Butterbaugh, bowlegged and buck-naked with a blood stripe on his forehead, jumping up and down on the terrace brandishing a firestick and screaming the University of Georgia's Bulldog Fight Song.

It's fair to say they were stunned.

Either 'Nica or Hazen had the wit and timing to send another flare arcing over the jaguar temple. It exploded and came down slowly, drifting smokily in the wind, the hot light forming a double halo above my head. Many of the Maya fell to their knees. Others covered their eyes, and lamentations filled the night.

I went up two more flights of steps to a terrace strewn with flowers and the freshly cut branches of trees arranged in front of four small houses. I had to stop to catch my breath. None of the Maya from the plaza forty feet below were attempting to follow. They all seemed to be kneeling, wailing, praying.

I looked up to see how far I had to go.

A figure in a long robe had appeared from the doorway of the structure on top of the pyramid. Smoke billowed around him. He wore funereal black and a white horned mask with a jutting, snout-like face. He was carrying a staff or a lance in his right hand, and a three-pronged object in the other. I had no idea who he might be.

I started up the central staircase. The limestone steps were only a few inches deep, and worn in the middle. It was a much tougher climb than I had anticipated, and the steps were slippery in places with half-congealed blood. Animal blood? I wondered how much slaughtering had gone on here already. The rifle lay across my hunched back, giving me one hand free, but I had nowhere else to put the pistol. The figure in black, standing at the top of the stairs watching me, had not moved. But the only thing I was afraid of at the moment was falling. If I'd been wearing shoes, I probably would've lost my footing. For the only time in my life I was glad I'd been born with big feet and monkey toes.

I tried to keep him in sight while I was climbing the stairs. He seemed to be chanting something, in low tones. Then I saw him raise the lance, slowly, as if he were taking aim. The lance was tipped with a gleaming, honey-combed piece of bone or quartzite. Whatever it was, it had an evil, useful look.

I flattened myself against the steps and tried to draw a bead with the automatic. His bestial headpiece glowed in the moonlight. I thought I saw a liquid movement of eyes in the deep spaces on either side of the exaggerated, curling snout.

Then, abruptly, he lowered the lance, turned and, with a dismissive shake of the three-pronged instrument in his left hand, vanished into the cloud of smoke rising above the terrace.

I began creeping up again.

The first stone I put my hand on was a loose one. It almost pulled free of the temple stairway, and that would have left me grasping at air with my other hand as I plunged head over heels all the way to the plaza below. It was my first unmistakable warning that the pyramid, fifteen centuries old, was not the solid structure it appeared to be from a distance, no matter what measures had been taken to preserve it.

Or—another thought, while I froze and recovered from that jolt of pure terror—maybe the damned thing was booby-trapped.

I was about to move again, with the desperate caution of the condemned, when a singsong, operatic voice from the terrace above me echoed around the plaza. It was an announcement, or exhortation, coming perhaps from the unseen figure in black. He spoke for almost a minute, or close to sixty violent pulse beats in my throat.

Then the drumming resumed in the plaza. I had to look down. It wasn't what I expected: the dancing had begun again.

Whatever he'd told them, they no longer seemed bothered by my presence, as if I were just a fly on the wall. That meant something. I wished I knew what.

I tried to swallow; my mouth was too dry. I moved over to the other side of the stairway and continued climbing. At this height there were places where the layer of stucco had come off in patches, and I found no mortar at all between a few of the stepstones. I avoided putting all of my weight on any one step as I hauled myself higher. I kept an eye on the edge of the terrace for the black-robed man, but all I saw was swirling smoke and the figure of the crouched, looking-down jaguar on top of what Glen Hazen had called the major house. Now that I was this close to it, I realized just how enormous the jaguar was. If it had been carved from a single block of limestone, then it had to weight at least a couple of tons. I wondered how the Maya workmen had raised it, and the carved stone roof lintel and facade of the house, in an age long before the invention of the block and tackle.

At last, the terrace.

There was a stone altar, flanked by tall braziers of burning incense, in front of the major house. And on the altar, the source of the blood I had been tracking through on my way up: the body of an eight-foot jaguar, so large it hung over both ends of the altar. Blood from its cut throat had drained down the slightly raked terrace to the steps. I could smell it, in spite of the strong odor of incense. On my knees, I unslung the Uzi from my back. There were torches on the terrace, adding more smoke than clarifying light to the scene. The doorway of the major house, less than six feet high, was a black void framed by representations of the mountain-monster.

I'd never been superstitious, never read my horoscope in the papers, and the Methodist preachers I'd listened to in my youth seldom mentioned hell or the devil; it wasn't that kind of religion. But when I rose to my feet on the terrace my knees were shockingly weak and I thought of what 'Nica had said about lines of magnetic force, the migration of souls from their world to this one. I was shaking from cold and plain old primitive fear, not knowing what I was going to see next. Then I got my emotions under control and dialed up the rational mind. Gritted my teeth. If something was going to kill me here and now, it wouldn't be a household god or a cosmic thunderbolt.

I was back on alert just in time to receive a brief warning, sense movement above me in the smoke, as if the stone *Balam* were stirring in preparation for an act of retribution for the slain brother-animal on the altar. A loose piece of stone fell, then by torchlight I saw the flicker of the hurled lance.

The instinctive act is to throw up an arm when something's coming at you, and there's no time to get out of the way. I also managed to twist side-on to the trajectory of the lance, which turned out not to be such a good thing.

The lance head was deflected by the Uzi in my hand, which slowed it down a little and probably kept it out of my armpit. It sliced into my right side instead, wedging between ribs and stopping. Otherwise it might have gone right through me. The lance still had enough force, like a hard karate kick, to knock me down. The Uzi went flying out of my hand, along with a piece of the shattered lance. About a foot and a half of the shaft was protruding from my side.

He appeared beside the head of the *Balam*, still wearing the horned mask with the long snout and a mouthful of sharp teeth beneath it. He had taken off the robe. He was naked except for a breechclout, a pair of boots brightly twined around his lower legs like coral snakes, and shingled epaulets on both shoulders framing the jade of prestige which he wore on a chain around his neck. He was broad through the chest. But he looked a little fat to me.

I was lying in blood with my left hand twisted under me, the broken shaft of lance sticking straight up. The Uzi had fallen a few feet away, unreachable in my condition. When you're hurt bad, you know. I knew; he knew.

He climbed deliberately down the facade of the major house, showing me the jiggling cheeks of his nearly bare ass. There were plenty of carved hand-holds on the facade. Small pieces of stone fell with him. I wondered, in the part of my mind not preoccupied with pain and fear of dying, just how close to crumbling the entire pyramid was.

He had the three-pronged instrument in his right hand, which he held up for me to see when his feet touched the terrace.

I coughed, and it was like being electrocuted; blood came up in my throat. I felt as if I were one lung short already. No way to know how much damage the wickedly serrated edges of the lance head had done inside the partly sawn-through ribcage. But any movement, even the shallow breaths I drew, brought more electric pain. Each successive jolt was the worst pain I'd felt in my life. I wasn't brave about it. I was crying, crying from rage and frustration, too.

He came around the altar in a catwise crouch to tear my throat out with the three-pronged knife, and I made sure he was too close to miss before I willed myself to move; arching my back just enough to pull my left hand free and kill him with the Firestar I had managed not to lose.

I did miss, with the first couple of rounds, aiming too high in my anxiety. Then I corrected as he tried to pull back and the next three whacked him hard, two on either side of the breastbone and another through the notch of his throat, and that one ripped out the back of his neck and sent him crashing down on top of his smashed mask. His outspread arms and legs shook as if he were trying to fly, to take off from the pyramid and soar away to the moon, and he seemed to be a long time quieting down.

I didn't trust that he was dead. I held the gun on him, staring, sweat and tears in my eyes, spasms that seemed to have their source at the lancehead going through me like ocean waves as I tried to sit up. Then I knew he was dead, all right, and he smelled bad from emptied bowels, and I was damn sure I was never going to get on my feet again.

But it wasn't Greg Walker lying there; it was Francisco Colon. So get on with it, Butterbaugh.

The drumming had stopped again, with the echo around the plaza of the last shot fired. Five shots, wasn't it, or—that left—uhh. I couldn't remember. Three more bullets in the clip, maybe. There was always the Uzi, but even from where I was trying very hard to stand I could see that the long magazine had been seriously dented by the flying lance. Maybe it would still shoot, chances were it would jam. The hell with it.

Now, I told myself, if you can stand up *this* high without passing out, you can probably straighten all the way. One lung's enough for anybody. Sharissa's waiting. Eleven-thirty yet? Get cracking.

"Francisco!"

A voice from the void—from a deep, hidden room, where, I supposed, the booming of gunfire also had been noted. Did he sound worried? The voice so distorted, as if in a well, I couldn't identify it as Greg Walker's voice, much less take a reading on his state of mind. And I still had a ringing in my ears from the Firestar, a reek of gunpowder in my nostrils stronger than the copal incense blanketing the terrace.

(Hey, still on my feet. This isn't so tough. Just don't ask me to straighten up. I've got a lance in my side.)

With my right hand I felt all around the wound. Oh-oh, a lot of blood on the outside, running down my leg. I nicked two of my fingers on the exposed edges of the lancehead. Just leave it alone. Let Doc Gúzman take it out, if I get that far.

Swaying on my feet, I started to tremble. No way I was going to get that far.

But I still had plenty to do, before all the life ran out and I was like the jaguar on the altar, drained slack and powerless and dusty-eyed in an ancient tomb.

I shuffled over to the door of the major house. Dark in there, except for the glow of a torch beside a flight of stairs.

"Francisco!" he called again.

More torches lighted the stairs to a passage below. There were ceremonial masks attached to the walls, affording handholds. My eyes were blurring. I knew I had to hurry, but each step took care and timing.

A room below. Ceremonial robes and headdresses, stone braziers of incense, a lot of smoke I didn't need.

Oh, God. More steps. Down and down and down.

A lighted room with picture walls. A passageway, so long, so unfairly long. A brazen light shining through a smoky doorway. I had to remind myself not to breathe through my mouth, not to shuffle my feet. Not to be heard until—

"Butterbaugh! I can't believe my eyes."

He appeared in the doorway as if it were the apron of a stage, flickering light behind him. He wore a regal golden headdress, but no mask. His muscular naked body was painted a ghostly shell-white from his hairline to his toes. Perfect in form, bizarrely grinning, frightening to me even in my depleted, nothing-to-lose physical and emotional state.

I raised the Firestar pistol, amazed at how steady I was. Although I had to lean heavily against the wall to keep from falling.

"Where . . . is she?"

"I can't believe my eyes," he said again. The pupils of those eyes were huge; he must also have had trouble focusing. From the deathly stiffness of his grin it seemed to me that he was slightly drunk, or drugged by conceit, by the empowerment that his theatrical stature lent to him. And—never to forget it—he was also, by any reasonable standards, insane. "Come in, C.G."

I flashed back then, to the house on Thornhill Road in Sky Valley, Greg Walker on his veranda in the jasmine-drenched summer night, his head bandaged in a flesh-colored turban.

"I'll know for sure when I start jogging again if I'm going to be a hundred percent. Would you like to come in, Sergeant? Sharissa's not home."

"Like . . . *hell* she's not home! Don't fuck with me, Walker! This is a nine-millimeter pistol. There are three shots left. You want them all in the face?"

He looked a little startled, and spoke quietly.

"You're not going to shoot me, C.G."

"What makes . . ." I started coughing. But I held the automatic steady in two hands, and his face, though blurred, remained in my sights.

"For one thing, I'd say you're bleeding to death from that lance in your side. You probably don't have the strength to pull the trigger. Did you kill Francisco?"

"Yes. Where's Sharissa?"

"Inside." He seemed momentarily unsure of what to do

with me, or himself. "I'm going to back up now. No sudden moves. You can come in."

It occurred to me that he wasn't all that confident I wouldn't be capable of shooting him. I knew I ought to do it—no more talk, just kill him. But I hadn't seen Sharissa yet. And if he was lying, and she wasn't in that room behind him, if he'd hidden her somewhere until the hour of the sacrifice, whether he was dead or not I might not have the time to find her on my own.

I had given up being concerned about the loss of blood. I was bloody all over, inside and out. I would know, I told myself; just before the last mortal weakness, I would have enough warning to kill him first. If bullets were enough to do the job.

He backed slowly away from me, frowning, his black-rimmed eyes fixed blandly on my face. He might have been thinking, *I walled him up, and he got out. I sent Francisco, and Francisco's dead. Maybe it's worthwhile not to take old Butterbaugh too lightly.*

With a turn of his head, looking backwards as if at a vision of Sharissa coming down a flight of stairs wearing the corsage I'd sent ahead, he said, "Here she is, C.G."

He had backed well away from the entrance. It was another richly ornamented, smoke-blackened room, with a centuries-old blood-stained slab of altar on which too many young people had died. The altar, featuring a fresco of gnomelike creatures squatting or sitting crosslegged, all of them looking to their right, exuded a stifling evil. Sharissa lay there now, on her back, wearing only a filmy white shift that covered her from her fragile-looking collarbones to her knees; but the insides of the globes of her breasts were revealed. Her hair was brushed and shining by torchlight. Her eyes were closed, darkly purpled, and looked sealed.

I groaned at the sight of her. Greg had circled the altar, light on his feet like one of the dancers in the plaza, careful not to turn his back to me. He placed a whitewashed hand lightly and tenderly between Sharissa's breasts.

"No, no," he said. "Don't you see? She's breathing. She's only asleep." His expression changed without really softening, to a rapture made obscene by the stark fierceness of his makeup, and raised his hand to stroke her dry forehead.

I thought I saw her eyelids flutter at his touch, and the concerns of a dream tighten the corners of her pale lips. He saw it, too. He shook his head slightly, as if any movement at all distressed him, somehow disturbed a perfection he demanded of this moment.

"God . . . damn you, get away from her!"

His bland, unfocused gaze.

"C.G., I have to admire you. Such incredible spirit. I haven't met many men like you, in my lifetimes. But you have to be realistic now. From the look of things, you're mortally wounded. I can't help you. This is as far as you go. Oh, you might get off one shot. You might . . . injure me. But you won't kill me. And you won't change what must happen here tonight. Look, I want you to see something. Because . . . maybe you've wondered, how does he know when it's time? Let me show you."

He walked around the end of the altar, slowly, claiming my full attention with the power of his eyes. In the smoky air he seemed to be vertically levitating. Then I saw that he had mounted a couple of steps hidden behind the altar. This brought his crowned head near the ceiling, which was decorated with what might have been a map of the stars, discs of many sizes in gold and silver, images of celestial deities. He gave me another glance, then reached up and moved a small lunar figure to one side.

A shaft of light slanted into the room, falling on a corner of the altar about two feet from Sharissa's head.

"The light of the full moon," he said. "Reflected by mirrors into this chamber. The shaft moves slowly across the altar as the moon rises to the moment of culmination of the eclipse. Notice the orientation of the altar. When the eclipse begins, the light will be centered on her forehead. I can't describe to you the energy that flows into the room at that time. Flows into her body. And out again, through her shed blood, through the beating heart I will be holding in my hands."

"Why . . . a virgin?"

He stepped down again. "The goddess of the moon, in her best form, is a virgin in all surviving religions and the mythologies of ancient peoples. The goddess is Artemis, or Diana, or Mary. For a few moments tonight, her name will be—Sharissa. She is worshipped because her blood is pure, her body uncontaminated by any man's seed. The purity of body and blood is the rejuvenating power of the ritual."

What about Lilith? I thought, but I couldn't speak. I coughed again, wiped my mouth with the back of my free hand. The gun in my other hand was very, very heavy. He saw that. He glanced at the precise circle of reflected and magnified moonlight on the altar, creeping imperceptibly toward Sharissa. He looked back at me, his hands relaxed at his sides. He had time. He would wait patiently for me to pass out.

"Tell me something," I said. "Did you kill Bobby Driscoll?"

He nodded, as if it were a trivial thing. It had never occurred to me before this moment. Now I wondered why, when it was so obvious. The only enemy Bobby had in the world was the father who jealously coveted Bobby's girl. Who had a compulsive need to preserve her virginity.

On the altar, Sharissa's outstretched hand trembled.

Distracted by this movement, he glanced at her. "She shouldn't be—maybe I had better give her—"

"You killed Bobby, because you were afraid they were about to become lovers? Is that it? She loved him, and she was vulnerable. That scared you. You conceived and raised her . . . for this day. You couldn't let some high school kid . . . cheat you out of your immortality."

"I always trusted Sharissa," he said proudly. "It was Bobby I couldn't trust. Because—"

"Because you're a man, and you know. You know how

easy it is ... to persuade a sweet, innocent girl who's in desperate need of understanding and reassurance that sex ... is what she wants. Oh, man, yeah. It's ... so easy. Even for a short, bowlegged nobody like me. Sometimes all you have to do ... is be there. At the right time. When you're needed. Greg, you damn fool—*you got the wrong guy.*"

I had to laugh. And laughter put me on my knees, I couldn't hold the Firestar any longer. It made a blunt metallic sound hitting the stone floor.

He moved a step closer to me. Torchlight glinted on the gold headdress he wore, gold of the gods. But at that moment he looked, despite his getup, pathetically human.

"What are you saying, C.G.?"

"Don't you know ... Greg? You remember. I was Sharissa's best friend after Bobby died. Night after night ... I was there for Sharissa. I was the one she turned to. And I was so crazy about her, God, I didn't have any scruples. It was easy, Greg. So goddamned ... easy."

"You're a lying son of a bitch! You never touched my daughter!"

"It happened ... only a day before the accident. That was the last day we played tennis. We played so many sets we were both nearly exhausted, then Sharissa ... invited me home to have something to eat. You'd gone to Atlanta ... the house was empty. We talked and talked. She didn't want me to leave. Somehow ... she was seeing me differently, that day. She wanted to be held. I don't know ... what was on her mind. She was in a dazed state. I think she desperately ... needed to get away from the horror of Bobby's death. Far, far ... away. We hadn't ... turned on any lights in the family room. You know, it's strange, but ... there was a full moon that night, too. I know it was Bobby who had ... prepared her, made it possible for me. Her eyes were closed, she smiled, she never tried to stop me. Afterward I think ... she just blocked our lovemaking from her mind. It only happened once, but once . . . is all that's required. Your party's over, Greg. Sharissa's not a virgin."

There was a bulge of tension in his throat, a look of savage hatred in his eyes. My executioner. He shook his head slowly, giving me a few moments to recant, to admit it was just a desperate lie to save her.

I shuddered; then I smiled at him.

"She has a . . . small birth-mole in an unusual place. A place . . . only a lover would know about. You might say . . . it's like a second clitoris. Look for yourself . . . if you don't believe me."

"No!"

The room seemed to be vibrating from the force of his denial. That was ridiculous, of course. But there was a powerful noise of thunder outside the temple. I thought, *the gods must be angry.* I tried to keep him in focus. He had turned to the altar, where the circle of light from the sky blazed at the edges of Sharissa's spread hair. With his back to me he put his hands on her, and, in a couple of moments, knew that I was no liar. Then he lifted and shook her.

"Sharissa! Sharissa!"

Kneeling, hearing the reverberating thunder fade slowly, I touched with my right hand the lance in my side.

"Sharisssssaaaa!"

Her head was flying back and forth. Her eyes were open, but blank. I was afraid he might break her neck, he was shaking her so hard.

"Tell me! Tell me! Did you? With him? Don't you understand *what you've done to me?*"

Put her down, I thought. *You can't treat her that way! Put her down or I'll—*

I don't know how tightly the blade of the lance was seated between my ribs. I only know that all of my rage at him was concentrated on the wound in my side, and when I put both hands on it the broken lance slid out very easily, like Excalibur from the stone. There was a fresh welling of blood from the hole it left, but I paid no attention. I was on my feet and moving toward Greg, stumbling a little across the uneven floor, Greg oblivious as he continued trying to arouse the daughter he had drugged. He heard nothing. He saw no one but her. I don't think he felt anything but his own rage and terror, even when I raised the bloody lance with the honeycomb blade the size of my palm and brought it down on the back of his neck.

The blade looked fragile, but it didn't break. It split cleanly the spine at the nape of his neck, cut almost all the way through to the carotid artery.

He lost his hold on Sharissa and crumpled at the base of the altar. His eyes looked frozen and dazzled in the beam of light from the port in the ceiling of the temple room. Then so much blood came out of his open mouth I couldn't bear to look at him any more, even as I hacked and hacked at what was left of the muscles that held his head to his body.

When that was done I found a little more strength and crawled up onto the altar with Sharissa and put a protective arm around her, my face against her throat. I kept track of the strong steady pulse with my lips, until they were too numb to feel anything.

Love you.

Somebody was calling my name. But I couldn't open my eyes, much less answer him. It didn't seem important anyway.

I will love you forever.

Forever . . .

EPILOGUE

November, 200-

I was never able to tell Sharissa that I was the one who had killed her father or, in fact, tell her that he was officially dead.

Years after the bloody business in the Guatemalan biosphere, in the place later identified by Glen Hazen as Kaxtún, a business trip took me from Florida to Nashville, and I wondered if I had the nerve to see her again.

Sharissa was, by then, in her last year of law school at Vanderbilt. I phoned Adrienne Crowder, who, after we had chatted for a minute or two about everyone's health, asked me if I thought it was such a good idea to revive "provocative memories."

"What has she remembered?" I said. When I was whole again, after five months of persistent infections and operations performed in three hospitals, Sharissa's grandmother had demanded a full account of what went on down there. It hadn't seemed necessary to me; Sharissa had been returned, safe and almost sound, to her grandmother's home in Sky Valley, and was taking summer courses in college. She'd had psychological counseling. "Is it something about her father?" I persisted, when Adrienne was slow to answer.

"Nothing that I know of. Sharissa seldom mentions him

anymore. I believe she's accepted the fact that his body will never be found." She paused then, to clear her throat. Her voice had coarsened since the last time we'd talked; still a hearty whiskey drinker. "When I spoke of reviving memories, I was thinking more of the . . . obsession that inspired you to take such costly risks for Sharissa's sake. Or is it merely a memory?"

"I haven't seen or spoken to her for almost—"

"That doesn't address my concern. How do you see yourself nowadays? As the unappreciated hero of a drama that still lacks a happy ending?"

She was beginning to irritate me; but I had to wonder if it was a grit of truth in her assumption that rubbed me the wrong way.

"I'm no hero, Mrs. Crowder. I have trouble keeping my weight down. I still get twinges when I go up a flight of steps too fast. I don't have any adolescent urges to involve myself in new and bigger adventures. All of my memories of Sharissa are good memories. I just want to know how she is. And I want to get it from her, if that's all right."

"You will give nothing away. Say nothing that could harm her."

Adrienne Crowder was old. She had lost a daughter and her husband, and Sharissa was all she had left; all the more dear to her because of it. I promised to be on my best behavior. She gave me the unlisted number of the apartment that Sharissa shared with another law school student, a woman.

When I called I got an answering machine, the unfamiliar voice of Sharissa's roommate. I left my message, telling her where I'd meet her, if she was able, and when.

I flew to Atlanta, changed planes for the short hop up to Tennessee, checked into the hotel which the company I worked for already owned in Nashville. No messages waiting. I had a leaden feeling of disappointment. I thought about calling her number again, but it was nearly one o'clock. She knew I was coming; she'd be there, or she wouldn't. I looked up the university on the map provided by the rental car agency and drove out West End to the Parthenon. The campus was across the street.

It was a warm day for November, but windy. Most of the leaves had been stripped from the trees. Occasionally the sun broke through fast-moving clouds as I walked from the parking structure to the student center.

I waited outside near the entrance, feeling strangely uncomfortable and alienated from the crowd of college kids coming and going with their bookbags, satchels, and Walkmans, a cultural clique I had once devoted four years to and which now seemed quaint, without much relevance to the world in which we grade ourselves, and from which almost nobody graduates cum laude.

Out of the context of this free-flowing crowd—on foot, on skates, on bicycles—I might have known her right away. But she was different, I had to stare to be sure, and by then she had looked up and noticed me; her recognition was instant. She left the side of an academic stork balder than I was and hurried up the wide flight of steps, a well-stuffed briefcase in one hand, calling to me.

Then we met, and embraced, a little awkwardly, with her kiss grazing my cheek.

"Your hair," I said. She was wearing it very short, except for a comber of cowlick in front like a fiddlehead fern. Full makeup, the clear, watered-amber eyes highlighted. Diamond-stud earrings, a rust wool suit, a floppy cream-colored bowtie, she looked even older than twenty-four. Then, reaching up, brushing at the stylish cowlick with the back of one wrist, her grin released all constraint; it was an unabashed and sunny grin of late adolescence, a look that I hadn't realized till then I still cherished.

"Oh, yeah, I'm not used to it, myself. Just had it cut last week. You don't like it?"

"Well, sure, it's—a new you, isn't it?"

"But you're the same. Haven't changed. Not getting a little pudgy, though, are we?"

"The hell we're not. Hey, how've you been?"

"Oh—" She gestured. *"Busy."*

"All dressed up; not on my account?"

"Oh, no. I'm working part time at Beekman, Roberts—that's one of the big law firms in town. Probably the biggest in entertainment law. My boss handles Denny Mahaffey, Sylvia Burns—" I shrugged. "Two of the hottest country acts right now. So, how long are you here for?"

"Just today. I'm interviewing applicants for Security at the resort we're building over by Opryland."

"Darn. Well, that gives us—I don't go to work until four today—"

"Time for lunch anyway," I said, smiling.

She steered us away from the student center, to an off-campus organic place four blocks away. Tuna sandwiches on whole wheat, heavy on the bean sprouts. She had carrot juice, I had lemonade.

"Wish we could get in some tennis while you're here. How long has it been? Lord—*five* years?"

"I had to give up tennis," I said.

"Oh." She looked crestfallen, sipping her carrot juice through a straw. "You came close to dying, Grammer said."

"We both did, I guess."

Sharissa nodded, picking up the cue. "Hey, how is Veronica?"

"With child, and crabby. Otherwise I'd stay overnight."

She clapped her hands. "C.G.! You're gonna be a *daddy?*"

"Again." So I got out all the pictures, of me and 'Nica and the twins, who by any standards were adorable.

"For which 'Nica gets all the credit," I said.

"Which one is Miriam, and which is Damiana?"

I pointed out the minute differences in the eighteen-month-old girls.

"And the new one?" she asked me.

"Haven't chosen her name yet."

"But it's definitely—"

"Yeah, another girl."

She clapped her hands again, beaming, then reached out and put a hand on my wrist, maybe more urgently than she intended.

"Are you happy, C.G.?"

"Yes. Yes, I really am. 'Nica's great, and I like my work. There's a lot of travel involved, though; I'm Security Chief for the chain, and there was a vice-presidency tossed in a few months ago."

I found one of my embossed cards and gave it to her. She studied it proudly. I basked in this moment of glory. One lucky guy. 'Nica's share of Francisco's majority interest in the Itzá Maya would make us comfortable the rest of our lives. Through the new owners of the hotel, one of the big luxury chains, I had gained employment once I healed. And that led to more responsibility, to my corner office at company headquarters in Sarasota.

"Hey, Butterbaugh! You and Veronica. I mean, doesn't life take some twists and turns?"

"All you can do is hang on and grit your teeth. So. How about you? Any special guy?"

She moved her shoulders a little uncomfortably, and looked away.

"Not right now."

"Things didn't work out with Hazen?"

"Well, you know—I guess we woke up one day and saw how it was going to be, he had his career and I wanted mine. I made one trip with him, down—down there." The fingernails of one hand tried to dig into the Formica tabletop. "I'm sure I was a major disappointment to Glen. I mean, I couldn't—I didn't last. The animals, the insects, the heat—everything came back to me; Daddy—I just unraveled. I was ashamed of myself, but that's how it is. Maybe I'll never get over—"

"Listen, it's okay, you don't have to—"

"When you called, I got kind of a chill. Not that I didn't want to see you again. I owe you so much—my life; but I—"

Her shoulders trembled again; she grimaced, catching

herself at the brink of tears. Snuffled and looked up apologetically.

"C.G.?"

"It's all right," I said again, but her eyes had drifted off. She looked apprehensive, defenseless.

"Maybe only a couple of times a year now. When I'm really stressed out, lonely—I don't know. That awful goddamned dream. Only it's more real than any other dream I've had. I have to go through it again, step by step. The rebel soldiers in the road. They were so young, they didn't seem to mean any harm. Then I see Cora Randall, her face is cut and bloody, she's looking up at me so helplessly. But Daddy is yelling, 'Run!' So I run, but that's when the dream goes out of whack. There's something wrong with my body. I can only run—backwards. Very, very slowly. Daddy is right there with me. And then they just—shoot him. In the back. They kill my father, right in front of me, and I can't do *anything*."

I almost shuddered. I had a different, indelible image of the last moments of Greg Walker.

"Don't be so hard on yourself, Sharissa."

"But when—will it stop?"

She fumbled in her purse for a tissue. Then, after slowly dabbing at her eyes, she took out her wallet and put that on the table.

"And the next thing I knew, I was—in a hospital. With you and Veronica. And she told me—you were probably going to die. She was crying when she said that."

Sharissa frowned as she sorted through her own wallet-album of photographs. She slid one out of its transparent envelope.

"Here's a picture I took of Daddy with Mr. Colon—he owned the hotel, the Itzá Maya. Veronica's cousin. You remember him, don't you?"

I took the photograph and glanced at it. "Oh, sure."

She was busy sorting through other photos, and didn't see what must have been plainly visible on my face. "I thought he was a very interesting man. He and Daddy got to be real good friends."

"I know."

"And he was killed trying to rescue me."

"We couldn't have found you without Francisco, and what Veronica calls the 'Maya wireless.' The rebels had probably been using Kaxtún as a base for a couple of years. Most of them had gone off on a raid, otherwise I don't suppose any of us would have got out of there alive. Hazen deserves a lot of credit for the way he handled himself. He carried both of us down a steep flight of steps to the helicopter."

She smiled, having come across a photo of the archeologist. "He just never would talk about it, though."

"Take it from me, Glen was a very brave guy."

"Well, they're still hoping to restore that temple at Kaxtún, the one that collapsed. But it takes a lot of money."

"Yeah, that was a shame. The vibrations from the helicopter's rotors must have caused the whole thing to cave in. If they ever do dig it out, they ought to find some interesting artifacts. But my memory's a little hazy as to just what I saw in there. I was about two quarts low on blood."

Sharissa shook her head, chidingly, and smiled again.

"I never was all that sure what you were doing in Guatemala."

"Blame your grandmother. She just wouldn't leave me alone. 'I *know* she's not happy, I *know* something's wrong, and it would make me feel *so* much better if you just went down there for a day or two—' Okay, I had some time coming, I thought it would be fun, get in some tennis at the Itzá, have dinner with Greg and Sharissa. Twenty-four hours after I get off the plane, I'm in a firefight in the Guatemalan—"

I don't think she was listening. She stared down at a photo in her cupped palm with an expression so close to heartbreak I almost bit my tongue.

"Sharissa?"

She swallowed hard, and nodded, then held out the photo for me to see.

After so many years, I still felt considerable shock looking into Greg Walker's eyes. And a tightening on the side where four inches of scar tissue partly filled the space of a missing rib.

"That's my favorite of Daddy," Sharissa said. "I guess it's true what they say. C.G.?"

"Oh. I—what's true?"

"That girls look for their fathers in the men they go out with. If that's the case—I guess I'm going to be awfully hard to please. Because he meant so much to me. And I loved him so much. He took such good care of us. He worked hard, and never really made a lot of money. But he didn't want a thing for himself. We had to drag him to the mall to buy a new shirt, or a pair of shoes. Everything was for *us*. So unselfish! Such a kind, decent man. And I will love him . . . love him forever."

Her eyes closed slowly, and there was a moment's tremor in her face, barely noticeable, that produced a single tear, and this time she didn't care about her makeup, she let it roll, slowly, down her cheek.

It wouldn't have mattered what words I spoke then, what sound of sympathy I made, because I wasn't there, in that sunny corner of the restaurant. Only Sharissa was there, with the spirit of Greg Walker, his small imperishable flame visible only to her. And I realized, with a sad stirring in my heart, that blood had been spilled for nothing, that she was alive, but trapped for the rest of her years. He had sacrificed her in a way he never intended.

Soon the pressure of time weighed on us. On the short walk back to the campus we said little, a couple of times meeting each other's eyes, each wondering if the other would say good-bye; but neither of us said it. She kissed me instead, with just a little linger to the kiss that reminded me of the August day and the first kiss she'd given me, and what she'd meant, and all that had followed that never-to-be-repeated night. The night Sharissa chose not to recall; or did she ever think about it? No reason to, it had been the briefest interlude in a month of huge, unsupportable sorrow.

We promised to stay in touch with smiles that might have seemed genuine to any but us, and parted. I went through my interview chores only partly focused, caught an American flight to Tampa that evening, and went back to the rich life by the Gulf of Mexico I enjoyed with 'Nica and the babies. The lights of my life, my imperishable flames. C.G. Butterbaugh. *Un hombre con buen suerte* as 'Nica would remind me when she was in one of her unfathomable moods. One lucky guy. The only thing that kept me from worrying about my luck was, probably I'd earned some of it.